RF

MAID

MAIDSTONE — 8 DEC 2011

19 OCT 2010

472
429

27 OCT 2010 — 4 MAY 2012

20 DEC 2010 2 2 JUL 2016

22/4/10

26 FEB 2011 2 4 NOV 2016

28 MAY 2010 3 MAY 2011 25 oct 22

23 JUL 2010 GOULDING.

18 AUG 2010 28 JUL 2011

24 SEP 2010 24 SEP 2011

Please return on or before the latest date above.
You can renew online at *www.kent.gov.uk/libs*
or by telephone 08458 247 200

JACARANDA VINES

From the Sussex Downs in the 1830s to modern day Australia, Tamara McKinley's novel traces the lives of several generations of one unforgettable family.

Cordelia Witney, widow of the tyrannical head of Jacaranda Vines, is determined not to sell the corporation. If she can persuade her granddaughter, Sophie, to change her mind, Cordelia feels they may win over the other family members. Sophie agrees to accompany her grandmother on a road trip to the Hunter Valley, site of the company's first vineyard. In order to get Sophie to understand exactly what she is fighting for, Cordelia must confide family secrets and ancient history. She begins her story with Rose, a young girl running from her native England hoping to find a new life in Australia...

JACARANDA VINES

Jacaranda Vines

by

Tamara McKinley

Magna Large Print Books
Long Preston, North Yorkshire,
BD23 4ND, England.

British Library Cataloguing in Publication Data.

McKinley, Tamara
    Jacaranda Vines.

    A catalogue record of this book is
    available from the British Library

    ISBN   0-7505-1781-6

First published in Great Britain in 2001
by Judy Piatkus (Publishers) Ltd.

Published in Large Print 2002 by arrangement with
Piatkus Books Ltd.

Magna Large Print is an imprint of Library Magna Books Ltd.

Printed and bound in Great Britain by
T.J. (International) Ltd., Cornwall, PL28 8RW

This book is dedicated to Thelma Ivory and Marion Edwards who are no longer with us, and missed. And to Alan Horsham and Dan Newton, who are still fighting with more courage than I would ever have.

Acknowledgements

With grateful thanks to Kevin Lewis for his tour of the Barossa Valley. The knowledge of this wonderful place's history is astounding and I couldn't have hoped to have learned so much if it hadn't been for him. I would also like to thank Robert Crouch for his help in researching the Romany history of their language and customs, and for his endless encouragement.

No book is ever published without the advice and enthusiasm of an editor, and I regard myself fortunate to have Gillian Green at Piatkus. Her keen eye and helpful advice is always appreciated. Last, but never least I want to acknowledge the work done by my agent, Teresa Chris. Her friendship and profound belief in my work is amazing, and I'll always be grateful.

Extract from *The Australian*

Melbourne, January, 1990

As the estranged wife of a secretive and notoriously difficult tycoon who dominated South Australia's wine industry, Cordelia Witney has learned to live with public humiliation, but even she is embarrassed by the very public row that has erupted following her husband Joseph's death last month at the age of 91.

While Joseph Witney was alive his family lived under the shadow of his violent temper and despotic management style that turned a once ailing Jacaranda Vines into one of the wealthiest corporations in Australia, with world sales of $A 12.5 billion a year. Now that he's dead, some company insiders believe Jacaranda will implode and his heirs will take the company public or split up the conglomerate and sell the businesses individually.

'There were a lot of people who wanted him dead,' says a former insider. 'Now he's finally gone, they'll get their revenge by killing the company instead.'

Others say his widow Cordelia, Co-president of Jacaranda, has taken up the cudgel and will fight her family to the death rather than allow them to split up the company or introduce more open management.

Now the King of the Vineyards is dead, many wonder what will become of his kingdom. Two years ago the French wine producer Lazare was defeated in its bid to buy Jacaranda Vines, but with the internal power struggle currently being waged between Cordelia, her brother Edward, and their respective children and grandchildren, we may yet see the biggest wine sale in history.

Part One

1

'Goodbye, Sophie. Take care of yourself out there.' Crispin's plummy, public-school tones were almost drowned by the announcer calling passengers for the Qantas flight to Melbourne.

Sophie leaned into his familiar embrace and felt a pang of remorse that things should have gone so wrong for them. Marriage was supposed to be for life, not a fleeting three years. Yet they had both quickly realised their mistake, and when things deteriorated to the point of no return, it had been Sophie who'd had the guts to face the truth and call a halt. In the end, it had been a relief to them both.

She drew away from her ex-husband and looked into his face. That disarming smile and those sexy grey eyes no longer had the power to make her senses flip, but she couldn't deny how attractive he was or how much she would miss him. 'Friends?' she said softly.

His fair hair flopped in his eyes as he nodded. 'Always. I'm sorry things didn't work out, Sophie, but at least we called it off before we grew to hate one another.'

She could feel the tears threatening and hastily turned away. 'It was nobody's fault, Cris,' she mumbled. 'Mistakes happen.' She lit a cigarette, the last she would have for the next twelve hours until the plane touched down in Dubai. It would be a real test of her will-power, and although her arm was already covered in nicotine patches, she wasn't at all sure how she would cope. 'Like booking on a non-smoking airline,' she joked wryly.

'About time you gave up, Sophie. You can go for weeks without a ciggie so why not today?'

She dragged the smoke deep into her lungs, her gaze trawling the bustling passengers who filled the concourse. 'I'm stressed out. This helps,' she said shortly. Smoking had been one of the things about her that had irritated him, but not nearly as much as his penchant for other women had irritated her.

Crispin dug his hands into his tweed jacket pockets. Tall and straight, he was every inch the ex-Army officer. 'You shouldn't let your family get to you like this. I know your grandfather was a bastard, but he's gone now – he can't rule your life any more.'

She raised an eyebrow. 'Can't he? It was his money that saw me through law school, his influence that got me the partnership at Barrington's. He might be dead but we're all still running around after him because of that damn' will of his and the mess he's left behind.' She stubbed out her cigarette in an overflowing metal bin. 'Besides, you're a fine one to talk. You wouldn't have gone to Sandhurst if it hadn't been for family tradition. Wouldn't have taken over that mouldy old pile of rubble in the country your mother laughingly calls the family seat. You'd have been much happier tinkering with cars.' She sighed. They were picking over old quarrels. 'Don't let's row, Cris. Time's too short.'

He drew her back into his arms and kissed her forehead. 'Take care, old thing, and I hope you find what you've been looking for. He's out there somewhere, you know.'

Sophie stilled. 'One mistake is enough, Cris. From now on I'm going to concentrate on my career. Men are no longer an option.'

He drew away from her, but maintained his hold on her arms as he looked deep into her eyes. 'You might think you're tough but you weren't meant to be on your own. Find Jay. Talk to him. See if you can't patch things up. You're still in love with him, you know.'

Sophie stared back at him. 'Jay's in the past,' she said through a constricted throat. 'I wouldn't have married you if he hadn't been.'

Crispin smiled sadly and then gave her a swift hug. 'Take care, darling, and write when you can.'

Sophie picked up her hand luggage and, after blowing him a kiss, went through passport control. Her pulse was racing, with both excitement and trepidation. It had been ten years since she'd left Australia. Twelve since she'd seen Jay – her first love – and although their parting had been a brutal wrench, she knew Cris had always suspected there was a part of her that still loved her first boyfriend.

The departure lounge was brightly lit, the duty-free shops busy, but she turned her gaze to the windows and peered out through the January rain. You're thirty years old, she told herself sternly. A corporate lawyer with one of the most prestigious firms in London – albeit with no illusions about why they nearly snatched your arm off once you'd qualified.

With an upward tilt of her chin she stared out of the window. She had kept her place on her own merits. The promise of Jacaranda's business had merely been a stepping stone. It was tough out there, especially for a woman – and she'd proved she was as good as, if not better than, some of her male colleagues.

The gate number was called and she gathered up her things and began the long trek to the plane. I am a woman with a bright future, she silently determined. I won't look back. I'll never look back.

Yet as she settled into her seat and waited for take-off, she watched the rain streak the windows and her thoughts turned to how it used to be all those years ago when she and Jay were young and still at college in Brisbane. Where are you now, Jay? she thought wistfully. Do you still think of me sometimes?

Cordelia Witney had disconnected the call, but her hand remained on the receiver as she mulled over the conversation she'd just had with her brother Edward, and the consequences it might have for the future of Jacaranda Vines.

'Problems?' Jane had always been able to tell when something was worrying her, but that was hardly a surprise considering how long they had known one another.

'You'd think that at ninety my opinions would be treated with respect,' she said bitterly. 'But

16

Edward seems determined to thwart me.'

Jane sipped her sherry, then placed the glass on the table beside her. 'You should have taken my advice and sold your share of the company, Cordy. Then you wouldn't be bothered by it all now.' The rather bossy tone was one she used when she considered others were in the wrong, and although this particular argument had been replayed many times over in the past twenty years, she still seemed determined to bring it up at every opportunity.

Cordelia refused to rise to the bait. With her glasses firmly perched on the end of her nose, she leaned back into the soft leather chair and stared out of the window. The company building might not be as tall as the Rialto, but the glass walls of Jacaranda Towers' penthouse gave her a 360° view of Melbourne, and now she had her new glasses, she could fully appreciate it again.

The city stretched out to the horizon in every direction, and on a clear day like today she could see beyond Westgate Bridge to the west, the Dandenong Ranges to the east, and the expanse of Port Phillip to the south. It was a far cry from the family's humble beginnings, but it had become impossible to remain at the château, and after a while she'd grown used to it. Even learned to love it.

'Did you hear what I said, Cordelia?' insisted Jane.

'There's no need to shout. I'm not deaf,' she retorted.

Cordelia turned from the window and eyed the immaculately groomed woman who'd shared her apartment for the past two decades. Jane was almost seventy-five but on a good day, in the right light, looked years younger. She used her wealth to keep old age at bay, and with a harsh regime of exercise and diet, retained the kind of figure women envied and men admired. No wonder my husband fell in love with her, thought Cordelia without malice.

Our relationship is a strange one, she admitted to herself. For who would have thought the two of us could ever grow to like one another after all we've been through? We are so different, Jane and I. She is the champagne whereas I'm the *vin ordinaire*. And yet there is always one bond that ties us.

'It's all very well for you to pontificate on the rights and wrongs of my decision, Jane,' she said firmly. 'You never understood the importance of those holdings or bothered to learn the history behind them.'

Jane shrugged elegant shoulders and smoothed the lapels of her designer jacket. 'You've always preferred living in the past, Cordelia,' she said dismissively. 'I really can't see why you remain so stubborn. Why not relinquish your hold on the company now Jock's finally gone? Let them sell the damn' corporation and leave the others to fight over the bones for a change. You're a wealthy woman, Cordy. The future lies with your children and the next generation. Let them decide what's best.'

'I might be old but I'm not senile,' she snapped. 'Just because Jock's dead doesn't mean I'm incapable of making my own decisions.'

Jane took a gold powder compact out of her bag and checked her appearance with a critical eye. She ran her fingertips over her surgically tightened chin and neck, smoothed one severely plucked eyebrow and snapped the compact shut. 'So what's the crisis this time?'

'Nothing I can't handle,' Cordelia said firmly.

Bright blue contact lenses made Jane's gaze cold. 'It's always secrets with you, isn't it?' she murmured. 'Aren't you ever going to trust me?'

Cordelia sighed. 'You know that's not the case, Jane, so don't let's argue about it.' She noticed how her friend's gaze shifted with impatience, how her mouth had set into a thin line, and knew she must try to mollify her before things got out of hand. 'This latest crisis is company business, and although I trust you implicitly, I cannot discuss it outside the boardroom.'

Jane stood up and smoothed her linen skirt over slim hips. 'Have it your own way,' she snapped. 'I'm going shopping.'

Cordelia turned back to the window. Shopping was Jane's answer to everything. The decisive rap of her Cuban heels across the parquet floor spoke volumes in the ensuing silence. The slam of the outer door was the exclamation mark to the end of their disagreement.

Cordelia sighed and closed her eyes. These past few weeks had been trying enough without Jane going crook on her, and she was getting too old and weary to have her life disrupted. Perhaps her friend was right after all and she should hand things over to the others?

'Like hell she is,' Cordelia muttered aloud.

19

History seemed to be repeating itself, she thought sadly, for this wasn't the first crisis to hit the vineyard. Her thoughts turned to her late, unlamented husband. Death might have taken Jock's body but his malevolent influence could still be felt, and as she thought of his once handsome, strong face, she remembered how different it had been when they were young and in love and the future had held such promise.

She could remember that summer morning as if it were yesterday. Could still feel the heat, hear the annoying buzz of the flies and the trill of the skylarks. It had felt good to be alive on such a day. The war years had taken the men to fight in the alien fields of Gallipoli. The women had been left to do battle with the powerful, wayward elements of South Australia, the enemies of leaf mould, parasites, drought and flood. Yet the wars had been won on both fronts, and despite the terrible toll they had taken, Cordelia's father and brother would return to a flourishing vineyard, for the vines the women of Jacaranda had tended over those long years were thriving on the terraces of the Barossa valley.

She was standing on the brow of a hill overlooking the patchwork landscape that rolled far into the distance. The harvest would begin tomorrow, and although she was impatient to get started, today she was taking a much-needed rest before the chaos of the next few weeks. A heat haze shimmered on the horizon as the sun beat down on the ripening grapes. The grass at her feet was bleached almost white, and the lonely cries of the rooks in the nearby trees were a dark reminder of how quickly the delicate harvest could shrivel and die if it wasn't picked at just the right moment.

Cordelia was hatless as usual, her long dark hair free from restraint, her feet bare. The white cotton dress was stained with the cinnamon red of the earth, and much to her mother's disgust, her arms and face were tanned. She raised her hands to the sky, lifting her face to the sun, eyes closed as she breathed in the scent of ripening grapes and hot earth. This was her reward for all those hours of labour in the terraces. This was her land, her inheritance, and nothing and nobody would take it from her.

'Persephone the bare-foot goddess of fertility,' drawled a male voice.

She whirled to face the speaker, the warmth in her face having little to do with the sun. 'You should learn not to sneak up on people like that,' she reproved.

'You should learn to wear a hat,' he said mildly. 'Didn't your mother warn you about the dangers of sunburn?' Blue eyes gleamed with humour as he looked down at her.

Cordelia glared at him, but she was more embarrassed than angry, aware how ridiculous she must appear. 'It's too hot to wear a hat,' she declared stoutly. 'Besides, what business is it of yours?'

'None. But it would be a shame to spoil such beauty.' His smile etched creases around his eyes and mouth, and as he took off his bush hat and scratched his head, she couldn't help noticing

21

how thick and curly his brown hair was.

She snatched up the discarded shoes and the hated hat. He had no right to be so impertinent just because he was handsome. 'You're trespassing,' she snapped. 'This is Jacaranda land.'

He replaced his hat, tugging the brim low over his eyes, but his booted feet remained firmly planted in the silvery grass. He tucked his thumbs into the pockets of his moleskins and stared out over the patchwork fields to the clapboard homestead that glimmered white behind the delicate purple blossom of the jacaranda trees. 'I know that,' he said softly. 'Just thought I'd take a look at my neighbour.'

The blue eyes were directed back on her, and Cordelia experienced a strange kind of fluttering in the pit of her stomach. 'Neighbour?' she stuttered.

He nodded and stuck out his hand. 'Joseph Witney,' he said. 'But me mates call me Jock.'

Cordelia's small hand was enveloped in his large, rough paw. So this was the new owner of Bundoran. The man who'd returned from Gallipoli earlier than most, with a shattered knee, and had been the subject of local gossip for weeks.

She looked past the checked shirt and up into his face, determined he wouldn't see how his touch and his nearness were affecting her. 'You don't sound Scottish,' she countered.

He released her hand and laughed. 'Me dad's family came out from Glasgow and I reckon the name just stuck.' With his head cocked to one side, he let his gaze wander over her. 'You must be Cordelia,' he said finally.

She twisted the ribbons of her hat around her fingers. It wasn't just the heat making her feel uncomfortable. 'How do you know that?'

He leaned towards her so their faces were on the same level. 'Everyone's heard of the beautiful Cordelia,' he murmured. 'But the gossip doesn't do you justice.'

She lifted her chin and returned his stare, determined to appear dignified and unflustered. Was his flattery genuine or was he just teasing? 'You seem very certain of yourself, Mr Witney.'

He smiled that devastating smile again as he straightened. 'Oh, I am, Miss Cordelia. In fact, I'm so certain I'll wager we'll be married before the new season's planting.'

Cordelia's smile was grim as her thoughts returned to the present. Jock always got what he'd wanted. Their wedding had been held in the tiny church in Pearson's Creek one week after the end of that harvest and it had taken only five years for her to regret her haste.

She was reminded of the time by the delicate chimes of the ormolu clock Jock had brought back from one of his trips to the Loire Valley. Almost an hour had passed as she'd been daydreaming, but with her memories had come an idea. She wondered if at last she had found a solution to the problem of Jacaranda Vines.

'It's a gamble,' she murmured. 'And if I lose...' She couldn't bear to voice her fears. For to acknowledge them might somehow invite them to come true.

A whispered riposte seemed to come from deep within her. 'But you've gambled before and won, so why not give it a try?'

Cordelia smiled. She knew in that moment of reflection she still retained the fighting spirit which had kept her sane over years of torment. Jock could not be allowed to reach from the grave and destroy everything she held dear. Tomorrow, once her grand-daughter Sophie was back in the fold, Cordelia would fire the first salvo in her fight to save Jacaranda Vines.

Excitement had built in Sophie as the jumbo jet droned over the vast red wastelands of the Northern Territory. She remained fixed at the window, drinking in the sight of her homeland, longing to see something familiar for her years in Australia had been mostly spent in cities. The outback was a daunting wilderness recognisable only from books and photographs. Yet how beautiful it was as the rising dawn set it on fire and the shadow of the plane chased across the sparse gum forests and glinting billabongs. What a pity she would have no time to explore her country – to discover the hidden mysteries of its vast and ancient sprawl – for her days would be spent in the boardroom of Jacaranda Vines, her nights spent poring over contracts and reams of figures.

As the plane travelled further south and the landscape became less harsh, her thoughts turned to her mother. It was unlikely she would come to the airport to meet her, but stranger things had happened and perhaps she'd changed.

Sophie's mouth twisted wryly. There was as much chance of that as finding a snowball in hell. After the divorce from Cris, Mary Gordon couldn't wait to point out that Sophie had failed yet again in the romance stakes. It had been done with consummate subtlety behind a fixed, false smile on one of her rare visits to London, but then such cruelty was nothing new and even though it had hurt, Sophie had managed to brush it off with the thought that her mother hadn't done too well either. Not with three divorces behind her and a string of lovers.

Mary Gordon, the petite, slim socialite, had made it plain from day one that she was horrified by her tall, wild-haired daughter, and had done her best to make young Sophie feel even more awkward and clumsy by pointing out their differences. The subtle nuances of speech as she discussed Sophie's shortcomings with her gaggle of friends, the direct hints that maybe a diet might help in those awful puppy-fat, pre-teen years, had all had the effect of water dripping on stone, and although Sophie was now confident in her work, her personal life and self-esteem were a shambles.

Why can't I just not care what she thinks? Sophie wondered as the plane landed and taxied to the terminal building. It's obvious she doesn't want to know what happens in my life. Obvious that no matter how hard I try there will never be anything between us.

Impatient with her thoughts, she gathered her things and prepared to step onto Australian soil for the first time in a decade. She shouldn't let her mother spoil the occasion, she told herself silently. Don't expect anything, and when nothing turns up you won't be disappointed.

Two hours later she was pushing through the doors of a new high-rise complex overlooking Melbourne's Royal Botanic gardens and the tannin-stained water of the Yarra Yarra. As she stepped into the air-conditioned glass elevator that ran up the outside of the building she shook her long black hair free from its pins and leaned against the cool wall. No one had been there to meet her but at least Gran had sent the limousine to pick her up and bring her here to the company apartment block.

It had been one hell of a long flight despite the stop-overs and she was looking forward to putting her feet up with a glass of wine and a cigarette before she snatched a few hours' sleep. The rest of the day would be spent checking the mound of paperwork she'd brought with her. She didn't want any hitches at the board meeting tomorrow.

As the lift rose swiftly to the fifteenth floor, she gazed out over the lush green of the Botanic Gardens to the riverside city. The essence of it hadn't changed at all, and even the new additions to the skyline seemed to blend with and enhance its beauty. The clock tower of Flinders Street Station gleamed mellow ochre in the early sun, and the glass tower blocks around it stood like sculpted blue and pink stalagmites amongst the sturdy terracotta stone of the earlier buildings. The spires of the two cathedrals were delicate fingers pointing to the lightening sky from the surrounding forest of modern Melbourne, and the graceful white bridge linking the two sides of the city was already busy with commuters. The long, slender tourist boats were tied up to the jetties, gulls circled for scraps above the esplanade of cosmopolitan restaurants and bars on the South Bank, and black swans glided gracefully in and out of the dwindling shadows cast by the willows. It was a summer morning in a city that rarely slept.

Sophie couldn't hear the rattle and clang of the trams from up here, or the sounds of a city preparing for another busy day, just the bland piped music from the speakers in the elevator ceiling and the soft hum of the air-conditioning. She hitched the weighty briefcase to a more comfortable position against her chest and, despite knowing how much work she still had to do, felt the stress of the long journey wane. She had finally come home.

2

Cordelia had been awake since dawn, despite the late night before having dinner with Sophie. There had been a great deal to catch up on even though their letters and telephone calls had been frequent over the years, and it was only exhaustion that had sent her back to her own apartment and bed. Yet she had lain there sleepless, her thoughts and plans for the future refusing to let her rest as the clock ticked away the hours. Now she was running late.

She watched the numbers flash past as the lift descended. There was an almost imperceptible jolt as it came to a halt. She took a deep breath, eyed her reflection in the mirror-bright stainless steel walls, and gripped her walking sticks. 'Curtain up,' she muttered as the doors slowly opened.

'Where have you been, Mother? We've been ringing the penthouse for the last half an hour, and I was getting worried.'

Cordelia stepped out of the lift and eyed the sharp-faced, skinny woman before her. She had decided long ago that she didn't like her youngest daughter very much, and what she saw this morning only compounded that. Mary was dressed in expensive clothes that would have looked better on a woman half her forty-nine years. Her make-up was thick, her jewellery genuine but over-done, her nails too long and too red, her heels too high. 'Nice to know you were concerned, Mary,' she said drily.

Mary's nails raked the assortment of gold chains around her neck, her blue eyes hard with anger. 'Sarcasm at this hour of the morning? You *have* been sharpening your claws.'

Cordelia shrugged off the cold, rather clammy hand at her elbow. 'I'll make my own way, thank you.'

With an impatient sigh her daughter strode away down the corridor to the boardroom. Cordelia gave a grim smile as she noticed how the too-slender hips swayed beneath the tight

28

black skirt in the effort to maintain her balance on those high heels. Poor Mary, she thought. I might not like her, but I do feel sorry for her. With three marriages behind her and too much time and money on her hands, she was fast becoming a cliché. The latest in her long line of lovers was reported to be at least twenty years too young for her and she was in danger of making a complete fool of herself yet again.

The boardroom was sparsely furnished but bright with cream paint and vases of fresh flowers. Portraits of the founders of Jacaranda Vines were grouped together on one wall, and vast picture windows ran the length of another. In the centre of the room stood a table carved from Huon pine that had been brought especially by sea from Tasmania and which gleamed with the lustre of many years' polish. Ten chairs had been placed around it and only one was unoccupied.

'At last, Cordelia. We've been waiting for almost an hour.'

She glanced from her brother Edward up to Jock's portrait and could have sworn he glowered at her. She turned away before he could shake her resolve, kissed her other two daughters, hugged Sophie and took her place at the table. 'Age has its compensations, Edward,' she said to her younger brother. 'My time is precious so I do with it as I see fit.'

He cleared his throat and eyed her with reluctant affection. 'As you say, Cordelia, time is of the essence and we need to get on.' He sat back in his leather chair and steepled his fingers under his chin. His eyes hadn't faded in eighty years; in fact they were a startling blue beneath the shock of white hair, and the face of a handsome young man could still be seen in the high cheekbones, firm chin and sensuous mouth. Cordelia was sharply reminded of their eldest brother, long since buried in the family plot. He'd been so young when he'd returned from Gallipoli, but the strength of youth had been no defence against the injuries he'd received there and within a few short months he'd passed away.

Edward cleared his throat, bringing Cordelia's thoughts back to the present.

'As Chairman of Jacaranda Vines, I have called this extraordinary board meeting to try and find a consensus over our future as a corporation.'

Cordelia hooked her walking sticks over the arm of her chair and settled back to study her family as Edward droned on. There would be fireworks, there always were, but it would be interesting to see how they all stood on this most important subject. She shivered as though Jock had come into the room to watch the outcome of a lifetime of manipulation, then firmly dismissed the thought. His influence might still be felt but he no longer had the same hold. Jacaranda's future was back in their hands now.

She and her brother Edward had five children between them – although to call these particular offspring 'children' was laughable, she supposed. They were all middle-aged now. Cordelia sighed. They were getting old, too old for the responsibilities Jock's death had placed on their shoulders, and not all of the grandchildren were cut out to take the vineyard into the next millennium. In fact, she acknowledged, the family corporation had become more of a means to an end for some of them than a living dynasty to be carried on through the generations, and she was almost glad she wouldn't be around to see what the future held for them all.

As Cordelia and Edward had the same proportional share in the company they had come to an agreement as to who would be Chief Executive after Jock's death. Cordelia had stepped aside, trusting Edward's judgment, knowing her brother would be the more acceptable face in the world of high finance. Perhaps, if she'd been younger, she would have taken responsibility, but she was content to use her influence from the sidelines. There was only so much women's liberation she could take. Personally, she thought it had all gone too far.

Yet, as she regarded Edward down the length of the table, she realised neither of them would be around much longer, and although her brother had relinquished the day to day running of Jacaranda to his son Charles, the question of a successor would have to be broached sooner rather than later. To use an analogy, she thought as she surveyed the more aged of the family members, the vines were slowly dying, and if they couldn't find the right cure, then the French might as well take over.

She felt the familiar rush of impatience at her own meandering thoughts. The fight hadn't even begun, and here she was, throwing in the towel. She eyed her brother's family who were lined up to his left.

There was Charles, his eldest son, fat and pompous and much given to pontificating on any subject regardless of whether he actually knew anything about it or not. He'd been a precocious child, and greedy too. Still was if his figure was anything to go by, she thought acidly. And yet, behind that irritating façade was a keen mind that was encyclopaedic when it came to the wine business, and Jock had exploited that knowledge to the full by putting him directly in the firing line if things went wrong.

Cordelia's gaze drifted to his brother Philip who was younger by five years, limp-wristed and becoming more so as it became socially acceptable to be gay. The two men had never been close, not even as boys, and although she couldn't understand why Philip should be the way he was, she knew how much it had cost him to declare his sexual preferences, and admired him for his courage. For his father, Edward, had all but disowned him, Charles was sneering to say the least, and Jock had unashamedly used blackmail to keep Philip tied to the company.

Her own three daughters were together for once. Mary was as close to the head of the table as she could get without actually sitting in the Chief Executive's seat. It wasn't her way to be sidelined halfway down a table, even if she was the youngest.

Then came Kate, dear, acerbic Kate who called a spade a shovel and didn't give a damn what people thought of her. She might not have inherited her sister Daisy's looks but she'd more than made up for that with her quick mind and sharp intelligence. Two of her husbands had died, making her very rich indeed, and the third had run off with her best friend taking a sizeable chunk of Kate's fortune with him. But the greatest loss of all had been her son Harry, killed in a football accident while still in his teens.

Cordelia knew her eldest daughter had suffered terribly over this, yet despite the set-back, Kate had managed to keep herself together and had forged a career as a fund-raiser and was now on the board of several prestigious charities. Jock had gone to his grave unable to cow her and for that Cordelia admired her.

Daisy was the beauty of the family or had been. Middle age was cruel, Cordelia thought sadly. It makes fools of us all, but for Daisy it must have been even harder to lose the looks and confidence she'd once accepted as her birthright. No wonder she appeared bewildered most of the time now.

Last but not least came the grandchildren. There, looking tired and dark around the eyes, was Mary's daughter Sophie, Cordelia's favourite and only grandchild now, and Charles' twins, James and Michael, still inseparable, still unmarried.

Cordelia sighed as her gaze swept over the faces. Not much to show after six generations in this wonderful country. But maybe it would be enough.

'The future of Jacaranda Vines is sitting around this table, Edward. I don't see what there is to discuss,' she said, cutting through the murmur of a dozen voices.

'The future's not always as cut and dried as that, Cordy,' he said, his deep rumbling voice reminding her so much of their father. 'The French have come back with a spectacular offer.'

'Jacaranda is an Australian winery,' she snapped. 'The French should stick to their own. Even Jock disliked the idea of them in charge.'

'Dad hated anyone else being in charge. At least let's hear what Uncle Edward has to say, Mother.' Mary's voice was high with impatience, her blue eyes cold.

'It doesn't matter what Edward has to say, Mary,' Cordelia replied firmly. 'He won't change my mind.' She looked around the table and saw she had some support, but there was dissent as well. Jock had done a lot of damage over the years. It would be difficult to make them change their minds and fire them with enthusiasm. 'But if you all want to waste the morning, so be it.'

Edward cleared his throat. 'The board of St Lazare has approached us with an offer of two hundred and fifty million dollars.' He paused as a gasp went around the room. 'This offer encompasses the vineyard itself, the château and bottling plants, as well as the wholesale outlets.'

'Just like the French,' Cordelia muttered. 'They always were greedy.'

'If they're willing to pay that much, then why not?' snapped Mary. 'I vote we accept.'

'Me too,' seconded Philip. 'Just think what we could do with all that lovely money.'

Cordelia eyed Edward's foppish son. His fair hair was sleek and expensively streaked, clothes designer and immaculate as ever. Only the family

34

knew of his brushes with the law and the expensive cocaine habit he'd once had.

'You get into enough trouble with the money you already have,' she said drily. 'Keeping Jacaranda proudly Australian and in this family's hands is far more important than high living, and as you are not fully involved in day-to-day company business, I suggest you keep quiet and let those who are have their say.'

'I have what Jock left me in his will,' he said softly. 'That gives me a right to my opinion.'

Cordelia knew this to be true but now was not the time to get into an argument. She turned to the twins. 'What do you have to say about this offer?'

The two men sat side by side, their sun-baked faces lined by the years they had toiled in the fields, for despite their wealth and position, they were truly men of the soil and understood little else. Their only concession to their enforced visit to Melbourne was a change into pristine mole-skins and checked shirts. Their battered, sweat-stained Akubra hats rested on the table, their scuffed boots were hidden beneath it.

James, ever the spokesman for the pair, glanced at his twin and cleared his throat.

'Reckon we like things the way they are,' he drawled. 'Jacaranda Vines has been going long enough without any interference from the French, and me and Mike don't see why it shouldn't stay that way. The proportional share in the corporation Jock left us won't make any difference to our opinion.' He lapsed into silence and looked down at his work-roughened hands.

'It is an awful lot of money, Mum,' said Kate as she glanced across at her sister Mary. 'I know Mary isn't the only one who thinks we should sell. We all had a bellyful of Dad and his bloody company while he was alive. Selling up and walking away seems like a bloody good idea to me now. But I suggest we think about what it would mean to us all if we don't.' She looked around the table. 'This could be our chance to take Jacaranda into a future we all want. A future without having to look over our shoulders, waiting for Dad to pounce. We've worked too long and hard just to let it disintegrate. I vote we remain as we are, at least until we've given it a go.' She turned to her sister Daisy. 'What do you think?'

Daisy seemed to have her mind elsewhere for she blinked rapidly behind her steel-framed glasses as if to wake herself from a day-dream. 'I can't think why Dad left me those shares in the corporation. He never let me have anything to do with it before and it's a bit late to start now,' she said breathlessly.

'Dad only split his fifty percent amongst us all to cause trouble,' said Kate acidly. 'He knew exactly what he was doing, and I wouldn't mind betting he's watching us now and thoroughly enjoying the spectacle of us at each other's throats.'

Daisy shuddered. 'You shouldn't say things like that about the dead, Kate.'

'It isn't anything I wouldn't say to his face,' she retorted. 'He was a bastard when he was alive, and dying is the one decent thing he ever did.'

'This is all riveting, darlings, but could we get on? I have a rather important meeting at my club.' Philip was leaning back in his chair, languid and perfectly at ease in his beautifully cut Italian suit and silk shirt.

'God forbid you should keep a bunch of old queens waiting while we discuss something really important,' snapped Mary.

Philip's expression was malevolent as he eyed his cousin. 'Takes one to know one, ducky, and with that outfit, you're beginning to look more drag than Dynasty.'

Mary was about to retort when Edward interrupted. 'I think this has gone far enough,' he rumbled, pushing away from the table and standing up beneath his father's portrait. 'This meeting was called so we could discuss the French offer and the other options open to us, not so we could fight amongst ourselves,' he said sternly.

'Why not? It's what we do best,' said Mary tartly.

'Shut up, all of you.'

Silence fell like a sledgehammer as they all turned to Sophie in amazement. It was as if they'd forgotten she was there. Forgotten she was an important player now – not a college kid.

'My, my. Someone's got out of bed on the wrong side this morning.' Mary tilted her head to one side, her eyes gimlet sharp in her narrow face. 'Missing not having a man around, are we?'

Cordelia noticed the momentary flash of anger in the girl's eyes but applauded her silence. 'If you haven't anything constructive to say, Mary, then I suggest you hold your tongue,' she snapped.

She folded her hands on the table in front of her. 'I know that to sell would be the perfect chance to take our revenge on Jock for all the years he bullied and blackmailed us. It's also the chance to have more money than any of us ever dreamed of – but what earthly good will it do us? We're already independently wealthy from the vineyard. We own tens of thousands of acres of prime land as well as property in most of Australia's major cities. Our shipping company is booming, and our road and rail transport companies are entering an era of growth and expansion. The new retail outlets are doing well since we took over from Ozzie's, and the planned expansion of our supermarket chain is almost complete.'

'We have to move on, Gran,' said Sophie.

Cordelia's pulse began to race. This wasn't what she'd expected. 'But I thought you understood what Jacaranda Vines means to this family, Sophie?'

The dark head nodded. 'I understand what it used to mean, Gran. Things are different now Jock has gone. Times are changing.'

'And we have changed with them,' her grandmother said firmly.

Sophie's dark eyes looked steadily back at her. 'Not enough. The world market is a tough place, Gran. The French have been undercutting us, and with the majority of our wines earmarked for foreign markets, our home trade is suffering.'

'The French are only undercutting us because

they can't compete with the quality and price of our wines,' Cordelia said stubbornly. 'Our champagne is as good as any of their highly priced fizz.'

'It's not just the French we're competing against, Aunt Cordelia,' interrupted Charles. He tucked his thumbs into his waistcoat pocket and puffed out his chest. 'South America, South Africa, Yugoslavia, Romania ... even the English are breaking into the market now.'

Cordelia grimaced. 'Crook stuff it is too. Only fit for cheap bars.'

'Not at all,' he said dismissively. 'There's a growing youth market for cheap late vintage, and we've failed to corner it despite taking over Ozzie's Bottle Shops.'

'Then something should be done about it – and quick. Why wasn't this discussed at the last board meeting?'

'My dear Aunt Cordelia,' he replied with a patronising smile, 'one cannot discuss everything in an afternoon, especially with so much else at stake.'

'We're getting side-tracked, here,' said Sophie. I don't think we have a choice but to sell – Uncle Charles can explain better than I, and I think you should all listen very carefully to what he has to say.'

'Quite so, m'dear,' he agreed, puffing out his chest like a pouter pigeon. 'Cordelia is under the impression that all is well with Jacaranda Vines. I'm sorry to say that is not the case.'

There was a murmur of surprise from the others, and he waited for it to subside before carrying on. 'We are only just discovering the full impact of Jock's questionable business practices. In the last few years it appeared that all was well, but under that veneer of success lies a pile of trouble.'

He had their attention now.

'The takeover of Ozzie's, the upgrading and modernising of the winery and the money ploughed into the expansion of our supermarket chain and wholesale outlets, has effectively wiped out the profits for the last two years. The shipping and transport side of the business is booming but cannot produce enough profit to counterbalance our outlay. The Australian dollar has taken a battering in the world markets since the Indonesian and Japanese troubles, and our exports are only holding on by the skin of their teeth.'

He held up his hand for silence as loud protests greeted this summing up of their position. 'Although we have invested heavily, the home market has taken a downward turn and our competitors smell trouble. There are several other wineries the French are interested in, and if these smaller companies come under the Lazare umbrella, we're going to find it even harder to compete without another serious injection of capital.'

'Rubbish,' Cordelia exploded. 'If we're in such dire straits, how come my monthly income hasn't been cut?'

Charles looked at her from beneath his bushy eyebrows. 'Your other investments have kept you afloat so far, but sooner or later, if you persist in ignoring the true state of the affairs, your income will dwindle.' The murmur rose to a climax with everyone talking at once. He again held up his hand for silence, and when finally it was achieved, he continued his catalogue of woes.

'Jock ran this company for almost seventy years. You don't need me to tell you what a bastard he was. In the beginning we saw him as a saviour, but in his last few years it seemed as if he was determined to leave us with nothing. In his will he left shares in the company to family members, giving some a vote on the future they'd never had before. But that will be worthless if we hang around much longer and ignore the truth. We all live in luxury, as Cordelia has reminded us, and that is part of the problem. The company has to support the ten of us, plus our dependants, as well as any modernisation and expansion to the plant. What with divorces, drying-out clinics, private airplanes and high living, the money is fast disappearing. If we don't do something, and quickly, we will all go down.'

Voices were raised in sharp protest and anger but he commanded silence immediately when he began to speak again. 'If we vote not to sell Jacaranda Vines, or at least part of the corporation, we will need capital to invest for the future. We have two alternatives. One is to go on the stock market and become a public company...'

'Never,' interrupted Cordelia. 'This is a family concern. Everyone will just have to tighten their belts. We can sell off the supermarkets and the bottle shops, even think about getting rid of some of our real estate. We've been in trouble before, we'll get over this.'

41

Charles took a deep breath, pressing his lips together as if to keep his temper and his retort under control. 'No, we won't, Cordelia. The knives are already out, and we won't get the full market price. Going public might mean handing over the family business to strangers, but if we wish we can still retain a majority share and have a say in how the company is run.'

He mopped his brow with a very white handkerchief and she suddenly realised how much this in-fighting was costing his health. 'So what's the other alternative, Charles?' she said quietly.

'Sell the whole damn' shooting match. Get rid of it once and for all. Lazare can have the bits they want, and if anyone here wishes to maintain a say in the running of the new company then I'll make sure they'll be guaranteed an executive place on the new board. We can sell the other companies off piecemeal once the dust settles,' he finished.

Sophie took up from where he'd left off. 'There is a third choice and that is to do nothing,' she said firmly. 'But if we do that, we'll be playing into Jock's hands and be broke within the next five to ten years.'

Everyone leaned forward, their expressions anxious as she carried on. 'Either of Charles' two alternatives will see Jacaranda Vines into the new millennium. The price will be the loss of its original character as a family corporation, and I admit it will be hard to see the end of an era. But other vineyards have gone the same route, and flourished. If we sell to Lazare it will mean some of us will have a place on the board of a prestigious company which has proved in the last ten years to be a strong force in the marketplace. It is from that position that the reputation of Jacaranda Vines can be steered into the next millennium. For those who no longer wish to be a part of the company, it would mean a hefty windfall, giving them the freedom to live their lives out of the shadow of Jacaranda Vines.'

Cordelia stared at her beloved granddaughter. 'A shadow over your life? Is that how you see your inheritance?' Her voice was soft and cracked with emotion.

Sophie looked around the table before turning to her grandmother. 'Sometimes,' she confirmed. 'It's all I've ever known, Gran. Grapes and vines, fermenting and bottling, storage, picking, tasting ... they were all learned before I could even read or write. My life was mapped out for me before I had time to consider what it would mean, and sometimes, although I love what I do, I feel there's no escape from Grandad's influence.'

Cordelia watched her face. Sophie was animated now she'd revealed her true feelings, and as she hurried to explain how much she was looking forward to working for another company, and what it would mean for her career, Cordelia realised she was in danger of losing her. The dreams she'd held so dear were drifting further away with each word. Jacaranda Vines was doomed unless she could make Sophie see things in a different light.

'I say we take an informal vote now and meet again in twenty-four hours.' Edward looked around the table. 'All those in favour of selling Jacaranda to St Lazare?'

Cordelia watched as Mary, Charles, Philip, Sophie and Edward raised their hands. No surprises there, but the odds were stacking up against her. She and her brother Edward had the majority holding; Mary had her own, plus what Jock had left her. Sophie owned six percent through Jock's legacy, Philip eight. He was a force to reckon with if it came down to an all-out battle and the proportional share was added up with the votes.

'Those against.'

Cordelia lifted her hand and was swiftly followed by Kate and the twins. She glared at Daisy who after a swift glance at Mary, timidly raised her hand.

'We have a hung decision,' Cordelia said triumphantly. 'There will be no changes made. Jacaranda Vines will remain a family corporation and proudly Australian.'

'It's not as simple as that, Cordy,' Edward said regretfully. 'The charter Jock drew up all those years ago states that in the event of a draw, there must be a further meeting called within the next twenty-eight days. And if a decision is not reached by then, the Chief Executive must look to the holdings in the company. If the result is still hung, I have the casting vote.'

'Over my dead body,' she said firmly.

'Probably will be,' Mary mumbled.

'I heard that,' Cordelia snapped. 'I might be old, but I'm not bloody deaf. Neither am I about to be shoved six foot under.' She pushed away

44

from the table and grasped her walking sticks. 'Sophie, would you come with me up to the apartment? The atmosphere in here is intolerable.'

Sophie nodded. 'But if you think you're going to change my mind, you're wrong. I'm quite determined to accept the French offer.'

Cordelia smiled inwardly as she headed for the lift. We'll see about that, she thought.

The meeting had thrown up few surprises for Sophie. This family of hers had a predictable kind of loyalty, and even something as serious as Jock's deliberate destruction of the company hadn't shaken them from their customary stance. After a lifetime of being bullied into submission it was hard to change, and Sophie had warned Edward and Charles of how the voting would probably go. The only surprise was that Philip had voted on the same side as his brother Charles, but she wouldn't put it past him to change his mind at the next meeting out of spite.

'Dollar for 'em?'

Sophie smiled down at the old lady who had more or less brought her up. 'There's a lot to think about, and with a family like ours it's enough to give anybody a headache. I'm sorry if they wore you out with their squabbling.'

Cordelia shrugged. 'At my age just being alive wears me out, but I must say I do like a good row. Airs all the grievances, shows us in our true colours. Can't pretend to be proud of my family on the whole, but some of you have redeeming qualities, and for that I suppose Edward and I should be grateful.'

Sophie stood in silence as the elevator took them up to the penthouse suite. As far as she could see, her mother Mary's only redeeming quality was that she lived several hundred miles away in Sydney. Dad had shot through before she was born, and apart from a grainy photograph Sophie knew nothing of him. Mary had never enlarged on the subject, and Gran knew even less. As for her own generation, the twins lived in a world of their own and were difficult to get to know. The aunts were fun, especially Kate with her sharp tongue and soft heart, but Uncle Charles was pompous, and Philip was all right only in small doses. His 'in your face' homosexuality was frequently tiresome, and she wondered if it was his way of defending himself.

Jane was waiting for them, a glass of gin and tonic in one hand, a cigarette in the other. They kissed the air at each other's cheek. Sophie had never understood Gran's decision to share her home. The two women seemed to have little in common, and although she quite liked Jane there was something secretive there which made Sophie distrust her. Yet it was none of her business what Gran did, and Jane had always been kind and friendly whenever Sophie had spent the school holidays at the apartment.

'Meeting go well?'

'Not what you might call a resounding success,' sighed Cordelia as she put her walking sticks aside and sank gratefully on to the couch. 'Pour me a brandy, Sophie. There's a good girl.'

46

Jane's finely plucked eyebrows lifted. 'That bad, eh?'

Sophie poured the brandy from the cut-glass decanter and handed it to Cordelia. 'The usual sniping – nothing out of the ordinary,' she said firmly.

Jane looked at them both, stubbed out her cigarette and drained her glass. 'Glad I'm out of it then.' She eyed the slim Patek Philippe on her wrist. 'Time I was gone. I've got lunch with the Arts Council to discuss the forthcoming exhibition at the National Gallery.'

'What is it this year?' Sophie used to love visiting Melbourne's state gallery, and would spend hours wandering through the beautiful high-ceilinged rooms with their exhibits of silver and bronze and exquisite paintings. It would be wonderful to take time out and visit again.

'The Australian bush painters. McCubbin, Roberts, Streeton.'

Sophie had an instant recall of McCubbin's wondrous triptych, *The Pioneer*. It was a painting she'd seen first as a small child, and it had never failed to tug at something deep within her as she gazed upon it. 'Let me know when the exhibition's on. I'd love to see it.'

Jane smiled warmly and nodded. 'I'll see you get an invitation to the preview. Be quite like old times. You and me in the gallery.'

There was silence in the room after she had left. Sophie eyed her bulging briefcase. She still had a lot of work to do before the deal with the French could be fully formulated and laid on the table, and she wondered how soon she could reasonably take her leave.

'Is there nothing I can do to change your mind, Sophie?' Cordelia's tremulous voice broke the silence.

Sophie shook her head. 'It's the only way forward, Gran. I'm sorry.'

The old lady was silent for a long moment, her mouth pursed, her gaze fixed on a distant point out of the window.

'I can't pretend I wasn't hurt to realise you thought of the winery as a shadow on your life, Sophie,' she said at last. 'But, having thought about it, I suppose I can understand why you should feel that way. After all, it is what we are, what we've been brought up to understand as our birthright, our future, and in turn our legacy to those who follow. It must be daunting for those whose hearts are not fully committed to take on such a demanding inheritance.'

Sophie was about to reply when Cordelia added thoughtfully, 'The vines are a harsh task-master – far harsher than Jock ever was. They've caused death and divorce, heartbreak and near bankruptcy – but they have also brought untold wealth which in itself can become a burden if not fully understood and managed.'

'It is a responsibility, Gran. Though not one I ever found daunting. But I need to spread my wings. To find different challenges. There's a great big world out there and I want to escape Grandad's shadow. Stand on my own two feet without Jacaranda opening doors for me.'

Cordelia eyed her for a long moment. 'I'd like you to do something for me,' she said quietly. She held up her hand to stem the protest. 'It has nothing to do with the meeting this morning – but something I've wanted for a long time.'

Sophie wondered what she was cooking up now. She wouldn't put it past Gran to have a scheme up her sleeve, and if she wasn't careful, she'd be caught up in it with no means of escape. 'What is it you want, Gran?' Her tone was wary.

'I want to visit the place where the first vines were planted,' Cordelia said firmly.

'You want to go to the Barossa? But I thought you swore you'd never return to the château after you and Grandad split up?'

Cordelia shook her head. There was a glint in her eye and a secretive smile playing around her mouth. 'Jacaranda in the Barossa Valley is the present, Sophie. It began a long time before that, in another place and another time.'

Sophie was bewildered. Like the rest of them she knew the family's sparse history. Knew the story of the early years when Gran's parents and grandparents had struggled to make the vineyard profitable. 'How come I haven't heard about this other vineyard?'

'People have short memories, my dear, and old family history can be easily forgotten once those involved are no longer with us.'

'What about the story of how your great-grandmother came to the Barossa with her children and helped to found Jacaranda Vines? It's a legend lapped up by the tourists when they visit the winery. There's even been a book written about it.'

'It's true as far as it goes,' said Cordelia wearily.

'But the real story behind Jacaranda began a long time before the Barossa Valley. In fact, you could say it began way back in 1838 in a small country village in England.'

'You want to go to England?' Sophie couldn't take it in. She sank into an armchair and stared in amazement at her grandmother.

Cordelia shook her head. 'It would be nice, but I think that's pushing my luck, don't you?'

'Too bloody right,' Sophie muttered as she remembered the endless flight. 'So where exactly is this mysterious vineyard, then?'

'You'll find out,' her grandmother replied, her gaze steady and defiant. 'But not until tomorrow. I expect you to be here by nine o'clock, with your bags packed. Bring only what you will need for travelling through the outback, and leave your work and that briefcase behind.'

3

Sophie changed gears so the camper van could negotiate the steep climb through the pine-covered hills. It was the end of their second day in the heat and dust of the Australian hinterland, and although they had long left Melbourne far behind them, she still couldn't quite believe she'd let her grandmother persuade her to make this journey. She was a city girl, more familiar with the boardroom and law courts than bed and board in a camper van, yet here she was, thirty years old, in the middle of nowhere, in sole charge of a woman fast approaching her ninety-first birthday. This must rate right up there with her disastrous marriage to Crispin as one of the daftest things she'd ever done.

As the camper crested the hill, Sophie took a hand off the steering wheel and hooked her long hair behind her ears. She'd forgotten how hot it could get out here. Forgotten how the sun bleached the green from the grass and made the pale leaves wilt on the white bark of the gums. If it wasn't for the air-conditioning, they would be roasted alive.

Yet, as she stared out at the panorama, she felt a tug of something within her that was akin to falling deeply and irrevocably in love. For this was her country, her inheritance, and she couldn't fault the awe-inspiring splendour of its primal beauty.

The horizon shimmered beneath a sky of incredible blue, the heat laying its watery mirage over the hundreds of miles they had yet to travel. Mountains soared out of the parched earth, hazy with the blue of the eucalyptus that filled the air with its perfume. Golden fields stretched beyond human sight, slashed by great sweeps of paprika earth, lone, blasted gum trees standing sentinel as reminders of the power of the elements.

As Sophie smeared away the perspiration that had gathered beneath her eyes and on her top lip, she caught sight of something that made her pulse race and her foot ease off the accelerator. Gently drawing the camper to a halt, she sat and stared in wonder, knowing this was a scene that had been repeated for centuries in this wild, untamed landscape, knowing she was witnessing something the ancient people must have seen – and although she was sitting in a modern camper van, it was as if she'd been transported to a time long past when magic still happened.

A pair of Wedge-tailed Eagles hovered in the empty sky above her, their powerful wings barely moving in the torpid heat as gimlet eyes searched the fields beneath them. They were so clear, so close, she could almost hear the rustle of their feathers. Then, in slow, graceful unison, the great birds swooped away, and as they disappeared from sight Sophie experienced a pang of indescribable sorrow. For despite her previous misgivings, she was experiencing something she could never have hoped to see back in the city. For like so many other Australians who'd cut themselves off from their roots by living abroad, this was a side to her country she had never got to know except through television and magazines.

Her sigh was a mixture of pleasure and regret as she resumed the journey. Perhaps there was more magic ahead, she thought, but she wished the eagles had stayed a little longer.

Later that day Sophie had washed up their supper dishes in the camp kitchen and been pleasantly surprised at the range of facilities in what could only be termed a country campsite. There were gas barbecues and tables and benches set throughout the site. The camp kitchen was fitted out with microwave ovens, irons, kettles, and all the utensils you might ever need, as well as a fridge, a freezer, a toaster and stainless steel sinks with lashings of hot water at the turn of a tap. It was all somewhat different from the English campsites with their freezing breeze-block showers and cold stand-pipes.

Perhaps this camping lark wasn't so bad after all, she decided. But if anyone had told her a week ago she would end up in the middle of the outback on a long journey with her grandmother, she'd have laughed in their face. She liked the shops and the neon lights, and the city pavements steady beneath her feet, where the only wild-life was the birds in the park and the drunks on a Saturday night.

She collected the washing up and headed for the camper van. It was a monster, gleaming in the yellow of the dimmed site lights, the drawn curtains silhouetting her grandmother as she sat reading by the internal light. Yet it was equipped with everything they could possibly need, and the bunks were surprisingly comfortable.

Sophie climbed into the back. 'I thought you'd be asleep by now. It's way past ten and the rest of the camp is as dead as a dodo. I'm amazed at how early everyone settles down. Back in England they'd be drinking and talking, with their kids running about making a row way past midnight.'

'Australians know what's good for them,' Cordelia said brightly as she put down her book. 'But you look worn out. Is the driving too much for you after that long flight? We've covered a lot of miles since yesterday morning.'

Sophie shook her head and began to get ready for bed. 'Driving doesn't bother me, Gran. I just

53

haven't slept very well for the past couple of nights, that's all.'

Cordelia's voice was soft and full of sympathy. 'Crispin, I suppose?'

Sophie pulled a long T-shirt over her head and began to brush her hair. 'More like jet-lag,' she said with a laugh. 'Cris and I are friends, Gran. Neither of us bears a grudge.'

'I never thought he was right for you, darling,' her grandmother said comfortably from her nest of pillows. 'Far too English.'

Sophie smiled. 'Yes, he was. But that was what attracted me. The smooth voice, the nice manners, the way he opened the door for me and treated me like a lady.'

'Good thing he had his own money,' sniffed Cordelia. 'At least you didn't have to fork out like your mother did every time she got divorced.'

'We signed a pre-nuptial agreement. Both his mother and I insisted – it was about the only thing we ever agreed upon.' Sophie put down the brush and crawled into her narrow bunk. 'The English are a funny lot, Gran,' she said thoughtfully. 'They have these rules for everything, and unless you've been born into the so-called upper classes, they can catch you out over the slightest thing – like wearing the wrong perfume or jewellery, or calling the dunny the toilet instead of lavatory. It's like living in Alice's Wonderland without a script.'

Cordelia took off her glasses and snuggled down beneath the duvet. 'But you were happy over there, weren't you? Your letters sounded as if you were.'

Sophie laughed. 'My accent didn't help of course, but yes – I suppose you could say I was happy.'

'You haven't got an accent,' said Cordelia stoutly. 'It's been swamped by English plums. I can see I've got a lot to do before you can call yourself Australian again.'

'Don't you start,' she teased gently. 'Cris's mother said that the first thing they would have to do was get rid of my "ghastly" Colonial whine and teach me to speak the Queen's English.'

'She didn't? Good thing I never met her – I'd have given her a piece of my mind. Colonial, indeed.'

They both leaned back into the pillows and laughed, but Sophie could still remember the humiliation of having elocution lessons to please her future mother-in-law, and the ghastly hour she had to spend with her every Saturday and Sunday to learn the etiquette of morning tea, luncheon and cocktail parties. It had been a nightmare, but one she'd seen through grimly because she'd thought herself in love with Cris. Don't look back, she reminded herself. Both Cris and Jay are in the past. It's time to move on.

She decided to change the subject. 'Where exactly are we going, Gran? All you've given me is the next day's route map.'

'All in good time, darling,' muttered Cordelia sleepily. 'Learn to live each day as it comes, then you'll derive more pleasure from the surprises it brings.'

That's all very well, Sophie thought crossly, but my life has been charted since day one, and it's difficult to change the habits of a lifetime. 'Don't you think we ought to tell someone where we've gone, Gran? They'll be frantic with worry by now.'

'I left a note with Jane, whom I trust implicitly, but knowing Edward he's already let the cat of the bag. He never could keep his trap shut for long,' muttered Cordelia sleepily.

'So Edward and Jane know where we're going?'

'Of course,' came the muttered reply.

Sophie bit her lip. Without Cordelia around, Mary was a loose cannon, and as Sophie lay in the darkness and listened to her grandmother's steady breathing, she wondered how soon it would be before her mother got wind of this trip and began to cause trouble.

The first stirrings of unrest had begun earlier that day in a restaurant on the South Bank of the River Yarra and were to have a far-reaching effect on more than one member of the family.

Mary snapped the menu shut. She would order a green salad and a glass of mineral water. It was hard work keeping her figure as she was naturally greedy, but as the years had worn on she'd become so used to the regime she hardly noticed what she ate any more. The binges were in-frequent, the bulimia almost history.

The three women were sitting beneath the canvas canopy that shielded them from the glare of the afternoon sun and bathed them in the cool green light suffused by the lush greenery of the potted palms that surrounded the outdoor eating area. The wrought-iron tables and chairs were placed strategically so the diners could look out over the Yarra and watch the passing cavalcade of boats and pedestrians. It was a favourite meeting place for Melbourne trend-setters, and Mary congratulated herself on her choice as she recognised several well-known faces.

'So what do you want?' Kate's blue eyes watched her sister through the inevitable cigarette smoke.

'I thought we could have lunch,' replied Mary. 'We don't meet up often, so why not make an occasion of it?'

Kate's bark of derision made heads turn. 'Don't give me that bull, Mary. Haven't you heard the one about a free lunch?'

'Keep it down, Kate,' hissed Daisy. 'People are looking at us.'

'Then they should mind their own bloody business,' she snapped, glaring at her audience.

Silence fell as the waiter brought their drinks and took their orders. 'Cheers. Here's to Mum. I thought she put up a good fight yesterday.' Kate raised her glass of wine.

Mary's glass remained firmly on the table. 'I found the whole scene embarrassing,' she said. 'Mother's far too old to know what's best for the business. She really should step down and let Charles and Edward make the decisions.'

'Why? Because they're men?' Kate's direct gaze settled on her youngest sister. 'Mum knows more about the winery than all of us put together. She has every right to her own opinion.'

Mary tapped her long nails against the glass of water. 'Of course she has. But didn't you think there was something a little off-key about the way she carried on yesterday?'

'Such as?' Kate's tone was dry.

'No sane person could go on like that with everything stacked against her. It's obvious the company's in trouble, but she seems determined to ignore that and stir up a hornet's nest.'

'You can't say things like that,' protested Daisy.

'Mum's got all her marbles,' rasped Kate. 'She's probably more sane than you ever were.' She leaned across the table. 'Remind me, sister dear. Who was it who had to have counselling for eating disorders? Who went to pieces and made an exhibition of themself when their last husband shot through by taking up a lover who was young enough to be her son?' She rested back into her chair. 'You of all people should think twice before questioning Mum's state of mind.'

Mary took a sip of mineral water. This was going to be more difficult than she'd thought. She would have to tread carefully, for apart from Kate's scathing cynicism, her decision to vote with their mother had come as a shock, and if she was to get her sisters on her side, it would take some finely tuned manipulation to get them to see things in a different light. She decided to change tack.

'Uncle Edward said something interesting after the meeting.'

Kate raised an eyebrow.

Mary forced a smile. 'I know you think he's a bit of an old woman but I find him most informative.'

Kate sighed and put down her glass before

stubbing out her cigarette. 'You're obviously dying to tell us your gossip so get on with it. Some of us have things to do this afternoon and I don't know why I let myself be dragged here in the first place.'

'Neither do I,' said Daisy as she fiddled with her spectacles. 'I hate scenes, and if all you're going to do is snipe at one another, I might as well go.'

As the waiter brought their orders, Mary looked at her two sisters, felt the familiar surge of impatience and struggled to hold on to her temper. 'Edward and I were discussing Mother after the meeting and he let slip that she's planning a trip.' She sat back and waited for their reaction.

'What's so unusual about that? Mum used to make lots of trips.' Kate prodded the pasta with her fork before adding a healthy spoonful of Parmesan cheese. She was one of those infuriating women who can eat what they like and never gain a pound.

'Used to, Kate. She hasn't really left the penthouse since Daddy died.' Daisy unfolded her napkin and proceeded to screw it up into a ball. 'I expect she's going down to the beach house at Lakes Entrance. It'll be cooler there than in the city.'

'Not Lakes Entrance, Daisy,' said Mary ominously. 'She's planning something far more adventurous.'

'For heaven's sake!' Kate put down her fork. 'Either tell us your gossip or shut up. You're spoiling a delicious Marinara with your amateur dramatics.'

Mary shook her head. 'This isn't gossip. In fact you could say it's from the horse's mouth.' She paused just long enough to earn a glare from both sisters. 'Mother is taking Sophie on a trip to the Hunter Valley.'

'What?' Daisy and Kate dropped their cutlery and stared at their elder sister.

'Thought that would surprise you,' she said smugly.

'Why?' demanded Kate.

'Mother evidently wants to return to her roots before she dies. Though why she wants Sophie along, I can't imagine.'

'Probably because she's more of a daughter than you ever were,' Kate said drily. 'But why now? There's only a month before the second vote and...' Her expression cleared and she grinned. 'The old so-and-so! She's using this trip to turn Sophie to her way of thinking over the French offer.' She resumed her attack on the pasta. 'You've got to give the old girl credit, she's got balls.'

Mary shivered at her sister's crudeness but decided to let it pass for once. 'Mum hasn't a cat in hell's chance of changing Sophie's mind. She knows what's best for the company even if you don't.' She paused for a moment. 'Why did you vote against the offer, by the way?'

'None of your bloody business,' retorted Kate.

Mary sniffed and picked up the thread of what she'd been saying. 'I don't care if Mother wants to visit the Hunter. She can go anywhere she likes if it keeps her out of my hair, but I do think it's a bit odd she's decided to travel in a camper van.'

Kate's bark of laughter caused the other diners to turn and stare. She ignored them. 'You've got to be kidding. Mum in a camper van? Why isn't she using the company plane?'

'How the hell should I know?' snapped Mary. 'Nothing Mother does these days makes sense. That's why I'm worried about her.' She leaned across the table to emphasise the solemnity of her words. 'I don't think she's at all well, Kate. In fact,' she confided, 'I have a suspicion she's going senile.'

Daisy balled the napkin in her lap and proceeded to shred it into a soggy paper mess.

'I can see where this is leading, Mary, and I'll have no part in it,' Kate warned.

Mary swallowed her disappointment. She should have known Kate was too smart to see through her plan. It was time to go for broke. 'I'm only concerned about Mother's welfare,' she lied. 'And the welfare of the company,' she added hastily. 'If this is the onset of senile dementia, then we should seriously consider Mother's place on the board, and what we should do with her shares if she's classified incompetent.'

Daisy threw the remains of her napkin on the table. 'I won't have you talking about her like this. You always were greedy, Mary. What does it matter about the shares? We're wealthy enough however the vote goes next month, and Mum's health is more important than anything else.'

'It matters a great deal,' murmured Kate. The pasta had been pushed aside and she'd lit another cigarette. 'Mum and Uncle Edward have the major shareholdings, and it matters who she

61

means to leave them to, or who will have power of attorney if she does become incapable of running her own affairs. Have you any ideas, Mary? You seem to think you know more than anyone else.'

'Mother doesn't take me into her confidence,' she said huffily. 'But I suspect she'll leave them to Sophie. She always was her favourite,' she added bitterly.

'Sophie's a capable girl. The company won't suffer if she becomes one of the major shareholders.' Kate stabbed out her barely smoked cigarette and stood up. 'But I disagree that Mother's gone soft in the head. She's just outspoken when it comes to things that matter to her and I won't have you casting doubt on her sanity.' She took a deep breath. 'When's Mum due to take this damn' trip? I think I'll pop in and see her first.'

'Uncle Edward clammed up the minute he realised he'd said too much. But it must be soon because they have to be back here in twenty-eight days' time for the second vote, and the journey there and back by road will take a good chunk of that.'

Kate leaned towards her youngest sister. 'Keep your suspicions to yourself until I've found out a bit more,' she warned. 'I don't want you causing trouble until I know all the facts. This could just be an old lady's whim to return to the past before she dies, and God knows that could be any minute. Don't spoil it for her, Mary, or you'll have me to deal with.'

With her salad barely touched, Mary leaned

back in the chair and sipped her mineral water. If Sophie did inherit Mother's share of the business, then she would become a very wealthy, powerful young woman. And if the company were sold, or went public, that wealth could be tripled. Another stab of jealousy gave her heartburn. It wasn't fair.

She looked at her watch. Time to go. She had an appointment to arrange this afternoon. An important appointment which just might turn things her way for a change – or at least give her the satisfaction of exacting revenge for all the past hurts she'd suffered.

Morning had dawned with a sky the colour of bleached denim, promising another day of blinding sun. Sophie had made their breakfast of fruit and toast, now they were sitting at the camp table under the awning drinking strong black coffee.

'Everything tastes so much better in the open air,' said Cordelia with relish as she speared another slice of melon and popped it into her mouth.

'I love the sound of the birds,' murmured Sophie. 'Listen to those kookaburras, and the wonderful warble of the magpies. Combined with the heavenly smell of those wattle trees, and the colours of the rosellas, it's all too perfect. London could be a million miles away.'

'It would be shame to move on then,' said her grandmother. 'Perhaps another day here wouldn't hurt. We've made good time so far.'

'Are you sure, Gran? Sophie looked back at her

across the table and smiled. Cordelia noticed how her face glowed with fresh air and happiness. She nodded, then drained the coffee cup and settled it into its saucer. 'I think we could both do with a bit of a rest, and it will be a chance to tell you about the people behind Jacaranda Vines.'

'But it was so long ago, Gran. How can you be sure what really happened?'

Cordelia smiled as she remembered asking the same question all those years ago. 'My great-grandmother Rose began to tell me about her life when I was twelve years old. It was a story that bound me to her in heart and mind, and one I'll never forget. In fact, it's so real I can picture the characters and the parts they played as if they are on a stage.'

Sophie put down her coffee cup and tucked her long hair behind her ears, her eyes wide with anticipation. Cordelia thought she looked very beautiful without a scrap of make-up to mar her complexion or the clarity of her eyes, and her bright red T-shirt and crisp white shorts were a refreshing change from the sombre black she usually favoured.

Cordelia smiled. 'Great-grandmother Rose must have looked a great deal like you when she was young,' she declared. 'You share the same dark hair and eyes. The same heart-shaped face and high cheekbones. But there the resemblance ends for she was a tiny little woman with a fragility about her that belied her tremendous strength and courage.'

'Thanks,' said Sophie tartly. 'I've had enough of

Mum telling me what a hulking great thing I am without you starting.'

Cordelia reached out and laid her hand on Sophie's warm arm. 'I didn't mean it like that and you know it,' she said firmly. 'You're tall and graceful, with an elegance your mother could never hope to achieve. Her nastiness is all about jealousy, and you should learn to ignore it.'

Sophie stared out at the surrounding bush. 'I know, but old habits die hard and when you're told something often enough, you learn to believe it.'

Cordelia kept her thoughts to herself. There was no profit in raking over cold ashes and she didn't want to spoil the mood. 'So, do you want me to tell you about Rose?'

'If it won't tire you too much, Gran.' Sophie leaned towards her, elbows on the table, hands cupping her chin. She was like a child waiting for a story, and Cordelia felt the same ache of love for her she'd first experienced the day she'd been brought home from the hospital.

'Then I want you to imagine an English village nestled beneath the range of chalk hills called the South Downs. It is very green, for they have lots of rain, and the sun is rarely hot enough to leach the colour from the landscape. Dark, rich soil is ploughed by blood-red oxen in the fields below the Downs, and sheep roam the higher land where the wind comes straight up from the sea. There are cottages in the hamlet with roses around the door and weeping willows shading the village pond, but although it's a cosy scene there is terrible poverty beneath those thatched roofs. Medical care was crude back in the eighteen-thirties. The farm labourers' diets consisted of bread and ale, and cheese if they were lucky. Children died young, women died in childbirth, and dirt and ignorance were rife. At the end of the village is a Norman church with crooked headstones peeking out of the long grass and wild flowers. The spread of an ancient yew shades the rough stone paths. The hills dominate the church and the village and the figure of a chalk giant is spread-eagled on one side of that hill, left there by the ancient Britons as a symbol of fertility. It is called the Long Man of Wilmington.'

Sophie nodded. She could picture it so clearly after her time in England.

'Down the hill from the church is the Manor house. It is owned by Squire Ade, and it is where the thirteen-year-old Rose Fuller works as an apprentice lady's maid to his eldest daughter Isobel. There are guests staying at the Manor who, unknown to Rose, are about to change the lives of both young women. We meet her and the people who coloured her life in the early spring of 1838. It's a sad time for Rose. Her father has been gored by the Squire's bull, and this is the day of his funeral.'

Rose and her mother moved silently around one another as they prepared breakfast that morning. The range was smoking as usual, and there had been a heavy fall of debris from the thatching. Rose was almost relieved to have something to do as she scrubbed down the table and benches and

66

swept the floor for her mother. Kathleen had barely acknowledged her presence, moving like a wraith around the cottage, seeing to the baby and the daily chores with her mind elsewhere.

At first, Rose had tried to lift her from her gloom by chattering of inconsequential things, but this had merely elicited a frown and a tightening of her mother's lips. So, with a heavy heart, the girl decided to stay silent rather than risk another rebuff.

The sun rose, melting the frost, and to ease the fug of the smoking range and the smell of death, Rose opened the window and set the door ajar. She stood on the step for a moment to breathe in the clean, fresh air, and looking up at the folds of the South Downs, she thought of John Tanner. The Romanies had been moved on by Squire Ade and she wondered when she would see him again for she needed to feel his arms around her. Needed to hear his words of love. Yet she understood that at seventeen John had to make his way in the world until she was old enough for marriage – but that didn't quell her impatience.

'Stop your dreamin', girl. There are things to do.'

Kathleen's voice startled her, and Rose turned back into the cottage. She looked up at her mother, almost afraid to voice the concern that niggled so persistently. 'What's going to happen to us, Mam?'

Kathleen eyed her for a long moment. There seemed to be no compassion in her face, no softness or light – merely an acceptance of her lot. 'We'll discuss that later,' she said sharply. 'For now I want you to take Davey next door. 'Tisn't fitting for him to see what's afoot today.'

'He should be told, Mam. It isn't fair.'

Kathleen's mouth thinned. 'There's enough troubles on our shoulders without Davey having one of his turns. Do as you're told.'

The day was barely started but to Rose it already felt as if it had lasted forever. She crossed the hard-packed dirt floor and grasped her brother's bony wrists until he stopped his tuneless humming and looked up at her. 'We're going visiting, Davey,' she said softly.

Poor boy, she thought as she stroked back the lick of hair from his forehead. His blue eyes and black hair should have made him handsome, but there was a vacancy behind that stare and an uncoordinated droop to his mouth that were the legacy of a childhood accident. A kick from the huntsman's horse had meant he would never hold down a proper job for people didn't take to his queerness, didn't understand his childlike babbling and endless singing. Davey would always be four in his mind despite his sixteen years.

'I want me da,' he said stubbornly. 'Not going.'

Kathleen's skirts rustled with impatience as she snatched away his bowl and spoon and roughly dragged him from his seat. 'You'll go when I tell you,' she said sharply.

Davey frowned but let Rose lead him out of the cottage to next door where Mrs Grey was waiting to walk to market. Rose sighed as she watched the long, lanky figure stride along next to the dumpy little woman, and almost envied his ignorance.

Returning indoors, she pulled the sacking curtain tight over the bedroom doorway, stripped to her petticoat and wriggled into her coarse brown dress. It was meant for work at the Manor but was the only one she had that would be half-way decent for church. Money didn't stretch to buying mourning, even hand-me-downs. The bodice was tighter than ever and the sleeves were short of her wrists, but it was clean, and still covered most of her boots because she'd let down the hem the night before.

The scant bristles of her much-used hairbrush caught in the knots of her black hair as she released it from its pins and hung it over her shoulder. Yet it wasn't the tug of the brush, the lack of decent clothes, or the want of a few extra pennies that made the hot tears roll down her face – but her frustration and hurt at Mam's coldness. Death should have brought them closer, bonded them so they could face the future together, but all it had done was tear the family apart and Rose had an awful feeling this was only the beginning.

The rumble and creak of wagon wheels drew near as she returned to the kitchen. Kathleen came from her room to gather baby Joe in her arms and stand beside her daughter, but she was an island in her sorrow, distanced by the thoughts she kept in her head and the rigid control with which she held herself.

Rose collected their shawls and, almost hesitantly, placed her mother's on her shoulders. There was no acknowledgement, merely a shifting of Joe from one arm to the other as

Kathleen adjusted the heavy black cloth.

Once the coffin had been laid on the wagon, the carter flicked his reins and Brendon Fuller began his last journey down Wilmington Lane to the church of St Mary and St Peter.

John Tanner had been tramping the hills around Lewes since dawn, his thoughts on Rose. He understood how she must be feeling today for although his mother had died when he was just three years old, the loss of his father haunted him still.

Max Tanner had lived life to the full if the stories were to be believed. He liked the women and they liked him, and sometimes this had brought trouble to his Romany clan and they'd had to move on. Yet he'd been a respected horseman and trader, with a cunning to match the most wily of minds, his lack of fear bringing him general respect. It had also brought disaster.

John could still remember that day. It had been a wild sort of morning with the wind howling in the trees, flattening the grass against the earth and sending the clouds scudding over the sky. The stallion had been bought at the Lewes horse fair and, like the weather, it was untamed.

There had been a full moon the night before, and much to his disgust six-year-old John had been made to go with the women to collect mushrooms. He'd waited until they were engrossed in their work then dodged away through the trees. He could hear their shouts but ignored them, and soon there were only woodland sounds following him.

The men were in the valley. Surrounded on all sides by trees, it was a natural arena for the breaking of new stock. A rough barricade had been erected in the centre and the young John had approached this as close as he dared then hidden behind a fallen tree. If the men caught him watching they would probably send him back to the women – and that was not a humiliation John was prepared to suffer for even at that age he had a fierce pride.

Max stood in the centre of the makeshift corral, his waistcoat and trousers dark against the bright red of his shirt. Gold glinted at his earlobes and throat and the wintry sun gleamed blue on his long black hair. He wasn't a big man but more compact than most, with arms and legs thickened with muscle and shoulders that squared up to trouble.

To the watching boy, Max and the stallion shared the same freedom of spirit, the same wildness. It was there in the flying mane, the bunched muscle, the strength of man and beast as they vied for superiority. The stallion stamped and snorted on the end of a long rope, his mane tossing, eyes rolling. John couldn't hear the words his father used but knew they would be the Romany words that by tradition were used to calm a wild horse. He watched in awe as Max took his time with the beast.

Poised lightly on the balls of his feet, he moved like a dancer this way and that, touching the whip in a gentle caress against the animal's flank to guide it in his footsteps. The rope was shortened measure by measure until man and horse were almost touching. Max was still talking, still crooning as the stallion trembled and fretted. Then he breathed into the velvet nostrils and ran his hand over the quivering neck.

The stallion flinched, jerking his head up, ears flat. But there was nowhere to go. Nothing to sense but the calm of the man before him whose smell had become familiar – whose voice and touch seemed to soothe his fears.

John crouched behind the log, spell-bound. One day he would have the courage to face such an animal. His father would teach him the skills he'd learned from his father and his father before him. It was the Romany way – his future. But for now he was content to watch and admire.

Afternoon shadows had fallen across the arena as the bit and bridle were eased over the stallion's head. He tried to toss them off, backing away, skittering and weaving to escape. But the man held fast, still talking, still exchanging breath for breath as he eased the bit between the snapping teeth. After a long while Max led the horse into the corner of the corral. The stallion was still, but the quiver in his sweat-sheened flanks warned he was poised for flight.

Max stroked his neck, running his hand over the strong back as he lulled the animal. Then, inch by inch, he climbed the makeshift barricade, talking all the while, his hand always in touch with the chestnut coat.

The stallion shifted uneasily as the man lay softly across his back, but the hands still caressed, the voice still crooned as the weight was shifted and the slack was taken up in the halter.

The reins tightened, pulled at the hated thing in the stallion's mouth. The man was astride him now, heels pressed to ribs, knees pressed tight as hands gripped his mane.

The other men leaped clear as the stallion reared. Max clung on, his chest tight to the animal's neck, his feet and knees gripping the heaving ribs as his face was whipped by the flying mane.

John forgot about hiding in the sheer exhilaration of the moment. He stood up as the stallion took off in a whirlwind of fury. Grass flew in muddy clods from the flying hoofs, the wind carrying the sound of the animal's whicker and the man's shout of triumph. The horse skidded, whipped round in a vicious circle, dropped his head and bucked.

Max was unseated, his hands torn from the reins, his body tossed in an arc over the beast's head. He fell against the railings with a crack that echoed in the surrounding trees.

Now John stopped walking and sat down on the remains of the old castle wall. It was as if he could still hear that terrible sound. Still feel the shock of what had happened. As Brendon Fuller had died instantly, so had Max Tanner.

He stared out over the hills, yet it wasn't the distant roofs of Lewes he saw but the black funeral pyre of his father's *vardo* wheel. Not the scent of damp grass and earth but the stench of burning wood. They had buried Max beneath an elm tree deep in West Dean forest, his gold earrings and chain clasped in his lifeless fingers. They were his talismans, the sign of his earthly

73

achievement. They would remain with him as was the Romany way, so his spirit would be at peace.

John shivered as he thought of that vital man lying beneath the earth. Death followed them all but fate determined its time and place. It could come secretly and silently or with obscene swiftness – but always inflicted a scar on those left behind.

He'd been fortunate, he admitted silently. His grandmother, the *dukkerin*, had taken him in, and there was always someone around to offer comfort and advice as he was growing up. But Rose? What would happen to her? He chewed his lip as he remembered how distant Kathleen Fuller was – how uncaring of her daughter. There was no large family to surround Rose with love and support – no constancy in her life now her da was gone.

He smiled as he thought about their early years. Even as a boy he'd felt something special for her, and as the years had passed the bond between them had strengthened. He found himself watching for her, waiting to catch a glimpse of her in the lane of an early morning as she made her way to the Manor. Sneaking her gifts of freshly caught trout or snared rabbit. The events of the past few days had brought all those feelings to the surface and he'd become impatient for the time when he could declare his feelings and make her his wife. He knew there was a man staying with the Ades who'd bothered Rose and couldn't wait to get her out of harm's way.

Thoughts of failure, of her rejecting him, never

figured. Although she was still very young, he knew the day would come – for he'd had the dreams, seen her face in the campfire flames and knew fate's hand had touched them.

The rusty caw of the rooks brought him to his feet. His thoughts had occupied him for too long; the sun was already rising, the shadows chased from beneath the trees. He hurried through the woods until he reached the clearing then stood for a moment, watching the morning ritual.

The *vardoes* were drawn in a wide circle around the camp fire, and he could smell the rook stew simmering in the black metal pot. Children played around the wagons and tents, their shrill voices echoing through the trees as they called to one another. The men were grooming the horses which were tethered off to one side of the camp, or sat smoking clay pipes as they waited for breakfast. The women chattered like starlings as they divided bread into chunks and threw vegetables into the pot.

John stepped into the clearing. His grandmother Sarah Tanner was waiting for him on the steps of her *vardo*. Despite her great age she still wore the traditional bright red skirts and petticoats and ornately embroidered waistcoat and blouse she'd favoured in her youth. Her long grey hair was tied back with green ribbon and gold glinted at her ears and in her mouth. She had propped one foot up on the shafts, leaning her elbow on her knee as she smoked her clay pipe.

John was all too aware of her keen scrutiny. Those eyes missed nothing.

The pipe was clamped between her remaining

teeth. 'So, you are planning to see her again?'

With hands deep in his pockets, John returned her direct gaze. 'I must. She has no one else and it's Brendon's funeral today.'

Sarah took her pipe out of her mouth and grimaced. 'She's *kairango*, boy. None of your business.' When John remained silent, she spat at his feet. 'Rose Fuller's trouble. Stay away from her.'

He decided it would be useless to argue. The *dukkerin* wouldn't listen anyway. He ran his hands through his hair and eased his shoulders. They were still aching from a boxing match the previous night.

'Look at me, boy.'

The soft demand was impossible to ignore and John reluctantly obeyed. His grandmother's dark eyes were fathomless and he knew she was seeing things from another dimension. A shiver of apprehension raised the hairs on his neck. The *dukkerin*'s power was rarely flawed – and he had a feeling he wouldn't like what he was about to hear.

'Your destiny lies along a different road, John. And it is a long journey. When Orion rules the heavens and Gemini splits asunder – then you will know the terrible price you pay for defying fate.'

John didn't want to believe her but as her eyes cleared and her gaze remained steady on him the dread returned. 'Rose is in me, Grandmother,' he insisted. 'I've seen...'

'Don't vex me, boy,' she snapped. 'You see what you want to see. Listen to me. Her path is

76

troubled, but she will not travel alone.' She paused for a moment, then wiped the spittle from the corners of her mouth. 'She travels with another,' she said softly. 'Your destiny is here, amongst your own.'

He shook his head but love and respect for the old woman kept him silent. She could believe what she wanted. He would never abandon his Rose.

Rose heard the earth fall with a thud on the coffin lid, saw the Parson brush dirt from his hands and turn to pay his respects to the Squire and Miss Isobel. It was over.

She stood beside Kathleen as the cottagers and farm labourers offered their condolences before hurrying to the table tombs for their share of ale and cake. Death was no stranger to any of them for accidents happened on farms; typhus, cholera and dysentery attacked the very young and very old in their humble cottages. It was the price they all paid – and as no one could do anything about it, it was accepted.

The cold had found its way into her bones. Her fingers and toes were numb with it, and when the Squire and Miss Isobel approached, Rose could barely find the energy to bob a curtsy.

'Thank you for providing all this, sir,' Kathleen's voice was clear and steady as she indicated the grave-digger, the horse and cart and food for the mourners. 'Brendon would have been pleased at such a grand wake.'

Rose dug her hands under the shawl. Da would have preferred to be alive – not six foot under in the cold earth, she thought bitterly.

'My wife sends her condolences, madam. And I have arranged for the carter to call the day after tomorrow to help with your move. You can be assured young Rose will be well looked after at the Manor and the confidences you have entrusted me with will remain private.' The Squire doffed his top hat, sketched a bow and walked away with his eldest daughter.

His words took some moments to sink in, but when the full import of what he'd said finally made sense, Rose grabbed Kathleen's arm. 'What move?' she demanded. 'Where are you going? And what did Squire mean about me at the Manor?'

Her mother hitched Joe higher on her shoulder, her gaze drifting over the gathering by the church door. 'We'll talk about it when we get home,' she said firmly.

'No.' Rose pulled her mother to face her. 'I want to know now, Mam.'

'This is not the place,' said Kathleen coldly. She wrested her arm from Rose's grip, but it seemed to expend the last of her energy and she didn't move away. 'Leave it, child,' she said wearily. 'Better not to discuss our business with so many listening.'

Rose eyed the mourners. Their mouths were full, their cheeks bulging as they lifted their pots of ale and watched the scene before them. She didn't care if they were listening, for the hurt Mam had inflicted was so deep, she was numb.

'Rose?'

She turned at the sound of a wonderfully

familiar voice. 'John,' she sighed. Then his arms were around her, holding her close, giving her the warmth and comfort she'd so desperately needed. She clung to him, burying her face in the folds of his greatcoat, breathing in the manly scent of tobacco and hair oil.

'What are you doing here?' Kathleen's icy demand broke the spell.

John kept his arms around Rose, but she could feel the tension in him as he faced Mam. 'I've come to pay my respects to a man I liked,' he said simply. 'And to make sure Rose was well.'

A rough hand tore her from his embrace and Rose stumbled on the grassy mound of an old grave. Having regained her footing, she stared from Mam to John in puzzlement. Mam's face was white, her dark eyes hostile, her mouth a hard line of disapproval. John was flushed, the tic in his jaw evidence of suppressed rage.

'Your respect for my husband would be better served if you left my daughter's well-being to those who have the right to guide her.'

'He was only being kind, Mam,' Rose protested.

'It's all right, Rose,' he said softly, his eyes so dark and fathomless she could see her reflection in them. 'Yer mum's only looking out for you.'

'Indeed I am, John Tanner,' said Kathleen stiffly. 'And I'll thank you not to bother Rose again.'

'Mam, she protested. 'Me and John almost grew up together. You can't do this.'

Kathleen looked down, her eyes cold, her expression inscrutable. 'Yes, I can.' She turned back to him. 'If I find you've been bothering my girl, then I'll have the Squire do something about it.'

John's fists were tight at his sides, a muscle in his jaw working hard to keep back the angry words. 'And just how are you doing to do that, Mrs Fuller?' he asked with the deceptive calm Rose recognised as a danger signal.

'She will be living under Squire's roof from Friday. As her employer and guardian, he will have the right to protect her from vagrants,' Kathleen said spitefully.

Rose was hauled down the path, the hand on her wrist so tight and determined there was nothing she could do but follow. But as they skirted the church wall, she looked back.

John was standing where they had left him. She could see by his expression that despite her Mam's warning, he would not give up on her.

She just had time to sketch a small wave before Kathleen dragged her out of sight and down the slope to the gate. Kathleen set a furious pace as she strode down the lane. Rose wondered where she'd managed to dredge up the energy.

'Slow down, Mam,' she panted. 'I can't keep up.'

'The quicker I get you home the better,' replied Kathleen. 'We've talking to do.'

The row of cottages was silent, their occupants either at the churchyard or in the fields. The rap of their boot heels on the cobbles echoed in the silence like hammers on nails, and Rose remembered the undertaker and the terrible noise that had come from the bedroom as Da was put in his box.

'Get inside,' said Kathleen, shoving her and slamming the door behind her.

Rose had had enough. She stood in the centre of the dim little room with her hands on her hips, hair tumbling over her shoulders. 'All right, Mam,' she said firmly. 'What was that all about?'

Kathleen laid Joe in his drawer and took off her shawl. 'I have work at the Dame School in Jevington. There isn't room for you there so I've asked the Squire to let you live in at the Manor. We leave here Friday morning.'

'Why didn't you ask me what I wanted to do?' the girl stormed.

Kathleen eyed her dispassionately. 'You might think you're almost a woman, Rose, but you have a lot to learn before you can be allowed to make decisions like that.'

'When have you ever asked my opinion about anything?' she said bitterly. 'Or cared if I was happy working for the Squire?'

Kathleen shrugged as she put the kettle on the hob. 'Life isn't about being happy, Rose. It's about surviving. I did what I thought best.'

'I'd be safer with John,' she stormed. 'Captain Gilbert Fairbrother might be a gentleman, but he's dangerous.'

'What's Miss Isobel's fiancé got to do with anything?' Kathleen said coldly. 'You been disgracing yourself?'

Rose bit down on the anger. Mam was in no mood to hear about the Captain's fumbling attempts to get her alone, or the lies she'd had to tell to keep it from Miss Isobel. 'No, Mam,' she said finally. 'But it's awful hard to keep out of his way.'

Kathleen slumped down on the bench, her head in her hands. Joe was yelling again, filling the little cottage with his angry demands. 'You'll just have to take care then. This is where you belong, Rose. You were born here in this cottage, and have seen nothing of the rest of the world.' She looked up then, her dark eyes shadowed with weariness. 'Trust me, Rose. It's for the best you stay.'

She eyed her mam, and despite the dragging weariness in her face could feel no pity. For Kathleen had rarely shown her affection, and when she had it was grudging. 'Why don't you like me, Mam?' Rose asked finally.

'What a thing for a girl to ask her mam,' Kathleen snorted. She thrust herself away from the table and picked up the baby. 'Of course I like you. You're my daughter.'

'That's not reason enough,' Rose said thoughtfully. 'Did I do something bad, Mam?'

'Lord have mercy, will you listen to the child,' Kathleen muttered as she changed the baby's sodden clothes.

'And what of John Tanner,' the girl asked quietly. 'Why were you so nasty to him? He was only there to pay his respects, and you know how we feel about each other.'

Kathleen's gaze slid away and came to rest on her lap. 'If you learn nothing else today, Rose, I want you to remember this. Things are different now. You're almost grown up and I have watched the way it is between you two. Your father would not have approved, Rose, and neither would the *dukkerin*. I want you to promise not to see the boy again.'

'I can't do that, Mam,' she gasped. 'John and I have been friends since I was not much older than Joe. He and I look out for each other – and now Da's gone...' She trailed off, not wanting to invite another blast of her mam's anger.

Kathleen stared at her for a long moment, tears dry, determination in the set of her mouth. 'If you don't promise never to see him again,' she said calmly, 'I'll not forgive you. The earth on your da's grave is still unsettled and his soul is in Purgatory. It was his wish you and John should go your separate ways. Do you defy your da's last wish, Rose?'

Rose shuffled from one foot to the other. Fear of hell and damnation, of her da's soul forever trapped in Purgatory, was too well entrenched. And yet she still couldn't understand why her father should be so against John. Had there been some kind of falling out between them? Her thoughts whirled until she became giddy and had to sit down. If she promised not to see John again, she would be bound by it – for if she broke the promise made on her da's funeral day, she would burn in hell for all eternity.

'I promise not to seek him out,' she said finally. There was a lump in her throat and a heaviness around her heart, and she wondered if she would ever be at peace again.

Sophie was so deep in the past with Rose and John that it took some moments to realise her grandmother had stopped talking. She blinked and reluctantly dragged herself back to the present. The sun still beat on the awning. The kookaburras still chortled, and the surrounding bush still wilted in the heat. It didn't seem real any more and she half-expected to see Squire Ade come riding past – for she had seen those green hills so clearly, felt the frost nipping her fingers and watched as John waved farewell to his Rose.

'Did he come back for her?'

Cordelia cleaned her glasses with a corner of her cotton dress and stared myopically into the distance. 'You'll have to wait and see,' she murmured. 'There's no point in telling a story all at once. Anticipation is half the fun.'

'How come you know so much of what went on all those years ago? You make it sound as if you were there.'

Cordelia perched her glasses on her nose and yawned. 'I was in a way,' she said finally. 'Rose was a great storyteller.'

'But you couldn't have known all that just through her, surely?'

'Not at first,' Cordelia admitted. 'But as the years went on and I matured enough to understand the complex weave of our family history, I was given access to other sources that filled the important gaps. The rest is logic and imagination.'

Sophie shifted in her camp chair. 'What sources?' she asked impatiently.

'This and that,' the old lady replied airily. Then she yawned again. 'Time for tucker and a stiff brandy. All this story-telling has given me an appetite.'

Sophie and her grandmother had started out early the next day so they could cover a good part of the journey before the sun made travelling uncomfortable, and were rewarded by the sight of a mob of roos bouncing over the pale green grass before they disappeared into the dappled shadows of a stand of gum trees. The road was deserted, the land stretching for endless miles around them. Distant mountains were dusky blue clouds along the horizon, and stands of eucalypt and stringy bark danced in pools of heat haze.

Sophie drove along the deserted Newell highway, aware of her surroundings and of her grandmother in the seat beside her. Yet her mind constantly returned to the dreams she had had the night before, and as a companionable silence fell between them, she compared the landscape of her dreams to that of reality.

She had dreamed of a chalk figure embossed in the lush grass of a gentle green hill above an English village, and of the people who had once lived in the Manor House and tied cottages that lay in its shadow. Her years in England had given her a taste of the scenery that must have surrounded Rose and her family, for Cris had wanted her to see as much as possible of his country and they had spent a great deal of time exploring the south coast of England and the tiny villages there time seemed to have forgotten. Now, as her grandmother unfolded the story of her ancestors, she felt those memories come alive, as if she too had witnessed the turns of fate that must have brought Rose to the other side of the world.

'I wonder what Rose felt when she first saw this country,' she murmured. 'It's so big, so empty – so stark compared to her tiny village. She must have been very lonely after living in such a close community.'

'Rose was made of stern stuff,' pronounced Cordelia. 'She might only have been a girl who knew nothing of the world outside her village, but she was clever and quick-witted and made the best of what life dished out to her.'

'How?'

'You'll find out later,' said Cordelia with a smile.

Sophie knew she had to be satisfied but it was hard not to show her impatience. 'Thank goodness things have changed,' she said as they approached the next camp site set on the edge of the Herveys Range. 'These days she could have sued her employers for sexual harassment.'

'Yes,' agreed Cordelia. 'It was a tough kind of justice in those days. Rich and poor alike were tied within their classes with little or no means of escape. For a pretty servant girl like Rose it was even tougher. The gentry looked down on them, if they bothered to look at all, and used them quite shamelessly without a thought for the consequences.'

'Why did you let mother go off on this hare-brained trip in the first place?' Mary demanded.

'I didn't know anything about it until she came out of her bedroom that morning with Sophie and her suitcase,' retorted Jane as she poured herself another drink.

'You could have stopped her.'

She turned from the bar and eyed Mary. 'Have you ever tried to stop Cordelia from doing anything?' Her tone was conciliatory. She had learned long ago not to rise to Mary's bait. If it was a fight she was looking for, she'd come to the wrong place.

'You could at least have called one of us to come and reason with her,' said Mary stubbornly. She drained her glass and helped herself to another gin and tonic.

Jane watched anxiously. Mary didn't usually drink much, there were a lot of calories in gin and tonic, but today was obviously proving more stressful than usual. Yet if she carried on drinking like this, she would soon be drunk and impossible to reason with.

'Cordelia is not someone who listens to reason when her mind's made up about something,' Jane said quietly. 'You should know that, Mary.'

'But to go off to the Hunter with Sophie is sheer madness with the crisis at Jacaranda looming over us all. What on earth possessed her?'

There was no reply from Jane for the trip was as much of a mystery to her as it was to the others. As she watched the younger woman pace the floor, she wondered why it should matter so much.

'What was her mood when she left, Jane? Was there anything odd in her behaviour? Any sign something was bothering her?'

Janet twirled her glass and watched as the light caught the crystal. 'She was the same as always,' she replied. Then she looked back at the pacing Mary. 'I do wish you'd sit down,' she said quietly. 'Wearing a path in the carpet isn't going to change things or bring them back any faster.'

Mary turned to face her, the glass in her hand almost empty now. 'Of course it would suit you if Mum never came back, wouldn't it, Jane?' she said thoughtfully. She waved a hand to encompass the apartment. 'You stand to gain quite a bit when she goes.'

Jane stood up. 'That's a spiteful thing to say, Mary.'

'But it's true, isn't it?' Mary closed the gap between them, her cold gaze sizing Jane up with calculated rudeness. 'You wormed your way into this family, lived free and easy on Mum's handouts. Now you're sitting tight, waiting for whatever she leaves you.'

It took all Jane's acting skills to appear calm before such vitriol – but the veneer was thin and wearing thinner by the minute. 'I don't have to justify myself to you or anyone,' she hissed. 'The arrangement between me and Cordelia is none of your damned business.'

Mary smirked. 'Not for long. If Mother's left you so much as a cent, I'll contest the will. You deserve nothing.'

Jane took a deep breath. 'You'll find there are no grounds to contest Cordelia's will, and you'd be better occupied minding your own business and looking out for your daughter.'

Mary's eyes were suddenly watchful and sharp. 'So you know what's in Mother's will? Helped her write it, did you? Made sure you weren't wasting your time?'

This was intolerable. Jane slammed the glass down on the table and heard the sharp crack as the crystal shattered. She stared at the deepening puddle of gin and tonic on the polished wood but made no move to clear it up. It reminded her of something that had happened a long time ago and, coming on top of Mary's tirade, it was almost too much to bear. 'You'd better go before I say something we'll both regret,' she said softly.

'What could you possibly say to me that I'd find remotely interesting, let alone regret? We're hardly close,' Mary sneered.

'Perhaps the lack of closeness is the best reason for silence.'

Mary frowned and Jane could see she was puzzled. She looked away, almost afraid of the questions that would surely follow for there were things Mary didn't know. Things she wouldn't understand – and this was not the time to reveal them.

'I'm not going anywhere until you tell me where Mum's will is.'

Jane almost breathed a sigh of relief before she looked into the stubborn face. This was something she could handle. 'I have no idea where it is,' she lied.

'I don't believe you.'

'Then we're at an impasse,' said Jane quietly as they stood facing one another. Her pulse was hammering, and she could feel cold rivulets of sweat running down her back. She wanted Mary gone. Needed silence and space so she could drop the façade of cool detachment.

Mary snatched up her handbag and headed for the door. 'This isn't the end of it,' she snapped. 'You'll be sorry you crossed me, Jane. Very sorry.' She didn't say good-bye, merely slammed the door behind her.

Jane sank into the chair and stared sightlessly into the distance. Mary had unwittingly scratched the soft underbelly of her lonely existence within this powerful family, and Jane found that more painful than she could ever have imagined. It had taken years to build up that defensive wall, but only moments for Mary to tear it down. Now she was left feeling vulnerable and lost, her conscience troubled.

4

Kate smiled as she left the meeting of the charity trustees and ran down the steps to the car. She had managed to persuade them to apply for a grant from the Lottery, and with the funding she had already raised, her dream of providing a special facility for young paraplegics was about to become a reality.

Australian Rules football was a tough, physical sport and, like her son had been, there were dozens of youngsters maimed or killed by it each year. Those who survived often had to live out their lives in wheelchairs or nursing homes. One put a terrible strain on both the patients and their carers; the other often took the youngsters miles from their families to places where they felt isolated and forgotten.

Kate's dream was to build a nursing home with a difference. She had found a plot of land on the Mornington Peninsula, and an architect who was willing to give his services free. The building would be constructed along the lines of a luxury hotel, with rooms set aside for visiting relatives and friends of the patients. There would be a medical wing, of course, and all the usual chiropractors, masseurs and physiotherapists, as well as a state-of-the-art entertainment centre with its own cinema that could double as a theatre. Indoor and outdoor pools, a restaurant and small shopping mall would make the complex completely self-sufficient. All profits from the retail and entertainment sectors would be ploughed back into the charity.

The project was ambitious and would cost millions of dollars. The trustees had been slow to commit such a vast sum, but once she'd raised more than half of what they would need, they'd had to capitulate.

Kate slammed the car door and took a deep breath before lighting a cigarette and starting the engine. If her meeting with Charles went half as well, she'd count this as a successful day.

The first spots of rain splattered on the windscreen as she drove down Nicholson Street, past Parliament House and the Hotel Windsor. Typical, she thought. Sun one minute, rain the

91

next. It only needed the wind to get up and it would be like winter again. Turning right into Flinders Street she had to brake sharply and wait, nails tapping on the steering wheel, for the rattling brown and yellow tourist tram to pass before she could turn left onto Princes Bridge.

Charles and his second wife Vipia lived in a six-bedroomed mansion off the Toorak road, and as Kate finally turned the car into the driveway, she was struck, as always, by the sheer grandeur of the place. It was big and rambling behind the remote-controlled wrought-iron gates, its balconies and terraces bright with flowers and tropical palms. The front door had once graced an old church in oak studded with iron. Stone lions guarded the steps leading up to the door, and as Kate passed them she patted them on the head and smiled. Even they looked smug.

The Italian maid opened the door and showed her into the lounge. 'How're the English lessons coming on, Angelina?'

'Is-a good. Fair dinkum.' She grinned. 'I getta de *maestro*.'

Kate raised an eyebrow. Charles must love that, she thought wryly. *Maestro* indeed. Whatever next?

'Kate, good to see you. Drink? Vipia will be with us shortly. Just seeing to lunch.'

She eyed her cousin with exasperated affection as he bustled about serving the drinks. He might be pompous and overbearing in the boardroom but at home he was just a bumbling fool. 'So you've got her doing the cooking now, have you?' Kate teased. 'Saves on the housekeeping, I should imagine.' Charles had a reputation for meanness when it came to servants.

'Now, now, Kate,' he said with a knowing wink. 'Vipia likes to feel she's in charge of her own home. Refused to let me hire any more servants, you know.' He shook his head, his brows meeting in a frown. 'Extraordinary woman,' he muttered.

Kate sipped the drink he handed to her but was saved from any caustic comment by the almost silent entrance of his young wife. The tiny, graceful Thai woman bowed a greeting and went to stand beside her husband. Her almond-shaped eyes were watchful, a smile playing only around her mouth. Her long black hair fell to her waist, her skin was the colour of milky coffee and her dress was a whisper of silk held up by threads of ribbon.

Kate smiled back, feeling as ever awkward and clumsy in the company of one so young yet so composed. Charles had never divulged his wife's age, or where he'd found her, saying only that they'd met in Bangkok through an acquaintance. Kate reckoned she was not much past twenty-five, and judging by what Vipia had confided to her when she'd had too much to drink, had probably been working in a bar or strip club.

'I suppose you want to talk about your mother?' Charles always came straight to the point.

'Then let's do it over lunch.' He put a proprietorial arm around his wife and gave her a squeeze. 'Vipia has prepared Thai chicken with rice and steamed vegetables.'

Kate remembered the last meal the girl had

cooked and could already feel the onset of indigestion. Vipia's idea of home cooking was to chuck in as many chillies and hot peppers as she could find, then send out for more. 'Great,' she said with forced enthusiasm.

The table was superbly set with linen, crystal and silver, with a delicate arrangement of one rose, one twist of something that looked dead and a few leaves as a centrepiece. Kate had to hand it to the girl, she knew how to make a table look nice – even if she did burn the lining of her guests' stomachs with her cooking. No wonder Charles was constantly red in the face.

Kate did the best she could with the lunch, eating as little as possible and shifting the rest around the plate. It reminded her of when she was a child. She used to do the same thing with Brussels sprouts, and could almost hear her mother now telling her to stop making a mess. She finally gave up and drank a long glass of water.

'As you seem to know why I'm here,' she said as she manfully tried to get her numbed tongue to work, 'I assume Edward told you what Mum's up to?'

'Dad did mention it, and although he thinks she's crazy to go off like that at her age, he agrees with me that she's free to do as she pleases so long as she gets back here in time for the next vote.'

'It's unfortunate you and Edward should choose to use the word "crazy" to describe what Mum's doing, Charles,' Kate said solemnly. 'Because that's just what Mary is trying to prove.'

94

He put down his fork and took a long drink of lager. 'I know,' he said finally. 'She turned up here last night.'

'You didn't believe her?' Kate was disturbed to feel her pulse start to race. If Mary had convinced her cousin, then it would indeed be an uphill battle to protect Mum.

'Fair go, Kate,' he blustered. 'Aunt Cordelia's one of sanest people I know. If you ask me, that sister of yours is the one who should be locked up. She's gone too far this time.'

Kate sighed with relief. She should have known her cousin had more sense. 'Mary's not demented, Charles. Merely greedy and spiteful. But I know how to spike her guns. I'd like you to draw up an affidavit to confirm your opinion of Mum's competence. I already have one from Daisy, and I'm seeing Jane later. Perhaps you could approach your father, Philip and the boys?'

'That's a good idea, Kate, but our opinion isn't a medical one. Won't hold water in a court of law.'

'It might only be a small dam, but it's better than no dam at all,' she said firmly. 'I phoned her solicitor this morning. He visited Mum at the beginning of the week, and he's willing to swear she's of sound mind. If we all agree, in writing, then Mary will find it almost impossible to prove otherwise.'

'I'll do my best, Kate,' he said thoughtfully. 'But what if we're wrong and this trip really is the first sign that all is not well with Cordelia? Bloody strange thing to want to do right in the middle of a crisis.'

Kate felt a surge of impatience. 'You saw her the other day. Didn't she impress you with the way she handled the meeting?'

He nodded and grinned. 'She certainly gave as good as she got, I'll grant you that.'

'Mum's solicitor could see no deterioration either. In fact he was impressed by how sharp she was when it came to putting her affairs in order.' Kate looked across the table at her cousin. She had to persuade him to sign that affidavit. 'Daisy and I see her most days, and Jane lives with her. We know her better than anyone, and would be the first to notice if something was off-key.'

'Take your point.' He nodded sagely and stuck his thumbs in his waistcoat pockets as he leaned back in his chair. 'I'll get on to the others straight after lunch.'

'In my country we have respect for our elders.' Vipia's light voice broke the silence.

'We do in this country, too,' said Kate sharply. 'That's why it's so important we block Mary's trouble-making before it gets out of hand.'

Charles patted Vipia's shapely thigh. 'All this talk of business must be boring for you, dear, and as it doesn't concern you, why not get my chauffeur to drive you into town? I know you want to shop for something to wear to the Vintners' Ball.'

The glance she shot at Kate was venomous but Vipia said nothing, merely rose from the table. Having deposited a kiss on her husband's balding head, she bowed to Kate and left the room.

Charles followed her with his eyes then turned back to Kate. 'Artful little thing,' he murmured.

'Better not to discuss the family business in front of her. She was quite put out that Jock didn't include her in his legacies, you know.'

Thank God for small mercies, thought Kate.

Charles eyed her solemnly. 'Anything else I can do? All this trouble couldn't have come at a worse time. Selling out or going public are our only options, and if the opposition get to hear of any in-fighting, they'll begin to circle like rooks on a dead dingo.'

'The family have been at each other's throats for years. I doubt the press will think it news-worthy. Jacaranda Vines has a reputation that will stand up just fine when it comes to the crunch.' She took another drink of water. 'Who has Mum's power of attorney, Charles?'

'Dad. He and Aunt Cordelia arranged it several years ago so that if something happened to her, the business could still run smoothly and the overall power of their share of the corporation would remain in his hands.'

Kate let out a long breath of relief. 'Thank God for that.' Then she had another thought. 'What if something happens to your father?'

Charles raised one bushy eyebrow. 'I have power of attorney over his business affairs, and I can assure you, Kate, they're in safe hands. If he should die, my brother and I will each have fifty percent of Dad's share.'

Kate noticed how he managed to avoid calling Philip by his name. 'Does he know how it's divided up?'

Charles shrugged. 'I haven't told him and I doubt if Dad ever has.' He paused for a moment,

97

deep in thought. 'You don't really think that sister of yours can throw a spanner in the works, do you?'

'I wouldn't put it past her. But if the rest of us stick together on this, she won't get far.'

The water in the pool at the next campsite was icy despite the heat of the sun, and had become a graveyard for flies, cockroaches and ants. Sophie had swum warily from end to end, but had had to give up when a particularly large fly almost went up her nose. Towelling herself dry, she closed the child lock to the gate and wandered back to the camper.

They had parked beneath a tree which offered some shade from the sun, but which was close to the shower block and toilets. Children played football in the dust, barbecues were being lit, and stubbies dug out of vast eskies to oil the throats of the men sitting around listening to the cricket on the radio. The Test was almost over, and England as usual was about to be defeated. This site was basic after the luxury of the last few days but the atmosphere was friendly, and Sophie smiled and said 'G'day,' in reply to shouted greetings as she headed back to the camper.

Her grandmother was sitting beneath the awning, the electric fan Sophie had plugged into the camper's supply purring on the table beside her as she gazed out over the limpid water of the lake. 'Good swim?'

Sophie grimaced. 'Don't ask,' she muttered. 'I need a shower to get the creepy crawlies off me.'

'That's the trouble with outdoor pools,'

Cordelia said wisely, despite the fact she'd never had one and had probably never swum in one.

Sophie showered and changed into a T-shirt and shorts. Then she poured herself a stubby and her grandmother a brandy and soda.

They sat in companionable silence and stared over the lake. It wasn't very attractive, and the bird-life appeared to be almost non-existent. The red earth was heaped in dusty mounds round the edge, the grass spindly and pale, and there was scum floating on the surface.

'Not the best view in the world,' muttered Sophie as she slapped at a mosquito. 'We should have looked around for another site before booking in here. The mozzies are bad enough now. They're going to be a nightmare once the sun goes down.'

Cordelia handed her the repellent and Sophie liberally sprayed them both. 'Right, Gran,' she said brightly. 'You've got a drink, you've been sprayed, and it's fairly cool under this awning. Perhaps you'd better carry on with the story before that brandy kicks in and you doze off.'

Cordelia eyed her mischievously. 'Are you suggesting I can't hold my drink?' She shook her head. 'I don't know what the youth of today is coming to when an old lady like me is shown such little respect.'

Sophie laughed. 'Fair go, Gran. I just want the rest of the story.'

Cordelia smiled, and her gaze grew distant as she once again returned to that small village in Sussex. 'Then perhaps we should now return to Milton Manor and Squire Ade and his wife

Amelia. For their daughter Isobel and Captain Gilbert Fairbrother play an important part in the founding of Jacaranda Vines.'

Captain Gilbert Fairbrother of the 7th Hussars was bored. He'd agreed to accompany his parents to this ghastly parochial back-water of Sussex only because Papa had paid off his tailor's bill and settled his outstanding account at the Beargarden. Otherwise he'd have spent his time in town visiting his favourite haunts – and his mistress.

An officer's life was a good one, and as long as his mother supplemented the half pay the peacetime Army dished out to men who lived in town, he could see no reason to remain in barracks. Father of course didn't approve, but as a matter of pride he'd stumped up the necessary amount for his son's commission and would do so again if he wanted Gilbert to rise higher and avoid scandal.

He yawned as he made his escape from the dining room and headed upstairs. He'd forced himself to endure the mindless prattle of his hostess, the boorishness of his host, and the fawning stupidity of Squire Ade's two daughters, but as neither of them promised a good tumble, he could no longer hide his impatience and had given up flirting with Isobel. It was definitely time to return to London and the pleasures of more sophisticated society.

Isobel and Charlotte Ade were passing presentable – if a little countryfied – but despite Mama's rather obvious attempts to matchmake, he'd managed to avoid being left alone with either of them. The little maid Rose was another matter, though. She was a fiery piece, as he'd learned to his cost when he'd cornered her the other day. The bruises on his shins were evidence of that, but if he ever managed to get hold of her alone then this entire sojourn in the country might not be such a bore after all.

A soft tap at the door interrupted his thoughts, and before he could answer his mother swept into the room.

'We need to talk, Gilbert.'

Clara fingered the halo of curls at her forehead. Gilbert thought how ridiculous they looked on a woman of Mama's age, but as usual she seemed to have forgotten she was well past her best.

'You really should be more careful, Gilbert,' she began. 'Your reputation for plundering the servants' halls is well known, but I do wish you'd contain yourself when we visit friends. Rose is far too young, and a scandal at the moment will put paid to all my plans...'

'What is it you want, Mama?' he said, his tone resigned.

She stood up and eyed her own reflection in the pier glass. 'I have managed to persuade that silly woman Amelia to agree to your formally courting Isobel.' She held up one hand to silence him as they eyed one another in the mirror. 'I will not accept any argument from you, Gilbert. It is time you were married,' she finished firmly.

'But she's impossible,' he spluttered. 'Really, Mama, this is beyond a joke.'

She turned to face him. 'What is beyond a joke

101

is a son of almost thirty who still looks to his father to pay his debts. What is beyond a joke is your continually trying to seduce housemaids and carrying on liaisons with married women. Isobel's father will pay a handsome dowry for his rather insipid daughter now there's a chance of capturing young James Winterbottom for Charlotte.'

She came closer and he could smell the overpowering scent she favoured.

'Isobel has no brothers, and her grandfather on her mother's side has no heir. He's immensely rich and it is said he's loath to leave his money to Amelia or that country clod of a husband of hers. Isobel is his favourite.'

She paused just long enough for Gilbert to take in what she was saying. His mother never failed to astonish him. How the devil did she come by her information? And what kind of tortured mind could play such terrible games when she knew how abhorrent a match with Isobel Ade would be to him?

'Who do you think would stand best chance of all that money and land?' She laughed. It wasn't the girlish trill she usually favoured but a deep, almost sensual chuckle. 'Why, his favourite grand-daughter's husband, of course.'

Gilbert sank on to the window seat. 'There's no guarantee, Mama. You may think you have all the answers, but how do you know he'll leave everything to Isobel? She has a sister.'

Clara came to stand beside him. 'I know a great many things, Gilbert,' she said softly. 'But it wouldn't be wise to tell you all my secrets.' She stroked the fair hair from his eyes. 'Charlotte will marry her suitor and become Lady Winterbottom with a vast fortune and a goodly slice of Berkshire. I doubt her grandfather would see the need to give her more.'

He looked at her, saw the glint of mischief in her eyes and knew immediately she had something on Amelia Ade's father. 'But I don't care for Isobel. She's dull and drab and far too bookish for my liking. She's more fit for a farmer's wife than an officer of the 7th Hussars.'

Her claw-like fingers grasped his chin, forcing him to look into her eyes. 'I'm not asking you to like her, Gilbert, but marry her you will. Your papa can no longer afford to keep you in the manner to which you've been accustomed. Your brother Henry is to inherit, and I will not have his legacy frittered away by your extravagance.'

He was about to protest when he saw the resolute expression in his mother's eyes and knew he was beaten.

It was as if she sensed his capitulation, for she kissed his cheek and held him close for a moment. 'You won't regret it, Gilbert,' she said softly. 'After all, you will be master of your own home, Rose is Isobel's maid and therefore will be at hand should your appetite require more meat than milksop – and who will think twice if you should take a mistress? It's quite the thing for married men you know.'

Isobel stared at her reflection in the mirror and wondered why a handsome fellow like Captain Fairbrother should find her attractive. The brown hair was mousy, the nose too long, the mild grey eyes not wide enough in that round, rather plain face. Her lack of beauty was something she'd accepted as a child, and her dismal seasons two years ago had merely confirmed it. Yet Mama had said he'd asked permission to court her, and although they had barely spoken, she had been flattered and pleased when he'd paid attention to her as they walked the estate, or flirted mildly over a game of cards in the evenings.

'I was born to be a spinster,' she said. 'So why should someone like Gilbert want to court me?' She and her sister were in their room, choosing clothes they would take to London.

Charlotte twirled in front of the glass, her silken skirts rustling busily as she primped and preened. 'Nonsense,' she said sharply. 'Why shouldn't you have a chance of happiness? Really, Izzy, you are such a mouse at times.' She wet a finger and smoothed it over her eyebrows, then pinched her cheeks to bring colour to them. With her head tilted, she eyed the effect in the mirror critically, found it to her liking and smiled.

Isobel eyed her thoughtfully. There was only a year between them, but the difference was startling. She loved her sister but sometimes wondered if Charlotte realised how much it cost her to put on a brave face, to suffer the agonies of shyness and the terrible effort of trying to appear frivolous in company when all she felt was terror. For Charlotte was naturally sunny with a strong personality, and although she wasn't a conventional beauty, her demeanour was such that no one seemed to notice or care.

Isobel returned to the subject of Gilbert. 'His interest does not necessarily mean my status as a spinster will change,' she said wistfully.

Charlotte flounced her petticoats and sat down with a thump on the stool beside her. 'Then you must do more to attract him, Izzy,' she said with exasperation. 'All those long silences between you are hardly encouraging, and look at your dress. It's so plain.'

'Lace and frills don't suit me, Charlotte,' she said as she smoothed the lines of her grey silk dress. 'And when Gilbert and I are together, I can never think of anything to say that might amuse such a worldly man.'

'Do you care for him, Izzy?' Charlotte's wide blue eyes were serious for once.

Isobel could feel a blush spread across her face and looked down at her hands. 'He's very handsome, and I'm flattered he shows interest in me – but care for him?' She paused, her thoughts confused. 'I don't know him well enough to decide one way or another,' she said firmly.

Charlotte picked up a bottle of perfume and pulled out the glass stopper. 'Mama says he's quite a catch,' she said slowly. 'His family is very well connected, you know. You'll have entrée to some of the most sought-after social events if you marry him.'

Isobel was in an agony of indecision. She wanted to please Mama, knew how important this match would be, but she had serious doubts regarding Gilbert's feelings. 'You don't think he's a little ... conceited?' she asked hesitantly.

Charlotte laughed. 'What man isn't? Especially one so handsome. He does cut a dash in that uniform.'

'But I wouldn't be marrying a uniform,' Isobel protested. She turned to her sister and took her hands. 'Charlotte, what if he's only after my dowry?' There, she thought. She'd voiced her one true fear.

Charlotte was still, her eyes steady on Isobel's face. 'Of course he isn't,' she said calmly. 'Gilbert comes from a wealthy family, and your dowry isn't much bigger than mine.'

Isobel wasn't convinced. 'I think Mama and Lady Clara have put their heads together, and he sees me as a convenient way to acquire land and capital. After all, he's the younger son. He will not inherit his father's title or estates.'

'Nonsense,' replied Charlotte firmly. 'He's positively smitten, Izzy. Why, he never left your side last night or this morning. You should be grateful someone wants you after your dismal season in London,' she added impatiently.

Isobel gave a wry grimace. 'Yes,' she said softly. 'The Captain is very aware of protocol. His manners are faultless. But does he care for me?'

'Of course he does, you silly goose. For heaven's sake, Isobel, stop dithering. It can get awfully wearing, you know.' Charlotte flounced from the room, the heavy door thudding shut behind her.

Isobel stared into the mirror. Grateful. That was a terrible word to use to a sister, she thought. Grateful to be bartered off to a man she hardly knew just so Charlotte could marry James

Winterbottom. Grateful that someone wants me – even if it is only for my dowry. If only I didn't care so much for him. If only his presence didn't make my heart flutter so madly I find it difficult to speak. How hard it was to be shy and awkward when one was so plain.

5

'Good-bye, Mam,' Rose called after the cart.

There was no reply from Kathleen, not even an acknowledgement she'd heard as she left for her new life in Jevington with her two sons.

Rose picked up the small bundle that represented all she owned, and with a heavy heart, set out for Milton Manor.

As her grandmother's voice faded into silence, the first hot tear rolled down Sophie's cheek. 'Poor little girl,' she breathed as a wave of misery swept over her and memories of her own childhood flooded back. 'What a terrible thing to do to a child.'

Cordelia's hand rested lightly on her arm. It was if she could see the parallels between Sophie and Rose's lives. 'At least you had me,' she murmured. 'Poor Rose had no one.'

Sophie eyed her through the tears. 'And I love you for that, Gran. But there's still a part of me that wants Mum to notice me,' she sniffed.

Cordelia stroked her arm. 'I can understand that. After all, a mother's love is supposed to be the strongest. But sometimes, even in the animal world, a mother will reject her off-spring. It's through no fault of yours, Sophie – just as Rose wasn't to blame for her mother's coldness.'

'Rose wanted Kathleen to love her, needed her to see she was a good and loving daughter. Why? Why do we feel like this when there's no hope?'

'Hope is all you both had, darling,' Cordelia said softly. 'It was the only weapon you could use, for if that failed you, the bleak truth would have been unbearable.'

Sophie smeared away the tears and blew her nose. It had been a long time since she'd cried. Years since she'd been made to face the unpalatable truth. 'You're right. Mum will never regard me as more than a nuisance, a mistake.'

Cordelia brushed the long black hair from Sophie's face and tucked it behind her ears. 'I understand how painful all this must have been for you,' she sighed. 'But you have to try and understand the way things were with Mary thirty years ago.'

Sophie had heard it all before, but she listened anyway. Perhaps, now she was older, she could understand.

'She married in haste and they were both far too young. Their marriage was already on the rocks when she found she was pregnant. She was very much in love with your father, you know, and wanted to use you to keep him. He went anyway. She kept up the hope he'd come back once you were born, but it wasn't to be. From that moment on she lost all interest in you and I took over.'

Sophie found the pain was less than she'd expected. For there was a part of her which sympathised with Mary. But she found it difficult to understand how any mother could reject her baby so thoroughly.

It was as if Cordelia could read her mind. 'Mary should never have had a child. She's too selfish to share any part of herself. It's why her marriages didn't work. Why she's always searching for the unattainable. There are times when I feel sorry for her. Times when I wish she could see the damage she causes not only to herself but to those around her.'

There was still a hard knot in her throat, and Sophie had to swallow before she could speak. 'I just wonder how a person can go through life completely unaware of others. Was she always so self-centred? Always so angry at the world?'

Cordelia looked thoughtful for a while. 'Mary was the youngest, and I probably spoiled her. But she was a demanding child, often sly and cruel. She saw something and wanted it. Took it, then discarded it. It was always the acquiring that drove her, never the actual possession. I can remember many toys being deliberately destroyed so no one else could get pleasure from them.'

'No wonder the aunts don't like her,' sniffed Sophie. The sadness on Cordelia's face made her reach out. 'I'm sorry, Gran. She's your daughter and you must love her.'

Cordelia's sad expression deepened. 'I don't know that I do,' she admitted softly. 'I suppose, deep down there has to be some remnant of

109

feeling, because I've never given up with her. But I find myself disliking her for what she's done, and what she's become. And yet I'm sad for what she might have been. Mary has spirit. She's clever and inventive. What might she have achieved if all her anger had been directed elsewhere?'

'But why is she so angry? What happened to make her the way she is?'

Cordelia closed her eyes as if the question was too painful to face. 'Perhaps I didn't love her enough when she was little,' she said finally.

'That's rubbish, Gran,' Sophie retorted. 'If you cared for her half as much as you cared for me, then she has no excuses.'

'But did I?' Cordelia whispered. 'I wonder if somehow, Mary realised she...'

Sophie touched the fragile arm as Cordelia's voice tailed off. 'Realised what, Gran?'

'Nothing,' she said firmly. 'I'm letting my thoughts run away with me. Mary had everything a child could want both materially and emotionally. There are no excuses for her behaviour, and I should be old enough by now to stop blaming myself for what she's become. That girl will never accept responsibility for the harm she's wreaked, and she'll go on blaming everyone else until the day she dies.'

Cordelia blew her nose, tucked her handkerchief into her sleeve and made a visible effort to regain her composure. 'It's probably genetic,' she said firmly. 'Goodness knows there's enough manipulative, greedy ancestors in the gene pool to provide an entire family with Marys.'

'That's what life's all about, isn't it? Manipulation. From the minute we're born we twist people to our will. The baby's tears to bring an anxious parent. The child's tantrums and wheedling to wear down opposition. The teenager's wilfulness. The adult's emotional blackmail.'

Cordelia smiled. 'How right you are. You've come a long way from the schoolroom, Sophie. I hope you didn't find the lesson too harsh?'

Sophie shook her head. 'Living in the shadow of Grandad taught me about manipulation. Yet, I think it's your story of Rose that's finally underlined those years of Jock's influence, and shown me how vulnerable we all are. Rose is manipulated by her mother and her circumstances. So are Isobel, Charlotte and Captain Fairbrother. Amelia Ade is both manipulated and the manipulator. Her social class and upbringing the defining factor. John Tanner is influenced by his origins, the squire by his wife.'

'And Kathleen? What do you suppose was the defining influence in her relationship with her daughter? She obviously loved her sons, so why not Rose?' There was a curious intensity in Cordelia's eyes as she waited for Sophie's reply.

Sophie thought about the woman she couldn't help but compare to Mary, and shook her head. 'Kathleen's an enigma. She was educated and conducted herself in a way that belies her social standing. Her marriage appeared strong and loving and her affection for the boys was never in doubt.'

She gave a wan smile, the image of Rose

traipsing along that lonely, pitted village lane still so clear in her mind. 'Sentiment must have been a luxury for people of her class in those days. Perhaps she saw Rose as a younger version of herself, and was trying to harden her for what she knew must lie ahead.'

Cordelia nodded. 'Maybe,' she said softly. 'But perhaps we shouldn't condemn her for that.'

'Why not? If it hadn't been for your loving influence when I was little, God knows how I'd have turned out. Rose had no one.'

Cordelia laughed. 'You'd have been all right, Sophie – whoever reared you. You have it in you to be a success regardless of anything Mary or I might have done. Just like Rose.'

'How can you be so sure of that, Gran?'

'Because I've watched you grow and mature. Seen the determination you have to succeed regardless of the pitfalls. It's almost as if you want to prove something to the world.'

'Maybe I just wanted to prove something to myself,' she replied. Suddenly it all seemed so clear, that she was amazed she'd never realised it before. 'Maybe I needed to prove to myself that I was worthy of something far more than I could have got from Mum, or Crispin, or anyone else,' she said quickly. 'Maybe it was my revenge for all past hurts and slights and I need to stick two fingers up at those who doubted me.'

Cordelia's smile was sad. 'You could be right, Sophie. But I hope you don't see your victories as vindication. See them for what they are. Your success in the business world is the result of hard work and a keen mind, nothing less. Be proud of who you are and what you've achieved by all means – but regard your success as a triumph of self-esteem, not revenge.'

Sophie's spirits lifted as she saw the pride in the old lady's eyes. All the hard work and sleepless nights were worth it just to see that expression. Yet she suspected she might never have achieved so much if she hadn't had the spur of her mother's rejection to instil that determination to prove herself.

'It's late, Gran. Perhaps we should get some sleep?'

Cordelia shook her head. 'I want to finish this part of the story tonight, Sophie. There isn't much more left, but it will tie up a few ends before we move on to the next section.'

John Tanner was sitting on the steps of the *vardo* in the late-afternoon sunshine. It had been a good day at the fight booth in Lewes fair. Most of the horses had been sold, the stock of pegs and baskets and bits of lace were low, and the fortune-telling booth had been busy all day. And yet he felt restless.

Grandmother Sarah jingled the coins in her purse and grinned. 'Plenty more where that came from,' she said.

He didn't reply. His mind was on Rose and the confrontation in the churchyard.

Sarah nudged him. 'Look who's here. Ain't she a sight for sore eyes?'

His spirits sank even further. Sabatina was a Zingaro – a gypsy of Italian birth – who was distantly related. And Grandmother obviously

113

had her sights set on pairing them off. 'Ciao Sabatina,' he called. 'What you doing here?'

Her black hair glistened blue in the sun, reminding him of Rose's. Dark sloe-shaped eyes regarded him mischievously beneath the circlet of *galbi* – gold coins – she'd fixed in her hair. She was beautiful and she knew it.

'The *famiglia* thought it was time for me to catch up with you,' she said huskily.

Sarah eased her joints as she climbed down from the *vardo*. 'Take this. John's got another week of fighting to do. Rub that into his back and shoulders for me.' She handed over a dark blue bottle with a wooden stopper. 'Get your shirt off, boy. I got to visit my *niamo*.' With that she turned and shuffled away, her bright petticoats fluttering in the brisk breeze that swirled around the ring of *vardoes* and tents.

John and Tina looked at one another, smiling with shared understanding. 'Our *puri daj* doesn't change, does she?'

Tina shook her head, her gold earrings swinging. 'Grandmothers never change,' she giggled. 'But to respect them is our duty.' She looked at the bottle and unplugged it. 'Phew,' she gasped. 'What is this?'

'Horse liniment,' he said gruffly as he took off his shirt. 'It's Gran's special concoction and although it stinks to high heaven, it works wonders.'

The almond eyes slid over his torso before returning to his face. The *galbi* glittered in the dying embers of the sun and her skin had taken on the soft hue of a ripening peach. She was more beautiful than he remembered, he admitted silently, but his feelings for her had never gone beyond those of kinship.

Tina's long hair feathered his chest as she began to massage his arms and shoulders. He could smell her scent, the oils she used in her hair and on her sinuous body, and as her fingers worked their magic, he thought he could feel an almost magnetic power drawing them closer.

He closed his eyes and imagined it was Rose touching his skin. Rose who sat so close to him he could feel her body heat.

Sarah returned from her reunion with the other members of her extended family an hour later. She smiled with satisfaction when she saw the *vardo* door closed and no sign of the young ones. John was so like his father Max, she thought. Healthy, handsome and strong with an appetite for life – he couldn't stay *shav* forever. It would take greater will-power than his to resist a beauty like Sabatina Zingaro – especially since Sarah had coached her so well.

Tina was the daughter of the Zingaros' *dukkerin*, and therefore royalty. A match with John would bring the two sides of the powerful family together again, and her father had already agreed so long as Tina didn't object. And Sarah knew she would never do that, for she had eyes for no one but John. If the girl had done as she'd advised, then their one night together would lead to a wedding and all this nonsense over the Fuller girl would come to an end.

Sarah was about to pass by when the door opened and John came out on to the steps.

115

'Where's Tina?' she demanded.

He frowned. 'How should I know?'

His grandmother was grim-faced as she grasped the railing and pulled herself up the steps. The boy had to be made of stone. What on earth had gone wrong? She cuffed him round the ears. 'Don't mess with the fates,' she snapped. 'Tina's meant for you – and I'll do everything in my power to make you see sense.'

Squire Ade was leaning back against a pile of pillows, lavishly spreading butter and honey on his bread, when his wife Amelia entered his room without knocking. That she had come to his bed-chamber at all surprised him, but to enter fully dressed at this time of the morning, and without warning, meant something was afoot and he had a strong feeling he wasn't going to like it.

'There's no time for breakfast, Charles,' she said busily. 'Gilbert will be back soon.'

'So what if he is?' the Squire mumbled through his bread. 'Prefer me own company up here where I can be left in peace.'

Amelia eyed him with contempt. 'No doubt,' she said waspishly. 'But this is more important than your need for solitude.' With her hands folded tightly at her waist, she tilted her chin and met his gaze squarely. 'Gilbert has asked to speak to you regarding Isobel,' she said triumphantly.

His appetite vanished and he dropped the remains of his breakfast on the tray and shoved it aside. 'Does she know?'

His wife clucked impatiently. 'Of course. We had a long talk last night, and she is delighted.'

Charles looked into her eyes. He could see no sign of deception here, no clue that underhand manipulation had been used on Isobel – and yet he had his suspicions. Amelia was devious, and his daughter too pliant and meek to stand up to her.

'I wish to speak to my daughter first, madam,' he said firmly. 'For if, as I suspect, she is against this match, then I will refuse my permission.'

'That is quite impossible, husband,' she said hurriedly. 'Isobel is dressing and the Captain is expected at any minute.'

Charles threw back the covers and climbed out of the four-poster. He was at a disadvantage lying in bed with Amelia standing over him. Drawing a dressing gown over his night-shirt, he tied the belt around his waist. 'Then the Captain will have to wait until Isobel and I are ready,' he growled. 'I will not be bullied in my own house, madam.'

'But, Charles dear...'

'But nothing,' he roared. 'Isobel must be consulted. She's a sensible girl. She'll listen to reason once she understands that scoundrel isn't good enough for her.'

Amelia stood before him, arms akimbo, green eyes filled with tears. 'Don't you dare spoil this for our daughter, Charles. She's in love with the Captain. This will give her a chance to live the kind of life we've always wanted for our girls – a chance to blossom. If you go storming in, you'll terrify her into submission and she'll lose her one chance of happiness.'

Charles was uneasy. He hated to see Amelia cry

117

– didn't know how to handle it. And although he couldn't be sure of its authenticity, his wife's argument was strong and he did want Isobel to be happy. But there were things about the Captain she should know before she tied herself to him. Things he found repellent and which would surely devastate his daughter and shatter what little confidence she had left after that humiliating debut in London.

Amelia reached for his arm, perhaps sensing his hesitation and his thoughts. 'I know you want the best for her but she's mature enough to know her own feelings in this matter and I don't wish her to be hurt again, Charles,' she said softly, tears trembling delicately on her eyelashes. 'Remember how she was after London? It quite destroyed her confidence. Now she has hope again. Would you wish to destroy that?'

'Of course not,' he replied gruffly as he patted her hand. 'But I don't like the fella. Never have. Isobel could do better, don't you know.' His gaze slid away from her, acknowledging the truth that Isobel's chance of finding a husband at all was a slim one.

'But she loves him, Charles,' his wife coaxed. 'If she sees Gilbert's faults, then she accepts them willingly.'

He thought of the report he'd had from the stables about the beating Gilbert had given his horse when it threw him. Remembered the to-do when he'd tried to get his way with Rose. 'He won't be faithful to her, Amelia. Won't look after her properly. He's not a gentleman.'

'Gilbert is smitten with her. Of course he'll be

a faithful, caring husband,' she said firmly. The scrap of lace and linen was dabbed delicately at her tears.

Charles doubted that, but for Isobel's sake he would listen to what the Captain had to say and make up his own mind. 'There are times, madam, when I wish I knew my daughters better,' he said regretfully.

'It is a rare father who knows everything about his children, Charles,' she murmured. 'Especially daughters. But you would take great pleasure in them if you could see them now. They are both so excited at the news, and their bedchamber is a positive riot of dresses and ribbons and petticoats. I haven't heard Isobel laugh so happily with her sister for a long time.'

Charles watched as she swept out of the room. His judgement had had no part in the decision foisted upon him. Amelia had, as usual, outwitted him. For if he was to refuse the Captain, then he would condemn both his daughters and never be forgiven.

'What to do, what to do?' He muttered as he stared out of the window. Was a man ever so put upon? If only he'd had a son. A man knew where he was with sons.

'It is all arranged, my dear. Your father is delighted to grant Gilbert an interview this morning. Quite the best news he's heard in a long time, so he said.' Amelia bustled into the bedroom and began to pull dresses from the cupboard.

Isobel plucked at the ribbons on her petticoat.

Her corset had been fastened so tightly she could scarcely breathe, and Rose had fixed her hair so firmly with pins she knew she would soon have a headache. But that was nothing compared to her agony of indecision over the forthcoming proposal.

'Papa approves then?' Her voice quivered with doubt and excitement. It was a heady mixture.

'Of course he does,' Amelia replied vaguely. 'Now, the yellow silk or the green stripe?' She eyed both dresses, holding them up to the light of the window.

'The yellow is Charlotte's, Mama. You know the colour doesn't suit me.'

'Neither does grey,' muttered Amelia as she discarded dress after dress and threw them to the floor. 'But that doesn't seem to stop you wearing it.'

'Mama,' she protested, reaching down to pick up her favourite dove grey silk from the floor. 'Please, Mama. Let me choose what to wear.'

Amelia eyed her thoughtfully. 'With your colouring, you need to have something to liven up your complexion. What about this? You've hardly worn it at all since it was delivered by the dressmaker.'

Isobel looked at the rose pink gown and chewed her lip. The embroidered bodice was cut so low she felt naked when she wore it, and the lacy frills at the elbow and around the décolletage were fussy enough without the silk rosebuds stitched to them. 'It's a little...'

'It is perfect,' stated her mother. 'I'll get Rose to help you dress and you may borrow my suite of

120

pearls. Rubies would be too much for daytime.'

'Mama.' Isobel reached for her hand to still her fussing. She was in an agony of doubt. 'Gilbert does love me, doesn't he? Truly? It's not just the dowry?'

Amelia gave a soft laugh and embraced her. Then she drew back and held Isobel's hands, her expression indulgent. 'You silly goose! How could he fail to love you when you look so charming? I do declare, Isobel, love has put colour in your face and a sparkle in your eyes. Why, you are almost a beauty.'

She turned as she reached the door. 'Take your time my dear. Mrs Patterson has prepared the morning room for you, so make your way down there when you're ready. I shall come back in a while to see you have not forgotten anything, then wait for Gilbert to finish with your father and escort him to you.' Amelia blew her a kiss and, with a wide smile, left the room.

Isobel was used to her mother's lack of tact, and the veiled insult about her almost being a beauty was lost in the first tremor of excitement. She had been silly to suspect Gilbert's intentions for Papa approved the match – and his judgement was always good. She had no more need to fret. The dreams she had hardly dared believe in were coming true at last.

The new gypsy camp had been set up in a narrow valley called Kingston Hollow. It was some way from the town of Lewes, but experience had taught the Romany it was better to be outside a town if their man should win the fight.

121

John sat alone in the silent *vardo*. His chest was bare and all that covered him was a pair of loose cotton leggings tucked into his most supple leather boots, yet he was warm, his pulse steady. A flutter of anticipation squirmed in his belly as the night breeze carried the distant murmur of voices from the fairground. The other men had told him it was a lively crowd tonight, with money to wager and beer in their bellies. The gents were turning up in their carriages, the whores were doing a brisk trade, and there would doubtless be trouble before the night was through.

He took a deep breath and looked around the only home he'd ever known. The *vardo* was partitioned into two halves, one for cooking, the other for sleeping. The kitchen area at the front had a stove with a narrow chimney passing through the roof, which worked well as long as the wind didn't blow in the wrong direction and fill the enclosed space with smoke. There was a larder, several chests full of grandmother's special bits of crockery and linen, and the walls were strung with copper pots and cooking utensils.

He was sitting in the back, on the broad, double berth he would share with the old lady until he married and could afford to have a vardo built for himself. It was draped with the same snowy lace that hung at the windows, and the collection of fans and tambourines on the walls above it enhanced the cluttered feeling. The lamps had been lit some time ago, and their diffused light softened the jarring colours of the rugs and cushions his grandmother loved so well. The brightly decorated jars and pots gleamed on the narrow shelves, and the intricate vines and leaves Sarah had painted so many years ago on the roof still had the power to convince him they were real.

This was all he'd ever known, all he'd ever wanted – until now. But his travels had shown him a glimpse of different worlds and he knew that if he was ever to capture his Rose he must leave this sheltered place and find his fortune elsewhere.

John eased his well-oiled muscles and flexed his fists. The sinews and veins coiled proud beneath the tanned flesh. He could feel his strength course through them. Tina had done a good job this evening, he admitted silently. Grandmother had taught her well in the arts of massage and healing.

He grinned as he smoothed back his long hair and tucked it behind his ears. The two women were hardly subtle and, truth be told, he was enjoying the attention. Tina was certainly a fine catch for a man. If his affections hadn't been elsewhere, he might have taken advantage of the situation. But this was not the time to think of Tina and Rose. He had a fight to win.

He knew of his opponent but they'd never met. Mad Jack Jilkes was a seasoned fighter with an impressive number of victories behind him and a large band of followers. There had been a time when Jilkes was considered good enough to contend for the British championship, but his fondness for the drink had ruined his chances and now he was forced to find his fights in the bare-knuckle arenas of the country fairs.

John flexed his fists, breathing deeply, concentrating all his energy on thoughts of his opponent. Mad Jack was almost fifteen years older than him, and despite his legendary past, John had seen his last two fights and knew he could beat him. He felt strong, almost invincible, and was impatient to step into the ring.

The *vardo* rocked as heavy footsteps climbed the steps to the door. The sharp rap was followed immediately by his cousin Tom Wilkins' voice. 'You ready, John?'

He nodded and stood up, mindful of the low roof. 'About as ready as I'll ever be,' he said firmly.

Tom's round face split into a grin. 'Should be easy pickings tonight, John. Mad Jack's been drinking and his crowd are laying heavy bets. Reckon you only need show up to win.'

John's hand clamped down on his cousin's pudgy shoulder. 'Don't ever underestimate the opponent, Tom. Jack might be drunk but he's an alley cat. He'll fight until his last breath, and fight dirty and all. This won't be no walkover.'

'Have you looked at yourself, lately, John?' Tom didn't wait for a reply but rushed on, his eyes bright with admiration. 'You got muscles bulging all over you, and your belly is as ridged as a wagon rut. You gleam, John, as if you were made out of copper, and I wager any man facing you tonight will know he's beaten before he lays a fist on you.'

John rather liked the flattery, but knew it for the

hero-worship it was and could therefore dismiss it. 'It ain't the way I look, boy, it's the way I handle meself. Now get out of me way. I got a fight waiting.'

Tom's hand stilled him. 'There's something I gotta tell you, John. And it's important.'

He sighed as he pulled on a thick jacket against the cold. 'You're stretching me patience, Tom,' he warned softly.

The boy shrugged, his face eager to share his news. 'Dad said he saw Big Billy Clarke come in with Jack's crowd and you know what that means, don't you?'

John stood still, excitement and hope high in him. 'Big Billy?' he repeated. 'Jack's manager?' He shook his head, reason taking over. 'Probably only here to keep an eye on his fighter.'

Tom rushed on. 'Dad reckons word's got out about you, and the man himself has come to take a *shufti*. Mad Jack's had 'is day is what Dad says, and 'e reckons Big Billy's looking for another fighter to put up for next year's British title fight.'

John tamped down a flutter of excitement. He had to remain calm and focus on winning. 'Better give 'im something to watch then, hadn't we?'

'Gentlemen,' shouted John's Uncle Harry, Tom's father. 'I present this evening's entertainment for your pleasure. In the red corner – Gypsy John Tanner.'

John raised his eyebrow at his young cousin. 'Since when have I been called Gypsy John?'

'Since Dad thought it up about five seconds ago,' Tom hissed back. 'You know what he's like

– anything to get the punters going.' He grinned. 'Good luck. I got a few bob on yer meself.'

'And in the blue corner, gentlemen, I present – Mad Jack Jilkes. Champion of the ring in over forty fights.' Harry's voice was drowned in the roar of welcome as the big man stepped into the ring.

John watched as Jack raised his arms to acknowledge the crowd. At first sight he had lost none of his awesome height or width. But although the fists were still the size of hams, John could see that the other man's face bore the scars of too many fights. The once iron-hard body was running to fat and the leg muscles were wasted where once they had been mighty pillars. Yet the impression of a man at the end of his fighting career was a false one for as Jack turned with a sneer to face him, John could see the killer gleam in those yellowed and blood-shot eyes. Mad Jack might be past his prime and ale-sodden, but he was still a fighter who would hold on to his glory for as long as he had breath. This would not be an easy fight.

They squared up to one another as Harry Wilkins stood between them, milking the moment until the crowd reached fever pitch. He recited the meagre list of rules that governed a bare-knuckle match but his words went unheard as John returned glare for glare, his pulse slowing, his mind and thoughts cooling with icy purpose for the task that lay ahead.

'So they send me a gypsy cur to put out of its misery,' Jack growled through the remains of his teeth. 'I'm going to enjoy this.'

126

John would not rise to the bait. It had been tried many times before and he'd learned to deal with the insults. His gaze was steady as he flexed his fists and balanced lightly on the balls of his feet.

Jack spat on the floor, inches from John's boots, but there was a gleam of something in the older man's eye that told John his calm demeanour was getting to him.

He tensed, waiting for Harry's signal to begin. Mad Jack was known to be a dirty fighter and John would have his work cut out to avoid the steel-capped boots Jilkes wore as extra weapons.

The right hook came from nowhere with such speed and ferocity that as John dodged out of the way, he felt the wind of it sail past his ear. Mad Jack was fighting true to form by beating the bell.

With Jack unbalanced by the punch and his body exposed, John connected with the man's flabby gut in a series of hard jabs. The bruising, vicious blows appeared to have little effect on the big man, and as John closed in, he was caught by a meaty fist in an upper-cut that almost lifted him off his feet and left his ears ringing.

He was thrown into the arms of his handlers who had thirty seconds to get him back into the three-foot square. They shouted encouragement as he tried to clear the flashing lights from his head. The breath was trapped in his lungs, sweat stung his eyes, and as his handlers shoved him back into the centre he felt real fear. He had lost sight of his opponent.

John shook his head, met his opponent's fist with his chin and staggered. The coppery taste of blood and the baying of the crowd seemed to bring him to his senses. He began to dance around the square, making the big man lumber after him. Time was what he needed. And the chance to catch his breath and clear his head.

Jack's strange yellow eyes were shot with blood and rage as he swung futile punches at the air between himself and the dancing man before him. 'Stand still, you mongrel,' he growled. 'Fight like a man.'

John danced lightly on the balls of his feet, his gaze now clear and steady on his opponent as they circled one another. His long arm shot out, the fist catching Mad Jack's cheekbone. A slash of red opened up and blood mingled with sweat on the punch-drunk face.

Another blow, another cut. Bone jarred, splintering beneath his hammer blows. But it did nothing to quell the rage in those feral eyes.

The kick caught him just below the knee, making him stumble and lose his rhythm. Mad Jack closed in, fists like hammers as they found the soft flesh beneath John's ribs. He danced away, gulping air into his battered lungs, favouring his injured knee. Mad Jack would have to be dealt with swiftly before he caused further damage. The bastard might be ale-sodden, but he was mean and strong and far more dangerous than his condition and age had led John to believe.

With sweat slicking his face, he dodged another swinging punch, then closed in quickly for a series of hard, quick jabs to the other man's exposed belly before dancing away again.

Mad Jack stumbled. He was off balance and

winded, his punches flailing the air. He swatted away his handlers who shouted for him to take the permitted thirty seconds, and bellowed with rage. Raising his fists to ward off further blows, he shook the blood and sweat out of his eyes and lurched around the square after the dancing figure. 'You're dead, you bastard,' he yelled.

John threw a dummy punch.

Mad Jack lifted his arm to deflect it and didn't see the upper-cut sledgehammer that caught his chin such a glancing blow he was rocked off his feet. He crumpled, swayed for an endless moment, then hit the floor with a crash that sent shivers through the soles of John's boots.

The crowd were on their feet. A roar of anger exploded like a tidal wave over John's head as he danced around the fallen man. 'Come on then, loud mouth,' John yelled above the noise. 'Get up and fight.'

Mad Jack was hauled to his feet by his handlers as Harry Wilkins began the count, but the ageing fighter had survived too many bouts to be disorientated for long, and soon shrugged his minders off. Blood, snot and sweat flew into the baying crowd as he shook his head like a great hound. But the man's evil temper made him careless. Mad Jack's punches were flailing wildly now, missing their mark, throwing him off-balance.

John neatly side-stepped, caught the older man off-guard, and with every ounce of strength he had left, swung a mighty punch to his chin. It hit square on, snapping Mad Jack's head back, making his eyes roll, his mouth drop open in shock. The mighty shoulders sagged as the arms drooped and the fists uncurled.

The crowd fell silent. A deathly hush enveloped both men as they faced one another, and John could feel the animosity suspended in that terrible silence.

Mad Jack swayed, his eyes unfocused, his once mighty legs trembling.

There was no time for pity, no place in the boxing ring for complacency. John hit him again. A swerving, accurate punch that caught the giant square in the face.

The big man tottered, blood streaming from his nose. Then he fell to his knees as if in homage to the younger fighter. His great bulk trembled, and like the chalk face of a cliff in a high sea, he slowly collapsed on to the ground.

Harry began the count. Jack's handlers had thirty seconds to get him upright and back in the ring. John stepped away. The silent crowd leaned forward as one, every eye on their fallen hero.

'Time's up,' yelled Harry into the ominous silence. 'We got a winner.'

The crowd erupted. Rotten fruit sailed into the ring, swiftly followed by the wooden seats and benches. Cushions were followed by ale pots and shoes as Mad Jack Jilkes was lifted by his handlers and hauled ignominiously out of the marquee.

Harry ducked a flying chair leg. 'Time we got out of here, boy,' he yelled above the uproar.

John didn't need telling. Surrounded by his handlers, he leaped out of the ring and tore through the canvas curtain into the night. The darkness was absolute after the light of the marquee, but the Romanys who'd been waiting for this moment had their night-sight and John and Harry were guided swiftly to the hidden horses.

As John spurred on his horse, his thoughts were bitter. The pattern would be repeated tonight as always. His victory meant his people had to hide, for the disappointed locals had no respect for their women or their property. If their camp was found, there would be fires set, stock stolen or set free, and their lives put at risk. The game was not worth it.

Tonight the camp was well hidden, and as John and the others turned their horses into the valley, they were certain they had not been followed.

Tina and Sarah were waiting for him. 'Drink this, boy. It'll put life back into you,' Sarah handed him a foul-smelling brew which he knew had magic powers to heal, and heal quickly. He gulped it down.

'John Tanner?' The voice rang out, clear and demanding from the darkness.

The men formed a protective line in front of the women. They had been so certain of their escape – now they were compromised. 'Who wants him?' John stepped forward but could see only shadows shifting in the darkness.

'Billy Clarke,' came the answer.

John and the others exchanged glances. 'Light the torches,' he whispered. 'And be ready if it's a trick.' He took another step away from the protective line. 'Show yourself, Billy Clarke,' he called.

The silhouette of a man on horseback moved against the starry sky and began the descent into the valley. The flickering torches showed a tall man, squarely built, who sat easily on the back of a thoroughbred.

John waited, his pulse racing. He could hear no other horses, could feel no aura of danger surrounding the visitor – perhaps it really was Big Billy Clarke.

The man swung down from the saddle and stepped forward, his hand outstretched in greeting, his expression friendly. 'I'm sorry to intrude like this, but you left so swiftly, I didn't have time to catch up with you at the fairground.'

John heard the murmur of the others behind him, but all he could focus on was the other man. Billy Clarke's eyes were steady in an honest face, his handshake firm. 'No point hanging around when there's a mob after your hide,' John said. 'But you took a risk coming here like this.'

The big man smiled as he looked at the circle of people before him. 'I didn't expect *pachiv*, certainly, but I see no risk in visiting my *niamo*.'

There was a stunned silence followed by a murmur of suspicion. '*Pachiv* is a ceremony given only for honoured guests,' said John solemnly. 'And although you say you are visiting relatives, your accent is not of our tribe, but *Lomavren*.'

Billy Clarke took off his hat to reveal thick black hair. 'My tribe came from Armenia, but surely as Romanys we are one family against the *gadjikanes*?'

John laughed. 'So that's how you were able to

132

follow us without being discovered! The *gadji-kanes* would have made a lot of noise, crashing about on the downs with their clumsy horses and yapping dogs. But you surprise me, Billy Clarke. I didn't know you were of the blood.'

Big Billy Clarke smiled, his dark face creasing into a thousand lines. 'Old habits die hard, boy, and although I've been living amongst the *gadjikanes* for a long while, I still have a few tricks up my sleeve.' He looked around him. 'As for my blood, sometimes it isn't politic to reveal my ancestry.'

There were nods and murmurs from the others as they crowded around the big man, and after introductions John led the way to his *vardo*. The men and women of his tribe followed, squeezing into the confined space until they were spilling out on to the steps or left to look through the windows.

Heat rose from the press of bodies as lanterns were lit and the ale was passed round. Voices rose and fell as pipes were smoked and the evening's fight was discussed. There was finally a lull in the debate and Billy turned to John. 'How would you like your next fight to be in a real boxing ring in London?' he said casually.

The lull became a heavy, expectant silence as all eyes turned to him.

'Depends what you can offer – and who the fight's with.' John's voice was calm but his thoughts were in turmoil. The famous Billy Clarke was offering him his dream – yet dreams could be won or lost in a moment's carelessness. He had to remain clear-headed despite the thrill of anticipation that shot through him.

The big man smiled. 'That is something we need to discuss, John. Because I see you as the next contender for the British title.'

6

Cordelia was more weary than she'd ever been. The retelling of the history of Jacaranda Vines was draining, and coming so soon after the crisis Jock had left behind, she wondered if perhaps she had made a mistake in coming on this journey.

You're an old fool, she berated herself as silence descended and Sophie's soft, even breathing accompanied the sighing of the wind in the gum trees. The story could have been retold back in Melbourne. Yet, as she lay there, her mind too active for the sleep she so desperately longed for, she knew this was the only way. There were people in the Hunter who were the final link to the past. People who might be willing, after so many years of silence, to heal the breach and bring life back into the broken, dying vines. It was a gamble she had to take. The last gamble in her bid to save her granddaughter's inheritance. And she knew that if she failed this time, Jock would finally have won.

Cordelia closed her eyes as the first rumble of thunder drifted overhead. The breeze had dropped and now, as the air thickened and the copper sharpness of an electric storm tainted the

134

softer scents of eucalypt and wattle, she was taken back to those first years of her marriage. The past was catching up with her, dimming the present, coming alive with such clarity that it was almost as if the intervening decades had never been.

Jock had been a patient, gentle lover in those early years, and she'd felt herself blossom as she explored her own sensuality and been surprised at the hidden depths he'd set free within her. Finally she had found an outlet for all those pent-up frustrations. Finally she had found someone who understood her need to run free and feel the earth between her toes and the wind in her hair. They shared the same dream, strove for the same goals, and when she gave birth to her precious twin boys, the future had never looked so bright.

Then her father had died, and as if that wasn't bad enough, the long dry arrived. Endless and exhausting, it drained the energy from the land and the people who tended the wilting vines, limping from one year into the next, and then the next. The sun was merciless, the winds hot, the sky scorched of colour as they trudged the long rows of vines with buckets of water. They might as well have spat into the wind for all the good it did.

Cordelia had been torn between two loyalties during those terrible five years, and even now she wondered if perhaps it had been the drought that had caused the first cracks in her marriage. For just as it split the earth beneath the vines and blew dust spirals along the terraces, so it parched her dreams and laid bare the roots of her relationship with her husband.

Jock's Bundoran was a smaller vineyard than Jacaranda, and easily managed with the terraces occupying less than a couple of thousand acres. He'd set up a watering system of pipes from the bore holes and depleted rivers, and as long as there was some water in the underground springs, Bundoran would survive.

Jacaranda Vines was another matter. It sprawled over thousands of acres, making it almost impossible to water on the same kind of system. The work was labour-intensive – hopeless against the onslaught of the drought.

Jock had known Jacaranda would fail to bring in a harvest, and couldn't understand why Cordelia insisted upon rising before dawn every day to cart water back and forth along the dying terraces of vines before returning, exhausted, to tend to Bundoran. His winery might be smaller than Jacaranda, with less history behind it, but it would come through the drought with minimal loss if he and Cordelia put their backs into it and didn't give up. He resented her stubborn determination to fight for Jacaranda's survival when his own vines needed just as much attention, and their arguments became more bitter as the heat increased.

The drought had finally broken with torrential rains that flattened Jacaranda's surviving vines and pounded them into the rich black earth. As Cordelia joined her brother Edward and her mother in that first, devastating walk through the terraces after the downpour, they knew they were finished. There would be no harvest this year, as there had been none for the five previous years. They had lost everything. Jacaranda Vines was dead.

Cordelia had returned to Bundoran on that damp, bleak morning, her skirts muddy, her spirits low, to find Jock jubilant.

'We're safe, Cordy! The vines have survived despite the downpour. I knew that staking system would work.'

He must have seen the lack of enthusiasm in her eyes for his joy was swiftly replaced with cold anger. 'I told you Jacaranda wouldn't come through. If you'd put as much energy into looking after our vines as you did over there, we might not have lost the Sauvignon.'

'Jacaranda is more mine than Bundoran will ever be, Jock,' she said quietly. 'My family have worked that vineyard for four generations. Now it's gone.' She could feel the tears threaten but refused to let them fall. She wasn't about to let him see how much the failure meant to her. 'I'm just glad Father isn't around to see it.'

Jock had looked at her then, his expression kindly. She was bedraggled, her hair stuck damply to her face and dripped down her back as her muddy boots stained the polished floor, yet her chin was up, her mouth set in determination. He'd put his arm around her and held her close. 'I know how much Jacaranda means to you, Cordy, and I'm sorry if I was insensitive. But this way of life we've chosen isn't for the weak. Your father knew that, and wouldn't condemn you.'

'I know,' she sniffed against his waistcoat. 'But without a harvest for five years, Jacaranda has no money to buy in more seedlings. Mum has lost the will to fight since Dad's death, and Edward's still too young to take over. If I don't do something, and quickly, Jacaranda will go under for the last time.'

She could hear the beat of his heart against her ear. It was steady and comforting in the silence that followed her outburst, and she burrowed into his embrace.

When he spoke some minutes later, his voice was thoughtful. 'Our harvest will make enough this year to invest in new vines for Jacaranda. If you're up for a challenge then so am I. Let's see if we can salvage something from this disaster.'

Drawing back from his embrace, she looked up into his eyes. 'Do you mean it, Jock?' She could hardly bear to hope, for this seemed like an answer to her prayer.

He nodded. 'I'm willing to invest in Jacaranda Vines, but that investment cannot be a gift, Cordy. I want something in exchange.'

Her pulse hammered as dark suspicions tempered hope. 'What?'

'I want a fifty percent stake in the vineyard.'

Cordelia sighed in the darkness as sleep finally descended. The vines Jock had planted all those years ago might have rescued Jacaranda, but in doing so, he had sown the wind. Now they were reaping the whirlwind.

The wooden swing-seat creaked as Daisy sat there in the darkness on the verandah. The air was still, as if poised for the coming storm, and scented by the night stock and jasmine that she'd planted many years ago. Ordinarily she would have been taking pleasure from the soft stillness of her garden, but tonight, as she gazed myopically out towards the ocean, she was barely aware of her surroundings, for her mind was elsewhere.

She still missed her husband Martin, even though it had been almost five years since his death. She supposed it was the manner in which he went that hadn't allowed her to get used to the idea. The cancer had gone undetected for years, and when it was finally diagnosed it was too late to operate. Three months later he was gone, and she still couldn't accept the void he'd left behind. Still found things she wished she'd said to him. For theirs had been a truly happy marriage despite her father's disapproval.

She smiled as she remembered how furious he'd been when she'd stood her ground and refused to marry anyone else. It had been her one act of defiance, and she had never regretted it.

With a long sigh, Daisy untied the cord of her cotton dressing gown and shrugged it off. It was too warm for even the lightest of clothes, and although she was normally shy, she knew no one could see her sitting there in her nightdress, for the verandah was shielded from the road by distance and a line of flowering red gums.

She sat there in the darkness thinking about her life, wondering how it would have been if she and Martin had been able to have children. Maybe, if she had someone else to care for, she wouldn't feel so isolated. Yet there were no guarantees in this life, and she couldn't be sure that any children she might have had would have wanted to be bothered with her. Elderly lonely parents could become a burden.

'But I'm not old,' she whispered into the darkness. 'I'm fifty-one. No age compared to Mum. No age at all.'

She thought about that for a long movement, the realisation coming like a thunderbolt. It was time to face up to reality. Time to stop wasting her life in mourning and self-pity. Martin had always protected her from Jock and Mary. Had cocooned her against the harsh realities of the family corporation and the attendant business worries, even though she'd been perfectly able to cope with such things. And she had willingly let him do it because it was easier to give in than fight to be heard.

Her father had seen her natural reserve as a lack of intelligence and had instilled in her a crisis of confidence so that she was terrified of large gatherings and awkward with strangers. His bullying tactics had cowed her and she'd come to believe very early on that her looks were her one redeeming feature. Now, as the toll of Martin's death was etched in every line of her face, she had come to believe she had lost even that saving grace, and like a timid mouse hidden herself away to become more grey than ever.

She stood up, the forgotten dressing gown slithering to the wooden floor of the verandah. Her pulse was racing as she opened the screen door and walked into the lounge to look in the mirror. If she could believe in herself again then perhaps the years of Martin's steady influence

140

wouldn't be wasted. If she could see in her reflection one glimpse of the young girl who had defied her terrifying father and married the man she loved, then she had a future less grey – less empty.

Daisy's hands were trembling as she switched on the lights. No negative thoughts must cloud her judgement, she decided, and after a deep breath dared to face the woman in the mirror.

Of course there were lines on her face, but in her imagination they had been far worse than the reality. There was grey in the wavy dark-blonde hair, but that could easily be dealt with. Her eyes behind the steel-framed glasses were surprisingly clear and steady, the grey irises ringed with black, the lashes perhaps not as dark or as long as they once were. Contact lenses and mascara would help – she'd see about that tomorrow.

Her fingers traced the high cheekbones and long, slender neck. She'd lost the youthful roundness from her face but the look suited her and her neck was still unlined. The mouth could do with a bit of lipstick and it had been years since she'd bothered to have a manicure. Her once long, perfect nails had been ruined by the frantic gardening she'd done to fill in the lonely hours since Martin's passing.

She blinked and blocked out the negative thought, lifting her chin defiantly at her reflection as she stepped away from the mirror to take stock of her figure. She had always been slender, even if she wasn't very tall, and although she could do with putting on a few pounds, the silhouette through her thin nightdress was still shapely and untouched by stretch marks or scars.

'It's time you stood up to be counted, Daisy,' she said firmly to her reflection. 'No more dowdy clothes. No more second best. And no more being bullied.'

They were brave words for one who had accepted long ago that her place in the family was at the end of the queue. The grey eyes looked into themselves for a long moment as if she was waiting for someone to deny this newly found courage. But there was only silence.

'You still have a life, Daisy,' she told herself. 'Dad can't hurt you any more – only you can do that by doing nothing. So go on, get out there and make yourself heard.' She smiled at the silver-framed photograph that always stood on the mantel.

Martin smiled back, and in the silence of that empty room – seemed to whisper encouragement. 'You defied him once – so do it again.'

Daisy nodded. Her husband's loving spirit was alive within her. She had taken the first step towards self-belief and tomorrow she would begin her emergence from the shadows of her family to campaign against the destruction of Jacaranda Vines.

It was cool and pleasant in the first few hours after dawn and Sophie had returned from her swim refreshed and full of energy. She had slept well the night before, her dreams full of Rose.

'You look chipper this morning, darling. Good night?'

Sophie nodded as she towelled herself dry and

changed into bikini top and shorts. 'Haven't slept so well in years. Must be the fresh air.'

'So you're not sorry you came along then?' Her grandmother's smile was sly.

Sophie laughed. 'Not at all. It was time I had a holiday.' She paused, knife hovering over a tomato as she prepared breakfast. 'Do you realise that barring the two weeks Crispin and I spent on honeymoon, this is the first holiday I've had since leaving uni?'

'All work and no play,' sniffed Cordelia. 'Can I have two slices of bacon? I'm feeling peckish this morning.'

'The doctor said you should go easy on the animal fats, Gran.'

'Stuff and nonsense. What does that old coot know about anything? Two rashers, and I'll have a fried slice as well.'

'Your funeral.'

'At least I'll die happy,' she retorted, and they both laughed.

Breakfast was eaten outside under the awning. It was still cool and the flies were not yet swarming so it was a leisurely, pleasant meal. As they ate they talked companionably of this and that and nothing in particular.

'Why are we making this journey, Gran?' Sophie asked finally. 'Couldn't you have told me the history behind Jacaranda without leaving Melbourne?'

'I could have,' she agreed. 'But I've long had a wish to see a particular place once more before I die, and I could think of no one I'd like better to come with me than you.'

143

'And what place is that exactly?'

'You'll find out soon enough,' Cordelia said as she lathered butter on her toast.

Sophie sighed and gave the old woman an impatient look. 'Why's it so important to keep our destination secret? What's there that's so special?'

'People. Memories. Part of my youth,' Cordelia murmured.

'When was the last time you visited?'

Cordelia's smile was sad as she looked into the distance. 'It was a long, long time ago, Sophie. Before I met your grandfather. I hope it hasn't changed too much, it would break my heart not to recognise it.'

She looked back at Sophie and must have seen the questions in her eyes for she patted her hand and smiled. 'I'll tell you more when we get there, darling. For now you will have to be satisfied with the story of how Rose came to Australia.'

Despite Amelia's objections that it would seem unnecessarily rushed, the wedding was planned for late summer. Isobel and Gilbert would be married in Wilmington Church with the Bishop of Lewes performing the ceremony. The reception would be at the Manor.

Outside in the grounds Rose tucked the latest of her mother's infrequent letters into her apron pocket. It had been read many times over the past four weeks and she wondered when she would hear from Kathleen again. With a wistful sigh she stared out over the kitchen garden. The early-summer sunshine had brought warmth to

144

the mellow brick walls that surrounded this peaceful haven and she lifted her face to the last of it, welcoming this moment of quiet after the bustle of the household. She could dream here, conjure up memories of her mother and brothers and the home life she still missed so terribly.

There had been only two opportunities in the past five months to visit the Dame School in Jevington, and when she had, she'd found an awkwardness had grown between herself and her Mam. Not that she was unkind, just remote. Rose gave a tremulous sigh. The family ties had been broken since she had moved into the Manor. Davey was wary of her and there was never enough time on her hurried visits to rekindle his trust. Even the baby didn't recognise her any more and would screech and struggle when she tried to hold him.

Not that she didn't like living in the Manor, she reminded herself. The food was plentiful, the beds comfortable, and when the long days of work were over, the company of the other servants made her forget her aching feet. To her relief, the Captain had kept his hands to himself recently when he made his frequent visits, and she'd only caught a glimpse of him now and again as he rode out over the Downs.

Rose's thoughts turned to John as the sun slowly sank. She'd heard nothing from him since Da's funeral and wondered if the rumours of his success in the boxing ring were true. And yet she couldn't believe he would go all the way to London without first coming to say goodbye.

Her spirits ebbed as the sun disappeared. It was

as if she'd been abandoned by everyone, and it was at times like these, when she had a few moments to herself, that the sense of loneliness seemed hardest to bear. She missed John's company almost as much as she missed her own family, and hoped the rumours were untrue, or merely an exaggeration of the truth. Perhaps, now summer was here, he would return to the village for the horse fair the gypsies always held on the common before harvest.

'Miss Isobel wants you, Rose.'

She was startled from her thoughts by a fellow maid, Queenie's, voice. She straightened her cap and smoothed her apron before hurrying indoors.

Isobel Ade was flushed with excitement as she turned from the window in her room. 'I have good news, Rose! Mama has agreed you may accompany me to London when I am married.'

Rose's spirits sank. 'Thank you Miss Isobel,' she murmured. 'But I know Queenie was hoping to go with you. She'll be disappointed.'

'Queenie isn't my personal maid,' Isobel said with a frown. 'Are you not pleased to be coming with me, Rose? I thought you would like the adventure of London and all it has to offer.'

The girl bit her lip. London was an exciting prospect – it was just unfortunate that the Captain was to be part of the deal. 'London sounds wonderful, Miss Isobel,' she replied with as much enthusiasm as she could muster. 'Will you be taking any of the other servants up with you?' At least if there were several of them, it would be safety in numbers.

'Alice from the kitchen, and I'll also be hiring a cook and housemaid.' Isobel took Rose's hands and looked into her face. 'What's troubling you, Rose? Is it the thought of leaving Wilmington or are you afraid of losing touch with John?' Isobel and her young maid had always been close and she knew most of Rose's hopes – if not all her fears.

She fixed on the excuse. 'If I leave here he won't know where to find me,' she said quickly.

Isobel laughed and turned away. 'You silly goose! Of course he'll know where you are, and as he's in London himself, I hear, you'll be able to see him on your days off. It's all settled, Rose, and I will not have any more argument.'

Rose bobbed a curtsy and left the room. Her mood was mixed. With John in London and a house full of servants, perhaps things would be all right. Yet she had the feeling the Captain, married or not, wouldn't change his ways, and the prospect of trying to avoid him all the time was daunting.

Gilbert emerged from the dining room, having drunk rather too much port after an excellent dinner, and caught sight of Rose through the long window in the hall. She was standing beneath the lantern in the garden, talking to some yokel. A letter passed between them and he wondered if she had an admirer who sent her love notes or whether the spotty, callow youth she was talking to was the focus of her affections.

At any other time he would have left them to it and joined the ladies in the drawing room. After all, she was just a servant, hardly worth noticing at all, except for that fine figure and fiery temperament. But something in her demeanour as she read that letter tweaked his curiosity and he made his excuses to the Squire and slipped out of the side door.

Rose's hand trembled as the meaning of the neatly written words hammered its way into her mind.

Rose, acushla,
The things I have to say to you will cause pain and I'm sorry I cannot be there to comfort you. But you are old enough now to follow your own path in life and will understand my reasons for leaving you in the care of strangers.

I can no longer live and work in Jevington, Rose. The dames are kind, but Joe is always sick with fever and Davey had made it impossible to remain here. He has taken to setting fires and I am afeared he will do real harm one day. But that is not the only reason for my leaving. I have never been happy in England, you know that. I have a deep yearning to be back amongst my own people in Ireland, and now your da is no longer by my side, I can return to my family.

You are wondering why you cannot make the journey with us. As a woman, I know how hard life will be for you, acushla, and my apparent coldness was only my way of preparing you for the future – a future that would not be possible in Ireland where work is scarce and a young girl cannot hope to have all the advantages you do

148

with the Squire. There are things I have done in the past that have brought shame – and worse – on my family, and by moving away from Sussex, perhaps those dark deeds will fade. Keep strong, Rose, and remember your promise to Da and me to stay away from the Tanners – for there are strong forces against such a union, and the *dukkerin* must not be crossed.

Rose's gaze swept over the spidery, blotched scrawl in horrified bewilderment and pain. She could see where Mam had shed tears as she wrote, but they couldn't have been half as bitter as the ones that rolled down Rose's cheek as the full impact of the words sank in.

'But why?' she sobbed. 'How could you just leave me? Didn't you love me at all?' The letter crumpled in her fist as she picked up her heavy skirts and ran out into the welcome darkness. She had no idea where she was going or what she was doing. She knew only that she had to get away.

Darkness enveloped her as she plunged down the hill to the line of rhododendrons that ran along the southern boundary of the Manor grounds. She didn't notice the whiplash of the branches as she tore through the thick, grasping bushes and fought her way out into the fields, or the sharp thorns and stinging nettles that snatched at her clothes and skin. The words of the letter pounded in her head as her boots pounded the newly sown field that glittered with late frost. For now she was truly alone. Truly abandoned amongst strangers who didn't care what happened to her.

Clambering over the stile at the bottom of the field, Rose headed for the river. The reeds sighed and rustled in the wind, the occasional sleepy call of a guinea fowl drawing her ever closer. She came to a shuddering halt, the toes of her boots sinking into the soft mud at the water's edge.

She looked down at the mirror-bright surface that reflected the quarter moon, her breath a sob, her shoulders heaving. The agony was almost too much to bear. She had lost everything tonight. Why not just end it here? No one would miss her.

'I wouldn't do that, little girl. The water's awful cold.'

Rose spun round, surprise and fear making her heart thud painfully against her ribs.

Gilbert was standing by the reeds, his arms folded, legs planted firmly on the frost-crusted grass at the riverside. His eyes and teeth gleamed in the moonlight as he smiled. 'Whatever it is that's upset you it can't be bad enough for you to plunge yourself into that filthy water.' He held out his hand. 'Come, Rose.'

Her tears had dried, but the agony of her mother's words bit deep. Rose looked down at the water lapping her boots then back at the man. She must not let him see how vulnerable and afraid she was. 'I mean nothing to you but sport. Why should you care?'

The hand wavered. 'If you are quite determined to throw yourself in that revolting mess of reeds and water, then I shall have no alternative but to jump in after you and play the hero. It's nothing to me if you live or die, but this is an expensive piece of tailoring and it would be a shame to ruin it.'

His tone was cold, emphasising the chill within her. 'I didn't ask you to help. Go away!'

An eyebrow arched and the smile flashed again. 'Temper, temper,' he admonished. Then he moved with a swiftness that took her by surprise and before Rose knew it she was plucked from the river's edge and deposited firmly on her back in the long grass.

She struggled to get to her feet but again he was too swift for her. As he sat astride her, his hands pinning her arms to the ground, she realised his intentions had always been dishonourable. It was suddenly important to live – to fight and overcome the night's evil.

'Get off!' she screamed, lashing out with her feet, struggling with every ounce of strength she still had after that mad dash over the fields.

His smile was gone, hands determined now as he shredded her clothes and tore at her flesh. His weight took her breath, pinning her to the ground as his own breathing became ragged and his eyes gleamed, not with humour but with lust. 'Not until I've had what I've come for, Rosie girl,' he vowed.

Rose screamed and struggled as he kneed her legs apart and swiftly entered her. The pain was like a knife, taking the last of her breath, and as he pounded into her the hard earth and chalk dug and scraped at her back until she thought there could be no flesh left. Silent tears rolled down her face and into her hair as her struggles grew weaker and the moonlit sky was eclipsed by pain.

Finally it was over. Rose felt him climb off her, and as she huddled away from him she watched through swollen eyelids as he brushed the dirt from his hands and knees. He smoothed his hair and, after straightening his coat, looked down at her.

'It will be my word against yours, Rose. Your messenger boy should take more care when he comes calling.' Then he smiled and set off across the field in the direction of the Manor as if he'd been out for a stroll.

Rose sobbed as she gathered the remaining tatters of her clothes. She was cold. So cold it was as if the grave had embraced her. What he'd done had stained her petticoats with the bright red of shame, and as she tried to stem the flow, she felt hot tears of humiliation splash on her hands.

Gone was the wish to end it all, and in its place had come a rage against Captain Gilbert Fairbrother. One day she would find a way to make him pay for what he had done.

7

Lady Clara Fairbrother was restless. She had noticed her son's prolonged absence after dinner, the heightened colour in his face and the mud on his shoes on his subsequent return. He'd been up to something, she knew the signs. Yet she had to admire the consummate ease of her son's comportment as he entertained Isobel and Charlotte with card tricks, even if there was rather too much of the actor in it to make her entirely comfortable.

The evening dragged interminably and she finally excused herself from the drawing room, pleading a headache and the need for an early night before the long journey in the morning. As she pulled the heavy drawing-room door closed behind her, she stood for a moment planning what she should do next. That Gilbert needed to be spoken to was imperative, but she knew better than to pounce while everyone else was still awake.

Clara glanced around the hall and made her way quietly into the morning room. She didn't bother to light the candles, could see quite well by the light of the moon, and as she sat in a chair by the long French windows, she stared into the gardens. She would wait until the house was still before going to Gilbert's rooms. It was better to sit in here than risk falling asleep on her bed.

The great sweep of lawn ran down to a high, thick hedge of rhododendrons, and she could just make out the narrow silver ribbon of the river on the southern boundary of the estate. It was peaceful here after the bustle of London but she was thankful to be leaving. There was only so much parochial pleasure one could take in a lifetime, and after numerous visits over the past months she was more than ready to return to the social whirl of a new season.

Her thoughts returned to her younger son. Gilbert was a fool, and although she had no idea of what he'd been up to this evening, Clara hoped it wouldn't bring any unpleasant surprises. She bit her lip as she stared out of the window. It was a great pity the wedding couldn't have been brought forward a few weeks – but there had been enough unseemly haste as it was, and she wanted no taint of scandal attached to the ceremony.

Something moved on the edge of her vision and Clara leaned forward, expecting to see a fox or badger in the grounds. There it was again. But that was no wild creature limping across the lawn. Her breath caught as she stood and reached for the window handle. Surely this could have nothing to do with Gilbert? And yet. And yet...

With her wrap forgotten, Clara stepped into the chill night. Her slippers were no defence against the frost on the paving or the dew on the grass, and her evening gown was too thin, but she was barely aware of the cold as she hurried to cut off the girl's escape to the back of the house and the servants' quarters.

Her voice was soft but commanding. 'You there – stop.'

Rose clutched the tattered remains of her clothes to her in an effort to hide her shame. She was shivering and her eyes were dark shadows in her white face.

Clara took it all in with one swift glance. 'Who did this to you?' she demanded.

'Captain Gilbert Fairbrother,' the girl announced with clear, unmistakable rage.

'Hush, girl. Do you want to raise the house?' Clara grasped her arm and looked furtively back to the open doors of the morning room. All was still, and she could now see candlelight flickering in the bedrooms above.

'If it means the Captain's punished for what he did – yes.' Rose glared at her through swollen lids, her mouth still stained with blood from where her lip had been gashed.

'You lie,' Clara said hurriedly. 'My son has been in the house all evening. I shall swear to it.'

Rose's look was one of pure hatred. 'So you defend him?'

Clara nodded. 'If it will avoid a scandal. Always.' Her grasp on the slender arm eased and her voice was deliberately less commanding. The girl had to be mollified. Perhaps bargained with. 'One word from you and I'll have you dismissed. But if you keep quiet, I'll see you recompensed.' She eyed the livid bruises that covered the girl's naked shoulders and arms. Gilbert was a fool to let his appetites run away with him.

'How?' Rose demanded, her voice still loud and clear in the still night. 'You cannot return what was stolen from me tonight, Lady Clara.'

'You would have lost it soon anyway,' she said impatiently.

Rose was obviously making an effort to take command of the situation, but she shivered so violently Clara was concerned she might faint. There was no way she could deal with her in that condition. Ignoring Rose's refusal of help, she put her arm around the girl's waist, and one firm hand on her arm, and pulled her around the side of the Manor to a door leading into what she discovered was the Squire's room where he conducted estate business. Clara breathed a sigh of relief as she lit a lamp and set it on the scrubbed table. There was no sign of the other servants, they wouldn't be disturbed here.

'Why do you defend him?' Rose asked baldly.

'Because he is my son and the scandal would break his father and ruin his brother,' she replied. Clara was bathing the girl's scratches with a piece of cotton and cold water from the garden tap. She had found an old coat of the Squire's in the corner cupboard and now Rose sat quietly at the battered desk, wrapped in the coat, her bruises livid in the lamplight. The flesh of her back had been gouged raw by the earth where he'd flung her, and as Clara listened to what Gilbert had done, she too wondered how she could defend him. But defend him she must if her eldest son was to have a future in Parliament.

'Then you are no better than him,' said Rose coldly.

Clara dropped the bloody cotton in the water and dried her hands. 'What is it you want, Rose?' She eyed the girl calmly. She had learned through bitter experience that there was always a price – no matter how lowly the victim.

'I want him to pay for what he's done. I want revenge.'

'It is not Gilbert who will pay,' said Clara calmly. 'It is his father who holds the purse strings. But I will see what I can do.'

Rose stood up, the coat drooping over her hands and falling to her knees, and Clara realised with a jolt that under the bruises and cuts she was beautiful in her anger, and could understand why Gilbert had taken such a fancy to her.

156

'It's not your money I'm after,' she hissed. 'You can't *buy* me.'

Clara's hands fluttered to the diamonds at her throat. 'Then what do you want?'

Rose touched the cut on her lip and hitched up the sleeves of the fustian coat. 'I want you to find me a post as a lady's maid. I can't stay here – and I certainly can't go to London with Miss Isobel. Not now. How could I ever look her in the eye knowing what I do about *him?*'

Clara sat down. It would indeed be a way out of the predicament. With Rose out of the house, Isobel and her family would never get to hear of tonight's disastrous events and Gilbert would have no chance of a repeat performance. 'But Miss Isobel is planning to bring you to London herself once she and Gilbert are settled in their apartments. How will you explain your change of heart?'

'I'll think of something,' said Rose firmly. 'But I will not go to London with the mistress to be used by your son.' The rise and fall of her chest couldn't mask the rage she was fighting to control, and although Clara was in no mood to prolong this intimacy with the girl, she felt a certain admiration for her courage.

'I take your point.' She stood up. 'But it will be some time before I can arrange suitable employment. You will have to remain here until you are sent for. Gilbert and I will be leaving early in the morning so there will be no need for your paths to cross again. If you keep tonight a secret then I promise I will have you out of here before the wedding.'

She took a step towards the girl, daunted by the cold distaste in her eyes but determined to take charge of the situation. 'One word from you and I will do nothing. Lady Amelia will have no recourse but to dismiss you without a reference and you will end up in the workhouse. I will see to that personally.'

Rose nodded. 'Keep your side of the bargain, and I'll keep mine.'

Five weeks passed before Rose was summoned to the Squire's room. Her cuts and bruises on the night Gilbert attacked her had been explained away as an accidental fall on the cobbles, and apart from a suspicious glance or two from Cook there had been no further discussion of the matter.

Now she stood in the doorway and bobbed a curtsy, brilliant sunshine at her back, the gloom of the Squire's room like a dark cavern ahead of her. 'You sent for me, sir?'

'Come in, Rose. Sit yourself down,' boomed the Squire. He dropped his feet from the cluttered desk and stood up.

Rose perched on the edge of a horsehair chair, nervously wondering why he should want to see her here. It was customary for Mrs Patterson to deal with the household staff, and she knew this must be something very serious indeed. She hoped Lady Clara had not broken her promise to remain silent.

'I explained to Mrs Patterson about the dress, sir,' she said quickly. 'Old one was just too tight and it split until it was indecent when I had me

158

fall. There was nothing left for it but to get another.'

The Squire frowned and chewed on his clay pipe. 'Dress? What should I know about such things, girl?' He lit a spill from the fire and put it to the tobacco. When he had a nice fug going, he leaned back in his chair and picked up a letter from his desk.

'I received this today, Rose. It is from a Lady Fitzallan of Grosvenor Square.'

Now it was Rose's turn to frown. She had never heard of the woman. 'Yes, sir?' she prompted.

'Lady Fitzallan is an acquaintance of Lady Fairbrother's and has written to me asking for a reference as to your good character.' The gimlet eyes peered at her over the thick vellum. 'I was not aware you wished to leave us, Rose.'

So, she thought, Lady Clara had kept her word. She could feel the heat in her face as she returned his scrutiny. 'It is for the best, sir. With Mam and the boys gone to Ireland, I feel I should leave Wilmington and seek my own fortune.'

He threw the letter back on to the cluttered desk. 'Fortune, is it, eh? And how would a slip of a thing like you seek a fortune by honest means? You're a country gel, and I've seen too many go bad to encourage you to leave.'

When Rose refused to respond, he gave a great sigh of exasperation. 'What has Lady Fairbrother to do with all this? How is it you were able to confide in her of your wish to leave Milton Manor?'

Rose ran her tongue over dry lips. She would have to be careful what she said. 'Lady Fairbrother must have overheard me talking with Queenie. It was the day I got that letter from Mam and I was upset and talking about leaving. This other lady probably mentioned she wanted a lady's maid and Lady Clara thought of me,' she finished lamely.

Charles Ade looked at her for a long moment, his eyes steady, his mind obviously troubled. 'That's a very complicated story, Rose. Are you sure there isn't another reason for your leaving?'

'Why, sir? Should there be?' Her expression was deliberately artless.

'Is there something you wish to tell me, Rose?' His tone was kind, his voice gentle. But his eyes held a piercing directness that made her feel uncomfortable, and she wondered if he had somehow guessed the truth.

'N-no, sir. It's as I said – I've a mind to try another place, that's all.'

He sighed. 'If you say so, Rose. But your mother entrusted me with your care and I wouldn't like to think you were hiding something from me.' He paused for a moment. 'Don't be afraid to confide in me. No matter how terrible a predicament you may find yourself in.'

She remained silent. The wedding was two weeks away. Lady Clara had kept her part of the bargain – and so must she.

His soft voice sharpened. 'You aren't in the family way, are you?'

Rose blushed. At least she hadn't suffered that humiliation. 'No, sir,' she whispered.

'Then what is it, Rose?' His tone was persistent, as if he suspected her reason.

The urge to tell him the truth was very strong, but she knew how it would hurt Miss Isobel, and once revealed the scandal that followed would destroy this family who had been so kind to her. Yet, by her silence, was she condemning Miss Isobel to a life of unhappiness? The quandary had been going round in her head for weeks. Now the moment had come to speak out, she knew she just couldn't do it. The revenge she sought was not against these people.

'You have been kind to me, sir, and I've been happy working for Miss Isobel. But I'm fourteen and I would like to see a bit more of the world.'

Charles Ade grunted and once more reached for the letter. 'You will certainly do that if you take up this post, Rose. Do you have any idea what it entails?'

She sat forward eagerly. 'Does the lady want a personal maid, sir?'

He nodded. 'More than that, Rose. She wants a companion, a lady's maid to accompany her on a particular journey.'

'Where to, sir? London? Scotland?' Her heart pounded. 'Ireland?'

'Further afield than that, Rose. Lady Fitzallan is sailing for the colonies in two months' time.'

'The colonies, sir?' Rose had heard stories of the adventures to be had on the other side of the world. Of gold and silver just lying in the ground waiting to be picked up. Of strange animals and savage people, of forests and deserts and great mountains that stretched right up to the sky. 'America?' she asked breathlessly.

'No Rose. Australia. The Dowager Lady Fitzallan is joining her son in Sydney.'

Rose couldn't imagine what this mysterious Sydney would look like or what she might find there. Yet her excitement was tempered by the knowledge that Lady Clara had planned her own revenge well. How convenient to send Rose to the other side of the world where no breath of scandal would reach London. Then there was the fear of the unknown. What would the future hold for her in the new world? Did she really want to go so far from all she knew and understood? And what of John? They would never see one another again – and yet he was already lost to her. 'What is Australia like, sir? Is it so very far?' she asked finally.

'Come, I'll show you on this globe.' He crossed the room and spun the wooden globe until he found Australia. 'It's at least three months away by sea – longer if you encounter storms. By all accounts it is hot and dry and populated by convicts and rough settlers. There are some who see it as an adventure, others who see it as an escape from scandal or the ignominy of being the youngest son or black sheep of the family. I understand the city of Sydney is now quite civilised, but of course it won't be anything like London.'

He pursed his lips, his fingers pressed to his mouth. 'Reconsider, my dear. 'Tis a long way from home, and I doubt you will ever be able to return to England. Your life would never be the same.'

'Your life would never be the same.' The magic words floated around her, bringing a dizzy, heady

162

pleasure she could no longer deny. Fate had given her a chance to change her life. Dare she take up the challenge? She looked at the globe and the blob of land set in a bright blue sea and thought about it. Then couldn't quite hide the excitement in her eager smile as she looked up at him. 'If Lady Fitzallan is agreeable, then I would like to go, sir.'

Big Billy Clarke had been as good as his word, and John was now the proud owner of three fine suits of clothes and a healthy stash of coins which he hid beneath the floorboards in his lodgings. The room he lived in was above a tavern in the centre of Bow. The floors dipped and swayed like the back of an old horse, the windows were tiny, the air foetid, and when John closed the door after another day in this alien city, he longed for the fresh air and freedom of the *vardo* and the open road.

The streets below his window were narrow, filled with the filth of the tenements, haunted by cut-purses, prostitutes, beggars and hawkers. The noise went on all day and night. The fights were violent and conducted with as much noise as possible. Drunks urinated freely against the walls of the King's Arms whenever the urge took them, and skinny, snarling dogs roamed the streets and alleys, foraging amongst the debris for food and fighting over the scraps.

Living amongst the *gadjikanes* made him feel *moxado*, unclean, and although he now had enough money tucked away to return to Wilmington and ask for Rose's hand, he knew he

163

would have to wait. He couldn't bring her here amongst the rabble of London. Rose deserved better. He was determined to save enough to buy their own *vardo*.

Night after night, regardless of how battered and bruised he was from the latest fight, he would sit on that mean, lice-ridden mattress and count his coins. Each one brought him closer to his dream. Each one represented another step towards the British title, and the kind of life he wanted for them both.

Yet patience had never been his strong point, and as the days turned into weeks, the weeks into months, the longing to return to the clean fresh air of the South Downs, and the familiar orderliness of the Romany camp was underlined by a deep, pervasive anger. That anger manifested itself in the ring as he faced his opponents and laid them out on the canvas amidst shouts of derision and slander, and he knew that if he didn't find release from it soon, he would lose control. Dreams were all very well, but the manner in which he had to earn those dreams was beginning to destroy his soul.

He stared up at the stained ceiling, then closed his eyes and tried to block out the noise from below. How good it would be to see Rose again – to walk with her over Windover Hill and hear the gulls shriek overhead. How pleasant to sit around the camp fire with the sound of the Romany language around him, the wind at his back, the smell of rabbit stew in the pot.

He sat up, his eyes snapping open as he realised there was nothing to stop him. His next fight was almost three weeks away in Sheffield, and Big Billy was out of town with another fighter preparing for a local bout. 'Why not?' he muttered. 'I can be down to Sussex and back before Billy even knows I've gone. I'm coming, Rose,' he murmured. 'I'm coming.'

Rose had said her goodbyes to Queenie and the others the night before. Miss Isobel had been kindness itself, even though she was puzzled by Rose's hasty departure, and had pressed a guinea in her hand. 'Take care, Rose,' she'd said. 'And if you want to change your mind, there's always a position for you in my London home.'

It was still dark as Rose climbed Windover Hill for the last time, but she didn't need light to show her the way. The wind sweeping off the South Downs was chilly and she drew the thin shawl more closely around her shoulders. Her long black hair was free from cap and pins and streamed behind her, enhancing the sense of excitement that had been building inside her for the past two weeks.

As she breached the hill she stood for a moment to catch her breath and gaze at the bright, cold stars. The sough of the wind in the gnarled trees and the crackle of early frost underfoot were reminders of the approaching winter she would never see. The cold air burned in her throat and her bare fingers tingled. She wished she'd remembered to put more paper over the holes in her boots. Her feet were icy and the hem of the brown dress sodden. Yet, as she stood in the stillness of the hour before dawn, she knew the discomfort no longer mattered. For this was home, and she needed to burn the image of it in her heart before she began the long journey to the other side of the world.

The tranquillity of the Downs embraced her as she walked, the scent of drifting wood smoke lingering as if the ghosts of the past had come to say their goodbyes. She closed her eyes and breathed deeply of those memories as the tears at last began to fall and isolation closed in. She had never felt so alone – so abandoned and small within the grandeur of the Sussex Downs – for the people she loved were gone and she would never see them again.

She wiped away the tears. Regrets must not be allowed to surface, for the decision to leave had been her own. Grasping her skirts, she plodded along the crest of Windover Hill until she came to the traditional winter camping ground. The Romany camp was deserted, its only remainder the ruts of their *vardo* wheels.

'Where are you, John?' she whispered into the stillness. 'Why didn't you come for me as you promised?' The ache for him was deep, the plans they'd made as cold as the ashes in the camp fire. Yet she yearned to see him again. Longed to feel his arms about her. For although their paths would never cross again, and their childish dreams never be fulfilled, they would forever remain a part of each other.

She turned away and as the sky began to lighten, looked out over the land. It was important to carry the image of this place with her to the other side of the world. To burn the sight, the sound and scent of it into her heart, so she could turn to them in moments of need.

The long, slender valley between the folds of the Downs widened out into the cattle pasture that dipped and rolled like the back of an old horse. Mist hung over Deep Dene as always, lending credence to the local belief that the steep, tree-lined gully was haunted. Sturdy Downland sheep grazed in a far-off field and the delicate white flowers of the blackthorn vied with the yellow insolence of the gorse. Rose felt the wind tug her hair and sting her face. After the stifling formality of the Manor she felt the headiness of freedom in her veins. She would never have to return there. Now she had the time to breathe, space to move, to be herself. The adventure had already begun.

The journey took John two days of hard riding. The mare needed rest as much as he did, and as he was not inclined to exchange her at the coaching inns, he had camped in fields and slept beneath the trees wrapped in a blanket. As the soft, gentle curves of the South Downs welcomed him home, he spurred his horse into a gallop. He could already make out the colourful tents and the flags fluttering in the wind.

The *dukkerin* was waiting for him, standing on the edge of the field, her hand shading her eyes as she watched him approach. 'I dreamed you would come, John. Welcome home.'

He kissed her brown cheek, and felt the frailty of her as he held her close. 'I've come for Rose,' he said finally.

She pulled away from him, her dark eyes looking deeply into his. 'The fates will not allow it, John,' she said solemnly.

'To hell with the fates, *puri daj*. Rose is the one I want and no one can stop me from having her.' He grabbed the reins, his foot already back in the stirrup. 'I'm going to fetch her.'

Her gnarled hand stayed his arm. 'Be still, John. She's gone. There was some unpleasantness up at the Manor. She's away to London.' Sarah must have seen the spark of excitement in his eyes for she shook her head and silenced his retort. 'But she won't be stayin' there, boy. There's a much longer journey ahead of her now. One that will take her beyond your reach even.'

Exasperation made him rough with her. Grasping her arm, he shouted into her face. 'Don't speak in riddles, old woman. Where's she going?'

Sarah glared back at him until, shame-faced, he let her go. Then she shrugged. 'Across the water is all I know.'

'When? When did she leave, *puri daj?*' His voice was softer now, a strange emptiness filling him so completely, it was hard for him to speak.

'A week ago.' His grandmother she took his hand and looked into the palm, tracing the lines with a dirty fingernail. 'You too have a long journey ahead of you, John, but there will be many months before you take the first step.' She looked up at him then, her eyes fathomless. 'That step will not be made with joy,' she warned. 'It will be made in haste and in fear.'

He snatched his hand away. 'I don't want to

listen to this,' he muttered.

'You'd do well to heed me, boy,' she snapped. 'The fates are giving you a choice. If you don't mind what I say, then you're a fool.'

'Fool or not, *puri daj*, I mean to find Rose and make her my wife. No matter how long the journey.'

The old woman sadly watched him lead his horse to the *vardo*. He had taken the first step on the road to hell, and there was nothing she could do about it.

8

Mary had spent the last two days in bed. She was experienced enough to know she'd gone too far in trying to beat the hunger this time and so forced herself to eat the meals she'd ordered from room service. The skinless chicken and green salads had been followed by a piece of fruit, and she drank pints of freshly squeezed orange juice throughout the day and night to rehydrate herself and make up for lost vitamins and her craving for sugar.

At first each mouthful had made her gag, but she had soon overcome that and was now feeling more in control. She'd had a great deal of time to think over the past forty-eight hours, and this morning was impatient to get things under way. Revenge would be sweet, and with food inside her, and a clear head, she felt strong enough to exact it.

She had made the telephone call earlier that morning. Now, as the noon appointment approached, she'd returned from the hairdresser's and was making her final preparations. She had dressed carefully in a pale lilac two-piece suit. The shoulders were padded, the lapels embroidered with deep purple irises. The narrow waistline and slim skirt emphasised her figure and she smiled as she realised she hadn't put on any extra pounds in the past few days despite the enforced eating. Slipping on a pair of high-heeled sandals, she examined her reflection. Her make-up was immaculate and she was pleased with the way the girl had coloured her hair, for she was always wary of new hairdressers and had been slightly alarmed when the colourist suggested using several tones of brown and gold instead of black. Yet, as she eyed herself in the gilded mirror, she had to admit the girl had done a good job. The softer streaks of colour had added depth and fire and toned in better with her skin.

You're getting old, she thought. It takes longer and longer to get ready to face the world, and there's hardly anything left of the real Mary under all that powder and paint and hair dye. Just how much longer can you go on nipping and tucking and running away from the years?

The depressing thoughts clamoured, threatening to take her down with them. Then the clock struck midday and the light tap on the door announced her visitor.

Turning her back on the mirror, she pushed aside the doubts. There was still enough fight in her for her to keep going, and she was damned if she was going to give in to old age. Just as she was damned if she was going to let the family walk all over her. This was her chance to get her own back, and she would see she did – in spades.

'Let's see how they like that,' she muttered as she went to open the door.

'Hi. How y' goin'?'

'Good. Come in, Sharon. Nice to see you again.' Mary led the other woman into the apartment and poured her a glass of Martini from the frosted jug she'd prepared earlier. She and Sharon Sterling had known one another for years, and although their knowledge of each other was intimate, it wasn't really a friendship – more a reciprocal business arrangement.

Sharon sat on the couch, her long, perfect legs crossed at the ankle. She was beautifully dressed as usual in a business-like suit, with just a hint of expensive gold jewellery at her throat and in her earlobes. The blonde hair was glossy and fell in a pageboy to her chin, framing her discreetly made-up face. Her rings sparked fire as she raised her glass in a toast. 'Here's to stirring the pot.'

Mary took a sip of the mineral water she'd poured for herself. She needed to keep a clear head for what she was about to do. 'As long as I'm not the one caught with the wooden spoon,' she said firmly.

'Haven't I always been discreet, darling?' Sharon's voice was almost a purr, the slanting green eyes feral as they flashed with malicious anticipation.

Mary nodded. There had been many interviews

like this in the past, and she hadn't been betrayed so far. Yet she had no illusions when it came to Sharon. She was a consummate journalist, a *doyenne* of dishing the dirt when it came to the rich and famous, and if she smelled a rat she'd be the first to pounce. The first to off-load any sense of fair play if it meant a bigger and better story.

'What I'm going to tell you today is dynamite, so you'd better make sure you don't reveal your source.' Mary's tone was grim, her gaze direct. 'And I don't want you recording this either.'

Sharon grimaced. 'Been a long time since I put my shorthand to work. But if you insist.' She put down her barely touched Martini and fished a notepad out of her capacious handbag. 'I've already spoken to my editor. Our team of lawyers will go through my piece before it's printed, and no journalist worth her salt ever reveals a source. So you've got no worries there.'

Mary took another sip of mineral water. She was suddenly nervous, her mouth dry, her pulse rapid. She had never dared go this far before, and wondered if, by doing so, she would lose more than she gained. What price would she have to pay for her spite?

'You're not backing out on me, are you, Mary?' Green eyes watched her as Sharon's pen hovered over the notepad.

Mary lit a cigarette, drew the smoke deep into her lungs then blew it out in a long stream to the ceiling. Sharon knew she was on the brink of a scoop and wouldn't let go until she had it all. The news blackout enforced by Mother and Father had long ago ensured the family's secrets remained hidden from the press. Until now.

Mary took a moment to gather her thoughts. She had come too far to back out now, she realised. The need for revenge was too strong.

'I think the world should know just what a bastard my father really was,' she began.

Daisy had barely slept, but when she did finally climb out of bed she felt more refreshed than she had done in years. After a long cool shower she chose her clothes carefully for the day's business. For this was the first day of her rediscovered confidence. The first day of asserting herself within her family.

Discarding the dowdy print dresses she'd taken to wearing since Martin's death, she chose a red shift dress. The colour enhanced her complexion and spoke volumes about her self-esteem. She added her three-strand pearl necklace and pearl studs, and swapped the usual sensible flatties for a pair of low-heeled black sandals. A touch of make-up and a dash of defiant red lipstick and she was ready. She didn't give herself time to doubt or allow the fears to surface but slammed through the front door, determined to recapture her life and put it in order. Too much time had already been wasted.

Charles was in his office waiting for her, and after his secretary had poured them coffee and left the room, he gave a bark of laughter. 'Bit surprised to see you here this morning, Daisy. What can I do for you?'

His sudden explosion of laughter would normally have made her jump. Yet this morning she seemed prepared for anything and merely smiled back. 'I want you to tell me everything you know about Jacaranda Vines Corporation.'

His eyebrows shot up and his pale blue eyes widened. 'You don't have to worry your pretty little head about such things, Daisy. Edward and I will make sure you don't lose out.'

She put down her coffee cup carefully on the polished desk. 'Don't patronise me Charles,' she said softly. 'I may have spent the last few years cocooned from the real world by Martin, but you'd be surprised how much I already know and understand about the corporation.'

Charles cleared his throat, clearly ill at ease. 'Martin used to discuss business with you?'

'You don't have to sound quite so incredulous,' she retorted. 'I'm not a half-wit.' She ignored his bumbling apology. 'He used me as a sounding board. I don't think he realised just how much of it I came to understand because he rarely waited for me to give an opinion. But he found it helpful to voice his concerns if he had a particularly difficult problem to tackle.'

'I see.' Her cousin looked thoughtful. 'Martin was an excellent distribution manager. He knew his market and could sell ice to the Eskimos – not that he needed to, of course,' he added by way of a joke. 'But to tell you everything about the company would take months, Daisy. It's impossible.'

'Nothing's impossible, Charles. Especially if you want it badly enough. I don't expect you to sit here and give me a lecture, but I would appreciate your letting me go through the

174

company files. I've had an idea.'

He gave her an indulgent smile. 'My dear Daisy, I hardly think you're in a position to know what's best for the company. After all, you're only a housewife. What would you know about high finance and corporate management?'

His tone made her prickle with anger. 'You're patronising me again, Charles,' she warned. 'I realise you all think I'm stupid and empty-headed, but I had a lot of spare time during my marriage to Martin and I didn't waste it.'

The eyebrows were raised again but he didn't speak.

Daisy was warming to her theme, and now she had him on the hook, she knew she couldn't let go. 'Just because I hate arguments and prefer to keep my mouth shut doesn't mean I'm thick,' she said firmly. 'I took a degree in business management, accountancy and statistics. It's amazing what you can do through the Open University.'

'You did what? Charles wasn't tactful enough to hide his astonishment. 'Martin never said.'

'He never knew.' Daisy smiled when she thought of how her husband would have reacted if he had. He'd have been shocked at first, then patronising, and would never have taken her seriously. 'I worked at my books while he was away at the office and hid them when he came home. It took me five years, and then another year to get my doctorate. I wrote a paper on the marketing and managing of a family corporation approaching the new millennium.'

She dug into her black patent handbag and pulled out the neatly bound thesis that had been hidden in the bottom of her underwear drawer for years. 'Perhaps you'd like to read it in your spare time? You might find it interesting.'

Charles eyed the thesis as if it was a King Brown snake. 'Strewth,' he hissed. Then he seemed to gather his wits, blood suffusing his face. 'Bloody hell, Daisy. Why didn't you tell anyone about this instead of sitting in at the meetings like a dithering idiot?'

'Because none of you would have taken me seriously,' she said quietly. 'Besides, when could anyone get a word in edgewise when you and Mum and Kate were expounding your theories? I knew that if I waited long enough, the time would come when I might be able to do some good.' She sat forward in the chair. 'This is the time, Charles. Will you help me or not?'

He spread his hands and let out a sigh. 'Things have already gone too far, Daisy. Your father seemed determined to destroy this company before he died. Couldn't take it with him, but he was damn' sure he wouldn't leave it behind. Dog in the manger bastard!'

'Good thing he died before he could see it through then,' she said firmly. 'But despite Dad, I'm sure there must be a way to rescue at least part of the business.'

'Better minds than yours or mine have already looked at the problem, Daisy. But if you think you can find a way, then of course you'll have a free hand. What will you need?'

Daisy relaxed. She'd been afraid that Charles would laugh at her. Afraid she wouldn't have the courage to stand up to him. 'Before we go any further, I want you to promise to keep this meeting and my intentions to yourself. There's been enough trouble already, and any more will only detract from what I might be able to achieve. I don't want the rest of the family poking their noses in until it's absolutely necessary.'

Charles nodded thoughtfully, amazement showing clearly in his eyes.

Satisfied she could trust him, Daisy took a deep breath. 'I want to see the books for all the companies under the Jacaranda umbrella. Sales figures, projected profits and employment records. Then I want to see the offer made by the French and any contracts that may already have been drawn up. I understand Sophie has already paved the way should we decide to go public, so I'll need to see what figures we have and the projected share price. But particularly, I need to look into the expansion programme Dad began. The bottle shops, the supermarket chain, and the plans for updating the winery.'

Charles' breath came out in a long, low whistle. 'That's a mountain of work, Daisy, and we only have a matter of weeks to come to a decision.'

She eyed him steadily. 'I have nothing else to do, Charles. Look on it as a challenge.'

Sophie had been driving for three hours, her mind still captured by the story her grandmother had begun to unfold. The thought of John and Rose bound for the opposite sides of the earth was almost too painful. They obviously loved one another, and it seemed cruel of the fates to keep them apart.

And yet, like the journey she was now making, perhaps that road would lead to unexpected encounters. To adventure none of them could have imagined. Perhaps fate knew what she was about, for who could have foreseen this trip she would take with Gran? What hidden purpose lay behind it? For Sophie firmly believed in fate. Everything in life had to have a purpose, even if the recipient couldn't at first understand it. It had been proved to her time after time when she'd wondered just where her own life was heading.

She eased her back and shifted into a more comfortable position behind the wheel. They had started out later than planned because Cordelia had been slow to wake this morning, and Sophie hadn't like to rush her through breakfast. She was still concerned by the old lady's pallor and shot a glance across at Cordelia, dozing quietly beside her. This whole journey was crazy. Who in their right minds would drive across this great emptiness with a ninety-year-old woman?

Sophie turned her attention back to the road. It was a question she'd asked herself repeatedly over the past few days, but she still had no answer. Logic didn't enter the equation where Cordelia was concerned, and she suspected the old lady would have made the journey with or without her. Yet that only served to make her even more frustrated with the whole episode, and she didn't like the feeling that although Gran was kindness itself she was manipulating Sophie.

As the camper crested yet another hill, they were treated to a breath-taking panorama, and with her gloomy thoughts wiped away, she suggested: 'Shall we stop and get a paper, Gran. It's Saturday, and you can read the gossip columns out to me as I drive. That Sharon Sterling's got a pen as sharp as a sword. I don't know where she gets her information from, or how people let her get away with some of the things she says, but it makes for fascinating reading. I made sure I had a copy ordered each week back in England so I could keep up with it all.'

'Nasty piece of work, if you ask me,' muttered Cordelia. 'Muck-raking is what I call it. Poking into other people's business like that isn't healthy.'

Sophie silently agreed, but still couldn't resist her weekly snoop into the gossip. She pulled up at a long, low log cabin, with a shady verandah running along the front. The yard was sheltered by pepper trees that hummed with bees, and someone had hung baskets of flowers from the verandah posts, bringing a splash of colour against the earthy tones of the wood.

The interior was cool, the shelves well stocked, and Sophie soon found what she was looking for. With fresh bottles of water still icy from the fridge, and a bag of apricots, she tucked the heavy wad of the weekend newspaper under her arm and headed back to the camper.

Five miles down the road Cordelia let out a gasp of horror. 'Bloody hell! I'll sue. I'll take the bitch to court and wipe her out.'

Alarmed by this uncharacteristic outburst, Sophie pulled into the side of the road. 'What is it, Gran? You've gone a real funny colour. Whatever's the matter?'

Cordelia's hand was shaking as she held out the colour supplement. 'That bitch Sharon Sterling has got us plastered over five pages. If I ever find out who talked to her, I'll ... I'll' She was so angry, she was obviously lost for words.

Sophie took the magazine, her eyes skimming over the lurid headlines and the familiar photographs. 'Strewth,' she said softly. 'Whoever it was certainly knew where to stick the knife.'

Cordelia snatched the magazine back. 'Carry on driving, Sophie. I need time and silence to digest this piece of venom before I decide what to do about it.'

She folded back the pages, settled her glasses on the end of her nose and began to read. It wasn't pleasant. Jock had been pilloried, and although he deserved most of it, there were things in the article that could only have come from a family member and were so private even she was shocked by the audacity of the informer in laying them bare. This could destroy the family.

9

Kate sat on her verandah, the colour supplement slithering to the floor from nerveless fingers as she stared out over the Dandenongs. The wounds of the past had been torn open, laid bare in black and white for all to pick over. The implication that she'd married her first husband for his money was hurtful and untrue, but to insinuate that her second darling man had merely been a further means to an end was plain wicked.

Tears blurred her vision and she didn't have the strength or will to wipe them away. She had loved Matthew, and although he'd been several years older than her, that first marriage had been loving and happy. His sudden untimely death in a car accident had devastated her. No amount of money could have compensated her for his loss, and she would gladly have scrubbed floors for the rest of her life if it could have meant his still being alive.

Jonathan had come along just as she'd resigned herself to widowhood and a burgeoning career that filled her lonely days and nights. They had met at a civic reception in Melbourne's Parliament House. He'd been an attractive man with a lively, inquiring mind who lectured in political sciences at the Victorian State University. He wrote books that were far too intellectual for her to understand and liked nothing better than a heated debate with his peers. Yet he was never once patronising and had encouraged Kate to expand her mind and see things differently. The birth of their son Harry had been a miracle, his death something that had brought them even closer. Thankfully the onslaught of Parkinson's hadn't been dragged out for too long, and Jonathan had died in his sleep just three years after it had been diagnosed.

The article was right about one thing. Those

two marriages had made her a very wealthy woman, but what good was money when you were alone? A single tear rolled down her cheek, trembled for a moment on her chin, then splashed unnoticed on to her blouse.

Yet it wasn't that particular accusation which had hurt the most. It was being dubbed a thoughtless mother with little time for her own son that really crucified her. The vicious article had suggested she'd been too busy with her social life and career, and had placed the blame for Harry's death squarely on her shoulders. Although she still felt an insidious guilt, she knew she wasn't the culprit, more the victim. It could have happened at any time. He'd been sent away to boarding school because he'd begged to go, not because she wanted him out from under her feet as the article suggested. Her fund-raising work had never been that important to her.

She sniffed back the tears and reached for the supplement. There was even a short piece on Phil. Trust that bastard to stick his two bobs' worth in. Probably demanded a fee for doing it too. She clenched her fist around the slippery, shiny magazine. Now there was the real culprit. He was the one who married for money, and she'd been the stupid, foolish woman who'd thought his flattery was love. Who'd believed his lies, and cried when he'd gone off with Leanne having emptied their joint account.

Thank God for some common sense, she thought. At least I always kept that account down to the minimum, and he only got away with a fraction of what Jon and Matt had left me.

She looked down at the ruined magazine, then spread it out once more on the garden table. Sharon Sterling was one piece of dirty work, and she'd been extremely thorough in her character assassinations. There wasn't one member of the family who'd escaped her vicious pen.

Daisy had spent the last two days and nights poring over the company books. The devastation of the corporation by her father was clear in nearly every page. He'd set out with clinical deliberation to destroy the business he'd spent a lifetime building, and knowing him as she did, she understood his reasons.

Jock Witney had come from lowly beginnings with not much more than a few acres of prime land to his name until he'd forced Mother and Uncle Edward to hand over fifty per cent of Jacaranda. He'd spent his life clawing his way to the top, and like a lot of successful men, hadn't cared about the people he'd trampled on to get there. When he knew he was dying, he'd looked at his achievements and had decided no one else was worthy of his life's work. So began the slow, insidious destruction of Jacaranda Vines and all its umbrella companies. The plans for updating and expansion were merely a ploy to empty the coffers, but had been masked by a clever campaign to take the company into the new millennium and a more prosperous future. The buying up of the bottle shops and supermarkets was unwise in a shaky economy now the Asians were in such financial straits, but he'd steam-rollered through the objections and gone ahead.

His tyrannical power had cowed the rest of the family. Those who'd dared object to what he was doing had been silenced with a demonic logic they had been unable to counter.

Daisy finally threw down her glasses and rubbed her eyes. It was Saturday morning and she was exhausted. Yet that exhaustion was tempered by a slow-burning excitement. She hadn't been wrong. There was a way to save Jacaranda Vines despite Jock.

She left the table, the books and papers strewn across it. A visitor might view the sight as chaotic, but Daisy knew where everything was. She made a cup of coffee and pushed through the screen door to the verandah. The paper boy had thrown the bulky Saturday paper on to the floor and it was spread everywhere.

As she bent to pick it up, her hand stilled and she was transfixed by the photograph of Martin staring back at her from the colour supplement. With trembling hands she gathered the supplement together and sank into the cushions of the verandah chair, her gaze trawling the headlines and sweeping down over the endless columns of print.

When she had finished, she felt nothing but a hot white fury. Sharon Sterling's article had torn into her, shredding her reputation and that of her husband. The insinuations had no foundation in truth, but their sly innuendo had made Daisy out to be an empty-headed, vain woman with no will of her own, who had turned away from a brutal, uncaring father only to marry a man just like him.

According to Sharon, Martin had constantly humiliated her, refused to allow her to have the baby she desperately wanted – even beaten her. He'd been mean with his money and his time, and had merely followed in her father's footsteps by bullying her into submission. What utter nonsense! Martin might have been the stronger of the two of them, but he'd never raised his hand or his voice to her. As for the lack of children – that was down to malformed ovaries and a reluctance to adopt.

Daisy felt like ripping the magazine apart until it was shredded so small it could be carried like dust out into the ocean. Yet, as she sat there, stunned by the sheer venom of the article, she found a deep well of calm within herself and concentrated on regaining her equilibrium.

Sharon must have got her story from somewhere. Or rather someone. The details were too vivid, the characters drawn too finely and assassinated too well for it to have been the work of an outsider.

Jane had already had a call from Edward. The poor man had been devastated by the revelations and was threatening to sue. Sharon Sterling had somehow found out about the time Jock had made him kneel on the hard boardroom floor for three hours while he ignored him and carried on with a meeting. It was Jock's way of punishing him for not noticing a rival's innovative expansion into new methods of bottling, and for having the audacity to ask for a day off to attend Charles' graduation. The incident had taken place many years ago, but Jane knew it still rankled and could quite understand how Edward must be feeling now it was splashed all over the papers for the world to witness.

Poor Edward. Jock had never forgiven him for inheriting the other fifty per cent of Jacaranda Vines along with Cordelia, and often used humiliation to get his revenge when the vote went against him. Yet her tears had little to do with pity for the rest of the family. They were for herself and the pain Sharon Sterling had caused.

The telephone was ringing again, and with a sigh she dropped the magazine on the floor and went to answer it.

'It's me, darling. Philip. I suppose you've already seen that scurrilous article?'

Jane swallowed back the tears. 'Yes. And if I get my hands on whoever spoke to that bitch, I'll kill them.'

'At least you came out of it fairly unscathed. Everyone already knew you were Jock's mistress, and of course you must be used to gossip-mongering after all your years in the theatre. But, my dear, to accuse me of pandering! I've never even been to those baths in Sydney, let alone picked up boys there. Not my thing at all, as you well know. And as for suggesting I might have full-blown Aids – well!'

Jane knew about Philip's predilection for older men in his youth, but she also knew his tastes had changed somewhat and that his latest lover was only just out of college. There had certainly been occasions in the past when scandal had been only narrowly averted by quick thinking and a fat cheque – but no hint of pandering or paedophilia. As for her coming out of this unscathed, he could have no idea of how wrong he was. 'You're not HIV, are you, Philip?'

There was silence at the end of the line, and when he finally replied Philip's voice was softer, more hesitant. 'I've never had the nerve to go for the test but I don't feel crook.'

'Then I suggest you go and have it done,' she said gently. The tears would not be stopped and she gripped the phone. 'I'm sorry, Philip. I can't talk now. Ring me later tonight when I've had time to take all this in.' There was a headache lurking behind her eyes, and her legs were shaking so badly she could barely stand.

'Fair go, Jane. This affects us all, you know. We have to do something. Today. Before Cordelia gets hold of it.'

'She's already been in touch, Philip. I've got an appointment with her solicitor this afternoon, but after having spoken to him on the phone this morning, there doesn't seem to be much we can do. That Sterling woman has obviously had a team of lawyers go over her piece with a fine-tooth comb. She's been very clever. Innuendo and personal opinion can't be construed as libel, and she's only come straight out with accusations she can prove.'

'I'd like to strangle the bitch, personally. And whoever it was who gave her the dirt to dish.'

'That's something we'll have to consider, certainly, and I have my own ideas about it. But not now, Philip,' she insisted. 'I've a migraine coming and I need to lie down.'

'Take care, Jane. I'm just sorry you got dragged into all this.'

'My fault for getting mixed up with Jock Witney in the first place,' she said sharply.

With the call disconnected, Jane slumped into a chair and stared out through the window. Poor Philip. He'd always relied on her for a shoulder to cry on. How dare that bitch rake up such filth? The anger mounted again and she picked up the magazine, leafed through until she got to the column related to her life, and read it once more.

Jane Bruce was only twenty when she began her long affair with the forty-year-old Jock Witney, and yet she was already the target for gossip in the tight-knit, louche world of the theatre. Miss Bruce was a very attractive young woman, and there were rumours of several liaisons with other thespians – not all of them free, white and single.

A player of insignificant parts before her affair, Jane Bruce was catapulted to stardom when she took the leading role of Blanche du Bois in *A Streetcar Named Desire* at the National Theatre in Sydney. A theatre sponsored heavily by the Witney family, though I'm sure this had no influence on the young actress' career. Miss Bruce's success was further enhanced by her screen role of Agrippina in the Australian Film company's version of *I, Claudius,* for which she won an award. Jock Witney was very coy at the time when questioned about his backing for the film, but this reporter has it on good authority that it was his money that saw the project through.

Jock's wife Cordelia must have known of her husband's philandering for it wasn't the first time he'd flaunted his mistresses and certainly wasn't to be the last. But this reporter wonders if she ever heard rumours of a baby? Perhaps she did and was part of the cover-up. For the truth is still so well hidden, not even the resources of *G'Day* magazine can get to the facts of the affair, and it is assumed that Miss Bruce will take the truth to the grave with her. But it is intriguing to think there might be someone out there who is unaware they have a right to claim from Jock Witney's billion-dollar estate. How jolly it would be if they could be found to add yet another piece to the puzzle that makes up the family behind Jacaranda Vines.

Jane could read no further. The pain behind her eyes was so intense she could barely raise her head from the cushions. She whimpered in anguish, invaded by memories she'd thought long banished. Yet there was a part of her which could still look with analytical calm at the whole scenario.

The article was venomous and spiteful – yet it proved one thing. Whoever the informant was, they hadn't known it all. For if they had, the truth would have been far more devastating for all concerned – and Sharon Sterling would have had a real scoop on her hands.

Charles didn't feel at all well. Despite the windows being open, he was finding it hard to breathe. He unfastened his collar and took off his jacket. The effort of doing this made his heart thud painfully against his ribs, and he rested his head against the cushions so he could catch his breath. Yet his mind was tormented by what he'd read in that damn' magazine, and he dreaded facing Vipia with it.

The magazine lay on the table beside him, the glossy pages open, the graphic photographs looming up at him. He had no need to read the article again, the words were etched too deeply in his mind for him ever to forget them.

There's no fool like an old fool. And Charles has certainly fulfilled the requirements to warrant such an epithet, for how else could one explain his extraordinary marriage to the young and nubile Vipia? This reporter wonders if he was aware of this young woman's past when he tied the knot – or if he knew and thought he could keep it quiet? Either way, it didn't take long for the research team at *G'Day* magazine to expose the truth.

Vipia was born in the north of Thailand into the poverty of a hard-working farming family. She was barely thirteen when she ran away to Bangkok and the bright lights and sleazy bars of that sinful city. She found work in a bar – not as a waitress but as a stripper, her wages supplemented by the men who flocked to Bangkok for the youthful sex trade. Vipia was eventually set up in an apartment by a rich American, but when he discovered she was using the premises to ply her trade, he threw her out. Vipia was resourceful, even then, and soon found another willing man to provide a roof over her head in return for her services.

This man was known as Leroy Texas, a maker of pornographic films the like of which cannot be found even on the top shelf of your local video store. In fact, *G'Day* magazine is reliably informed by the Australian Police Commission that such material is banned in this country, and Mr Texas, alias Fred Brown, is now languishing in a Sydney jail for trying to import his filth.

Vipia became a star of the screen where the parts on display had nothing to do with talent or even a hint of acting. *G'Day* magazine has managed to find one of these sordid tapes, and after viewing the scenes of degradation and multiple sex orgies that involve minors and animals, this reporter had to stand under a shower for a long time before she could feel clean again. The tape has since been destroyed according to police guidelines, and it is hoped the purveyor of this filth, Mr Texas, remains in jail for many years to come.

It is rumoured that Charles met Vipia in a sleazy strip joint in the red light district of Bangkok – not introduced by a business acquaintance as he insisted on his return to Australia. The corpulent widower had been a well-known habitué of Sydney's brothels before, during and after his marriage, so the whorehouses of Bangkok would have been no more than a busman's holiday for him.

My advice to Charles, who surely pays for his wife's services in the diamonds and pearls he buys for her, and the endless shopping expeditions she makes to the exclusive boutiques of the city, is to consider buying her a scold's bridle and a chastity belt as his next gifts. They might ensure her silence and continued loyalty – for there is rumour that Vipia's favours are no longer exclusive, and that she's getting far more than financial advice from a certain young stockbroker.

Charles' eyes snapped open as he heard the car pull up in the driveway. He looked through the window and watched the chauffeur hand Vipia out and follow her into the house, arms laden with designer label carrier bags. His pulse was uneven as he clenched his fists at his side and waited for her.

The door opened and there she was.

Charles looked at the doll-like features, the slender, almost childish figure in the wispy dress, and wondered why he'd never questioned her more closely about her past life in Bangkok. Never voiced his suspicions of her having another man here.

Because he was too much of a coward, he admitted silently. Because Sharon Sterling was right. He was an old fool who'd allowed his balls to rule his brain, and he hadn't wanted his suspicions confirmed. What he didn't know wouldn't hurt him so, like an ostrich, he'd buried his head in the sand and left his arse naked.

'I found that dress I was looking for,' Vipia said happily, obviously unaware of his anger or discomfort. 'They will have to take it in, of course,' she added smugly. 'My figure is so much more petite than the average Australian whale woman.'

There was no sign she was aware of the magazine article, but then that was hardly surprising. Vipia could neither read nor write, could only just about manage to sign her name. 'Shut the door, Vipia,' he said with far deeper calm than he felt. 'We need to talk.'

A few hours later, after tears, hysteria and offers of exotic sex had all failed to win Charles round, Vipia stood by in sullen silence as he wrote her a large cheque and vowed it would be the last money she received from him. There was no question of a divorce settlement after the lies she'd told him to cover up her unsavoury past. The pain in his chest was getting worse, but he chose to ignore it as he picked up the telephone and booked a one-way ticket for her on the next plane to Thailand.

The tears were flowing, the hysteria rising as she knelt before him and clutched his legs. 'Don't send me back. Please, Charles. I will lose face. Have to work in street again.'

He shrugged her off and rang for the maid. 'You've done it before, you can do it again,' he said coldly. 'But I've given you enough to tide you over until you can find another drongo to set you up.'

Angelina's eyes widened as she took in the scene, but she obviously knew better than to comment and for that Charles was grateful. This whole episode was humiliating enough without having to explain himself, and he wondered if the maid had already seen the papers and come to her own conclusions.

'Vipia is leaving,' he said firmly. 'See that all her

clothes and anything she brought with her from Thailand is packed within the next half an hour. You are to bring the jewellery and any credit cards you find down to me. She is to take none of it – not even her wedding or engagement rings.'

Vipia made to follow Angelina out of the room but Charles grabbed her wrist. 'You'll stay here. I no longer trust you not to steal from me. Sit down and stop that awful noise, it won't do you any good.'

Two hours later, as he watched her plane leave the runway, Charles muffled a cry of pain and turned to his chauffeur. 'You'd better drive me to the hospital,' he said gruffly. 'I feel real crook.'

Mary had treated herself to a rich *café latte* as she read the Saturday papers. She, of course, had had to be included in the catalogue of vitriol, but there was nothing new exposed, nothing too damaging, for she'd managed to keep certain things hidden and had merely confirmed one or two rumours about past lovers and indiscretions that she had no qualms about revealing.

She leaned back in the chair and smiled with satisfaction. Sharon had done a superb hatchet job, and she wished she could have been around when the rest of the family read about themselves. Dad was of course out of it, but even he might have taken some kind of pleasure in the way the knife had been twisted so expertly, and she chuckled to think of him looking down and watching them all squirm.

The touch about the baby had been a masterpiece. She hoped that bitch Jane was suffering.

She might have been a success once but now she was just a gold-digging has-been – an old tart with a taste for the good life.

Mary had no evidence to suggest there had been a child, just a feeling something had gone on between Jane and Dad that had caused a glitch in their affair. Mum was tight-lipped about the past, but Jane was definitely hiding something. There was also the mystery of why the two women now shared an apartment. She smiled as she sipped the hot sweet drink. Strange how speculation and imagination could come up with such a good story – Sharon had positively drooled as Mary spun it out.

'There's no place in this family for bastards,' she hissed. 'If the bitch had got pregnant, then Dad would have made her get rid of it.' The bitterness caught in her throat as she thought of her own pregnancy with Sophie. If she'd had her way, the kid would have been terminated or adopted. Given to the first person willing to take her. But she'd left it too late by the time Paul shot through and Mother had taken over as usual and insisted upon rearing the brat herself. Which meant the kid was a constant reminder of Paul – the one man she'd truly loved but who had never loved her in return.

Mary sighed and set the magazine down. She eyed the telephone. It was time to ring her sisters and put on the act of disbelief and hurt she'd rehearsed over the past two days. They would find it odd if she remained silent, and although she had no regrets over what she'd done, she couldn't afford to be found out.

10

Daisy walked into the boardroom and was hit by a wall of noise. She took in the scene with one swift glance and sat down at her usual place. Her absence would have been noted, but her presence would go almost unnoticed as usual. She gave a grim little smile. To be ignored had always given her time to take stock and judge the temper of the family. Her judgement wouldn't be sought, but it was surprising what you could learn from the outside looking in.

A heavy rap of the gavel on the table made them all turn to look at Edward. 'Sit down,' he roared. 'All this shouting will get us nowhere.'

'So what do you suggest?' sneered Mary. 'That we take this lying down?'

'It's what you do best, dear,' drawled Philip.

'What's that supposed to mean?' Mary's face was almost as red as the scarlet nails clawing the table.

Philip leaned back in his chair, assured of everyone's attention. 'I mean,' he said deliberately, 'that you conduct most of your business on your back. Sharon Sterling certainly got you pegged.'

'She didn't get you wrong either,' Mary retorted. 'Bloody shirt lifter!'

'Enough,' roared Edward. 'I will not have this meeting turned into a bitching match. My son's

196

lying in a hospital bed and my sister's out in the middle of nowhere worrying herself crook. We need to discuss this sensibly and calmly, not throw accusations about.'

'I agree,' said Kate. 'And the first thing we have to do is find out who spoke to Sharon Sterling.'

'What do you suggest? A lie-detector test?' Philip studied his nails. 'I hardly think the person responsible will put their hand up and confess, do you?'

'Of course not,' Kate retorted. 'But we can rule out certain members of this family.'

Daisy watched as her sister took a breath and hurried on through the chorus of denials. It was interesting to see the different expressions flit across their faces. Interesting to mark those who could hide their feelings and those who couldn't.

'Charles certainly wouldn't have done it, and neither would the twins. It's not in their nature,' said Kate firmly. She looked around the room. 'Where are they, by the way?'

'I tried contacting them, but they're both away from the vineyard and can't be reached,' rumbled Edward.

'Uncle Edward is definitely above suspicion, and Mum and Sophie were out of state when the story broke. To suggest Mum would do something like this is ludicrous, and Sophie isn't spiteful enough.' Kate took a breath. 'I know it wasn't me, and I hardly think Daisy would do such a thing.'

She smiled at Daisy and turned to Mary. 'Which leaves you,' she said coldly.

Mary threw her hands in the air. 'Typical!' she

spat. 'When in doubt, blame me. But haven't you forgotten just one or two tiny details? I'm not the only one with an axe to grind. What about Jane?'

Everyone turned to look at the woman who wouldn't normally have been in the boardroom – but these were exceptional circumstances. 'I have no axe to grind,' said Jane calmly. 'Cordelia's been good to me, and I certainly wouldn't repay her by trying to destroy her family.'

'Pretty words,' sneered Mary. 'But you don't get off with this so lightly, Jane. You've been leaching off this family for years. First Dad, now Mother. What hold have you got over her, Jane? Why has she given you a home when it was you who broke up her marriage?'

Daisy could see Jane was struggling to maintain her composure. But she was ever the consummate actress. When she spoke, her voice was calm. 'I have no hold over your mother,' she said quietly. 'As for your parents' marriage, that was over long before I was on the scene.'

'Was the piece about the baby true? Is there some bastard running loose out there who could claim a piece of our inheritance?'

Daisy held her breath as she saw how Mary's eyes gleamed. Then she noticed how Jane almost cringed from that venomous glare, and was shocked by how much Mary appeared to hate the older woman. She sat very still as she watched them, and for the first time she wondered if that animosity was merely the fear of Mary's losing part of her inheritance – or something far deeper.

'If it was, do you think I'd have told a cheap reporter after all these years? And if it wasn't, then why cause so much pain to Cordelia? Your argument doesn't stand up, Mary.' Jane's composure was still in place, but only just – Daisy could see the white of her knuckles as she bunched her fists in her lap.

'She's got a point, Mary,' Kate said firmly. 'I think you should drop it.'

'No way,' said her sister vehemently as she stood up. 'There's no smoke without fire, and I think we should know the truth once and for all.' She turned back to Jane. 'What did you do? Get rid of it? Have it adopted? Give it away? Was your career more important than your bastard – or did Dad know what a scheming cow you were and refuse to be blackmailed into paying you off?'

Jane stared fixedly at the table. 'I have already given you my answer,' she said quietly. 'I did not speak to that reporter, nor would I ever do so.' Her eyes were bruised with weariness as she finally looked up at Mary. 'If anyone at this table is capable of such vicious character assassination then it's you. You always were spiteful and grasping. How many pieces of silver did she pay you to betray your family, Mary?'

'I'm not staying around to be insulted like this,' Mary hissed.

'Then rack off,' drawled Philip. 'I'm sure you'll find plenty of other places where the insults are of a higher grade.'

Mary threw him a glare of pure malice. 'You can sit here and tell each other lies all night long, but you'll never get to the bottom of it because you're all too scared of the truth. Dad was right. You're nothing but a bunch of losers!' She grabbed her handbag and stormed out of the door, banging it with such ferocity that it resounded through the building.

They sat in stunned silence, each with their own thoughts. Daisy chewed her lip. That was a flawless performance by Mary but she had just noticed something she had never seen before, and as the truth dawned knew with absolute certainty that it couldn't have been Jane who'd talked to Sharon Sterling.

Cordelia had assured Sophie she was merely feeling tired rather than unwell after the shock of the article. Now the lights were out and she listened to her granddaughter's restless sleep, she could finally give rein to her own troubled thoughts and memories.

The article had painted Jock accurately, but there was a side to her late husband that no one else had seen. It was this knowledge that had sustained her through the bad times, and would sustain her now. For although their marriage had crumbled, and Jock had become impossible to live with, they had still shared an intimacy that nothing and no one had managed to break.

The first few years of marriage had been happy and fulfilling for Cordelia, their lives filled with work and plans for the future for their twin boys. With Jock's financial input, Jacaranda Vines was once again a success. The two vineyards had been combined, and as the workload increased they had taken on more men. The planting of new and stronger vines, and the five successive seasons of just enough rain and sun, had guaranteed good harvests with a promise of excellent vintage.

Each year's vintage saw the arrival of the pickers, women and boys mostly, with nimble fingers and strong backs, who trawled the thousands of acres of terraces from dawn to dusk. The heat was intense, the sky blue, the grapes black with a dusty silver bloom. Yet the back-breaking work was helped along by snatches of song and much laughter as the story-telling became more whimsical and preposterous, and Cordelia had never felt more at one with the earth than she did in those few short, hectic weeks.

It would take over a month to strip the vines, press the grapes and fill the casks before vintage was over, and during that time, although she was out in the terraces each day, she would only catch a glimpse of Jock in the distance as he observed, monitored and admonished the workers.

He would rise before first light and not return to the homestead until long after the sun had set. Yet he never seemed to tire, for the excitement of vintage filled each waking hour as he waited for the fermentation of the must in the scoured dark vats. After the first day's picking, it would be at least another twenty-four hours before fermentation began, but on the second day they would stand in the cool wine cellars and breathe in the wonderful sour aroma of new wine.

'It's a miracle, Cordy. A blessed miracle,' he breathed.

She felt his arm slip around her waist, and leaned into him. She too thought of it as a miracle, and the sight of those sweating red-faced men working the presses over the vats was something she would always hold precious. For fermentation had begun. The juice of the pressed grapes was seething, hissing and bubbling like a black porridge, the mat of the grape skins twisting constantly as gas bubbles broke through. It was as if it were alive.

'The secret, of course, is to know when to run the wine off into casks. For a Sauternes we have to keep the sugar content, so the fermenting period has to be brief. For the dry reds the process must be much longer.' Jock seemed to have forgotten that Cordelia had been born with the smell of new wine all around her, and knew as much about the fermentation and bottling process as he did, but she indulged him. This was the time she loved him the best, for he was young again, almost carefree once the picking was over and the casks were being filled.

She looked up at him. The sun had burned his skin to a deep mahogany, enhancing the colour of his eyes and bleaching fair streaks into his hair. He was very handsome, and she felt the lurch of passion he always aroused in her. 'Will this be a good vintage?'

He nodded and squeezed her waist. 'It will be an excellent vintage, Cordy. You and Jacaranda Vines have brought me luck.'

She sighed in the darkness. That had been the best year of their marriage, but it had also been the last time she'd been truly happy. She had clung to the memories of those first five years, hoping they would sustain her through the bad times that followed, yet the knowledge that Jock had had a succession of affairs throughout the following years was something that cast a deep shadow over that short episode of happiness.

That she hadn't known, hadn't guessed that her husband was unfaithful was not too surprising. Love was certainly blind, and although in hindsight she'd realised what a fool she'd been to trust him, she also admitted that her blindness might have come from not wanting to see the truth.

Their lives were entwined with the vines and ruled by the elements, and although her own journeys to Adelaide were rare, Jock would frequently leave her and the twins alone at the homestead to go to the city to sell their vintage and make contacts amongst the tradesmen.

He'd explained carefully that they needed to make room in their cellars for the new vintage, and the wine he sold to hotels and gentlemen's clubs, and various acquaintances who regarded themselves as wine experts, would go towards the upkeep of the property and wages for the men. Jock had even sent some of their five-year-old vintage to London in the hope of establishing Jacaranda as one of the leading wineries of the world. They were exciting times, those early years, and she'd been swept along in the wake of his enthusiasm.

Her marriage to Jock soured on one of her rare visits to the city, and from that day on they had only the vines and their children in common. She'd gone with him to celebrate their sixth successful vintage and had been looking forward to wearing some of the fine clothes she'd had made for the special occasion. The fashions had changed since the Great War and the dresses she'd packed for her trip were heavily beaded with handkerchief hems that danced just above the knee. They were very daring, but Jock had assured her she would be in the height of fashion, and although she doubted that a man so taken up with the vineyard would notice things like that, she had to believe him.

'But promise me you won't cut your hair, Cordy,' he'd whispered before kissing her neck as she prepared for the journey. 'I love it when you let it hang free. The new bob is all very well but I find it rather masculine.'

The ball at the Governor's house was a grand affair. Cordelia had been awed by the crystal chandeliers that hung from the highly decorated ceilings and by the jewels of the richly dressed women. But Jock had been right. Her dress was perfect, even if her hair hung right down to her waist.

Although she was a stranger amongst these people, Jock seemed familiar with many of them and before introducing her quietly told her that this man bought his wine, that man was on the board of the Australian Wine Commission, the other man and his wife were part of the social elite and had professed a liking for Jacaranda's wine. She had smiled and made polite conversation, even learned to dance the newfangled Charleston to the band the Governor had so thoughtfully supplied, but she was soon hot and out of breath and after making her excuses had looked around for Jock.

He was dancing vigorously with an animated dark-haired woman who looked up at him with the directness that came only from a long-established intimacy. Cordelia watched them for a moment, the joy of the evening crushed by the sudden knowledge that Jock and that woman were more than friends.

Although she felt sick, she took a glass of lemonade from a circling waiter and went out on to the balcony. She had to have some fresh air, time to think and put what she'd seen into perspective. Jock was a handsome man. Women were always flirting with him. It didn't mean it went any further, she insisted silently, refusing to listen to that still small voice that warned her it wasn't so.

The evening was blessedly cool after the heat of the ballroom, the breeze coming up from the ocean with a tang of salt to stir the damp hair that clung to her neck. Cordelia sank on to one of the stone seats that was almost hidden in an arbour and closed her eyes. The breeze was cooling her neck and shoulders like a caress, but nothing could quell the shock of her discovery or the ache that had settled deep within.

The light tap of heels on the terrace was accompanied by the rustle of beads against silk and a plummy English voice.

'My dear, he's the talk of Adelaide!' The statement was conspiratorial, uttered with a degree of malicious relish. 'But he's playing with fire this time. I don't know how he dared bring his wife along, knowing Leonora would be here.'

Cordelia wasn't really listening. She hated gossip and wished they'd go away so she could have time to herself to think about Jock. But the women had settled themselves on the steps leading down to the garden and seemed reluctant to leave. Although they hadn't seen her in the darkness, she had no wish to be discovered eavesdropping. She was about to reveal her presence by standing up and walking away when their voices stilled her.

'I pity Cordelia,' said the second Pommy voice. 'Poor woman.'

'Nonsense! With a handsome man like Jock as a husband, it's only to be expected he'll stray. Leonora certainly isn't the first, and I very much doubt she'll be the last.'

Cordelia sat bolt upright, her pulse racing, her hand to her mouth to stifle a gasp. She had to get out of here. Had to escape before she heard any more. And yet something held her there in that rose-scented arbour, and it had little to do with being caught eavesdropping. For she was transfixed by the need to know just how long her husband's affair with the mysterious Leonora had been going on.

'These colonial women have different standards from us, my dear. She's probably living over the brush with some dashing vintner up in the Barossa Valley. It's all that space and outdoor living, you know. I've heard it gives one a lust for nature. You only have to see all the hair to know she's quite wild.'

There were stifled giggles and Cordelia wanted to rush out and bang their stupid heads together. She could feel her temper rising, the heat burning in her face, yet she remained still. She would not give these simpering, ignorant women the pleasure of seeing her out of control. She would wait – regardless of how devastating their gossip was – regardless of the need to give vent to the bitterness and pain that lay heavy within.

'Mind you, *I* wouldn't mind getting closer to Jock Witney. They say that one day he'll be very rich indeed, and coupled with his looks, that can't be a bad bargain.'

'That's all very well, my dear. But I understand he's only making his fortune because he managed to get hold of half his wife's vineyard. It's even been suggested he married her for her inheritance. He was almost bankrupt when he came back from the war, you know, and although he was doing quite well at Bundoran, the land isn't half as rich as Jacaranda's. He might be a handsome rogue but I wouldn't trust him. He's too ambitious, too demanding.'

The women carried on chattering for another few moments then drifted back to the ballroom. Cordelia was suddenly cold, almost frozen to the narrow stone bench as she digested the full impact of the women's gossip. Jock had saved Jacaranda Vines. If it hadn't been for him they would have foundered and been no more. Surely that hadn't been his plan? His reason for marrying her? Had it?

Cordelia turned on her side now, face buried in the pillow as she remembered that awful night and the scene that had followed.

Jock had thrown off his coat before striding into the bedroom of their hotel suite. 'That all went splendidly, Cordy. The Wine Commission is going to review our first two vintages, and if all goes well, we'll earn our first seal of approval.' He smiled at her. 'You did well. It's nice to see you dressed up for a change. We should do it more often.'

Cordelia could barely suppress her anger. She didn't care about the bloody Wine Commission. 'Who is Leonora?' she asked bluntly.

Jock seemed unconcerned by the question but Cordelia noticed he couldn't quite look her in the eyes as he replied, 'The widow of a friend.'

'Wouldn't it be nearer the truth to say she's your mistress?' There, it was out, never to be taken back. She looked hopefully into his face, willing him to deny it, to prove the gossip she'd overheard wasn't true.

'So what if she is?' he said carelessly as he released his collar studs and eased off his shirt. 'Leonora is a very rich woman, and because of her late husband, she has all the right contacts in the wine industry. She'll help us to make our fortune, Cordelia, so don't rock the boat by getting prissy.'

Cordelia had to sit down. His audacity was stunning. 'So you don't deny it?' she gasped.

He looked at her for a long moment. 'Why should I, Cordelia? Would you prefer I lie to you?'

She shook her head. 'Of course not. But you seem so ... so cold and matter-of-fact about it all. I thought you loved me?' She looked up at him, pleading with her eyes for it to be so, but what she saw made her shiver. There was no gentleness in his smile, no attempt by him to reach out and comfort her.

'Of course I love you, Cordelia,' he said wearily as he undressed for bed. 'You are my wife. But a man has needs, and I see no reason why my being married should make any difference. I have always been discreet, have never wanted to hurt you in any way. Why can't you just be satisfied with what you have?'

The tears were streaming down her face. Who was this cold stranger? Surely not the husband who'd made love to her only the night before? 'Leonora isn't your first, is she?'

'No,' he said. 'And I doubt she'll be the last. Now come to bed. I'm exhausted and need my sleep before the meeting at the Vintners' Club in the morning.'

Cordelia stood up, rage tearing through her with such ferocity she could barely control her trembling. 'Go to hell!' she yelled. 'I'm not getting in that bed with you after this.'

He paused in the act of turning down the sheet. 'The hotel is full, Cordelia,' he said smoothly. 'There is nowhere else for you to sleep.'

She began to throw her clothes into a trunk. 'Oh, yes there is,' she panted. 'I'm going back to Jacaranda, and you'll be getting a letter from my solicitor. I'm leaving you, Jock, and taking my sons and my vineyard with me.'

He whipped round and had crossed the space between them before she could blink. His hand encircled her neck as his face loomed over hers. 'Don't you ever threaten me like that again, Cordelia. You are my wife.'

'No, I'm not,' she gasped as she clawed at his hands. 'I was just a means to an end. It was

Jacaranda you wanted, not me.'

The pressure of his fingers tightened momentarily, then he released her. 'Leave me and I'll see you never keep Jacaranda. Take my sons and I'll break you and your precious family. From now on, Cordelia, you will do things my way.'

She swallowed, her hands fluttering at her throat, remembering. She could still feel the pressure of his fingers around her neck, could still see the rage in his eyes and hear the icy determination in his voice. She hadn't left him that night, for she couldn't risk losing the boys or the vineyard. Yet a spark of determination was lit within her then and with a bravado that shocked them both, she'd locked herself in the bathroom and cut twelve inches off her hair.

They had returned home following that disastrous trip to Adelaide, and after many months of protracted silence between them, had found a kind of compromise – a truce. But as the years had passed and the catalogue of his various women had steadily lengthened, Jock abandoned any pretence of discretion and Cordelia had learned to regard them as unimportant – no matter how much it hurt – no matter how humiliating it became. It was that or risk losing Jacaranda forever.

With a sigh, she settled down to sleep. Jock hadn't had everything his own way, though, she thought. There were secrets of her own he might have suspected but never uncovered, and when she'd finally got her revenge, it had been delicious to sit back and watch him make a fool of himself.

11

'It's very beautiful here, Gran,' Sophie said as they settled down with a cup of coffee after breakfast. 'I checked the map. You didn't tell me we were coming to the northern boundaries of the Hunter.' She stared wistfully towards the rolling plains of the valley floor. 'Coolabah Crossing must be down there somewhere. Jay was always talking about it – now I understand why.'

'You were very much in love with him, weren't you?'

Cordelia's expression was artless, but Sophie noticed how watchful she'd become and sensed there was something going on in that devious mind. 'I suppose so,' she replied carefully. 'But we were both so young. What did we know about anything?'

'Probably more than you realised,' replied her grandmother.

Sophie placed the cup on the table, her expression deliberately blank to mask the rush of feelings Cordelia's question had aroused. 'What are you trying to say, Gran?'

She shrugged. 'Nothing,' she said airily. 'I just wondered if you ever heard from him once you both left college, that's all.'

Sophie eyed the old woman and wondered where this conversation was leading. 'You know I didn't, Gran. That was why we split. Then Grandad stuck his oar in and I went off to London and university.' She looked away, but the sunlight was making her eyes water and the horizon a blur. 'I always wondered why he disapproved of Jay.'

'He had his reasons – as he did for everything,' said Cordelia enigmatically. 'But I thought you and Jay went well together. You had so much in common, with your families owning vineyards, and I was disappointed when you married Crispin on the rebound.'

'I didn't,' spluttered Sophie. 'I adored him. He was everything I wanted in a man. Independently wealthy, handsome, charming, and from a good family.'

Cordelia's look said it all and Sophie blushed. 'Okay, Gran. I made a mistake and picked someone who couldn't keep his zipper up. But I was over Jay a long time before Cris came along.'

'I wonder,' murmured the old woman.

Sophie watched as she refused help to get out of her chair and hobbled off down the gravelled path to the wash block. Left alone to her thoughts, she wondered what Jay was doing now and whether he'd stayed at Coolabah Crossing. He could be married and have a brood of kids for all she knew. She'd followed the rise and rise of Coolabah Wines over the years, but there had been no mention of him in the business news or gossip columns, and she'd always been curious as to whether he'd fulfilled his ambition to take over the family vineyard.

She sighed. They had been soul-mates at

college, each one half of the other, sharing so much that they seemed destined for one another, and as she sat there in the early-morning sun, she had a clear image of how Jay had looked then. His dark hair and eyes were a direct contrast to Crispin's cool English fairness, and although he hadn't been as tall, she still had to look up at him. Jay's skin was darkened by the sun, his hands rough from work on the terraces during college holidays, and when he'd forgotten to shave there was a dark stubble on his chin that made him look dangerous and exciting.

She smiled sadly as she remembered how he'd meet her after classes and the way she would cling to his broad back as they roared down to the lido by the river on his motorbike. Evenings were spent talking – they'd had so much in common – and weekends exploring the bush where he would teach her to cook bush tucker and spot the koalas in the trees. And one memorable summer they had flown up to Lindeman Island on the Barrier Reef where they lived like castaways and carved their initials in the rough bark of a palm tree, promising to love one another for always. 'We were just kids,' she murmured into the silence. 'Of course things changed between us.'

The exchange of letters had been frequent during those first few months after graduation, then suddenly, and inexplicably, there was nothing – not even a phone call. She wrote twice more – made phone calls that weren't answered, left messages that were ignored – and had finally had to face the fact that he no longer loved her or wanted anything to do with her. His brother had been cold when he'd answered the phone, his tone brusque as he told her Jay had left for France for a year at a winery. She could still remember how hurt she was by his silence, how bewildered by his unexpected rejection – but she'd been too proud to beg an explanation.

She stared down into the valley, the familiar ache returning after all these years to remind her of that overwhelming first love she'd lost. Where are you Jay? Are you happy? Do you ever think of me?

'You're getting sentimental,' she muttered crossly as she cleared the breakfast table and stowed it away. 'Too many sleepless nights and too much travelling. Get a grip, Sophie.'

'Talking to yourself, dear? I thought it was only I who did that.'

Sophie turned and smiled. 'Just thinking aloud. Are you ready to leave, Gran? I'd like to finish our journey before the sun's too high.'

Cordelia settled herself in the camp chair under the awning. 'There's just a little more of Rose's story I want to tell you before we reach our destination.' She held up her hand to stem Sophie's objections. 'I know you'd prefer to travel before it gets too hot, but it won't take long. Besides,' she added with a smile, 'it will go some way to explain what you will find at the end of our journey.'

Sophie frowned. 'You're talking in riddles again, Gran.'

'Then perhaps I'd better get on with story and make myself clear.'

The *Hawk* sailed into Botany Bay on 22nd December, 1839. It had taken three long months to navigate the distance between London Docks and New South Wales, and Rose was almost sorry the journey was at an end. Now, as she stood on the wooden deck and leaned over the rails, she had her first glimpse of this new country that was to be her home – her future.

The hot wind tugged at the bonnet and dress Lady Fitzallan had bought her, the sun warmed her face and made her screw up her eyes, but the sight of the primitive buildings that clustered around the little jetty and the stretches of honey-coloured sand lapped by jewelled water made her pulse race. The beauty of the wooded slopes, so green against the glaring red of the earth and the blue of the sea and sky, was like something out of a picture book. So bright, so clean – almost unreal.

And yet, as she stood there in awe, she was soon to scent more familiar smells that reminded her of England, for together with the exotic aromas of the blazing flowers and strange-looking trees were the warm aromas of horse dung, cattle feed and hay that wafted out to sea on the hot wind.

As the *Hawk* settled at anchor, timbers creaking, canvas sails slapping against the masts, Rose listened to the shouts of the sailors as they climbed like monkeys up into the rigging and prepared the ship for her long stay in port. She knew many of the officers on board had brought their wives and families, and that some of them, like her, had come on this long journey to begin a new life in this new world.

The Dowager Lady Fitzallan was a pleasant employer compared to Lady Amelia, but though their long voyage had forced a certain intimacy between them, there was no guarantee she would need Rose's services once they landed. If that should happen, what would become of her then? She pushed the gloomy thought aside. There could be no going back, no regrets despite the sickness for home and a fear for the unknown.

'Rose. I've been hunting for you everywhere.'

She turned at the sound of the familiar voice. Lady Muriel Fitzallan was short and fat and seemed to float along the deck like a clipper in full sail, her grey skirts billowing from wide hips beneath a tightly corseted bosom. Her hat was broad-brimmed, covered in feathers and tethered beneath her copious chins with black lace. Her round face seemed unusually petulant today.

Rose bobbed a curtsy. 'I've been watching them sail into the harbour, Ma'am. Don't you think it's ever so pretty?'

Lady Fitzallan's frown relented and she smiled. 'Pretty is as pretty does,' she said confusingly. 'We'll see what's what when we get ashore.' She glanced out to the harbour, favoured it with a nod of approval, then turned back to Rose. 'I seem to have mislaid my fan, dear. Go and fetch it, there's a good girl.'

Rose bobbed another curtsy and hurried back to their cabin. Lady Fitzallan was always losing something, but she didn't mind the constant searching for she liked the old girl. In a way she reminded her of Cook. They shared the same shape and outlook on life, for like Cook the dowager's tempers soon blew over, and under that rather bossy exterior was a bustling energetic soul who spoke her mind regardless of the company or situation and was never knowingly unkind.

The dark panelled cabin was unusually tidy for Rose had packed the trunks the night before and now there were only a few last-minute things to be folded away in a portmanteau. She quickly found the fan which had somehow become wedged down the back of a chair, and after tidying away the last of the packing, she returned to the railings.

The dowager fanned her scarlet face and dabbed her brow with a scrap of handkerchief. 'My son warned me about the heat but surely this must be unusual? What person could survive in such temperatures?'

Rose, who was sweating profusely in her thick woollen dress, had no reply. She wished only to strip off the layers of petticoats and underthings her employer had provided and plunge into the water. It looked so cool, so inviting.

'Come along. It's time for me to disembark.'

Rose followed the billowing, portly figure along the deck to the rickety wooden ladder that ran down the side of the ship to the little boat bobbing beneath.

After a long argument, during which Lady Fitzallan refused to yield, a special chair was produced that could be swung down by ropes. Rose watched in concern as, with a great deal of fuss and last-minute instructions, Lady Fitzallan was hoisted high over the railings.

The dowager sat bolt upright, hands firmly gripping the ropes, her feet primly crossed. The round face had lost a little of its colour but those stubborn chins were valiant, nose firmly held in the air as the wind flapped the brim of her bonnet and ruffled her skirts.

Rose stifled her giggles as the old woman was lowered in stately silence and carefully deposited on a narrow wooden bench at the bow of the rowing boat. No master craftsman could have made a more fitting figure-head.

She watched as less particular passengers made their way down the ladder to the boat. When it was full, the sailors pulled on their oars and headed for shore. Lady Fitzallan's wave was regal and Rose smothered another giggle. The old girl was enjoying herself, and why not? It was an adventure for both of them.

Rose hurried away from the railings and after making sure all the luggage was safely lowered into the appropriate boats, carefully made her own way down the ladder and into the dinghy that had been reserved for the servants of the first-class passengers.

She grasped the side of the rowing boat. The wind snatched at her bonnet, sending it bouncing against her back on the ribbons that were tied around her neck. Her hair was ripped from its pins and streamed behind her, making her want to laugh with the sheer joy of it all. The creak of the oars was accompanied by the groans of the sailors and the shout of the boatswain as the little craft plunged through the waves. Gulls screamed overhead and salt spray cooled her as the bow lifted and sank with the roll and pitch of the swell.

Rose closed her eyes and lifted her face to the sun, breathed in the salt air and the warm scent of hot earth, and knew that, whatever her future held, she was content in this one moment of pure freedom.

The short trip across the bay was over too soon. The ropes were thrown to the jetty, caught and firmly lashed. Hands reached down to help them out of the yawing boat and on to the slimy green steps.

Rose climbed up to the cobbled quay, and as she stopped to catch her breath, swayed and would have stumbled if a strong hand hadn't caught her elbow. She laughed and looked up into a sun-reddened face and bright blue eyes. 'I feel as if I'm still on the ship,' she said.

'You haf the sea legs,' he replied. 'It vill soon pass.' He removed his dusty hat to reveal hair as red as the earth. 'Otto Fischer, at your service.'

Rose blushed, smeared the damp hair from her face and bobbed an unsteady curtsy. She had never had a gentleman doff his hat to her before and rather liked it, even if he was a foreigner.

'There you are, Rose. I thought you were never coming. The heat is appalling, and my son has arranged for us to stay in an hotel for a few nights before going on to the Mission.' Muriel Fitz-allan's eyes took in the length and not inconsiderable breadth of Otto Fischer. 'I don't believe we have been introduced,' she said haughtily.

He clicked his heels and bowed low. The

introduction over, his gaze returned to Rose. 'It is a lovely name for a lovely lady,' he said without a hint of false flattery. 'I am hoping we can meet vile you are in town.'

Rose blushed an even darker scarlet, but it was her employer who saved her from having to answer. 'Rose is in my employ, Herr Fischer, and as this is our first day in this god-forsaken place, there is much to do.' She turned her back on him. 'Come, Rose.'

She grinned up at the red-haired giant before ducking her head and hurrying after the bustling figure cutting a swathe through the jostling confusion of the quayside. She knew she would probably never see him again for they were due to leave Botany Bay in a couple of days for the interior, but she was very aware of his gaze following her into the crowd and wished there had been time to get to know him a little better.

'Henry, this is Rose,' proclaimed Lady Fitzallan to a tall, thin man with a drooping moustache and sad eyes. 'She's a little young, I know, but she's a good girl and has looked after me well during the journey.'

His hand was warm and soft as he took Rose's fingers and bowed over them, but he didn't speak and after only a cursory glance, turned back to his mother. 'I have arranged for the luggage to be brought directly to the hotel. Take my arm, Mother. The pavement is rough, and I wouldn't like you to fall.'

Rose gathered up her small bag and followed them. This new country certainly had some features that reminded her of home, she noted with a grin. Horses stood dozing in the sun, flies swarming around their eyes and flicking tails. Whores stood on street corners, as brazen as they were in the London alleyways, and skinny dogs foraged in the rubbish. The inns were doing a roaring trade, spilling out their staggering customers, and the bare-foot urchins running in the streets might have ruddy complexions, but as they watched the portly dowager stride along, there was the same knowing gleam in their eyes as in the London boys'.

Yet the comparisons ended there. For here the smog of London was replaced by a fine red dust that seemed to hang permanently over everything. It got down your neck and made you itch, streaked the sweat on your face and made your eyes gritty. To make things worse, it was stirred up in a choking cloud by coaches dashing by and a bullock team laboriously toiling up the hill. Rose wished she had a handkerchief to cover her nose and mouth as Lady Fitzallan had.

She trudged after Henry and his mother, her darting gaze taking in everything. Shops were crude wooden shacks, shaded by verandahs, their wares displayed in hectic profusion. There were the necessities of life, such as cooking pots and tools, stoves and clothing, but also brightly coloured parrots in cages, fringed shawls and highly lacquered oriental chests amongst the pottery, beads and native clubs and spears that caught her eye and her imagination. Rose eyed them longingly. What fun it would have been to explore! If only Lady Fitzallan would slow down a little.

As she hurried after them, she noticed how the wooden houses all had little white fences to separate them from the street and verandahs which offered a shady resting place out of the broiling sun. The flowers and trees were nothing like she'd seen before and the heavy sweet scent of their blossom almost disguised the stench of garbage and manure that littered the street. The birds too seemed to have been painted from a child's colouring box. Few dusty brown sparrows could be seen amongst the startling blue and yellow and pink and white of the circling, squabbling bird population.

She gripped her small bag and took a deep breath of excitement. There was an energy here, a roaring untidy lust for life that was almost primitive in its challenge. Yet she could already see the promise of this city in the broad avenues and the few simple sandstone buildings that were obviously the homes of gentry. The promise that one day it would become an important place in this raw new country. It just needed time, and the energy of the new settlers to make it so, and she was infused with just such enthusiasm.

A flash of something bright caught her attention and she stared wide-eyed at the straggling, ragged group of women who shuffled in their chains along the quayside towards a large wooden shed. Each woman was dressed in yellow. Mostly bare-foot, covered in scabs and sores, none of them looked as if they'd had a square meal or a wash in months. Some, she noticed, had had their heads shaved and looked even more cowed than the rest.

'Convicts,' muttered Lady Fitzallan. She shook her head in disapproval. 'The authorities dress them in yellow as a mark of shame. They shave off their hair if they've broken the law during the journey.' She clucked sympathetically. 'Poor souls. Most of them have never been outside the hovels of London. They must think they've been transported to hell. But I suppose anything's better than hanging.'

Rose's spirits fell even further as she noticed how many of them had small children hanging on to their skirts. 'But what about the children? Surely they haven't been transported?'

Henry cleared his throat and spoke over Rose's head. 'Poor souls indeed, Mother. But you must remember why they have been sent here. Criminals, the lot of them.' He wiped his brow with a white handkerchief, leaving red smears on the linen. 'As for the children.' He shrugged. 'Some of them are here under sentence, but for many others it would have meant begging on the streets in London, prostitution, starvation, probably death if their mothers had left them behind. Here they'll get an education, be taught a trade. This is a good country for those who are willing to put their backs into it. There's clean air out in the interior – plenty of space for a man to work his own land and prosper.'

Rose gazed up at him. It was a long speech for someone who was obviously spare with words, but his declaration had betrayed his passion for this new land and the deeply held belief that nothing but good could come out of it.

'What will happen to the women?' she asked

quietly. 'Are they being taken to prison?'

He shook his head, his hazel eyes flitting over her thoughtfully. 'They've just arrived off the *Posthumous*. They'll be found work in the homes of the squatters, on sheep stations or in business establishments. The authorities don't like imprisoning women – they cause too much trouble, and it means more barracks being built to keep them separated from the men.'

'What kind of work?' Lady Fitzallan asked querulously. 'I would certainly not employ a convict maid. I could never trust her.'

Henry smiled. His light brown eyes gleamed with humour, making him suddenly appear younger and less careworn. 'Every new arrival says that but they soon change their mind, Mother. Convict labour is cheap and there isn't a house or a business that doesn't have at least one convict servant. Most of them are ticket of leave – men and women who have served most of their time and are allowed to work to prepare for when their sentence is over. It gives them a chance to build something for the future. Very few return to England.'

'Aren't they dangerous?' asked Rose, shielding her eyes to watch a long line of men shuffling along the street, their legs chained, their heads bowed. They looked so pitiful, that even as she spoke, she knew it could not be so.

'Not the ones I mentioned before,' he said softly. 'But those men are the hardened criminals. That's a chain gang, off to the quarries in the hills. They will never be free.'

Rose watched them shuffle out of sight. The

grey pyjamas marked them for what they were, and with their bowed heads they seemed somehow degraded, as if they regarded themselves as less than human.

Henry must have noticed her distress for he sighed again. 'The same rules govern the body who stole a loaf of bread as the murderer with no remorse. If they break them, they know they will suffer several strokes of the lash and extra time put on their sentence. At worst, he or she will be sent to Port Arthur or the penal islands of Maria and Sarah.' He shook his head. 'None of them wants that. They are said to be hell on earth. But for those who work out their time with good behaviour, then this land is open to them to make a good life for themselves and their families. There are plenty of ex-convicts in the colony who are now leading honest lives, and those men and women have the spirit and courage to lead this new country of ours into the next century.'

Lady Fitzallan shuddered and grasped his arm. 'Convicts in charge? The Queen would never allow it,' she said stoutly.

'Her Majesty is a long way away, Mother, and if a man or woman can survive their years of penal reform to make something of themselves, then they are made of the right stuff to do Her Majesty proud.'

He smiled down at the two women. 'Enough of my lecturing. You look fit to drop, the pair of you. Come. We will have tea in the hotel and then you must rest. We have three days before we begin the journey out to the Mission.'

There were sixteen oxen in all, their broad backs rolling like ships in a sea of red dust as they trudged along the track pulling the loaded wagons behind them, on the way to Yantabulla, where Henry had his land.

Rose and her employer had soon learned from those more familiar with the colony, that it would be sensible to do away with the clothes they had brought with them, and dress in thin cotton. Rose was only too delighted to cast off the heavy woollen dress and hampering petticoats, but Lady Fitzallan had refused to believe a lady of breeding would ever dare to be seen without her corsets. It was only after a rather frightening fainting spell at the Governor's dinner party on their third night, and the earnest reassurance by the Governor's wife that nobody in the colony ever wore stays, let alone a dozen petticoats – that she had been persuaded to comply.

The dowager soon came to realise the wisdom of wearing as little as possible, but because of her fair colouring, had to wear a hat and thin gloves, and always carried a parasol to protect her from the sun. Rose on the other hand relished the warmth on her skin after all those years in the cold and damp of England, and she abandoned her hat along with her corsets and petticoats and was soon the colour of mahogany.

Rose sat on the bullock cart, rolling with it as she had done with the ship, the dust of the beasts' hoofs coating her in a veil of red. Mountains soared all around them as they left Sydney far behind. Cruel, shadowy gorges yawned within inches of the creaking wagon wheels, and the red and ochre hills loomed over them like ancient guardians. Exotic flowers blossomed in rock niches and trailed amongst giant ferns and tangling vines. Water poured down from the mountains to splash into verdant valleys that echoed with birdsong, and strange loping beasts hopped away into the bush or shyly watched from the shadows of ghost gums.

Lady Fitzallan became so exhausted by the heat and the dust and the long hours of sitting on a hard wooden seat that she no longer stared in awe at the beauty surrounding them and had long given up asking the names of the different birds and animals. She sat slumped beneath her parasol, chin resting on her chest, snoring softly. The once plump, bustling little body had grown thin, the round face drawn, and although she put on a brave show at the end of each day, Rose and Henry knew the journey was proving too much for her.

But Rose was full of restless energy as she watched the white cockatoos preen in the trees and the eagles soar above the gorges. Flocks of grey and pink parrots swooped and swirled overhead, and she smiled at a tiny blue wren with cheeky tail feathers cocked above its rump like an oversized windmill sail. This was a land of magic and wonder, as old as time itself, as new and fresh as the Garden of Eden, and she still experienced a thrill at knowing she was amongst the first to travel this winding, tortuous road that had been hacked by convicts through the mountainous bush. The ruts of their wagon wheels and the plodding of their oxens' hoofs were marking a new territory in a new land – one she was determined to make her own.

During those long but never interminable days and weeks, Rose had plenty of time to compare this new life to her old one. The scenery was more striking and startling than the soft greens and yellows of Sussex, but it was a lonely place, especially for women. This was a man's world, where muscle was needed to work the land, fight the elements and build an empire, and she felt very small and insignificant amongst the vast emptiness of it all. And yet she was old enough to realise that women had their place here, just as they had at home. For if this new country was to prosper, then it had to be populated – and that was something men couldn't do alone.

Perhaps the lack of women was the reason for Otto Fischer's persistence, and the admiring looks she'd received from the men in Sydney? She thought of the German and smiled. He was an energetic man, full of ideas and enthusiasm for his newly planted vineyard, and she had enjoyed his company during their short stay in the city.

She blushed at her own thoughts and looked across at her employer. Thrust into one another's company because of their sex, they had found they liked each other and had formed a friendship that would have been unthinkable back in England. To imagine Lady Amelia Ade making this journey made Rose's smile even wider, but her expression saddened as she thought of John in his brightly covered wagon. How he would have loved this journey into the unknown. To travel free and unmolested, to live as he pleased amongst people who saw the man not the gypsy.

Rose blinked and brushed away the tears. She must not think of John. He was in her past. The future was all that mattered now.

The bullockies were a brotherhood of the track, renowned for hard language and even harder drinking. The man who led the team of sixteen oxen wore the usual garb of red shirt, moleskin trousers and plaited cabbage tree hat. He rode a sure-footed, mean chestnut pony and carried a fearsome sixteen foot long whip which he flicked over the heads of the oxen to keep them in line and moving. He knew every water hole, creek and river on the outback track, and the stories he told around the camp-fire at night became more colourful as the journey progressed.

Rose loved listening to the stories, and although she wasn't sure whether she should believe them or not, she had decided to give him the benefit of the doubt. For Bullocky Bob made the most delicious bread which he baked in the embers of the fire, and the strongest tea she had ever tasted in the metal can he called a billy.

He was an ugly man, with a sun-creased face and his hands were rough, the nails broken and filthy. Yet there was a gentle side to him, and although he wouldn't have appreciated anyone knowing, Rose had seen him take the locket from his greasy trouser pocket and look at the picture inside it with soft eyes. She was intrigued as to what kind of woman waited for him at the end of this lonely track – but she never dared ask.

They had been travelling for weeks and were all

229

exhausted. The rain was heavy, drenching them in seconds, turning the dirt into a quagmire, veiling the bush in a curtain of water. The oxen bellowed, Bullocky Bob swore and cracked his whip and Rose and the old lady tried to shelter beneath the canopy. The heat was still intense, and as the rain persisted, the mosquitoes swarmed and steam rose from the bush, smothering them in fetid humidity. Paradise was suddenly showing how treacherous it could be.

Henry had ridden on ahead to see if the Darling river was passable, and returned in a flurry of mud and water, waving his hat. 'We'll have to be quick,' he yelled to Bob. 'It's about to run a banker.'

Bob chewed his tobacco, spat into the mud and cracked his whip. 'Don't tell me, mate,' he rasped. 'Tell these buggers.'

The oxen were reluctant to move, but the whip urged them on and they set off again with a lurch and a roll that almost unseated the two women. Clinging to the sides of the wagon, Rose peered through the downpour at the scene before her. The river was wide and swollen, the water rushing over giant boulders, frothing over small falls and swirling in dangerous eddies. The banks were slick and steep.

'You'll have to get off,' shouted Bob over the thunder of water. 'Wagon's likely to turn turtle.'

Rose helped Lady Fitzallan down, and with Henry's help, hoisted her up behind him on the saddle. 'Hold tight, Mother,' he shouted. 'Whatever happens, don't let go.'

The old woman looked down at Rose with fear

in her eyes, then she buried her face in her son's sodden back and clung on.

Rose climbed up behind Bob. 'You'll be right if you hang on tight, girlie,' he reassured her, folding her arms around his whip-thin waist. 'Sit still and let me do the work,' he warned.

The oxen stood morosely by the side of the river, their ears twitching, their bellows almost drowned by the sound of the rain and the torrent of water. Bullocky Bob cracked the whip, and Rose clung to him as he turned his horse this way and that to encourage the beasts to move. But not for her the whimper of fear or tightly shut eyes. This was an adventure, and although she was scared witless, she didn't want to miss any of it.

With ponderous reluctance the leading pair of oxen slithered and scrambled down the bank into the water. The others could only follow, and soon the whole team were splashing and bellowing their way across the racing swirl that reached almost to their shoulders.

The water was icy, reaching nearly to her knees, and Rose could feel the tug of the undertow threatening to tear her from the saddle. Yet the fear did nothing to dampen the excitement, and as she clung to Bob, she knew this was just another experience to add to all the others she'd had in the past few months – and if they survived – she would remember it always.

The great heads of the oxen gleamed damply and their horns were raised skyward as they struck out and headed for the safety of the other side. Their bellows were fewer now, for they needed all their energy to push against the rip-tide that threatened to sweep them downstream. If one lost its footing or stumbled, it would take them all, as well as the food, furniture and supplies that were stacked in the wagons behind them.

'Get on yer bastards, yer lazy mongrels. Move yer arses, yer flea-bitten buggers.' Bullocky Bob had worked too long and too hard to risk losing his prime stock, and he swore and spat and used his whip to keep the animals moving.

Rose clung to him, her wet hair plastered to her face and back. Steam rose from the beasts and from the banks, mosquitoes flitted and bit, and the water swirled around her legs. The tough little horse beneath her never lost his footing, pitting his wiry strength against the force of the water as he plodded alongside the complaining oxen. The wagons tilted, their precious cargo tightly bound by leather thongs and rope, creaked and jarred against the restraints. Wooden wheels jolted on hidden boulders, scraped and rumbled over the stony river bed until Rose thought they would surely snap.

Then they were clear, scrambling up the bank of mud and onto the scrubby grass. Rose slid from the saddle and sank into the mud, gasping from the cold, the excitement and the fear. She'd done it. She'd come through the first test.

Bob looked down at her. 'You're a dinky-di little sheila, I'll say that for yer,' he said gruffly as he pushed back the plaited hat and wiped his face. 'Y'came good when it mattered. But you'd better see to Ma over there. Looks crook.'

Rose hurried across to Henry and helped Lady Fitzallan down from the horse. She did look pale, but there was a fire of excitement in her eyes that surely mirrored her own.

'If I look half as bad as you, then thank goodness no one can see us,' she laughed. 'What would they say in the Governor's drawing room now?'

Rose grinned and smeared her wet hair from her face. 'They'd probably say you were a dinky-di sheila,' she yelled above the downpour. She saw the frown of incomprehension on the older woman's face. 'I'll explain later,' she said with a grin. 'Come on. We need to get you into some dry clothes. Bob's setting up camp down the road.'

In the late afternoon of the next day they arrived in the new settlement of Yantabulla. The sky looked fresh and very blue but the heat was unrelenting, striking hammer blows to the head and the backs of their necks.

As the oxen team ponderously plodded along the wide main street, Rose and Lady Fitzallan stared at the neat wooden houses with their red tin roofs, and the small parade of verandah-shaded stores that were festooned with all the necessities of life in the interior. Pots and pans, canvas for tents, spades and picks, axes, buckets, billies, saddles and bridles. No tourist geegaws here. No bright fans and fancy shawls.

There was a hotel, the only building on the main street that was higher than one storey. Its paint was white beneath the layer of red dust, the verandah and balcony shaded by wrought iron that looked like lace. Men sat in rocking chairs in the shade, eyes shadowed by their dusty hats as they watched the procession pass. Horses dozed at the hitching posts, tails and ears twitching to ward off the flies. The church was built of wood with a narrow steeple and a scrubby front yard behind a picket fence, the cemetery shaded by a vast pepper tree that was alive with bees and butterflies.

Rose eagerly looked for the Mission house amongst the neat new buildings, but the oxen trundled along the main street and soon the town was behind them, masked by a cloud of red dust. Ten miles further on they drew to a halt.

Henry swept off his hat and pointed to a rusting, dilapidated shack that seemed to be held up by the tree that grew beside it. 'Here we are. Welcome to Yantabulla Mission.'

Lady Fitzallan paled. 'It's a shed,' she whispered. 'You've brought me all this way to live in an outhouse?'

He smiled and shook his head. 'Only for a little while, Mother. See that plot of land behind it? And the building? That will be our home eventually.'

Rose followed her gaze. The rough frame of a large house was sitting in the middle of an overgrown field, but it seemed to have been in that state for a long time. 'There's no one working on it,' she said doubtfully.

Henry frowned. 'I had planned to have it finished before your arrival,' he explained. 'But the natives are impossible to train and have no skills. The convict labour only arrived a couple of months before I left for Sydney.'

He seemed unaware of the horror on his mother's face and carried on blithely. 'Good bunch of men. They seem to enjoy working with their hands after so many months on those terrible ships, and the carpenters are skilled artisans who take a real pride in their work. They also know how to get the natives working. Lazy lot the Aborigines. Prefer sitting under a bottle tree to earning their bread and baccy.' He pointed towards a strange-looking tree that did indeed resemble an upturned grey bottle. There in the sparse shade lounged a group of men and women with skin so dark they almost looked like shadows.

Lady Fitzallan was clutching her throat, her eyes wide with horror. 'You're employing convicts and savages? I won't feel safe in my bed, Henry.' Her jowls trembled. 'If I had known, I would never have come.'

'I tried to warn you, Mother.' His tone was exasperated as he twisted his soft felt hat in his hands. 'The natives are quite friendly, I can assure you. Not at all war-like until they get into the liquor store, then they only fight amongst themselves.'

Lady Fitzallan was close to tears. 'I didn't think anything could be this awful. When I think of my lovely home in London, of the country house in Berkshire and my tea parties on the lawn, I could weep.'

She proceeded to do just this and Rose put a comforting arm around her. 'I'll make the shack as comfortable as I can, Lady Fitzallan,' she said as brightly as she could in the circumstances.

Those black men looked awfully sinister with their white clay markings, wild hair and naked bodies. 'We have furniture and food, and look – there's a well so at least we'll have fresh water.'

Lady Fitzallan sniffed and permitted her son to lead her through the broken picket fence into the yard, but she kept a fearful eye on the group of curious native faces that watched their progress.

The door to the hovel was so old and broken it slumped drunkenly against the frame. The roof and walls were sheets of rusting corrugated iron nailed to a frame of rough timber, the windows without glass but screened with mesh to keep out the flies which swarmed over the rubbish in the yard.

As Rose picked her way over the rubble and debris strewn across the tough, spiny grass, the spirits that had been so high during their passage along the main street plunged. Never in her wildest imaginings could she have expected this.

The interior of the one-roomed shack was even more depressing, and furnace hot. There was a rough wooden truckle bed, a table with three legs propped up by a pile of stones, one chair that had seen better days and a range that hadn't been scrubbed for years. Washing facilities consisted of a stained butler's sink which balanced on a precarious wooden frame that looked as if a puff of wind might bring it down. It was filled with dishes that were hairy with mould and her entrance startled a large-eyed creature which scuttled away through a hole in the window mesh, its long fluffy tail waving behind it. Vermin had already made a start on the bed linen, and the dirt floor was littered with rat droppings and gnawed bones.

Rose took a deep breath, let it out in a sigh and began to roll up her sleeves. She turned back to the old woman and her son who stood woefully in the yard, a cheerful smile plastered on her face to give them courage. 'I've seen better, but it won't take long to clean up,' she said with forced cheerfulness. 'And with the things we brought with us, we'll soon have this looking like home.'

Six months later the tin shack in the bush still looked as if it was falling down, but the door had been fixed along with the screen mesh and Rose had persuaded Henry to get one of the convicts to patch up the roof and repair the chimney. The range had taken hours to clean, but as the layers of dirt and grease were removed, they revealed a fine, sturdy black piece of engineering that looked wonderful after she'd given it a good polish. It was hell to cook on, though, because the fire had to be alight most of the time for her to provide three large meals a day for the convicts and native workmen – and combined with the heat of the sun, the single-room shack became a sweat box.

The dirt floor had been swept and rolled flat, then covered with tightly fitting boards to discourage burrowing possums and curious snakes. Curtains fluttered at the windows, and clean sheets flapped on the clothes rope which stretched between trees. The contents of the bullock cart had been carefully stored under a thick tarpaulin at the back of the shack, for there was simply not enough space for a four-poster bed, heavy chests of drawers and a complete set of dining-room furniture.

Lady Fitzallan had been tearful at the idea of her expensive furniture rotting away where the termites and heat would destroy it but had had little choice until the house was finished. Her relationship with Rose had become even closer, and now she almost looked upon her as the daughter she'd never had.

Rose was fond of the old woman, but there were times when she wished she could see her own mother again. Kathleen might not have been the best Mam in the world, but she was the only one she knew, and despite the way she'd been treated, she would have given anything to have talked to her again.

Waves of home-sickness often swept over her at the least expected times – like when the heat bounced off the tin roof making her swelter as she worked – when spiders, as big as your hand and twice as furry, scuttled out of the dark corners, and when, in a moment of respite, she stared out at the endless wilderness that surrounded them. This was such a lonely place. So empty compared to the sheltering High and Over hills and leafy lanes of Sussex.

Rose stood in the doorway that afternoon to catch the breath of cool air that swept across the grasslands and empty wastes. She had been cooking since early morning and was taking this moment to rest before she had to prepare for the next day. Sweat soaked her dress and plastered her hair to her face and neck, for the kitchen was broiling, with swarms of flies settling on the merest morsel of food not stored in the wire-mesh meat safe suspended from the roof joist.

She'd kicked off her shoes some time ago. Now her feet were stained with the red earth, the soles hardened by walking bare-foot around the vegetable plot and back and forth to the wash tub and clothes line. Her hair fell in a tangled mass over her shoulders, damp with sweat and gritty from the dust which seemed to hang perman-ently over everything. How shocked Cook would be if she could see me now, she thought with a grin. Well, I might be bare-footed and poor – but at least I'm free. And that's got to be worth more than gold.

Leaning against the door jamb, she looked out over the cleared pastures to the stand of gum trees where Henry's few cattle sought shelter. The light had a quality so clear and bright that each feature stood out in stark silhouette against the cloudless sky. The pale shifting grass was silver against the harsh red of the earth. Lime green leaves of the pepper trees were startling against the dark olive of the scrub bushes, clashing with the impudent scarlet of the bottle brush and yellow wattle. Ghost-white bark trailed in shreds down the tree trunks to reveal scars of black and red, and in the branches between the sweet-smelling eucalyptus leaves flitted parakeets and budgerigars of every colour imaginable. A flock of galahs swirled overhead, their pink underbellies a glorious sunset sweep against the sky as they gathered to drink at the water-hole.

Rose sighed with pleasure. She might long for

the cool damp days of England, but there was a beauty about this place that enticed her. Something primal that echoed within herself and would not be denied.

She looked away and turned towards the sound of hammering and sawing. The fine new house was almost finished and reminded her of the grand residences she'd seen in London on her short stay before setting out with Lady Muriel. Built of wood, it stood two storeys high, with an elegant balcony and verandah fringed with wrought-iron lace. There were neat green shutters on the big windows, with fly screens fixed firmly over the glass, and a sturdy oak door to the front of the house which opened into a large square hall. The amber-coloured stone chimney took up most of the north-facing wall and would bring them warmth in the winter and draw the smoke. There were five bedrooms, a drawing room and dining room, a kitchen and pantry and a study for Henry.

Life had settled into an unending round of work for all of them – but it was work that made them stronger, fitter, and at the end of the day they were snoring as soon as their heads hit the pillow. Rose was in charge of the shack, the food and all household chores. Lady Fitzallan took over the convicts and natives with a panache that had startled her son after her initial repugnance and got them all working far more efficiently than he ever could. She had a way with the men that commanded respect, and although her manner was sometimes a little domineering, she had the sense to counteract it with downright straight talking and a no-nonsense attitude. The black fellas, as they called themselves, were taught hygiene and made to wear Western clothes to hide their nakedness. Unfortunately this wasn't always successful. Lady Muriel would sigh in despair as shirts were worn as head covers and petticoats used as slings for the babies.

When Henry remarked upon her amazing success, she merely shrugged and told him she'd been in charge of servants all her life, why should convicts and Aborigines be any different?

He did all the heavy work as well as run his Mission. The Aborigines loved stories and Henry used to try and convert people to Christianity, but soon realised they preferred Rose's cooking. He'd thought about it for a while and then set them working on the garden: digging, planting a new vegetable plot, clearing and burning the scrub and laying a cinder path up to the new front door. As they worked, he told them the Bible stories and just hoped they were learning something. He saw them as a simple people, used to living off the land, hunting and fishing for their food, searching for berries and wild honey in the bush. They wore few clothes, despite his mother's efforts to civilise them, and jabbered away in their own strange language that so far had proved unintelligible to him. He knew they laughed at him. Knew they came only because of the promise of food and tobacco. Yet he persevered. For he was called to do God's work in this wilderness, and nothing must stand in his way.

The evening was drawing in, the sun dipping low on the horizon, gilding the grasslands that stretched further than any eye could see. Cattle roamed contentedly now the flies had gone, rooks cawed and the smell of warm earth and cooking damper bread wafted on the cooling breeze. The fronds of the pepper tree hummed with bees, casting deep shadows across the cleared yard and carefully watered vegetable patch. A few dusty chickens scratched and fussed in the dirt and the cockerel strutted self-importantly back and forth amongst his harem, making sure they left him a few scraps for his supper. One of the convicts had erected a water pump and windmill, and this primitive wheel of rusty iron squeaked as it turned in the late breeze and drew water from the bore. It was a comforting sound, one she almost didn't hear any more – yet if it stopped, it was noticeable by its absence.

Rose yawned. This was the best time of day, when the heat was gone and the breeze came from the distant mountains to rustle the pepper tree and send the dust into drifting spirals across the dry earth. Work was almost over for the day, and tomorrow they would be moving the rest of the furniture into the new house. She looked over her shoulder at the gloom of the little shack. In a way she would be sorry to leave it for it had become home, and despite the heat, the dust and the flies, it reminded her of the cottage in Wilmington, for no matter how vigilant she was, the dust could never be banished, and cobwebs appeared overnight.

The thud of horse's hoofs on the dirt road made her look up, her hand shielding her eyes from the glare. The rider seemed to float in the watery mirage of the dying sun. He rode tall in the saddle, his broad shoulders and wide-brimmed hat silhouetted against the orange sky. There was something about him which seemed familiar, and yet she couldn't quite think what it could be.

He slowed his horse to a walk, the harness jingling as the animal snorted and tossed its head. 'Miss Rose,' he called. 'I haf found you at last.'

'Otto?' she murmured. 'Otto Fischer?' She pulled away from the door jamb where she'd been leaning and hastily tried to tame her hair. She must look a right sight. Her apron was filthy, her dress almost see-through with sweat, and she couldn't find her boots.

He swung down from the saddle, dropped the reins and strode towards her, his arms stretched as widely as his smile. 'Rose. My Rose. I haf come to rescue you.' He swept her up in a bear hug and spun her around until she was giddy.

'Put me down,' she gasped, out of breath because he held her so tightly to his vast chest.

He gently set her back on her feet, his whole demeanour reminding her of a playful oversized puppy. Rose backed off. He was too big, too loud, too overpowering. 'I don't need rescuing,' she stammered, desperately trying to find her shoes and her dignity.

'I think so,' he murmured looking over her shoulder at the gloomy hovel. 'You come *mitt* me, Rose. I have fine house. Not shack in desert.'

Rose put up her hands to ward off further boisterous attack, and was met with a wall of chest that seemed to block out the sun and any hope of escape. She looked up into the cheerful freckled face and friendly blue eyes. He had good teeth, she noticed distractedly.

'You can't just come round 'ere and expect me to drop everything and run off with yer,' she said stoutly, her confusion making her Sussex accent return with a vengeance. 'I got an 'ouse already.' She pointed proudly to the magnificent new building.

His arms dropped as did his smile. 'This is your house? You marry Minister?'

Not for the want of his trying, Rose thought. Henry had been making sheep's eyes at her ever since she and his mam had moved into the shack, and she'd been dreading the proposal she knew he was about to make. Lady Fitzallan had dropped enough hints and Rose already worried about how to reject him without giving offence.

She laughed, but even to her it sounded too high and brittle to be genuine. 'Gawd, no. It's her ladyship's house. But I got me own room,' she added defiantly. 'I'm like one of the family.'

He let out a great sigh. 'Thank *Gott*,' he breathed. 'I thought I had lost you, Rose.' His expression became serious, and although it was obvious he wanted to, he no longer attempted to touch her. 'I haf come from a long way to ask you to marry me. I think of no one but you since I am leaving Botany Bay.'

Rose looked up at him – she had to, he seemed at least twice her height. She could see he was serious and his intentions honourable, but had a sudden, painful memory of John. His dark eyes and hair, his laughing mouth and gentle voice. So different from this flame-haired giant with the strange accent and boisterous character.

She blinked as if to shut him away in the deepest, darkest part of her past. There was no use thinking of John. They would never see one another again. They had no future together.

If she went with Otto, it would mean a new start all over again – a chance to explore a different part of Australia with a man who made her laugh and who would protect her. She liked Otto well enough but although there was a spark of something between them, she knew she didn't really love him. Not with a passion – not in the way she'd felt for John.

'I don't know you, Otto,' she said finally. 'We've only met a few times. How do you know you want to spend the rest of your life with me?'

The big man put his hands over his chest. 'I feel it – here,' he said. 'Every day I see your face as I work in my vineyard. Every day I say, "Otto, you must find her".' He smiled, the creases at the corners of his eyes deepening.

'Now I have come. Please vill you do me the honour of becoming my vife?'

Rose smiled up into that homely, open face. He was a good man with a good heart and it mattered to her that she couldn't love him with the passion he deserved. He was too honest to be cheated like that. 'I like you, Otto,' she said softly. 'I like your smile and the colour of your hair. I enjoy your company, you make me laugh.'

'But?' His broad smile was gone and his eyes were troubled.

'I don't love you,' she said gently. 'I hardly know you. How can I come with you?'

He nodded, his bright head ablaze like the sunset. 'It is *gut*, Rose. I vill stay here in Mission until you know me. Then you vill see I am *gut* man. You will marry me and come to my vineyard.'

She was beginning to feel her resolve weaken against such a determined onslaught. 'But won't you be needed back at the vineyard?'

'Not as much as I need to be here vit you,' he said firmly. 'You more important.'

'Otto remained in Yantabulla for almost six months. He missed his harvest, hoping the man he had left in charge would see it through. He was lucky, for his manager was another German who shared the same passion for the vines as he did, and that year's vintage was to be the best they'd had for a long time.'

'A good omen for the future, then,' murmured Sophie. 'Did Rose marry him or did she decide to stick with the Minister?'

Cordelia winked. 'What do you think? Of course she married Otto. Muriel Fitzallan was a bit put out, but in the end she realised her son was too quiet and set in his ways for Rose, and wished them both well. She knew, I think, that Rose needed the freedom to go her own way, and she wouldn't have had that, tied to Henry and his Mission. She even gave them a present of her four-poster bed as a wedding gift, and they had a hell of a job getting it back to the Hunter Valley for this time there were no oxen to pull it and they had to strap it to the back of Otto's wagon.'

Cordelia smiled. She could still remember how her great-grandmother Rose had laughed as she recalled that journey – and how she'd blushed when she recounted their first night together.

'The road was rough as it had been on their previous journey,' Cordelia continued. 'Now, instead of a team of oxen and Bullocky Bob, there was just Rose and her new husband and a team of mules to carry the supplies and pull the wagon. The marriage ceremony had taken place in the little wooden church on the edge of town.'

Cordelia could still see that sepia photograph she kept in the family album. Rose had looked beautiful that day, so delicate and dark-haired against the robust strength and breadth of her husband.

'Rose wore a pale lilac dress that had been donated by Lady Fitzallan. She had altered it to fit the occasion, and when she appeared in the church, the old lady burst into tears. Her bouquet was a bunch of wild flowers, bottle brush and kangaroo paw mixed with fern fronds and tied with white ribbon. She wore a single spray of yellow wattle as a garland for her hair. The reception was small, attended only by Lady Fitzallan and Henry, the convicts and one or two curious Aborigines, but there was time to drink a toast with the rough wine Otto had brought with him before he swept her away to her new life in the Hunter Valley. Henry and Lady Fitzallan stood in the dusty road, watching until distance made them tiny specks on the horizon.'

'So Rose learned to love him?' Sophie smiled.

'I'm not surprised, he sounds a good man. I wish I could have known him.'

Cordelia dipped her chin and looked at her gnarled hands. 'I never met him either, and I've always regretted it.' She took a deep breath, as if to chase away sad memories, and carried on with her tale.

'Their wedding night was spent on the road in the makeshift shelter of a canvas awning strung between tree trunks, their bed a soft mattress of eucalyptus leaves, ferns and moss. Otto was a gentle lover, his natural passion and enthusiasm tempered by the knowledge that for Rose this must be an experience she could look back on with fond memories.

She had so far not told him of Gilbert's attack, and was tense – half expecting a repeat performance, for she had no other experience to judge. Yet Otto's soft love-making stirred something within her that made her forget Gilbert, and she found a warmth and tenderness for her new husband she'd thought she would never feel. Perhaps this was love, she thought afterwards when he was snoring beside her. Perhaps this feeling of quiet peace and contentment was what marriage was all about – not the childish passion she'd felt for John.'

Sophie smiled. 'I'm glad she came to love him. It would have been cheating Otto in a way if she hadn't.' She paused for a moment. 'The bed they took back to the Hunter isn't the same one you've got at the apartment, is it?'

Cordelia smiled and nodded. 'It will be yours one day, Sophie. A family heirloom. Did you know that five generations of babies have been born in that bed? One day it will be your turn.'

Sophie let it go. She knew she was through with men but didn't need an argument about it. 'I think we'd better get going, Gran. The sun's up, and I've still no idea where we're going.'

Cordelia stood and leaned on her walking sticks. 'I know the way from here, you won't need the maps any more,' she said quietly.

With her grandmother settled in the seat beside her, Sophie turned the camper van out of their night pitch and headed out on to the open road. It was half an hour before she spoke. 'Why are you making such a secret of our destination?' she asked. 'What are you hiding?'

Cordelia was silent for a long moment, and when she did speak, she didn't answer her granddaughter's question. 'It's rather wonderful to think men and women like Rose and Otto forged this path through the bush and the mountains so that we, the following generations, could discover the beauty they fought so hard to maintain.'

Before Sophie could reply, she sat forward eagerly. 'Turn here and drive up that hill.'

Sophie did as she was ordered, the camper van groaning its way up the rocky, rutted track in first gear. The engine was over-heating again, the sun was high, blinding against the dusty windscreen. She parked on the plateau and switched off the engine.

The view stretched from east to west as far as the horizon permitted. The gentle rolling slopes of the Hunter Valley were partly shadowed by the low protective hills that surrounded it. It was a stunning sight – one that almost took the breath away in its sheer magnitude.

'Help me out, Sophie. I need to see it as Rose must have done on that first day.'

Sophie handed her grandmother down, and with a guiding hand on her elbow, led her to a rough picnic bench and table that had been set beneath the shade of a spreading gum tree.

Cordelia looked out at the land she remembered so well from that one visit during her girlhood. It hadn't changed much. The terraces were laced with the dark green vines, the men who worked amongst them mere specks in the distance. The sun was dappled through the eucalyptus leaves and she could hear the chirp of crickets and the hum of flies. It was hot and still, not a breath of air disturbing the rich black earth or the pale green foliage of the gums. Tears blurred her vision as she remembered first coming here with her mother. It had been a long time ago and so many things had happened in the intervening years.

'Otto brought Rose here at the end of their journey. It had taken them weeks, but finally they were almost home. He drew up his weary horse beside Rose's and they stood right here, looking out at Otto's little kingdom.' Cordelia sighed. 'It was smaller then, of course, and the fine house you can see in the distance much less grand...'

'Look out there, Rose,' he said proudly. 'That is our land – our own little empire.'

250

Rose looked down into the verdant valley where row upon row of dark green vines climbed their way across the gentle terraces that were shaded by the pine trees and sheltering hills. It was a different kind of beauty from that of the outback – but no less inspiring.

'All of it?' she breathed. 'But it's even bigger than Squire Ade's estate.'

He cocked his head. 'Who is this man? He is vintner?'

Rose laughed. 'If you mean does he grow grapes, no. It's much too cold in Wilmington for that.' She turned once again to the sight before her, hardly daring to believe this was to be her future home. It looked so cool in the shade, so green and lush compared to the outback's dust and flies. Dreams were made of this – it was like coming home.

12

Kate had spent a restless night thinking about that meeting in the boardroom. It had come as no surprise to realise it must have been Mary who'd talked to the press, but the sheer venom of her attack had certainly shocked her, and she wondered, not for the first time, why her sister felt as she did.

Mary was the youngest and most spoiled of them all, and to her elder sisters it had sometimes seemed as if Mum had taken much more time with her than she had with them, had given in to her every whim, every tantrum. Even Dad had spoiled her, this unexpected child of his middle years, with a pony before she could even walk, numerous trips on his plane to exotic holiday islands, and a brand new Mercedes sports car on her eighteenth. No wonder she was such a grasping bitch now.

Kate grimaced. If anyone should feel aggrieved, it should be her and Daisy. For Mum and Dad had been too busy building up the legend of Jacaranda Vines to take much notice of their first two daughters, and it had seemed to them they had been pushed from one nanny to another throughout their childhood. Dad had remained a distant, domineering and very frightening figure right to the end of his life, Mum the buffer zone. Not for them the ponies and exotic holidays, but rusting bikes and second-hand utes to get them to the country dances in the bush.

Yet, with the hindsight of maturity, she realised Mum had always been loving. Had always had time to look at their drawings and tell them bedtime stories. Then there were the picnics at the water-hole, the days of helping bring in the harvest, with their mouths and fingers sticky from the sweet grapes they'd eaten as they picked. Walks in the bush, riding over the hills and out into the never-never where they hunted for pieces of opal and old spear heads.

Kate grinned as she sat on her verandah and watched a small grey wallaby make a meal of the lush grass she so carefully watered. No, there was no real grievance now as far as she was concerned. Mary might have been spoilt with material things but Mum had shown the other two how to have fun in simple ways. Had let them run bare-foot in the dust and swim naked in the water-hole where the frogs croaked in the rushes and the sun browned their skin. Had taught them the aboriginal stories of the Dreamtime, and drawn pictures of the magic spirits in the dust.

She could still remember the great rainbow serpent they'd drawn that stretched in endless undulating curves across the red acres of wasteland. It had taken them all day, and when they were finished, Mum had found a strange yellow stone for its eye and they had danced like natives around it to bring them luck.

She finished her coffee, the smile still in her eyes as she stared out over her garden to the city below. That Mary had been conceived at all was a surprise, she thought. Mum had moved out of the château and into the Melbourne apartment three years before she was born. Dad was an infrequent visitor, rarely staying for more than a night – and when he did, it was always in the spare bedroom, and nearly always finished up in a row. She remembered asking her mother once why she didn't go out and find a nice new daddy for her and Daisy, but Mum had just given a tight little smile and said she wasn't about to be the first person in her family to go through the disgrace of a divorce.

Kate understood later that their lives were necessarily entwined because of her and Daisy and Mary, but most of all because of Jacaranda.

Mum wasn't about to lose any part of her precious vineyard through a divorce settlement, and certainly wouldn't risk one of Dad's mistresses taking her place. She preferred to keep her hands on the reins, and her humiliation to herself. Jock was welcome to his philandering, but he would find no fault in her, no scandal he could attack her with. She was content to remain in peace with her children.

The cup rattled in its saucer as Kate carried it back into the kitchen. Her old memories stirred up so many mixed emotions, and since that awful magazine article, she'd often found her pulse racing for no reason and her hand shaking as she tried to write her reports. It was most unlike her to react so violently, but she realised it was only because she could do nothing about any of it and the frustration had to manifest itself somehow.

Returning to the verandah, she tried to settle down to her charity reports. The money was still coming in but there was a lot to organise. Yet her mind kept returning to that board meeting, sifting through what she'd seen and heard. For something strange had happened – something so fleeting she'd almost missed it – yet it remained hidden in the furthest reaches of her mind and she knew she wouldn't rest until she finally remembered what it was.

'Daisy,' she breathed at last. 'It was something to do with Daisy.' Kate gave up on the reports and leaned back in her chair, willing the memory of yesterday's meeting into sharper focus. Daisy had been her usual silent self, coming in quietly,

254

sitting down almost unnoticed during the initial hubbub of the meeting. But in that silence was a certain self-assurance, an unfamiliar watchfulness as the meeting went on around her.

The more Kate examined the remembered image, the more certain she became. Daisy had looked different. Not only in the clothes she wore, and the discreet make-up, but in the confidence that shone in her eyes and the way she carried herself.

Kate's thoughts whirled. Why? she wondered. What had happened to Daisy to make her more confident – to give her that sharper edge as she sat there listening to them all? She hadn't taken part in the argument, had given no opinion, no clue to what she'd been thinking. And yet... And yet...

Kate sat bolt upright as a flash of memory brought back those last few moments before Mary had slammed out of the room. What was it Daisy had seen then? And why had it made her eyes widen and her lips part?

Kate grabbed her bag and her keys and raced out of the house. She wanted to see her sister's face when she asked her the same question.

Mary had returned to the hotel, thrown her belongings into a case and taken the next flight for Sydney. Now she was on the couch in the lounge of her harbourside mansion surrounded by dirty plates, empty bottles and discarded clothes. The man she'd picked up on the plane was pulling on his strides, obviously in a hurry to leave.

She watched him for a moment, her eyes bleary from too much gin. She couldn't remember his name, and although she could remember how rough and demanding he'd been, his company was better than being left alone. She reached for the throw to cover her nakedness; the efficient air-conditioning was making her shiver.

'Do you have to go?' she mumbled. 'I could get the maid to fix us breakfast.'

He zipped up, fastened his belt and began to hunt for his boots. 'You told her to get out last night,' he said as he tied the laces. 'Besides,' he added firmly, 'I have to go. I'm late already.'

Mary reached out, the movement making her head pound so badly she sank back into the cushions. 'Stay a while longer,' she begged. 'I get so lonely in this great big house.'

He looked down at her then, his youthful face unable to disguise his repugnance. 'I'm not surprised,' he muttered. 'This place is a tip, and you look like shit.'

Mary winced. 'That wasn't what you said last night,' she retorted. 'You weren't so picky when you wanted to get your end away.'

His lip curled in disgust. 'Perhaps I should just put it down as doing my bit to help the aged,' he sneered.

'Bastard!' Mary threw the bedside clock at him.

He ducked, snatched up his hold-all and headed for the door. Turning as he stood in the doorway, he slowly shook his head. 'You should be thankful I was drunk and horny enough to screw you at all. The thought of it now makes me chunder. Goodbye.'

Mary swung her legs over the side of the couch and sat there for a moment, her breathing ragged, her head pounding. The door had been closed softly but she could still hear his footsteps on the pine staircase leading down to the ground floor and the slam of the screen as he made his way out into the street.

'Hope the bastard has to walk back to the city,' she muttered. The thought that he might steal her car, or any one of the expensive trinkets she had around the house, was something she preferred to ignore. She was insured. There were more important things to consider. Like her need for a drink.

'Here's to you, Dad,' she slurred as she held up a glass of gin in a toast. 'Here's to you and all the other bastards who've screwed up my life. May you rot in hell.'

With the bottle firmly grasped by the neck, she weaved her way back to the discarded throw. Unable to bend and pick it up, she slumped to the floor and sat cross-legged, the bottle and glass between her thighs. She shivered as she pulled the velvet throw around her shoulders, the tears streaming down her face.

'Why did you stop loving me, Daddy?' she asked the empty room. 'I know I was bad, but you didn't have to *ignore* me.'

The telephone was ringing, but she left it. She didn't want to talk to anyone – just wanted someone to hold her. With the throw around her shoulders she lay down and drew up her knees. Daddy had been the only man she'd trusted to love her without question. Now he was gone and there was only the memory of her banishment.

Jock had spoiled her, she knew that, and had played up to it – had used it as a weapon against her elder sisters and enjoyed their jealousy. He would buy her anything she wanted, take her away on wonderful holidays to the Barrier Reef and the Far East, treat her like a princess. She had known there would be a price to pay eventually – an arranged marriage to the son of a wealthy Catholic vintner which would make Jacaranda even more powerful than it already was – but was willing to go along with it because it was all a part of Daddy's master plan, and power was an aphrodisiac to both of them. But her close relationship with Jock had come to an end when he'd returned to the château unexpectedly one day to find her in her pink and white bedroom with one of his field-hands.

Mary was home from college and had quickly grown bored in her father's absence. Her life in Melbourne was an exciting one, with far more sophistication than the country drongos could offer, and now in the heat of the afternoon she'd become restless. The need for excitement laced with danger was impossible to ignore.

She'd gone for a walk around the château grounds and wandered out into the fields. The man was a stranger, an undergraduate working his summer vacation, but he was young and handsome, tanned by the sun and obviously flattered by her attention. It had been easy to lure him up to her room.

They had been too busy to hear Jock. Too lost

in the tangle of their bodies to notice him standing there.

'Whore!' he roared. 'You filthy slut!'

Mary and the boy whirled round to face him, all thoughts of pleasure swept away at the sight of Jock in the doorway, his face livid beneath a sweat-stained Akubra.

'Get out,' he yelled at the boy. 'You're fired!'

Mary sat up, the sheets covering her nakedness as the boy scrambled to find his clothes. Although she was terrified of her father's rage which had never until this moment been unleashed on her, and ashamed he should have caught her like this, she started to giggle as the boy ran bare-arsed past him, then roared with laughter as he dodged Jock's riding whip and scampered downstairs. 'Go for it, Daddy,' she gasped as the hysteria made her weak.

He marched to the bed, dragged her out by the hair and threw her to the floor. Shocked by the unexpected force of his assault, she lay there, stunned, tears dry, eyes wide with fear. There was no laughter now.

He stood over her, the whip still in his hand. 'You disgust me,' he roared. 'A daughter of Sodom and Gomorrah – that's what you are. And under my own roof with a farm labourer. You're no better than the alley-cats we keep in the barns.'

He raised the whip, his face suffused with anger and frustration.

'Don't, Daddy! Don't hurt me, Daddy,' she sobbed. 'I'm sorry. I won't do it again.'

'Too bloody right you won't,' he growled. The

259

whip hovered, then his arm sank, his rage replaced by weariness. 'Why, Mary? Why do this when we had such plans for the future? You could have had the world – *we* could have had the world. Now...' His cold gaze roamed over her, making her shiver. 'You're used goods. A target for gossip – a disgrace to the family. No decent man would want you now, least of all a son of the religious McFadyn family.'

She shook her head and pulled the sheet from the bed to cover her nakedness. For the first time in her life she was afraid of him. Afraid of his cold rage and what he might do next. Yet, before she could speak, he had turned away from her, his words falling like ice into the heat of the room.

'You have an hour to pack. Then I never want to see or speak to you again.'

She got to her knees, her heart hammering as she realised how deadly serious he was. 'He forced me,' she said quickly. 'I didn't want to do it but he was stronger than me – I had no choice.' She warmed to her theme as he hesitated. 'You were right to be angry, Daddy, but it wasn't my fault. He raped me. Forced me up here to make me do horrible, disgusting things with him. Don't punish me for that, Daddy. Please.'

'Don't compound your sin by lying,' he said grimly. 'I've heard the rumours about you. Up until today I refused to believe them.'

Mary was cold, so cold in the bitter light of her father's eyes. 'But, Daddy...'

It was as if her protest had gone unheard. 'You will live with Cordelia from now on, and when I visit, I do not want to see you – not ever. From this moment I have only two daughters. You no longer exist.'

'You can't do that,' she yelled. 'What about all the women you've had over the years? Why punish me because I'm like you.'

He turned in the doorway. 'A woman's reputation is priceless. You of all people should understand that once sullied, it can never be redeemed. Your worth lay in your looks and in your family name and what that stands for. You're of no use to me any more.'

That had been the last time they had spoken. The last time she'd seen him. The grim, upright figure in boots and moleskins had watched her traipse out to the plane that would take her away from Jacaranda. She had looked down from that plane until he was a mere speck in the vast landscape beneath her, and had known this was one breach she would never heal. For Jock Witney was not a man who forgave easily. Once betrayed, forever lost.

Mary curled up on the floor of her Sydney mansion and whimpered. The gin trickled unnoticed from the bottle on to the carpet, and somewhere, not too far away, the telephone kept on ringing.

Daisy had been to the hospital to see Charles. Her cousin was surrounded by humming machinery, wires and tubes, and had been too doped with drugs to be able to have a proper conversation. After a long talk with his doctor, she'd returned home. Now she was sitting on her verandah, looking out at the ocean, thinking how beautiful life was, and how precious. How silly she'd been to fritter it away by leading a vicarious life through Martin. Where once she had thought it enough, she now knew she had so much more to offer and was almost frightened by the surge of resentment she felt for all those lost years.

It was Dad's fault, of course. If he'd been supportive of her wish to go to university, how different her life would have been. But Jock Witney was not a man to change his mind about anything – even when he knew he'd made the wrong decision.

Daisy smiled grimly. She'd spent years living a lie. For although she'd been proud to achieve so much for the charities she'd worked for, she still yearned for something more challenging, where she could spread her wings and not fear her father looking over her shoulder. Now he was gone, and the fear with him. Once things had been set in motion over the future of the vineyard, then she would see about her own place in that future. Demand to be recognised as someone who had a great deal to give, and who no longer wished to remain on the side-lines.

Her thoughts were disturbed by the arrival of Kate. She swept up the driveway in her sports car, the gravel spitting from beneath the wheels into the flowerbeds. Daisy sighed. She did wish her sister would drive with more care. She'd only weeded those beds this morning, and now look at them.

'Glad you're in,' Kate said once she'd reached the verandah. 'You haven't heard anything from

Mary, have you?' She collapsed on the swing-seat, making it groan and tilt. 'Jeez, it's hot! Traffic's a nightmare.'

Daisy grinned and fetched her a glass of iced tea. 'Why should I hear from Mary? She doesn't make it a habit to keep in touch, and I can't remember the last time she phoned me.'

Kate drank the tea, the ice tinkling against the frosted glass Daisy had taken straight from the fridge. 'That's better,' she sighed. 'I was parched.' She put down the empty glass and scrabbled in her bag for a cigarette. 'Mary's left her hotel. I phoned earlier to give her a piece of my mind, but she'd already checked out. I suppose she went back to Sydney, but I can't get an answer on her phone and the messages are piling up on her answering service.'

Daisy frowned. 'You don't think she'll do anything silly, do you? She was right over the top yesterday at the meeting – almost out of control.'

Kate blew a smoke ring and watched it waft away in the warm breeze. 'She's probably either stuffing her face and making herself sick, or getting screwed and drinking herself into oblivion,' she said grimly. 'Either way, I don't know why I care but I'm worried she's not answering her phone.'

'Mary always did like to live dangerously. Remember that drover she lived with for a while who used to beat her up? She used to say she liked a bit of rough now and again, and it was a refreshing change from the soft city men she usually hung around with. If Mum hadn't done something, I reckon he would have ended up

263

killing her in one of their drunken fights.'

Kate smiled. 'Good old Mum. Always there in a crisis.' She smoked her cigarette in silence as they both looked out at the ocean. It was sparkling like diamond-encrusted blue silk, and the plovers were circling around a small fishing boat as it chugged back to the shore.

'I presume you've come to talk about something other than Mary,' Daisy prompted her several minutes later. She knew Kate. Mary had never been her number one priority.

Kate stubbed out her cigarette. 'Something about you is different and I want to know what it is,' she said with her usual bluntness.

Daisy smiled. She might have known nothing could get past her sister. 'It's called self-belief,' she said simply. 'I just realised I no longer had to live my life through other people, and you'd be surprised what I have planned for the future.'

Kate eyed her for a long moment, then nodded. 'I knew there was something. You seemed so in control, so sure of yourself yesterday – and yet to all intents and purposes, you were the same quiet, ineffectual Daisy.' She smiled. 'Good on ya, girl. About time you gave us a run for our money. So what did you see yesterday that knocked the wind out of your sails?'

Daisy looked away, the smile tugging at her mouth. 'I saw the truth,' she said quietly. 'And now I've had time to think about it there can be no doubt. Everything fits into place, everything's explained.'

Sophie eased the heavy camper down the steep

track, the engine complaining, the wheels throwing up scree and dust. She breathed a sigh of relief as they finally reached the road. 'This is too big for hill-climbing, Gran. I hope there aren't any more scenic spots you want to visit.'

Cordelia smiled. 'No more. Look. We're here.' She watched as Sophie changed gear and peered out of the window. Held on to the door handle as the camper braked sharply.

'You're kidding,' Sophie breathed. 'This is impossible. Why here? Why this particular place?' She turned to her grandmother, her face pale beneath its tan. 'I thought you said we were going to Rose's vineyard? The one where Jacaranda Vines began? What are you playing at, Gran? Is this some kind of cruel joke?'

Cordelia felt a tremor of unease. The last thing she'd meant was for Sophie to be hurt, but it was too late to change her plans now. 'It's no joke, Sophie. This is the right place. The vineyard where Rose and Otto laid the foundation of our family.'

'So the people here are related to us? They're another branch of the family I never knew about?' Sophie dashed the tears from her eyes and slammed the van into reverse. 'I'm going straight back to Melbourne,' she declared. 'There's nothing for me here, and I'm amazed you thought there would be.'

Cordelia put her trembling hand over Sophie's, stilling her. 'There's everything here for you, darling. Wait and see. Just be patient.'

They stared out of the window at the ornate iron arch above the dusty road, each with her own thoughts, her own memories. The black wrought iron gleamed in the afternoon sun, its message stark against the glare of the sky.

**Coolabah Crossing Vineyards
Est. 1839**

Part Two

13

Mary opened her eyes and lay there for a moment wondering if she'd died. She was surrounded by a glare of white and the quiet rustle of people moving just beyond her vision. Voices were hushed and there was a wonderful smell of flowers. She turned her head on the pillow, eyes watering from the glare, and saw who was sitting quietly by the bed.

'Daisy?' she mumbled. 'What's happened? What are you doing here, and where the hell am I?'

'Making sure you stay alive,' said her sister grimly. 'Though God knows why I should bother after what you did to us all.'

'I haven't done anything to you,' Mary protested weakly. 'It's me in this hospital bed, remember?'

'That article should have had your name signed at the bottom,' said Daisy with disgust. 'Only you could have dished the dirt with such venom.'

'You did it to yourselves,' she muttered. 'I only told Sharon the truth.' She ran her tongue over dry lips. 'I need a drink.'

'Here.' A glass of water was thrust into her hand. 'You should try it more often – does wonders for the complexion, and doesn't leave you with a hangover.'

Mary eyed her through half-closed lids as she

propped herself up on one elbow and sipped the ice-cold water. Her mouth tasted foul, and there was something about Daisy that made her feel uncomfortable. Exhausted by the effort, she sank back into the pillows. 'You didn't answer my question,' she muttered. 'What are you doing here?'

'We couldn't reach you by phone and, after talking to your housekeeper, I contacted the Paramatta police. They broke in and found you lying in your own vomit, naked and out for the count. Not a pretty sight by all accounts. You were brought here to the hospital under an assumed name – the last thing we need right now is more scandal. I caught a plane and arrived about two hours ago.'

Mary eyed her sister and realised it wasn't just Daisy's voice that had changed. There was something strong and composed about her – not like Daisy at all. She was usually such a mouse, so grey and self-effacing, and yet here she was laying down the law as if she'd been born to it. She was wearing make-up too, Mary noticed, and a smart dress and jacket that hadn't been bought off the peg. She closed her eyes against the sun. Daisy had to have a man lined up. It was obvious, for she wouldn't go to all that trouble for anything else, surely?

'Why, Daisy?' she asked finally. 'Why have you done all this for me?'

'Because you're my sister,' she replied simply.

'And?' Mary knew there had to be more. Even this new version of Daisy would find it hard to forgive her betrayal.

'You might be a gold-plated first-class bitch, but you don't deserve to die like a wino in your own vomit. There's unfinished business, Mary, and I'm determined you see it through.'

Mary groaned and closed her eyes. She felt like death, and the last thing she needed was her dim-witted sister coming on strong with this bossy, school-marm attitude. 'My personal life has nothing to do with you,' she hissed. 'You've all made it quite clear you don't want to have anything to do with me, and I don't care a damn what you think. Now clear off before I ring for the nurse and have you thrown out.'

She watched through slitted eyes as Daisy chewed her lip and dithered. 'Go,' she barked, making her sister jump. 'Piss off and leave me alone.'

Daisy stood up. There were high spots of colour on her cheeks, and her fingers nervously twisted the strap of her handbag. 'You can be as rude as you like but it won't change my mind,' she said with a firmness that surprised her younger sister. 'You're coming back with me, whether you like it or not. There are things you should know before the board meeting – and once I've told you them, you'll understand why I had to come.'

The homestead road to Coolabah Crossing was long and winding, smooth with concrete, fringed on either side by shady gum trees. Sophie's hand rested on the gear lever, reluctant to begin the journey back to the past. Jay had talked so much about this place, and although she'd never seen it before, she felt she already knew what awaited her at the end of that road.

'Do they know we're coming?' she asked nervously.

'I phoned before we left Melbourne,' replied Cordelia. She patted Sophie's hand. 'There's no need to be nervous, darling,' she said softly. 'I spoke to Jay and he's looking forward to seeing you again.'

Sophie stared through the window, her thoughts and emotions in turmoil. 'You shouldn't have sprung this on me, Gran,' she said softly. 'It wasn't your decision to make.' Yet to see him again was all she had wanted a few years ago. To talk to him, to ask him why he'd suddenly stopped writing. But they had both moved on, forged separate lives on opposite sides of the world. they might have been close once – now they would be strangers.

'I'm sorry, Sophie. I didn't realise how hard this would be for you,' said Cordelia softly. 'But Jay holds no grudges, so why can't you?'

Sophie gasped, all the old anger and hurt rising to the surface. 'He what?' she demanded hotly. 'He was the one who stopped writing, who didn't bother to call and explain why. It was he who broke every promise he ever made – not me.' Her hands were shaking as she scrabbled in her bag for a cigarette. It would be the first for more than a week, and as the nicotine poured into her system she rammed the gears into first and put her foot down on the accelerator. 'I'll give him no grudges,' she muttered through the cigarette smoke as they passed beneath the wrought-iron arch.

272

'I'd slow down if I were you,' said Cordelia mildly. 'You're missing some lovely scenery.'

Bugger the scenery, Sophie thought. But she took a deep breath and decided it might be a good idea to compose herself, and after a quick glance, had to admit Coolabah Crossing was impressive.

Gum trees swayed in the warm breeze, sending dappled sunlight over the road. Freshly painted fences surrounded the fields on either side, where a string of magnificent horses cropped in the long grass. As they turned the last gentle curve in the road, the vista opened out and Sophie couldn't help but gasp in delight. Sprawled along the crest of a low hill, the ochre bricks of the ranch-style bungalow were mellow in the sunlight against a backdrop of pine-covered mountains. A verandah swept its length, supported by graceful white columns and white iron latticework. Bougainvillaea splashed purple and pink against the red-tiled roof, and terracotta pots spilled feathery ferns along the verandah where comfortable cane furniture beckoned from the shade. A wattle tree drooped over the yard, its citrus yellow droplets almost touching the cinnamon red of the path which led around the house, and the lime of the pepper trees was in stark contrast to the darker green of the vine terraces that appeared to stretch into infinity.

'Bit different to Jacaranda,' she said grudgingly. She'd be damned if she'd let the old lady see she was impressed. She was still too cross with her.

'The château at Jacaranda was never really a home,' replied Cordelia sadly. 'It was too big and grand for that. But Jock wanted a status symbol to match his growing reputation as a successful vintner, so he pulled down the original house, built his monstrosity and once he'd filled it with expensive porcelain and fine art, it felt more like a museum.' She sighed. 'Nothing stays the same, does it? Even this place has changed beyond recognition. I remember when there was just a little wooden house on that hill – grand by early-twentieth-century standards but certainly not as prosperous-looking.'

Cordelia was lost in memories – not all of them happy. She had first come here with her mother just before the end of the Great War. They had travelled the long, winding roads between the Barossa and the Hunter in a horse and wagon, stopping at dusty outback hotels on the way where their fellow travellers were drovers and ringers, swagmen and fossickers. Cordelia had loved life on the open road – for surely Rose must have felt the same excitement, waking up each day not knowing what they would encounter, meeting strangers, seeing sights she would never have seen back at home? Yet this journey with Sophie had brought back so many memories. So many regrets.

She stared out over the verdant grazing pastures, but her eyes were focused on the past. She saw only the sturdy little clapboard house that had once stood on that hill sheltered by gums, and the people standing on the weathered verandah to welcome them.

Mother had been both nervous and excited, her

hands tight on the reins of the matching greys as they'd trotted up the dirt road to the house. 'The last time I came,' she'd confided, 'was with your great-grandmother.'

Cordelia remembered so well the way she'd looked across at her mother. She had never seen her look so pretty, so animated. 'Why don't they ever visit us?' she'd asked. For the news that there was another branch of her family had come as a surprise when she'd first been told of the planned visit.

Her mother's expression had darkened. 'There was a family row,' she said hesitantly. 'Your grandmother wasn't pleased when I told her about our journey, but great-granny Rose was delighted. The rift had grown too wide, you see, and she was glad someone was doing something before it was too late.'

'It must have been serious,' said the seventeen-year-old Cordelia.

Her mother slapped the reins. 'It was. And even though Mother refuses to back down, this visit is to try and heal the split. And there's no time like a wedding to put the past behind us.'

Cordelia looked away, disappointed. She'd have liked to know more about this intriguing split but Mum's expression told her she would have to wait. Yet her spirits lifted as the horses came to a halt in a welter of dust and sweat beside the verandah. For there, standing beside his weather-beaten father, was the most handsome man she'd ever seen.

Walter was eighteen. He'd gone to war by lying about his age and had returned wounded three years later. Now he stood lean and brown, crippled leg stiff from the hip which gave him a piratical swagger as he crossed the dirt clearing to greet them. Their eyes met over the steaming lather on the horses' backs, and Cordelia fell deeply and irrevocably in love.

She sighed as the present returned in a glare of sun. That visit had promised so much and yet it was to end in failure, for Walter's forthcoming wedding was the purpose of their visit, the excuse to heal the family rift – and although they had both immediately recognised their feelings, it was too late to do anything about them.

Her mother had seen the way they'd looked at one another – so had Walter's father – and to avoid further family squabbles, they'd been kept apart. Cordelia had had to sit and watch as he exchanged vows with his young bride, and she and her mother had left for the Barossa the next day. The visit had brought an uneasy truce between the two sides of the family, but her grandmother died still refusing to speak to her sister, and as the years passed and distance made it impossible to visit again, communication between the two sides dwindled to the occasional card at Christmas.

Cordelia took a trembling breath. Here she was back where it had all started and she was as nervous as Sophie. Would Walter be glad to see her after so many years? Would he recognise the young girl he'd loved in the old woman she'd become? Her pulse raced as the camper drew to a halt. The years might have rolled on, but some things never changed – and although she knew it was impossible, there was the young and handsome Walter waiting for her on the verandah.

Sophie's heart hammered as she brought the van to a halt. There was someone waiting on the verandah. He might have been in deep shadow but she would have recognised that figure anywhere.

Jay stepped from the shade into the sunlight. He was long and lean with a wiry strength that showed in his easy stride and broad shoulders. His slim hips were encased in white moleskins, brown, flat-heeled boots followed the curve of his muscular calves. He was perhaps a little more tanned than she remembered but his hair still shone blue-black in the sun, and his smile of welcome still had the power to make her pulse race and her legs feel weak.

She pulled her thoughts together and grabbed her bag. Goodness knows what he'll make of me, she thought as she climbed out of the van. It was too late to run a brush through her hair and put on some make-up, and although she was furious it mattered so much, she was thankful she'd put on clean shorts and T-shirt this morning.

His gaze took her in with one sweep of those long-lashed dark eyes, then he grinned and without a word went around to the other side of the van to help Cordelia down. Sophie stood there, bewildered and for once unsure of what to do next. She hadn't expected an effusive welcome but she had thought their meeting after so long would have been marked with more than silence.

Arrogant bastard, she thought, and reached into the camper van to snatch Gran's overnight bag from the floor. If polite indifference was his weapon, then two could play at that bloody game.

'How ya goin', Aunt Cordy? You look pretty beaut for someone who's travelled so far.' Jay's deep voice was as rich as dark chocolate as he bent to embrace the old woman.

Sophie watched, jealousy tearing through her as she remembered how she'd once been held in those strong brown arms, but she thrust the memory away and stared blindly out over the fields. She must not let him see how all this was affecting her.

'How ya goin', Soph? Been a long time.'

The voice was too close for comfort but she knew she would have to turn and face him. The deep-set, dark eyes looked down at her so steadily she could see her own reflection in them. 'Good,' she replied hoarsely. She cleared her throat, looking away from that sensuous mouth and strong chin. 'But if I'd known this was where I was heading, I wouldn't have bothered,' she said with a chill that belied the rapid beat of her pulse.

'Fair go, Soph,' he drawled. 'No need to be like that.'

He seemed unaffected by her coldness and she grasped the hold-all and handbag more firmly. 'As you say – it's been a long time,' she muttered.

He eyed her with amusement, dark eyes dancing over her, making her feel like a petulant child. 'Let's get this lady into the shade,' he said finally, turning back to Cordelia. He tucked the old lady's hand into the crook of his arm, and shortening his stride to match her pace, led her to the verandah.

Feeling somewhat isolated, Sophie followed them along the red path and up the steps. It was wonderfully cool, with a breeze stirring the ferns and making the bougainvillaea flowers dance against the white trellis. She watched as Jay settled Gran into one of the chairs and fussed over the cushions. Gran was thoroughly enjoying herself. But then Jay had always been attentive, Sophie remembered – only now it was especially to scheming old ladies. She dumped the bags on the verandah floor and plumped down into the nearest chair. If this act of his was meant to impress her then he was wasting his time, she thought sourly.

Once they had been handed long tinkling glasses of home-made lemonade, Jay dug his hands deep into the pockets of his moleskins, the open neck of his checked shirt gaping to give a glimpse of a brown chest and smattering of dark hair. 'Dad's out on the terraces with my brothers but they'll be back soon for tucker. Grandad's having forty winks but I expect he'll turn up right enough. He's been looking forward to seeing you again, Cordelia.'

'How is he?' she asked.

'He'll be right. Bit creaky round the joints now, of course, but he still keeps us on our toes, the old bastard,' he said fondly.

'And your mother?'

Jay grinned. 'Out riding as usual. Nothing

keeps her tied to the kitchen and the house now she's got the horse breeding up and running.'

As if to refute this remark, the screen door slammed back and a cheerful, sun-browned face peered out at them. 'G'day,' a woman said brightly as she strode out on to the verandah. 'You must be Cordelia. Nice to meet you at last. The name's Beatrice, but everyone calls me Beatty, and I'm responsible for this great hunk of manhood, God help me. And to think I went on and had four more. Must be something to do with all this fresh air.' Her words rushed out as if she'd been set a time limit.

Beatty wasn't wearing a scrap of make-up, and her blonde hair was tethered by an alice band. Her only jewellery was a simple silver locket around her neck and silver studs in her ear lobes. Jay's remark about her preference for the outdoors was borne out by the horse-stained jodhpurs, boots that were scuffed and worn and a faded checked shirt that had seen better days. But she was still a handsome woman, and as she stood next to her dark son, they made a striking contrast.

Sophie was surprised to hear the familiar upper-class Pommy bray. Jay had never told her his mother was English, and she could just imagine Beatty riding to hounds with the county set and wondered how she'd come to be living so far from home. Yet she seemed to be a part of this wild and demanding county – at home amongst the men and horses, the vines and the wilderness.

Very blue eyes were turned on Sophie, their appraisal swift. 'You must be Sophia. I can see why Jay was once so smitten.' The handshake was firm, the fingers rough from her work in the stables, but the smile was open and friendly.

Sophie knew he was watching her. She tried to ignore him and concentrate on his mother. 'Sophie, please. Sophia makes me sound like an Italian film star.'

'If you say so,' Beatty replied without malice. 'But I always thought Sophie a name for someone soft you could sit on and squash. And from what Jay's told me you're much too sensible for that.' Beatty laughed and palmed back the sun-bleached lock of hair from her broad, unlined forehead.

Sophie felt a lurch of recognition. It was a gesture that mirrored Jay's. A gesture she had once found endearing.

'Tucker's in about half an hour,' declared Beatty, lighting up a cigarette, oblivious to the anomaly of such an Aussie word being uttered in plummy Pommy tones. 'Jay, why don't you take Sophie for a walk around the property while Cordelia and I get to know one another? I'm intrigued to meet you both at last, but I have a feeling this isn't just a casual visit, and I'm nosy enough to want to find out more.'

Sophie looked to her grandmother for some excuse, but Cordelia was ignoring her, making a great show of fumbling in her handbag. She looked up at Jay who was leaning nonchalantly against a white column. No help there, she realised as she caught the challenging twinkle in his eye. 'It's a bit hot for a walk,' she said quietly. 'I think I'll stay here in the shade.'

'Nonsense,' Beatty said firmly. 'It's time you and Jay acted your age. Clear off and leave me and Cordelia to gossip.'

'Mum has spoken,' said Jay, the lines at the corners of his eyes creasing with humour. 'We have no choice.'

Sophie rose from the chair with as much grace as she could muster and followed him down the steps into the broiling heat of the midday sun. It felt strange to be walking beside him again. Strange and disconcerting as their bare arms feathered against one another and sent a shock-wave through her. She widened the gap between them.

Jay didn't seem to notice, or if he did was keeping his thoughts to himself as he strode around the side of the house, his flat-heeled boots ringing on the stone path. 'Dad pulled the old place down before it could disintegrate,' he said, his voice as emotionless as a tour guide's. 'This new place is bonzer but it doesn't have half the character. I can still remember sitting on the old porch, watching the fireflies at night as the house creaked and the wind blew round the rock pilings that held it up.'

Sophie blindly followed him. She shouldn't be feeling like this – not so soon. Had Cris been right about their marriage being a sham? A romance off the rebound that she hadn't had the courage to acknowledge for what it was? It had seemed unthinkable back in London – but the reality was far more difficult to digest. The sound of Jay's voice, the aroma of the stables and warm flesh that emanated from him were achingly familiar and far too enticing for her to believe anything else.

'Dad cleared the scrub and built the stables after he and Mum got married,' he carried on. It was as if he had no idea of the turmoil he was inflicting. 'Mum came from a wealthy county family back in England and was used to having horses around.' He grinned. 'According to Dad, they weren't too happy about her coming out here with a wild colonial boy, who could drink any man under the table and spoke with an accent that cut steel. But Mum loves it, and apart from an occasional visit back home says she's always pleased to get back here to Coolabah Crossing and her horses.'

'Why the name?' she managed at last. 'What's a Coolabah?'

'Strewth, Soph! You don't know much for a dinky-di Aussie. Been a Pom too long, I reckon, I'm going to have to educate you.' He grinned again as he palmed the black hair out of his eyes and made her senses race. 'The Aboriginals call all gum trees Coolabahs, but in fact it's one of the smaller eucalypts, with rough bark and thick foliage. The gum-nuts are much smaller than those of the bloodwood, red, yellow or blue gum, and it never grows much over thirty-five feet. When this land was first cleared, they left the Coolabahs as wind-breaks and shade.'

'Like Jacaranda,' she murmured. 'When that was first settled, the Jacaranda trees were in full bloom, and because of the wonderful lilac flowers, it was decided to use them as an emblem for the vineyard. We still do,' she said sadly. 'But for how long is anyone's guess.'

He stood there, his hands in his pockets, his eyes screwed up against the sun. 'I heard about your troubles. Can't be easy.'

'It's nothing we can't handle,' she said firmly. 'I didn't take up corporate law so I could sit wringing my hands.'

He turned towards her, blocking out the sun, the nearness of him making her breathless. 'What did I do to make you so crook, Sophie? Surely enough time has passed for us to be mates?' His eyes were deepest black as he looked down at her.

She glared back at him. 'If you don't know there's no point in discussing it,' she snapped. She turned and walked away – those eyes were having a strange effect on her. 'I'm going back to Gran.'

'You're running away again, Sophie.'

His soft, deep voice trailed her as she hurried down the path. Too right, she thought. And the faster the better. Gran should have realised it was a mistake to come here – a mistake to think she would be unaffected by Jay's presence and all the memories it brought with it. What the hell had she plotted in that devious mind of hers – and why?

Cordelia was enjoying herself. It was good to sit here on the verandah after a home-cooked dinner and reminisce with Jay's grandfather Walter. Her distant cousin was wearing well, and although he was almost ninety-one, there was still a sparkle in his eye that belied the grey hair and grizzled jaw.

Walter, or Wal as everyone called him, had never been a natty dresser, and this evening was decked out in scruffy trousers held at the waist with an old tie while his shirt had lost several buttons, giving a glimpse of a food-stained singlet and leathery chest.

'Jeez, it's good to see ya, Cordy,' he drawled as he put his tinny on the verandah decking. 'Quite like old times, eh?' He laced his fingers over the small mound of his belly and eyed her with pleasure.

'Too right, Wal. Should have done this years ago – but you know how it is.' She looked down at her own gnarled hands, the years that had passed heavy with memories.

'Wouldn't have done no good, not all the time you was married to that bastard. My Emily passed away almost thirty years ago, Cordy. You could have come back then. Brought the kids with ya. There was always a home for you here, you know.'

She patted his arm. 'It wasn't as simple as that, Wal. There was Jacaranda.'

He nodded, his eyes distant. 'Yeah,' he sighed. 'The vines have a way of tangling a bloke up, tying them to one place. But I'm rapt you've finally made it.'

'I should have done this years ago while I still had the strength to ride out over the pastures. But all the time Jock was alive...' She didn't finish the sentence. They were from a generation that lived with their mistakes, and understood why things could never have worked between them. Which didn't mean they hadn't been tempted.

It was seventy years ago – by God how time flew, how much living they'd both done – since that last night together. They'd been standing on the top of the guardian hill, looking down at Coolabah Crossing. The moonlight drenched the valley in silver, the dark shadows of the vines sprawling across the land. It was the night before Wal's wedding and they'd managed to sneak away while the family slept.

He'd been standing close but not enough to touch Cordelia – and yet she could feel his warmth and energy. She had known she would remember this night forever. Had known she would treasure it like a precious jewel. 'I wish...' she'd begun.

He'd stilled her, his fingers tracing her lips. 'I know, Cordy. But we'll always have this memory. Always think of each other when we stand in another moonlight, no matter how far apart we are. If we take what we both want now, then what we already have will be destroyed.'

He'd reached for her then and held her close, his mouth pressed against the top of her head. Cordelia had clung to him, breathed in the scent of tobacco and horses, of fresh air and hot earth. She wanted him, needed him – but knew he was right.

Wal's voice was soft, drawing her back to the present. 'Remembering the moonlight?' He smiled sadly, the once dark eyes misted with age and regret. 'There's many a night I've stood out there thinking – and it kinda helped knowing you was doing the same.'

She nodded. 'Reckon we've been living too

much in the past, Wal. Things change, nothing stands still.'

He smoked in silence for a while. 'I read about your troubles in the paper,' he said gruffly. 'How can I help, Cordy?'

Mary had feigned sleep for most of the day. Daisy was still sitting outside in the visitors' lounge, reading a book, but sooner or later she would need the bathroom or something to eat and that would give Mary a chance to escape.

'Bloody hell,' she groaned as Daisy pulled a neatly wrapped sandwich out of her bag, and poured a drink from a thermos. 'Trust her. Why doesn't the bitch just leave me alone?'

She slumped back into the pillows, thumping them hard with her fists. She was on the fifth floor which overlooked a concrete path and a rockery full of redstone boulders, and the only door in the room led straight to the corridor – and Daisy. She couldn't afford to leave it much longer. The doctor would be doing his rounds soon, and she knew from past experience they wouldn't keep her in another night. Daisy probably knew that, too. Which explained why she was sitting out there like a prison guard.

Mary began to peel the plaster off her hand and, with a grimace, pulled out the drip. Keeping an eye on her sister, she swung her legs off the bed and stuffed a pillow beneath the sheet. Hidden by the partially closed door, she tottered over to the cupboard and reached for her clothes.

Her head thumped, and her legs could barely support her, but it was amazing what a person could achieve if they worked at it hard enough, she thought as she pulled on the silk sweater and skirt Daisy had brought with her from the house. She struggled with her underwear and finally gave up on her bra and tights. Exhausted, she sat in the bedside chair and watched Daisy through the crack in the door. 'I won't go back with you,' she muttered. 'You can sit there all bloody day, but I'll never let you boss me around.'

It was almost an hour later when Daisy eyed her sister's hospital room, frowned and put her lunch wrappings back in her bag. Then, with one last hesitant look, she stood up and walked down the corridor.

Mary dragged herself to her feet, got to the door and looked out. She was just in time to see Daisy's back as she disappeared around the corner. The adrenalin rush gave her the energy to hurry in the opposite direction.

Down the corridor, around a corner, then another. There had to be a lift somewhere. She had no bag and no money, not even a credit card. But with a bit of luck she could reach the Paramatta house before the alarm was raised – throw a few things in a bag – pick up her credit cards and go into hiding until it was time to return to Melbourne.

14

Sophie stood on the verandah. It was barely an hour past dawn but the sun was already suffusing the land with an extraordinary light which brought everything around her into glorious focus. The men had been gone since before dawn, their clatter and deep voices bringing her slowly awake. Now, in their absence, the peace and tranquillity were almost tangible.

Shoving her hands into the pockets of the jodhpurs she'd borrowed from Beatty – they were more practical out here in the long grass than shorts – she breathed in the scent of eucalyptus, freshly dewed grass and sweet wattle that hadn't yet been smothered by the day's heat. This was a long way from the city with its sweltering pavements, bustling crowds and forbidding tower blocks. Even further from the gloomy, grey London winter. And although she hadn't visited Jacaranda château for many years, this place reminded her of its serenity, and the freedom to breathe and be herself – offered space and grandeur that no city could provide. If only Jay had kept his promise, she thought bitterly. Coolabah Crossing would have been a perfect place to raise a family.

Her thoughts soured by his broken promises she stepped down from the verandah and headed for the stables. At least his younger brothers had been welcoming, and last evening had been spent listening to their stories as they tried to outdo one another. She hadn't believed half of it, but then the Aussie man could always tell a tale, and she'd played her part and thoroughly enjoyed herself.

Three of the brothers were almost identical, with the same dark hair and eyes, the same smile. The fourth was blond like his mother, with blue eyes and the long black lashes of his father, John Jay. He and Jay were the only bachelors, the only ones who still lived in the house on the hill with their parents and grandfather.

Sophie stopped walking and looked out over the home pasture. There was something about this place that was drawing her in. Perhaps it was the story of Rose that made it seem so familiar – or perhaps it was only her memories of Jay's descriptions all those years ago? She watched a flock of rosellas swirl overhead before they settled in the pepper tree. Whatever it was, she thought, the magic had little to do with him.

She resumed her walk. The stables were over on the far side of the home paddock, well away from the house so the horseflies didn't get indoors. Gran was still sleeping, which wasn't surprising after last night, thought Sophie with a grin. She and Wal had been talking long after the rest of them had left or gone to bed, and although she couldn't hear what was being said, she suspected Gran and Wal had a history. It was something in the way they looked at one another – something in the easy way they were in each other's company. It was amazing how Gran could still surprise her.

The long grass swished against her boots, the fragrance drifting up to her as she made her way across the paddock. The intriguing split between the two sides of the family had so far not been explained, but she was fairly certain Gran would tell her before they returned to Melbourne. Gran never did anything without a purpose, and as Sophie already knew so much about Rose, it stood to reason that her grandmother would tell her the rest of the story.

The stables were clean and orderly, the yard swept clear of manure and straw. Inquisitive heads appeared over the half-doors, long eyelashes batting at the flies that had already begun to swarm. Sophie stroked the velvet noses and murmured to each of the horses as she passed. They were fine blood-stock, nothing like the hacks she'd sometimes hired back in London.

'See you've made friends already. Do you ride?' Beatty appeared around the corner of the stable block, water bucket in one hand, a bale of straw in the other.

Sophie retrieved the bale and carried it into an empty stall. 'Not as much as I'd like. We had horses in Kent but the city hacks don't really interest me, and I have so little time to ride I've sort of let it slip.'

'Can't have that,' said Beatty firmly. 'Come on. You can take old Jupiter out for a canter. He could do with the exercise – getting far too fat and lazy.' She tossed Sophie a hat and proceeded to saddle an enormous black stallion who snorted and stamped and tossed his head as she fitted the bit and bridle. 'Stand still, you old bugger,' she said bossily. 'You know this won't hurt.'

Sophie chewed her lip. The stallion was at least eighteen hands, and obviously full of oats despite his greying whiskers. 'I don't know,' she began.

'Nonsense,' said Beatty as she slapped the glossy black neck. 'Quiet as a mouse once you get going. He's just showing off. Up you get.'

Sophie was hoisted into the saddle. She grasped the reins, found the stirrups and fought to keep her balance as the stallion danced beneath her.

'Talk to him, let him get used to you,' ordered Beatty. 'If he doesn't do as he's told, give him a touch of the whip to show him who's boss. Enjoy your ride. Jay's out there somewhere,' she added vaguely as she returned to the stall and began to rake out the straw bedding. 'Get him to show you around.'

'Not bloody likely,' muttered Sophie as she finally got Jupiter under control and they made a regal exit from the yard. 'Come on, Jupiter. Let's get some exercise.'

The stallion seemed to understand, and as they left the home paddock and headed for the horizon, he stretched his neck and broke into a gallop. Sophie leaned over the graceful neck, the sun in her face, the warm wind at her back. She hadn't realised how much she'd missed the horses in Kent or the freedom of being in the saddle on a bright, clear day.

The rhythm of the horse beneath her and the sheer joy of freedom and space made her forget

Jay and her grandmother, even the troubles at Jacaranda. If only life could always be like this.

They eventually slowed to a walk, the horse's great lungs heaving like organ pumps, the sweat drying in salty foam on his neck. She turned his head and made for a stand of box and red bloodwood eucalyptus. Sliding from the saddle, she led Jupiter through the trees to the small stream she'd spotted. Birds chattered overhead, flies buzzed and crickets sawed in the humid green glow of the leafy canopy.

She knelt beside the horse and they both drank from the cold, clean mountain water that trickled through clumps of spinifex and giant grey boulders. Then, with Jupiter happily grazing in the undergrowth, Sophie leaned against the rough bark of a red bloodwood, tipped the bush hat over her eyes and settled down to listen to the birds.

'You'll get bit,' warned a deep familiar voice.

Sophie realised she must have dozed off for the sun was already high above her and as she sat up the hat fell over her face, the leather strap catching in her hair where she'd let it loose. She wrestled with it, teeth gritted as she heard Jay chuckle.

'You're only making it worse. Here, let me help you.'

Seething and embarrassed, she tried one last time to free herself, but her anger was short-lived as she felt the warmth of his fingers on her hands. She snatched them away, the breath coming fast as Jay knelt before her. He was too close for comfort, his eyes dark in that tanned face, and

293

she became fascinated by the tiny scar at the edge of those black brows which she'd never noticed before. He needed a shave and his shirt had lost a button. She looked away, afraid of what he might see in her eyes. Afraid of another rejection.

His own breathing was ragged as he finally freed her. 'There. No harm done.'

'Thanks,' she murmured. She took back the hat, mesmerised by him as he knelt so close. The tension was tangible; so much electricity sparked between them, that even if she'd wanted to, she couldn't have moved away.

She flinched as he reached out and stroked her hair. 'I'm glad you've never had it cut,' he said softly. 'It's so beautiful.'

Sanity fled. She was trapped like a butterfly in a web as his eyes held hers and his hand drew her close. Their breath mingled and their lips were a whisper apart. Despite all that had happened, she wanted him to kiss her. Wanted his lips on hers again, his arms around her.

Then she remembered the promises he'd broken and the way he'd just stopped writing – remembered how he'd simply put her to one side and forgotten about her. 'Stop!' she said hoarsely, struggling away from him and clambering to her feet. 'I can't do this.'

He stood there with his hands at his sides, his dark eyes full of mocking laughter. 'But I thought...'

'Well, you thought wrong,' she snapped as she grabbed the reins and clambered back into the saddle. It was easier to face him now she was high above him. Easier now she was on the verge of escape. How dare he laugh at her? Didn't he have one ounce of feeling in that testosterone-fuelled body of his? 'Don't follow me, Jay,' she warned as he reached for his horse. 'I have nothing to say to you.'

Cordelia was sitting in the shade of the verandah, watching the activity in the home paddock and admiring the mares and foals. With their silken coats and long, delicate legs, they were fine specimens. Beatty certainly knew her business. These were no half-tame droving ponies but pure-bred racehorses.

She leaned back in the cushions and sipped from the glass of lemonade Beatty had brought her earlier. Sophie still hadn't returned from her ride and Jay was nowhere to be seen, which augured well. Wal was out somewhere on his old nag.

Silly old fool, she thought fondly. He'll fall off and break his bloody neck one of these days. But at least he's still capable of getting on a horse. Despite his old war wound and stiff knee, he didn't have useless bloody legs that let him down. She eyed her own feet with disgust. Her ankles were swelling with the heat.

She closed her eyes and tried to picture how this place must have been all those years ago when Rose and Otto had first settled here. She remembered how it had looked back in the twenties, with the old wooden house on the hill that Rose had said was freezing in winter and a hothouse in summer. The terraces hadn't spread quite as far then, for the land was still mostly bush, and of course the stables were merely a series of corrugated tin shelters.

Cordelia smiled as she recalled how Rose had told her of Otto's enthusiasm which had swept her along and taught her so much. But despite Rose's cheerful account of her time here, Cordelia had sensed the years had been hard. They had seen many changes in this once untamed colonial outpost, not least of all in Rose herself.

The year was 1847 and Rose was twenty-three. The years of working in the terraces and helping to clear the scrub had taken their toll. She had been delivered of four children, but none of them had lived long enough to draw breath. Now she was in the last stages of her fifth labour and Otto could be heard pacing the hall outside. The atmosphere in the room was tense.

'Where's the doctor, Muriel? Why doesn't he come?'

Rose panted as another pain gripped her and made her cry out.

Lady Fitzallan, who had moved to Coolabah Crossing after her son Henry had died of a snake bite, shook her head, her grey eyes glancing worriedly towards the door. 'I sent one of the boys to fetch him but he's out with another patient. He'll come as soon as he can, my dear. Try and hold on.'

'I can't. I need him now,' screeched Rose as the pain tore through her and she felt the urgent need to push.

Muriel Fitzallan moaned fretfully, then seemed

to pull herself together and became the efficient bustling little person Rose and Otto had grown to love. 'If you want to push, then do it,' she ordered. 'But easy, easy.'

Rose gritted her teeth, grabbed hold of the ornate carved posts at the head of the preposterous bed and bore down. 'Please let this one be born alive,' she panted. 'Please, God. Please.'

The baby was impatient to be born and slid from her into Muriel's capable hands. 'There!' she said with triumph as she cut the cord and slapped the tiny bottom. The newborn's cries trembled in the air as Muriel deftly cleaned eyes and mouth and swaddled it in a clean cloth. 'It's a girl, Rose. A healthy girl who's very much alive.'

Rose's tears were of joy and relief, of triumph and thankfulness as she cuddled her precious, red-faced baby. Then without warning another pain ripped through her and she arched back into the pillows. 'What's happened?' she yelled, terrified something had gone wrong and she was about to die.

'Merciful heaven, Rose, there's another one!' shouted Muriel who stood flushed with excitement at the other end of the bed. She snatched the baby away and unceremoniously dumped her squawling in the basket on the floor before returning to help Rose.

She felt the urge to push again, and as she bore down a second little life slithered from her. There was a long silence. Although she was exhausted, she propped herself up to see what was happening. Her pulse raced and dread lay cold upon her.

She'd heard that grim silence before. Knew what it meant.

Muriel Fitzallan was hastily clearing the second baby's mouth and nose, then she held it up by the feet and sharply rapped its bottom. There was no answering cry. The colour left her face and her mouth fixed itself in a determined line as she tried again. Still no sign of life.

Rose burst into tears but Muriel seemed determined to defy fate. Without a word she plunged the newborn baby into the bucket of iced water she'd used to keep Rose cool during labour. As she brought it out, dripping and blue, the baby's tiny chest expanded and the first explosive yell filled the room to join that of her sister.

'She's alive,' Muriel breathed. 'Thank God, she's alive.' She turned back to Rose, the yelling baby held high. 'Rose,' she declared proudly, 'you have twin girls.'

Otto must have been listening for he tore into the room then and almost fell to his knees beside the bed as he looked from one squalling baby to the other. 'We haf two babies?' he said with such awe and disbelief that both Rose and Muriel burst out laughing.

'Too right,' said Rose proudly as Muriel placed both babies in her arms. The fear was over, the pain forgotten. There was no need for tears any more. 'This is Emily,' she said snuggling the first born. 'And this,' she said, kissing the soft, downy head, 'is Muriel.' She looked up at the stoic little woman who had become more of a mother to her than hers ever was. 'That's if you don't mind?' she added.

Muriel touched the soft cheek of the nestling baby with one trembling finger, the tears coursing down her face. 'Of course I don't mind,' she whispered. 'It's an honour.' She sniffed and pulled her handkerchief from her waistband to blow her nose. 'They are the nearest I will ever have to grandchildren, and I've already come to think of you as a daughter. Dear Rose. Dear Otto.' She hurried out of the room, the power of speech failing her for the first time in her life.

Otto made the great bed dip and sway as he sat down and put his arms around his tiny wife and even tinier babies. 'Now ve are true family,' he said proudly. 'And I promise you, Rose, that one day ve vill have the best wine in Australia.'

Cordelia surfaced from her thoughts to see Sophie striding down the path towards her. There was something about her that told her grandmother all was not well. There was anger in her stride, and a defiance in the set of her head. Cordelia sighed. It could only mean she and Jay had not patched up their differences. Perhaps this called for more drastic measures?

'Enjoy your ride?' she asked with deliberate innocence.

Sophie gave her a peck on the cheek and slumped into the chair next to her. 'Jupiter was wonderful,' she said breathlessly. 'And the scenery was fantastic.'

'But?' Cordelia eyed her with a mixture of exasperation and affection.

Sophie took her time to drink the last of the lemonade, her face carefully neutral. 'I'd have preferred to be on my own,' she said finally.

The silence grew and Cordelia waited for the outburst she knew would come. It didn't take long.

'He's got the cheek of Old Nick,' she exploded. 'There I was, minding my own business, and he comes along and tries...' She took a deep breath and bit her lip. 'He must think I'm stupid,' she finished lamely.

'Perhaps he just wants to make up for whatever happened between you,' said Cordelia mildly. She was trying hard not to smile. It was obvious Sophie was more furious with herself than with Jay.

'A bit late for that, Gran,' she muttered. 'Years of silence can't be made up for with a quick grope.'

Cordelia raised an eyebrow and sipped from her glass to hide the twitching of her lips. Things were looking promising. 'What exactly is it you're objecting to, Sophie?' she said quietly. 'Jay's obviously heavy-handed attempt at reconciliation or your own unwillingness to reject it?'

'It wasn't heavy-handed,' she retorted. 'In fact, it was rather romantic.' She looked away, the colour rising in her face as she realised how this must have sounded. 'You're right,' she said after a long silence. 'I'm furious with myself for letting him get to me again.'

Cordelia smiled and nodded her head. 'If the spark's still there, why not give in to it? Life's too short, Sophie. We all deserve a little happiness.' Good grief, she thought. I'm beginning to sound like one of those dreadful agony aunts. She glanced across at her granddaughter and realised the same thought had crossed her mind too.

'Fair go, Gran. The man dumped me. He can't just pick up where he left off because I happen to be the only convenient female around the place.'

Cordelia ignored the bitterness. 'What exactly happened between you two all those years ago, Sophie? You never really explained.'

She took a long, trembling breath then the words spilled out, tumbling over one another as the pain returned and memories flooded back.

Cordelia listened, her hand resting lightly on her grand-daughter's. When the tirade was over, she nodded. 'I think it's time you two had a long talk.'

'I have nothing to say to him,' muttered Sophie.

Cordelia tutted. 'Nonsense. You're still in love with him despite having married that idiot Crispin – and I think that if you both sit down and try and talk this through, you'll find things aren't quite as black and white as you think.'

Sophie's eyes were haunted as she turned to her, but in their depths Cordelia could see the first spark of hope. 'What do you mean, Gran?'

'You haven't thought this through,' she said firmly. 'There is a reason for everything, and I have no doubt you and Jay got your wires crossed.' She thought for a moment, her gaze roaming over the paddocks out to the distant hills. Something about Sophie's story didn't add up but her suspicions could never be voiced for their implications were too cruel. There was enough angst in the family already.

'Jay is obviously in love with you – I can see it

in the way he looks at you, the way his eyes follow your every move. He might not say much, but that's the way with men out here in the bush. Give him a chance, Sophie. For your own sake, if not for his.'

Sophie rose from the chair and stood at the verandah railings for a long moment. Then, without a word, she slammed through the screen door and headed for her bedroom.

Cordelia sighed. It was up to them now – but it wouldn't do any harm to nudge them along a little. She smiled as she waved back to Beatty who was approaching the house from the home paddock. With the rift slowly mending between the two sides of her warring family there was hope for the future of Jacaranda Vines. All she had to do now was persuade Wal and his family to see things the same way.

15

Sophie showered and changed and, with her wet hair cooling her neck, sat at the window enjoying the light breeze that wafted down from the hills. It was pleasant here in the shade of the back verandah, but although she found it soothing to watch the distant figures as they moved up and down the terraces, she couldn't dismiss her own troubled thoughts. What had Gran meant by her enigmatic advice?

She shook out her hair and roughly towelled it

dry. Her thoughts were getting her nowhere, but if the opportunity arose she would certainly ask Jay for an explanation. It was the least he could do after his behaviour that morning.

With her hair in a tangle, Sophie ran the brush through it as she looked out over Coolabah Crossing. The lay-out was similar to that of Jacaranda, but the ugly stainless steel storage tanks and bottling plant were out of sight of the house whereas at home they were the first thing visitors saw as they drove down the long drive to the chateau.

She was dreaming of how things must have looked when Otto and Rose first came here when there was a tap on the door and her grandmother came in.

'I thought it was time you learned a bit more about the family,' she said unceremoniously. 'Come on.'

'Where are we going?' Sophie wound her long hair into a knot and tethered it with a scrunchy. 'I'll need to change again if it means going for a walk.'

'You'll see. Hurry up. Wal's waiting in the trap.' She eyed Sophie's shirt and shorts. 'You're right as you are.'

She pulled on her sneakers and socks and by the time she'd tied the laces, Gran was already out on the front verandah, Wal helping her down the steps. She stood in the doorway and watched as the scruffy old man handed her grandmother up into the brightly painted pony-trap as if she was a queen. Wal might appear rough and ready but under that gruff exterior beat the heart of a true gentleman, she realised. Pity it didn't apply to his eldest grandson.

Cordelia was almost prim beneath the parasol as she sat on one side of the trap and waited for Sophie. But her granddaughter noticed that her colour was high and there was a sparkle in her eyes. Wal slapped the reins gently over the pony's back and they pulled away. The gentle sway of the old-fashioned trap, the creak of its wheels and the jingle of harness combined with the steady clip-clop of the pony's hoofs as they headed east. Sophie leaned back against the varnished wood, the sun on her face, the wooden trap warm beneath her fingers. She had never before known such contentment.

'Rose had a lot to learn when she first came to Coolabah Crossing,' began Cordelia. 'Otto was a good man but his chief passion was his vines and Rose knew that to understand her husband, she had first to master this strange new way of life.' She tilted the parasol against the glare of the sun. 'But everything has its price, as you will see in a minute.'

Sophie looked past Wal's shoulder out into the distance where a stand of wilgas drooped, their trunks lost in the shimmer of heat that rose from the earth. The white picket fence that marked the boundaries of the family graveyard were a familiar sight throughout the outback. She knew that here at last were the true roots of this family – her family.

They clambered down and, with Cordelia leaning heavily on Wal's arm, waded through the long grass into the shade of the wilgas and the peace of the little country graveyard. Butterflies of incredible blue darted between the headstones, crickets chirruped and flies hummed, but these small sounds merely enhanced the surrounding silence.

Sophie followed the two old people to the far side where the grave markers were crudely carved, their epitaphs faded by the elements and covered with lichen.

'Rose had four stillbirths before she had the twins,' said Cordelia softly. 'There were no more children after that. Just hard work, poverty and an endless struggle against the elements. But her daughters grew strong and healthy, with the same love for the vines as their father.'

Sophie dug her hands into her pockets as she slowly walked along the line. The mounds had all but disappeared back into the soil, but they'd been kept neat, the grass cut, the weeds pulled, the encroaching bush held back with judicious pruning and hacking.

They stopped by an old-fashioned table tomb with a marble inlay. 'Muriel Fitzallan never did return to England,' said Cordelia. 'She came to visit Rose and Otto after the Mission was taken over by another worthy young man, and never left.'

Sophie read the epitaph. Lady Muriel Fitzallan had certainly found a loving home here, and a final resting place that looked right over the great sweep of Coolabah Crossing. She wondered if the bustling, fussy little woman still surveyed her adopted kingdom with pride.

She moved on, frowned as she read the next

epitaph, checked to see she was not mistaken and turned to Cordelia. 'Surely that can't be right, Gran?'

Cordelia settled down on the rustic seat which had been built beneath the weeping fronds of the Wilga. 'Unfortunately it is,' she sighed. 'Who knows how things would have turned out if it had been different?'

'So what happened?' Sophie sat beside her as Wal wandered off to smoke his pipe and stare into the distance.

'Rose and Otto settled down to raise their family and improve their harvests. Lady Muriel became mother and grandmother, even making them a gift of enough money to build an extension to the house so they could live in relative comfort. Otto employed a couple of girls to help in the house, and several ticket of leave men to help clear the scrub and till the earth for his new seeding. These men lived in a series of shacks well away from the house. Rose could sometimes hear them howling like dogs when they got into the cellars and drank the raw wine after the harvest.'

Cordelia shivered. 'She said that sound lived with her right through her life, and she never forgot it was those men's labour that paved the way to future success.'

'It can't have been easy to live amongst men who'd been forced to come all this way,' muttered Sophie.

'It wasn't, but these men had almost finished their sentences, and some of them even stayed on afterwards, got married to local girls and made good lives for themselves. Towards the end there was quite a community here at Coolabah Crossing.'

Sophie frowned. 'The end? But it's still here.'

Cordelia mopped her brow. 'Don't rush me,' she said softly. 'I'll tell it all to you in time.'

Sophie watched the expressions flit across her face as she began to speak, and as the silent gravestones shimmered in the afternoon heat, felt herself drawn back to the days when this little corner of Coolabah Crossing was Rose and Otto's world.

With her babies to look after, Rose was tied to the house. Lady Muriel was a doting grandmother, with endless stories to tell and songs to sing, and would spend hours pushing them about in their baby carriage across the fledgeling lawn Rose watered so carefully.

The three housemaids Otto hired were the daughters of free settlers from Paramatta. They reminded Rose of herself when she'd worked at the Manor, but their lot was much harder for the heat was relentless, the work never-ending. She tried to be fair and made sure they had enough time to make the long journey back to Paramatta to visit their families, but the sheer distances involved meant their visits were rare.

She was pleased to have help in the house for there was always something to be done now they had Lady Muriel's fine furniture to polish as well as the stout German furniture Otto had brought with him. Because of the heat, the windows had to be kept open, and with the circulation of hot air came the dust. Fine, clinging and red, it whirled into spirals that whipped across the baked earth and covered everything: gritting the tongue, irritating the eyes, impossible to brush out of their hair. Yet she knew the dust would disappear with the autumn rains. It was all a part of the excitement heralding the ripening grapes and the next vintage.

Otto would rise before dawn, kiss her and the babies, and leave for the terraces. He ate his meals in the fields with the ticket of leave men and returned long after sundown, sweaty and covered in dust, to fall asleep at the dinner table Rose had taken such pains to make attractive. His skin reddened and peeled, his bright hair became dull with the dust, but his enthusiasm never waned. Although she rarely saw him, she understood his need to watch over their investment. Every penny they had was sunk into the earth and the vines, and in this house that was palatial compared to most outback stations.

Sundays were different. No one worked on Sundays, and Rose looked forward to leaving the house and travelling in the buggy with Otto to the tiny church five miles away that had been built to serve the newly settled area. It was like a holiday. Otto would wash the dust from his hair, clean the dirt from his nails and put on his suit. Rose and Lady Muriel took the opportunity to dress in their best hats and clothes, for this was their only social outing, and they would be meeting other vintners and their wives. The two-year-old twins, who were now quite a handful, were washed and primped and given strict instructions to keep clean and sit still.

They made quite a procession down that long, bumpy road, Rose thought as she looked back at the cart where the three house servants perched, clinging to their gaily flowered straw hats as the overseer Hans held the reins loosely over the quiet pony's back. Her gaze fell on the ticket of leave men who trudged far behind them, the dust rising from their rough boots, settling on the poor clothes that served as their Sunday best.

She felt the unfairness of making them walk so far – they had other carts. But Otto had insisted this was the way things should be done, and as time had gone on, she'd realised it was so, and although she still didn't like it, learned to keep her objections to herself.

It was the law for these poor wretches to attend church, regardless of their beliefs, and although their lusty singing was good to hear, she sometimes wondered if it was just an excuse to release some of the pent-up anger they must surely feel – for although they worked in the open and had comfortable quarters to return to at night, these sad-eyed, skinny men still bore the scars of their long internments and knew they would never really be free – would never see the misty damp of home again.

Rose looked away and thought about tomorrow. She had longed for the day when she too could return to the open fields and escape the restrictions of the house, for since the twins' arrival she too had felt like a prisoner. Not that she didn't adore her babies, but she missed those days in the sun, striding along the terraces, bending her back to hoe and cut and trim, with the endless sky above her, the earth warm beneath her feet. The restlessness had grown, and now, as her daughters began to take on personalities of their own, and learned to walk and talk, she felt she could leave them in the care of Bessy, the newest housemaid, under the watchful eye of Lady Muriel.

They were woken before dawn the next morning by a shout from below. Otto leaped from the big double bed and threw open the screens on the window. 'Vat is it?' he called.

''Roos. Bloody great mob up the north end,' came the reply.

Rose dashed out of bed, pulled on trousers and shirt, boots and socks. Otto glanced across at her as he tore off his nightshirt and pulled on moleskins and boots. 'Go back to bed. I deal with this,' he said shortly.

She ignored him, finished lacing her boots and reached for a belt to hitch up her trousers. 'They're my vines just as much as yours,' she said quietly. 'And I know what a marauding mob can do.'

Otto grinned, his eyes very blue in his sunburned face. 'Too right,' he said. 'Come on then, ve do battle.'

They hurried downstairs to find the house in uproar. The twins were crying, the maids were crashing pots and Lady Muriel was issuing orders. Rose and Otto hurried out and went to fetch their horses from home paddock. There was no one in sight, the light of a new day barely over the horizon. There was a terrible stillness in the air. A stifling weight that seemed to hang over everything.

'Ve haf storm soon, I think,' Otto said gravely as he looked up at the sky. 'Not good for grapes if too heavy.'

Rose clung grimly to the reins. She knew heavy rain could destroy the harvest, but she still hadn't fully mastered the art of sitting on the back of a half-wild horse and was fully occupied with staying put.

As they approached the northern part of the property, they were met by a devastating sight. The mob had trampled line after line of precious ripening grapes, their great feet and tails sweeping aside the year's work as they gorged on the fruit. The ticket of leave men were running between the terraces, flapping their jackets, shouting, waving pitchforks and hoes in an effort to scare them off.

Rose and Otto swung down from their saddles and joined in the fray. The great grey beasts eyed them laconically, hopped just out of reach and resumed their meal.

Otto ran back to his horse and took his shotgun from the saddle. Hans did the same, and as the shots echoed round the valley and animals fell in the dirt, the others got the message and bounded off. 'Get up there and mend the fences,' shouted Otto. 'Make them stronger, higher, or they vill be back.'

'But we'll never keep them out, Otto. They jump too high, and they're too strong.'

He looked down at her, his hair dark red with sweat, his eyes cold with fury. 'I haf here a year's work and all my money in this harvest, Rose. If this fails we vill haf nothing. Nothing. I can't let the 'roos just trample me into the ground.'

Rose nodded, knowing there were no words to console him. The grapes were easy pickings for the wombats and possums, the bandicoots and echidnas – it seemed as if every living thing for miles around depended upon those vines. 'Let's go and see how much damage there is,' she said softly. 'Perhaps it won't be as bad as you think.'

He shook his head and looked up at the lowering sky. 'If the storm comes in the next few days ve vill have lost it all anyway,' he said sadly. 'One cold night and all our work vill be for nothing.'

Rose saw the slump of his shoulders and knew he was right. All they could do now was pray the rain held off and the frost didn't hit. The grapes were ripening well, it promised to be a good harvest, despite the damage – but it was still six weeks or more away, and anything could happen before then. Not enough rain, and the grapes wouldn't ripen and grow sweet. Too much and they would rot on the vine. Frost would kill them, humidity would leave them mouldy and useless. Blight could wipe them out.

Perhaps Otto should have taken the other vintners' advice, and invested in a mob of sheep, or planted corn and wheat as back-up, she thought. But she knew he was not a man to put his money in sheep or corn. He was a vigneron, a grower of grapes and producer of wine. He had no time and precious little money to spend on anything else, preferring to leave it to fate and

Mother Nature to decide their future.

Two weeks later they were standing on the verandah, looking up at the sky. There was a slight wind and a drift of clouds sailing over the face of the moon on that clear, late-spring night. 'It vill be no colder than usual,' declared Otto thankfully. 'We can go to bed no worrying.'

They were fast asleep when the heavy tread of feet thundered up the stairs and their bedroom door was flung open.

Hans was breathing hard, his face ashen. 'It is freezing hard, Otto. I haf already got the men to light the pots.'

'Get them out on the terraces quick, Hans. I come *mitt* you.'

Once again Rose and Otto threw on their clothes and hurried outside. They had been alert all through the winter for frost. The slightest downturn of the barometer in the hall had Otto sniffing the air. He would even leave their bed at night to walk around the vineyard, testing the stillness, studying the stars for some clue as to what the weather would bring. A severe late frost could be deadly to the blooming vines.

The French had come up with the idea of coating the vines with smoke, and in the early years, Otto had used brush and straw with green leaves to make a smoky fire – and as the frosts hadn't been too severe, the vines had survived. Now he was better equipped with hundreds of frost pots filled with oil. As they hurried out of doors, Rose prayed this new method would save them.

She stepped out into the yard and knew they were in trouble. The cold goosed her flesh, bit deep into her bones. The housemaids came out shivering in their night clothes to join them, and Lady Muriel hovered in the doorway, her nightcap askew on the grey curls, the little girls peeking out from behind her voluminous nightgown.

'Stay with the children, Muriel,' Rose ordered. 'You girls put some clothes on and come with me.'

They joined the procession of men, each carrying the flaming, smoking frost pots up and down the terraces, dousing the grapes in a tarry film. Rose was soon black from head to foot, eyes stinging, choking from the smoke. It was a silent, desperate trudge in that glittering cold, no one daring to voice their fear.

The night dragged on and one of the maids stumbled in her weariness and Rose rushed to pick up the sticky, burning pot. A fire now would finish them.

Otto strode up and down, encouraging the exhausted men, bringing them water, relighting pots that had run out of fuel, trying desperately to reach all his vines before it was too late.

Rose watched him as she trudged back and forth coating the grapes with the smoke. He strode like a great bear along the terraces, a man still in charge, a man with hope, but she was afraid for him for she understood what it would mean if they failed.

Three hours later the darkness began to lift and in the faint glow on the horizon the yellow flames of the pots seemed to pale.

Otto called out, 'Sun is coming. Now ve vill see.' His voice was cracked with weariness and emotion and Rose went and put her hand in his to comfort him.

The smoke-blackened figures stood in exhausted silence as they watched the sky lighten. There was nothing more they could do. Rose and Otto stood side by side as the light on the horizon deepened to gold. He held her hand in his big paw, his eyes fixed on the lines of vines. Rose could feel the rapid thread of his pulse and knew how hard it was for him to disguise his anguish, his dread – the hope they'd done enough.

The mist dissolved in a burst of light from the rising sun and the people of Coolabah Crossing were finally faced with the night's outcome. Rose felt Otto flinch as they stared out over their hundreds of acres where frost rime glittered on the rows of blackened vines which drooped, defeated and dead, on their supporting wires.

Silence engulfed them as the sun rose in majestic splendour above the scene of devastation. Then one of the housemaids began to wail, and Otto took a deep, shuddering breath as the sound echoed round the blackened, dead valley.

Rose was galvanised into action. She strode across the ruined terrace and slapped the girl's face. 'Stop that,' she shouted. 'We haven't been beaten – not yet. Some of the vines might have survived. Go and look.'

She returned to the silent Otto. His shoulders

drooped as if the weight of the world was on them. His face was haggard beneath its coating of oily soot, tell-tale streaks of white evidence of the tears he'd shed. Her heart lurched and she threw her arms around him, holding him as she would one of her daughters. 'Come,' she whispered finally. 'Let's walk. Let's see if we can find something to keep us going until the next planting.'

They walked for over an hour as Rose counted the vines that had survived. A few acres on the lower slopes, and one or two patches amongst the older, more established vines. But the new planting had been entirely lost, as well as a large area of Sauternes.

She stood there with her husband surveying their loss. Her hard-earned knowledge had taught her to estimate how good a harvest would be, and judging by what she saw now, there would only be a quarter of their crop harvested this year. That was if the grapes didn't get too much rain or humidity or were eaten by caterpillars or locusts first.

'I vill not be able to repay the debts, Rose,' Otto said sadly. 'Nor vill I be able to replant unless the bank gives me the money.'

'So go to the bank and ask for more,' she said firmly. 'We have all this land and the house to put up as collateral. We aren't beaten yet.'

He smiled down at her, his spirits already rising. 'You are so small and yet today you are stronger than I, Rose. So much determination in that little body.' He took a deep breath that shuddered through his large frame, then squared his shoulders, his chin raised defiantly as he looked over the blackened remains of many years' labour.

'I am not defeated, Rose. I vill send to Germany for another consignment of vine cuttings immediately. I vill also go to the other vintners in the Hunter and see vat they vill sell me. I vill replant. I vill be patient. My plans are set back three years, Rose, but ve are young. There is plenty time.'

Neither of them voiced their fears. What if next year's crop failed too?

Otto rounded up the men and gave an order to Hans to issue them with rum. Rose could scarcely bear the sight of the vanquished vineyard. Now Otto seemed to have recouped his energy, she could return to the house with the other women and help with the food that would be needed. There would be time to mourn later, when she was alone and Otto couldn't see her.

Her skirts trailed in the dirt, her shoulders ached, and there were blisters on her fingers where she'd burned herself on one of the pots – yet she smiled as she saw the other women, for only the whites of their eyes were visible in the blackened faces. They looked at one another in shocked silence, then despite their weariness and the terrible loss they had all suffered, they burst out laughing. Rose finally knew at that moment why she loved this wild, untamed country. She was free here, equal to those around her regardless of their birth, bound to them in the endless struggle to survive in these lonely open spaces. Otto was right. They would not be defeated.

Cordelia's eyelids grew heavy and she fell into a doze. The breeze was warm, the sunlight dappled and dancing through the wilgas, but her dreams were dark, populated with people from the past who paraded before her in a cavalcade of memories. There had been frost at Jacaranda and they had spent all night out with the smoking pots, their hopes and fears all directed to that moment of dawn when all would be revealed. Modern methods had improved their chances against the deadly enemy of frost, but there were still so many other predators on the vines and their own lives seemed bound to the survival of those delicate grapes.

Then there was Jock, his face browned by the sun and wind, striding along the terraces issuing orders, lashing out with his whip at some poor soul whose work was too slow or careless for his liking. Labour laws might have changed the way he dealt with his employees in the later years, but she could still hear his raging voice as he bullied poor Edward, saw again the humiliation her brother had suffered at his hands. The light had gone from Jacaranda during those years. Now perhaps there was a glimmer of hope – a chance to begin again.

Her eyelids fluttered open and it took a moment to realise where she was. She sat there, unwilling to break the spell of her dream. The years had fled, taking with them her youth and her strength but never her memories. She had lived in a time that would not come again. A time of exploration and adventure in which she and Jock had made their mark. Strange how that seemed more real than now. Strange how the past was full of colour whereas the present appeared to have lost its substance.

'Cordy? How y'goin?'

She looked up at Wal whose face was creased with concern. 'Just wondering if it was all worth it,' she said quietly.

'Too bloody right it is,' he growled, pipe clamped between his remaining teeth. 'You and me worked hard, Cordy. This is our children's inheritance – got to be worth something.'

She shaded her eyes and looked out over the land. 'It's time I went back to Jacaranda,' she murmured. 'Back to where I really belong.'

'Not feeling crook, are yer?' He frowned, his calloused hand light on her shoulder.

She smiled and shook her head. 'I'm just like an old clock, Wal. Ticking away, slowly winding down. It won't be long before I stop altogether.'

'You and me both, girl,' he said with a sigh as he inspected the cold dottle in his pipe. 'But it ain't time yet,' he said firmly. 'There's unfinished business.'

The line of graves marked the final resting place of the ticket of leave men who'd lived out their lives in this distant corner of the world never to see the coast of home again. Most of them had been so young, Sophie realised. Too young to have been torn from their families and all they knew for this untamed land. They had come from London and Liverpool, from Ireland and Scotland and Wales, and she could almost feel their poor lost spirits in the earth that covered them.

No wonder so many of the towns and cities in Australia bore the familiar names of their mother country.

She watched as Wal put his hand on Cordelia's shoulder, saw the concern in his face turn to a smile. They had been cheated of the life they could have led together, she realised – cheated by circumstances and the stiff regulations of their times – just as the ticket of leave men had been cheated of their futures. Yet their feelings for one another had survived the years and the distance, and although there must be bitterness for what they had lost, they both hid it well in the joy of seeing one another again. It was good that Gran could make this journey before it was too late – just a pity she hadn't lived in a time when she could have packed her bags and chased her dreams.

Sophie jammed her hands in her pockets. Wasn't she doing the same, she wondered. By turning her back on Jay, by accepting his rejection without question, she was about to make the same mistake. But this wasn't the first half of the century, it was the last decade of the millennium – there were fewer restrictions – fewer barriers for them to breach.

She knew then she would have to face him. Have to ask why – for her own sake, and peace of mind. If things were as hopeless as she thought, then it couldn't hurt more than it already did. She would have to pick up the pieces and start over – but she had done it before, and although it had ended in disaster, she could do it again. Lessons had been learned – she wouldn't rush into another relationship.

Putting all thoughts of Jay to the back of her mind, she returned eagerly to her grandmother. 'Ready to tell me the rest?' she asked. 'Or are you too tired?'

'I'm always tired, darling – but that's what happens when you get to my age.' She patted Sophie's knee. 'Now, where was I?'

Sophie leaned back on the bench and closed her eyes. She could hear the crickets and the flies and the rustling of the grass and the leaves. Could feel the warmth of the sun on her skin and smell the earth and the sweetness of the ripening grapes. And as Cordelia once more took up the threads of her story, Sophie felt herself slip into Rose's world.

Coolabah Crossing was within the tribal lands of the Wiradjuric, and as the vineyard was cleared and settled, the curious natives came out of the bush and set up humpies. They had learned quickly that the coming of the white man meant food and baccy and the strange fruit drink that let them commune with their Ancestors. Otto tolerated them for he'd heard about the troubles on other stations when the owners had tried to force them away. As long as they stayed out of the terraces and did a bit of work now and again, he let them stay.

Rose was fascinated by them. Their skins were so dark it was as if the sun had sucked away all reflection, the eyes almost ochre in the broad faces. Yet it was their tribal markings, so different from those of the Wandjuwalku at the Mission, that really made her wish she knew more about these silent, watchful people with their earth-bound philosophy.

As the years had rolled past, she'd got to know them and some of their legends. She even learned a few words of their language and would often sit with Wyju and listen to his stories about the Dreamtime.

He was a tribal elder, a tall, slender man with whorls and slashes etched into his flesh and daubed with clay and ash. He wore a thin leather thong around his waist and another around his head. Yet his nakedness did not disturb her for it seemed natural in a proud man of the Never Never.

It was three days after the frost attack and Wyju had just returned from walkabout. Otto and Rose were sitting on the verandah watching the last of the sun disappear behind the hills.

'Where you been, you lazy bugger? We could haf done with you these last few days.'

'Been walkabout, Boss.' Wyju came and squatted at the bottom of the verandah steps.

'Vat is this, Wyju? You got another wife out there, I bet.' Otto laughed at his own joke but the native frowned.

'I been singin' up the country, Boss. Walkabout means treading in footprints of Ancestor, singin' his songs, making creation again.'

Rose had heard about these invisible song lines. 'How do you know what to sing, Wyju? And if you can't see them, how do you know where the lines are?'

The old man slowly shook his head. 'Dreamtime tracks, Missus. Ancestor walk over land scattering words and music in his footprints. A song is map given to baby by mother when first kicks in belly. Mother marks place and then it is totem for baby. Baby has dreaming with song lines, and he will meet brothers of the same totem if he does not stray from them.'

'It all sounds very complicated,' grumbled Otto. 'If you can't see the lines or hear the music how vill you know if you haf kept to your path?'

The smile was wide in Wyju's dark face. 'Australia like big music, Boss. Song lines along you all over from sacred site to sacred site. Only black fella know sacred sites.'

'So dreaming and song lines and totems are all a part of the same thing?' Rose was confused now. 'What happens if a man crosses from one line to another without knowing? Will he be in danger?'

'Dreaming is story. Every site has a dreaming. Black fella ask, Who's that? Whose story? A rock could be liver of speared kangaroo that Ancestor ate on his journey. A billabong the hiding place of fish totem.'

'So we could be walking over these sacred places without even knowing?' Rose felt a chill as the man's gaze turned to her.

'Bad thing happen if you destroy totem, Missus. Legend say man alonga here move sacred stones and fire dreaming come with spear to kill him.'

'Don't frighten the Missus, Wyju,' warned Otto. 'She's got enough imagination as it is, without you putting ideas into her head.'

'You have big trouble with farm, yes?'

Otto and Rose nodded.

'It is because you take away rainbow serpent's eggs.'

Rose frowned and Otto laughed. 'Snake eggs, my eye!' Rose saw the look of scorn in the black face and put a restraining hand on her husband's arm. 'I think we should take him seriously, Otto,' she murmured. 'There's a lot of truth in legend – I should know with the Irish in me.'

She turned back to Wyju. 'Where are these eggs? Can they be returned?'

'Come alonga me, Missus. I show you.'

Rose nodded to Otto and they followed the graceful naked figure out into the far eastern corner of the terraces. The land had been cleared several months back and new plantings sown. Now, because of the frost, there were only stunted black roots.

'Serpent dreaming here, Boss. Lay eggs. You take them away, away. Serpent angry along you. Song line broken.'

'It was just a pile of sandstone boulders, no use to anyone,' said Otto in exasperation. 'How the hell vas I supposed to know it was a totem or a song or a bloody dreaming?' He glared at Wyju before grasping Rose's arm and leading her back to the house. 'Take no notice of savages. They tell stories to frighten you. If we replaced every rock and tree, there would be no land for us, no home, no harvest.'

She could see his point but there was enough superstition in her to believe that perhaps there was magic in those song lines and discarded boulders, and Otto shouldn't treat Wyju's threat lightly.

Time moved on and Rose forgot about the strange story as they prepared for their harvest. Vintage after the frost was poor that year, a thin, mediocre wine they sold quickly to the less salubrious outlets in Paramatta and Botany Bay. Then they set to and cleared the terraces, turning the earth and digging the furrows in preparation for the new cuttings Otto had promised. Most of the furniture had been sold, the house mortgaged and the loan from the bank increased. Otto had travelled for days throughout the Hunter Valley, buying up stock from other vintners who were in financial straits. Now he was on his way back, his pockets empty, the precious vines carefully wrapped in damp sacking on the back of the wagon.

Rose was almost asleep on her feet as she stood on the verandah and watched the plume of dust approach the house. She had been up all night with Lady Muriel, heartsick to realise her old friend might not be with them for much longer.

Muriel had been unwell for weeks, the colour fading from her cheeks, the bustling figure slower now, the comforting curves whittled away as she lost her appetite. The doctor's round was enormous, spread over hundreds of miles, and they were lucky he happened to be visiting a nearby property – but it had still taken him a week to get here. He'd examined Lady Muriel, pronounced it was her heart and that she should rest, then left in his pony and trap for his next case.

Rose anxiously waited for Otto to climb down

from the wagon. As he swept her up in his arms, she leaned into him with thankfulness. He was her rock – the one certainty she had in her life – without him she didn't know what she would do.

His blue eyes dimmed as she told him about Lady Muriel, and without bothering to wash the dust and dirt from his clothes and hair, he took the stairs two at a time and went into the old woman's bedroom. She had become a mother to him, as she had to Rose. She was experienced and wise in the way of the world, and had supported them whole-heartedly in their enterprise, both financially and spiritually. They owed her much more than the guineas she had lent them to enlarge the house.

Rose stood at the bottom of the stairs, listening to the deep murmur of Otto's voice and the almost inaudible reply of the sick woman. The house would be lonely without Muriel, she realised. Even the maids would miss her, although there were times she knew the old woman irritated them with her fussy English ways and imperious orders.

The new cuttings were planted the day after a heavy rainfall and as the months went by Lady Muriel seemed to rally. Otto declared this would be the harvest that paid off their debts and gave them back their house.

'We vill celebrate, my Rose,' he said a month before the harvest was due. 'I vill buy you diamond ring, pearls, anything you vish. And for Lady Muriel, I buy new shawl and parasol so she can sit in the sun.'

Rose laughed and returned his hug. 'Just bring

us some new furniture,' she said with a chuckle. 'Apart from Muriel's bed, these old sticks we're left with are falling apart with mildew and termites.'

It had been a happy evening, with candles on the table, Lady Muriel's silverware glinting richly against the white cloth and a toast to the future with Coolabah wine. Otto held up his glass, swirled the ruby fire and sipped with enjoyment. 'Our first real vintage,' he said proudly. 'Chateau Coolabah Rosé, 1841, the year of our marriage. I laid it down after our first harvest together.'

Lady Muriel lifted her glass and took a sip as Otto watched and waited for her reaction.

'Perfect,' she said with relish, high spots of colour on her cheeks. The grey silk dress rustled as she struggled to stand. 'I give this toast to you and Rose. You have made an old woman comfortable, shown me love and understanding, even though I know I am sometimes trying. To you both. Long life and happiness.'

They weren't to know this would be the last evening they would all spend together. Weren't to know the terrible price they would have to pay for daring to ignore Wyju's warning.

Michael O'Flynn was working his ticket of leave and had come to Coolabah Crossing almost a year ago. He had served his time in Botany Bay after surviving the hell of a convict ship and although the wooden shack in the middle of nowhere was a far cry from the deprivation of his prison cell, he hated it. Hated the stench of the other eleven men in the shack. Hated being made to wear cast-off clothes and the walk to church every Sunday.

But most of all he hated the heat, the flies, the dust and the never-ending battle to keep the vines alive, for he knew that no matter how hard he worked, none of this could ever be his. His sweat was making the fat German rich – and when his time was up, Michael would be lucky to have a few coppers in his pocket and a piece of scrub land that would break his back and yield nothing for years.

He was restless that night. Now it was late, the lights no longer shining in the windows of the German's house, and the other men were snoring and snuffling in their sleep. Michael slipped out of bed, lifted the latch and stepped into the moonlight. It was hot, even now, the warm wind sweeping across the land, stirring the strange red earth into spirals that spun across the yard and out on to the terraces.

Michael eyed the cottages the free men had built once their time was served. They, poor fools, had decided to stay and take their chances here. It was easier than going out into the great wide world and fending for themselves. Marriage to local girls had supposedly brought them respectability, but he knew the taint of conviction would always hang over them – would even colour the lives of the many children they had sired.

He looked out across the lines of dark vines and spat into the dust. He needed something to help him sleep, and he knew just where to find it.

With the dexterous stealth of the seasoned thief

he'd once been in Dublin, he slipped through the shadows and made his way to the cellars. He knew where the key was hidden. Knew that if Hans the overseer caught him it would mean ten lashes. But the thought of all that drink just lying there waiting for him was too much. He opened the door and slipped inside.

It was cool in the underground cave he and others like him had hacked out of this impossible red earth. As he lit the lantern and held it high, he paused for a moment's reflection. The stones that lined the cave from floor to ceiling had been carried by wagon from the quarry at Paramatta. Each bore the mark of the tools the poor wretches of quarrymen had wielded as their chains clanked and their guards stood by with whips and guns.

He supposed he should count himself lucky he was out here in the middle of nowhere – but that didn't diminish his hatred for the people who had sent him here – and for the people who employed him. This was no life. He hadn't had a woman in years and apart from the odd issue of rum when the German bastard was feeling pleased with himself, hadn't had a decent drink since old One-eyed Pete had slipped him a fifth of brandy he'd managed to steal from the kitchen.

He lifted the lantern and let the dancing shadows flicker over the racks of bottles that lined the walls. Then he began to fill the deep pockets of his worn coat. It wouldn't do to take them all from the same place, he decided, choosing one here and one there. The German would certainly notice they were missing then.

Satisfied he'd left no trace of his night's visit, he locked the door and returned the key to its hiding place. Then he set off into the bush.

It was still dark when he woke. He lay there bleary-eyed, wondering what it was that had snatched him from sleep. Then he smelled something that made him sit up, fear rolling in his gut and sweat breaking out on his palms.

The empty bottles had left a trail as he'd wandered out into the bush, the last of them lying on its side close to his feet. He vaguely remembered having crawled under this bottle brush to get a bit of sleep before he had to return to the hut, but didn't remember what he'd done with the lantern.

As the smoke drifted skywards, grey against the black of the night, he heard the crackle and spit of burning grass and realised what he'd done. He remembered having stumbled and fallen, dropping the lantern and forgetting about it when he finally got to his feet again and reached for the next bottle. He must have walked on and in his drunkenness not noticed the lamp-oil and the flame spill into the long, silvery grass.

'To hell with the lot o' ye,' he shouted defiantly as he swayed on his feet and watched the smoke gather strength and swirl in the wind. 'Burn, ye bastards! Burn to hell and damnation!'

Rose turned uneasily in her sleep. Her dreams were troubled, and even the warmth and solidity of Otto lying beside her couldn't banish the fear that threaded through them. She stirred again

330

and opened her eyes.

Otto was flat on his back and snoring, his arms and legs splayed across the bed as usual, leaving her to cling to the edge. Aware of how tired he was, she lay still, staring into the darkness, trying to work out what it was that had woken her. There was certainly a distant noise, but that could hardly have disturbed her sleep, it was too soft, too much like the familiar moan of the wind as it swept down from the hills into the valley.

Horror made her sit up, her eyes staring into the darkness as realisation hit. 'Otto,' she screamed, leaping from the bed. 'Otto, wake up! There's a fire.'

He was thrust from sleep. In the same moment he threw back the covers and tore out of bed to the window. 'Oh, *mein Gott,*' he moaned.

Rose pushed past him to see for herself. A wall of flame was heading their way, riding on the swirling smoke that seemed to reach the stars. 'I must get the children,' she breathed as she snatched up her clothes and tore out of the room.

Otto struggled into his moleskins and charged down the landing, banging on the doors. 'Fire! Fire! Get out of ze house!' He tore into Lady Muriel's room. 'You must get up. Fire. Help Rose. I go to the vines.'

The old lady struggled to climb out of bed, her nightcap askew, her grey hair trailing over her shoulders. She didn't have time to reply for Otto was already halfway down the stairs.

Rose snatched the sleepy, frightened children from their beds and tore down the stairs and out of the house. They were screaming and tearful as she ran with one under each arm towards the wine cellar. It was underground and built of stone – it was the only place she could think of that might not burn.

'Stay here,' she ordered as she lit the lamp and snuggled them into the blankets she'd ripped from their beds. 'I'm going back to get Granny M.'

Two pairs of wide eyes stared back at her in fear and bewilderment. Rose hugged the girls fiercely. 'Don't be afraid,' she whispered. 'Granny M and I will look after you, but you mustn't come out of here until I say it's safe.'

She kissed them both. Their rounded cheeks were damp with tears but they seemed reassured and nodded confidently. Rose looked at her beautiful five-year-old twins, one so dark, the other as auburn as her father. They were precious, more precious than any vine, and although she knew she must, she was loath to leave them.

'Go and help your husband,' came a bossy voice from the doorway. 'I'll look after the girls.' Lady Muriel's face was ghastly by the light of the lantern and her breath ragged, but she still had an air of command about her despite the nightdress and shawl.

Rose kissed her girls again and put her arms around Muriel. 'Take care of yourself,' she murmured. 'Use those buckets of water to douse down the door, but if the fire gets too close, you must take the girls to the river. Sit down in the water and make sure you keep your head wet.'

Muriel gently pushed her away. 'I know what to

do,' she said firmly. 'Now go. Otto will be frantic.'

Rose kissed her soft, pale cheek and didn't allow herself to think how frail she seemed. Turning for one last glimpse of the people she loved, she closed the door and raced to join the stream of men and women who were heading for the terraces.

Otto ran to the make-shift stable. The horses were wild-eyed, screaming in fear as they kicked the weathered wooden walls and doors that kept them prisoner. He grabbed the nearest horse and threw himself on its back, then leaned down and opened all the doors so the rest could escape. Like everything else, they would have to take their chances.

He twisted his hands in the mane and kicked the animal into a gallop. The wall of fire was far enough away from the vines for him to try and do something about it. They had plenty of water, and this wasn't the first time he'd had to fight a fire on Coolabah Crossing. He still had hope.

'Ve haf to dig a trench,' he yelled as he joined the line of men who were already beating at the flames on the higher slope. They were armed only with sacking, spades and flat brooms. 'Follow me.'

He led them back to within several hundred feet of the first line of vines, took a spare spade and began to dig. The smoke was choking, the heat searing even from this distance, and as he worked, sweat stung his eyes. He couldn't afford to lose another crop, not so soon after the frost – not when everything depended upon it. He began to mutter prayers he'd thought long forgotten, in the hope that if there was a God, he would listen and do something about it.

With his head down and his arms and legs working on automatic, he dug furiously at the earth. The trench would have to be wide and deep enough for the fire not to leap across it. But did they have time?

He glanced up. The wall of smoke and hungry flames were even closer. He dug faster, harder, each spadeful of dirt giving him another inch or two of vicarious security.

'It ain't no good,' yelled Simmons, one of the ticket of leave men. 'Fire's catching up and there ain't enough of us.'

Otto kept on digging. 'You bloody dig,' he yelled back. 'Only way. It's the only way.'

The heat scorched his face, charred his hair and eyebrows and boiled the sweat. But still he kept digging. He was aware of the other men and women beside him. Aware of the children and old men who were handing buckets of water along the line. Aware he was losing the battle.

'Get outa there, mate. She's turning!' A rough hand yanked him out of the pit he'd dug and dragged him away.

Otto scrambled to his feet, his eyes wild. The smoke boiled around him and he could see the great orange heart of the fire as it descended on his beloved vines. He shrugged the hand from his arm and began to run. 'Buckets over here,' he shouted. '*Wasser* on the vines. Soak them!'

He ignored the shouts of warning – was deaf and blind to the others who tried to stop him as he grabbed a bucket and threw the contents on the shrivelling vine. The heat was already doing its work and the once luscious grapes were as wrinkled as raisins.

'More!' he shouted. 'More *Wasser.*' Tears of frustration combined with the soot in his eyes and he wandered blindly amongst the dying, burning crop, the empty bucket dangling from his fingers. 'Please, *Gott,*' he moaned. 'Let it rain.'

The sound of the flames crackling in the vines, the smell of sweet hot grapes bursting and the taste of cinders in his mouth were the last sensations Otto experienced. The wall of flame twisted with the wind and roared over him like a giant wave, engulfing him. Otto sank to his knees. He knew he would never see his beloved Rose again.

Rose was with the housemaids on the far eastern corner of the vineyard. Water was plentiful here, from a mountain stream running along the edge of the plantation. They passed the buckets hand to hand as the men beat at the flames with spades and brooms. They didn't have time to dig a trench, and she had long since lost sight of Otto.

Sweat soaked her, smoke was blinding, getting into her throat and making it raw. She could neither speak nor see in the swirling, roaring inferno, but she already knew this was a battle that couldn't be won without a miracle.

As she threw yet another bucket of water on the wilting vines, she refused to let herself think of the children and Lady Muriel. The house was still standing, she could see the dark shape of it when the wind blew a gap in the smoke. Therefore the wine cellar would also be out of the line of fire. She had to believe they would be all right. Had to believe Lady Muriel would have the strength to take the children to the river if it got too close.

Rose battled on. The heat crisped her hair and singed her brows, the smoke eddied, the flames spat sparks from tree to tree. She jumped as flames tore up the dry bark of a gum tree and exploded in a shower of sparks as it reached the eucalyptus oil. The tree split in half, tottered and swayed, then with an almost graceful movement began to fall.

'Look out!' Rose raced towards the girl who stood transfixed in its path.

The tree crashed to the ground, its tortured branches pinning the terrified maid to the earth. Flames licked at the leaves, tore up the gnarled branches and moved hungrily over the cotton dress and long fair hair. Rose was beaten back by the flames and the heat as the girl's screams were cut off with chilling suddenness.

She took a step back, covering her face with her hands to shut out the horror.

'We can't do nothing, Missus,' said a field hand's wife. 'It's turning. We gotta get outta here.'

Rose felt the tug on her arm and let herself be pulled away. The world was full of smoke and the orange destruction of the flames. The deep, ominous roar of the great beast rolled ever onwards. Vines were cringing from the heat, yielding to the fire, the sweet smell of the harvest hot in the choking air. She slid down the bank into the river and sank beneath the water that was as warm as if it had come straight from a billy.

The rising sun was masked by the black smoke and day had become as dark as night. The weeping, terrified men and women huddled in the water as the fire inexorably grew closer. Rose pushed her way through them, her heavy trousers and boots making it difficult to walk through the water. She had to find Otto and the children. Had to know they were safe.

Muriel knew she was in trouble. The pain in her chest was getting worse and she was finding it hard to breathe. She leaned against the cool wall and fought the rising panic. The children had to be protected. She mustn't let them know how ill and afraid she was. Her strength was ebbing fast but there were things that needed to be done. Smoke was already filtering under the door.

'Come along, girls,' she said in her most bossy manner. 'Pick up those buckets and keep the door wet.' She took off her shawl and rolled it into a long sausage, ramming it under the door. It might give them a little more time.

She put her arms around the little girls as they emptied all but one bucket against the door. They were wide-eyed and obviously terrified yet neither of them cried. Neither of them called for their mother – and Muriel felt the pride and love she had for them overcome all her discomfort.

The smoke coiled ghostly fingers around the shawl and through the knotholes in the wood. The pain in her chest was an iron band which ran down her arm and made her bite her lip. Sweat beaded her face and ran down her spine as her heart hammered against her ribs. They couldn't stay here. The smoke would kill them if the fire didn't.

Muriel waited for the pain to ease a little, then put her arms around the twins. 'We are going to play a game,' she said with forced lightness. 'First, we have to get wet.'

One pair of brown eyes and one pair of blue looked up at her in trusting innocence as she picked up the last bucket and drenched them both. With the last of it tipped over her own head, she snatched up the shawl and wrapped it over her hair to cover her mouth and nose.

'Stay back against the wall,' she ordered. 'As far back as you can.'

She waited for the little girls to cower damply at the far end of the cellar, then reached for the wooden latch. The wood was warm to the touch but she could hear no crackle and roar of flames, so carefully opened the door a crack and peeked out.

The outside world was grey. Filled with swirling, choking smoke that rolled like a great ocean over the land. The roar of this ocean was still distant, and there was no sign of the flames.

'Come,' she ordered. 'Take off your night-dresses and put them over your heads. Cover your mouths and noses, like this.' Pain shafted through her like a knife, making her head spin and her breath catch. She had to hang on. Couldn't give in to it, no matter how bad it was. The girls must be kept safe for Rose and Otto.

Muriel swayed as shadows of mortality drifted behind her eyes and into her head. She could feel the thread of life throbbing in her veins, could hear the thud of that aged heart as it struggled to keep her alive. 'Come, girls,' she whispered. 'Hold my hands.'

They emerged from the underground cellar to find the grass already alight on the roof, and Muriel knew then she'd made the right decision. If it caved in, the wine cellar would have become their tomb.

She held tightly to the little hands as she led the naked children across the clearing, over the crisped lawn and towards the willows. Each step sent a knife of pain into her chest. Each breath had to be fought for and expelled in the drum of agony that was her heartbeat. She could see the glint of water through the smoke. Could see the shadowy figures crouched there in terror as the fire bore down across the terraces.

One more step, she begged silently. Just one more. And another. And another. Almost there. Almost there.

Muriel dragged the children down the steep, trampled slope and slid gratefully into the murky water. She pushed the twins on until they were standing up to their necks.

'Keep your heads wet,' she ordered, her breathing thready, the pain all-encompassing. 'We'll have a competition to see who can stay underwater the longest.'

She watched as the children ducked beneath the water – then cried out as the steel band in her chest tightened and cut off her breath. It was as if her heart was trying to burst through her ribs, and she could no longer fight it.

Lady Muriel Fitzallan sank to her knees and slowly collapsed. The water enveloped her and she gave herself up to it. Her last thoughts were for the children and their parents, and this place called Coolabah Crossing which had become her home.

It was six months later when Rose and the children climbed the hill that overlooked Coolabah Crossing. She stood with them in silence, one child clinging to each hand as they surveyed the remains of their home.

The red earth was scarred black, the trees charred and gaunt against the insolent orange and yellow of the dawning day. The nearest terraces were almost bare, the tattered remains of the cremated vines a sparse lace across the scorched earth. Yet in the distance beyond the smoke-damaged house there was the lush green of re-growth and new plantings – the tiny figures of the surviving men and women trawling up and down the terraces. Life went on. Rebirth amongst death.

The little cemetery looked so isolated and lonely. The new stones they had carved in memory of those who had died glimmered in the glow of the rising sun, the fresh paint on the picket fence gleaming against the pale green of the new grass that had already sprouted from the ashes. Rose sighed. She might be leaving behind those she loved, but she knew her heart would always remain in this silent, desolate place.

'Why do we have to go, Mama?' asked Muriel with the same imperious manner of her namesake.

Rose smiled and stroked back the fiery red hair that was so like poor Otto's. 'Because Granny M wanted us to have an adventure,' she said simply.

The truth was, Lady Fitzallan had been an astute investor. Not only had she paid off Otto's debts, she had left them the deeds free and clear for both land and house, but she'd also bought large packets of land throughout South Australia, some of which were leased for healthy rents. Her will had left instructions for a particular parcel of land to be handed down to Emily and Muriel when they were of age, and then through the female line of the family.

Rose felt the time was right for her to travel and see more of this vast country. The ghosts at Coolabah Crossing were still too new for her to stay, and she didn't have the heart to begin here again, knowing Otto's ashes remained in the soil.

Hans would take over as manager. The land was already being cleared and new shacks built for the families and ticket of leave men who had fought so bravely on that terrible day and won their freedom. Wyju's sacred totem stones had been returned to their rightful place, the song lines of the legends restored, the Aborigine creation resung into being. Coolabah Wines would rise from the ashes.

The three of them stood on the hill, silhouetted by the rising sun, framed by the leafy branches of the delicate Coolabah trees as their skirts drifted in the dewed grass. Rose held her twins by the hand, as she thought of how things had changed since that night of Gilbert's attack back in England.

She had come here as a maid, with not much more than the clothes she stood up in. Now she was a woman of substance, with land and houses and money in the bank. A sad smile played at the corners of her mouth. Fate had demanded a heavy toll for that wealth, and although she would have preferred to have Otto and Muriel by her side and remain poor, she was wise enough to know their spirit would live on through her and the children, and she would guard her fortune wisely.

With one last, lingering look over Coolabah Crossing, she turned away and headed for the over-loaded wagon. Once the twins were settled, she climbed up onto the worn wooden seat and took the reins. With a gentle slap of leather on their backs, the mules began to plod along the rough track, taking them away for the last time.

16

Sophie hadn't seen Jay since the previous morning and she wondered if he was avoiding her. She couldn't blame him, she'd been a bitch to behave the way she had, but she justified that by telling herself he deserved it.

She returned to the homestead, pulled on jeans and boots and took Jupiter for a ride. The great wide spaces and endless sky gave her a sense of peace, with room to breathe and the chance to collect her thoughts – for the shadows of past generations still haunted her.

As they plodded over the rich grasslands she thought of Rose and Otto. They had come here with little more than hope and a raw energy which seemed instilled in that generation of adventurers and squatters who battled the bush and the elements to hack out an existence in these primeval surroundings. How easy it was for the following generations to reap their harvest. How easy to forget the hardships that had made their present wealth possible.

The silence of the Hunter Valley surrounded her as they took the winding path up the hill. The heat shimmered, making the trees dance in the watery mirage that sprawled across the baked earth. The essence of pine and eucalyptus filled the still air and the sibilant throb of the crickets and tree bats enhanced the feeling that this ancient land still held the spirits of those who had come before. It was here, out in the heat and the dust of the bush, that she could feel the power of the native legends – the rhythm of the song lines that to the white man's eye were invisible as they traversed the land. Yet their music could still be heard in the creatures that inhabited this earth, could still be felt in the waves of heat and energy coming from red soil and ghostly bark. The harmony of man and earth, of legend and the day-to-day struggle was such that the music of the song lines seemed to echo the pulse of her very being.

As they crested the hill, she slid from the saddle. With Jupiter cropping the grass beside her, she looked out over the valley and tried to imagine how Rose must have felt all those years ago when she had come to this hill for the last time. And as she stood there, she thought she heard the rustle of long skirts in the grass. Rose was with her.

It was in that moment she understood why it was so important to fight for her inheritance. The moment she finally realised this land, these sprawling terraces, were as much a part of herself as they had been for the generations that had come before – and she couldn't betray their trust.

'Reckon it's time you had these, Cordy.' Wal deposited the scrapbooks and photograph albums on her bedside table. 'I kept 'em in me grandad's old trunk. Seemed the most fitting place.'

Cordelia riffled through the pages, remembering how she had done the same thing all those years ago when she'd come here with her mother. She breathed in the musty smell of old paper as she sifted through the box of mementos Wal had placed on the bed. Everything was as she remembered it but, like herself, older and more decrepit.

She pulled out the largest of the mementos and held it to the light. The silver was tarnished, the leather cracked with age. 'I was always surprised they allowed him to keep it,' she murmured as she stroked the ornately tooled leather. It was heavy – too heavy for her arthritic fingers, and she carefully returned it to the worn velvet pouch.

Wal grinned. 'Didn't have much choice. He shot through before they could catch him, but then he was always light on his feet.'

Cordelia smiled, and as Wal left the room, lay on the bed, her eyes closed, the cool green light filtering through the shutters. The journey out to the cemetery seemed to have taken the last of her strength, sapped the vital spirit that had kept her going this far – and yet she knew she couldn't give in to this enticing drift of idleness, knew she must finish what she had started.

She opened her eyes and stared up at the ceiling fan that spun air-conditioned coolness into the room. Her life was turning rather like the fan – but in ever-decreasing circles back to the beginning – where the sounds, the smells and the memories were sharper than ever, where her life's pattern had been set.

Now she had almost come full circle, she felt the restless need to return to the Barossa where her life had been played out over the years, where her hopes and dreams had been forged in the rich black soil, to become withered in the furnace blast of Jock's ambition. Yet those dreams had never died – they lived on as they had done for Rose and her children, and her children's children. It was Cordelia's one triumph, and she wouldn't relinquish it for anyone.

Cordelia sighed. There was no point in wondering what her life might have been if she'd defied convention and married Wal – regrets only made a person sour – and there were so many things she was grateful for it would have been churlish to wish it otherwise. Her sons had been a gift that had been snatched from her too soon, but in their loss had come her daughters. Kate and Daisy had given her so much pleasure, so much love, and despite her failure with Mary, she had given her Sophie – the hope for the future.

Her gnarled fingers touched the scrapbooks that lay beside her. It was almost as if she could feel the power emanating from the man whose life was recorded in them. It was time for Sophie to learn why the family had been split apart.

Dinner was over and there was still no sign of Jay. 'He's flown down to Sydney with his father,' explained Beatty as they sat on the verandah with their coffee and brandy. 'There's a couple of things they need to sort out.'

Sophie raised an eyebrow but there was no further explanation. She didn't miss the warning look Cordelia shot at Beatty or the smile that hovered around the old woman's mouth. Something was going on – but she knew it was useless to try and discover what it was for Cordelia was a practised hand at keeping secrets.

'We begin vintage next week,' said Beatty. 'I hope you're going to stay for it?'

'Too right,' said Cordelia, and struggled from her chair, the brandy beginning to have an effect. 'I've got something for you Sophie,' she said mysteriously. 'It's in my room.'

She followed her grandmother through the screen door and along the passage to the back of the house. Eyeing the tattered scrapbooks with their garish covers and the battered, highly decorated red lacquer box, she frowned. 'What are they?'

Cordelia sank on to the bed with a groan. 'Damn' body,' she muttered. 'Lets me down every bloody time. Don't reckon I'll be much use at vintage.'

Sophie picked up a scrapbook, but before she could thumb through the pages, Cordelia stayed her hand. 'Take them all with you,' she said. 'Read them when there's silence, so you can hear the voices of the past, and feel them reach out to you – if you're very still, and concentrate hard, they'll come and tell you their story.'

John Tanner returned to London after his visit to Sussex, the fires within him stoked by the rage of knowing he'd been too late and by the hope his path would cross with Rose's in the bustling, stinking streets of the city. For no one had been able to confirm the rumour she'd left England for the other side of the world and he clung to the possibility that she was still here, breathing the same fetid air, hearing the same street cries.

When he wasn't fighting in the ring, he spent hours wandering the less crowded avenues of the wealthy, hoping he would see her emerge from one of the elegant houses that stood sedately behind their fine wrought-iron railings. These journeys into the cleaner, broader streets made him restless, for the reality of his own existence was a far cry from these wealthy corners of London, and when he returned to his room above the tavern, he would lie on the filthy bed and dream of the life he'd planned for them both with the guineas he was carefully hoarding from his fights.

Winter brought some relief from the stench of his lodgings, the cold winds ripping through the tenements, the frost riming the cobbles, making the horses' hoofs spark and slither as they dashed along the avenues of the fashionable parts of the city, carriages bowling along behind them, their occupants snuggled in furs and blankets. The poor, fleetingly free from the fever that was rife in the hovels during summer, now died of hunger and cold. Ragged children shivered as they begged bare-foot amongst the rotting, discarded fruit and vegetables in Covent Garden market, and the elderly and the hopeless gave up, their pathetic corpses lying where they fell to be picked over by the gutter vultures.

It was John's second winter in this Godforsaken city, and although he had spent some of his precious coins on a fur-lined coat, his breath still clouded the air as he strode along the frosted grass of Hyde Park. Gentlemen rode by on magnificent horses, doffing their hats to the ladies who perched side-saddle on high-stepping mares or sat swathed in furs in their carriages. Small children bowled hoops and scattered bread for the ducks as watchful nannies sat and gossiped on the benches or pushed baby carriages along the cinder paths.

John eyed each nanny, each maid who hurried past, but there was no sign of apple cheeks and rich black hair – no glimpse of the beloved little figure he so longed to see. He sighed and blew on his hands. Their knuckles were still bruised from his last fight and the cold had cracked the skin.

The snap of a whip made him turn and leap out of the way as a carriage came bowling down the track, a matching pair of greys in its traces foamed in sweat. John saw the face of the man who held the reins and then that of the woman in the carriage, so pale beneath the fur halo of her hood. His pulse jumped as recognition hit and was confirmed by the woman's eyes widening for the split second they were abreast of one another. It was the Squire's daughter, Isobel, and that bastard Gilbert Fairbrother.

Oblivious of the stares and exclamations of the strollers in the park, John began to run. The carriage was heading for the northern gates, and if he lost it in the bustle of the streets, it would be impossible to follow them. His boots crunched on the cinders as he tore after the carriage, his coat tails flapping, his long hair coming loose from its leather thong. His cousin had told him Rose was expected to move with Miss Isobel to London, and that the rumour she was off to Australia was just a story put about by servants' gossip. If that was true – and he hoped with all his might it was – then perhaps at last he would find her.

The carriage turned up Tottenham Court Road, Gilbert cracking the whip to set the horses high-trotting past the gloom of St Giles' rookery. Gilbert and Isobel's sensibilities were obviously far too delicate to withstand the sight of such poverty and degradation, and John wondered if they even noticed there was another side to this city.

The ornate gates of Bedford Square were closed as usual, and John groaned as his ribs ached and his breath became ragged as he forced himself on. The carriage was going past the gate keeper and out into the open country of Paddington.

It finally turned left along Walsingham Lane and pulled up in front of number sixteen. The house was three storeys high, surrounded by pleasant gardens showing early snowdrops and primroses. John leaned against the wall of the Victoria Tavern, his sides heaving as he tried to catch his breath. All he had to do now was wait – for surely this was Miss Isobel's new home – and if Rose was here, sooner or later she would have to come out.

He watched as Gilbert handed Isobel down from the carriage before climbing back into the driving seat and heading for the stables at the end of the lane. Isobel's slight figure was bundled in a velvet cloak that swept over the sawdust and horse droppings in the road as she hurried away from the carriage and mounted the broad scrubbed steps to the front door. A maid appeared, the gleam of her white cap and apron almost startling against the gloomy interior. Yet even from this distance John knew it wasn't Rose. Although he was disappointed, he still hoped it wouldn't be long before he saw her again.

The chime of a church clock startled him. He'd let time slip away and now he was late. There was a fight tonight. Big Billy would be waiting. With one last, lingering look at the house, he turned away. He would find it again – and soon.

Sophie leaned back into the pillows, a slender paperback book in her hands. It was a reissue of a nineteenth-century pamphlet on a prize-winning bare-knuckle fighter. Big Billy Clarke had certainly known his boxer, for he seemed to have caught the essence of John Tanner even though the English was old-fashioned and the prose inclined to be purple in this biography of his most famous fighter. Yet it was the line drawing on the cover that said the most and she found herself returning repeatedly to that face which reminded her overwhelmingly of Jay's.

John was bare-chested, his wide shoulders and muscular arms squared to an unseen opponent, fists raised, knuckles catching the light. But it was his face that fascinated her. The black eyes and dark brows, the sweep of the broad forehead and the mane of unruly hair that fell almost to his chest, spoke of an exotic strength and determination that belied his wiry build. It was a powerful image – one that defied the past and lived on in the present. Lived on in Jay and his brothers.

Bruiser Barnes had left John with a cut lip, a black eye and sore ribs, but he had finally won the fight and with the English Champion's belt still proudly displayed around his waist, Big Billy had taken him out to celebrate.

The next morning John woke before dawn with a sore head and a tongue the texture of a horse blanket, but all that was forgotten when he looked down at the ornate belt and thought of the amount of money he'd earned. He no longer kept it hidden under the floorboards for he'd been broken into several times already and knew it was only a matter of luck they hadn't found his hoard. So, on Big Billy's advice, he'd opened an account with a bank.

Climbing out of bed, he poured cold water from the cracked pitcher into the murky bowl and washed as best he could. When he had finished shaving and dressing, he tied back his hair and eyed his reflection in the fly-spotted mirror.

'Not bad for a gyppo,' he murmured. 'Not bad at all.' He grinned and jingled the coins in his pocket. Today was going to be a good day, he decided. He didn't have to defend his title yet and his time was his own. It was still early, he could make it over to Paddington in time to catch the servants as they ran errands.

Charing Cross and the Bermudas were a smoky warren, the filthy alleyways still rimed with glittering frost as he strode past the crooked, leaning tenements and into the Strand. Newgate Prison's massive walls loomed over him, black with soot and grime, but he hardly noticed any more. He bought a farthing dip from a hawker who stood in its shadows. John munched the bread fried in pork fat with relish and licked his fingers as he strode along the narrowing highway, admiring his reflection in the bow windows. He had no doubt he would see Rose today – no doubt at all.

The house gleamed in the early sun, frost still glittering on the window panes as shadows were chased from the narrow country lane. John wiped his greasy fingers on his coat as he leaned against the tavern wall and waited. The curtains were being drawn from the downstairs windows and a butcher's boy ran along the street and down the steps to where John guessed the kitchen would be. He waited for the boy to emerge again, and stepped out of the shadows.

'Know them well, do you?' he asked, the coin glittering between his fingers.

The freckled face and sharp features looked up at him. 'Might,' the boy replied tersely.

John held out the sixpence and let it glint in the early-morning light. 'Is there a maid in the house called Rose?' His pulse was so rapid he was finding it difficult to breathe.

The boy snatched the coin and tossed it in the air. 'Dunno,' he said cheerfully. 'This is me first day.' Then he laughed, dodged John's cuff round the ear and scampered off.

Despite his disappointment, he grinned. The boy reminded him of himself at that age – cocky and sly and too sharp for his own good when it came to fleecing idiots of their money.

He turned his thoughts back to his dilemma. The household was obviously busy, perhaps it would be best to wait until one of the maids was sent on an errand. But that could take hours, he thought impatiently. They might not need anything and the day would be wasted. Without giving himself time to think whether it was wise or not, he brushed his coat down, straightened his wing collar and cravat and strode down the steps. The lion's head knocker was small and tarnished and seemed to echo right down the lane as he rapped it twice. It was too late to change his mind now.

The girl's pinched face was red, her eyes agitated. 'Yes?'

John took in her skinny frame, the brown dress and reddened hands. There was something familiar about her but for the moment he couldn't quite place her. 'You the maid here?'

'So what if I am? We don't want no hawkers or gypsies,' she said firmly as she began to shut the door in his face.

John put his boot in the way. 'I ain't selling nothing, miss. Just enquiring if you got a Rose Fuller here.'

The door opened a fraction more, the maid suddenly inquisitive. 'Rose? What you want with her?'

John's heart hammered and his palms grew clammy. 'We come from the same village in Sussex,' he explained quickly. She was already edging the door shut again. 'I worked with her da. Good man, Brendon Fuller, shame he was killed like that.'

The girl's eyes sharpened, her thin mouth quivering with indecision. 'I knows who you are, John Tanner,' she said finally. 'But Rose ain't 'ere.'

He bit down on his impatience. 'She's away on a visit? Day off? What?'

'Looks like you're mighty keen to see our Rose,' she said as she eyed his expensive coat and the smart cravat. Her smile was roguish as she looked up at him. 'But I reckon you got a long ways to

354

go afore you see her again – she be in Australia.'

Big Billy had tried to persuade John not to fight again so soon after his title bout. He was now the English Champion with enough money in the bank to buy a good house and fill it with the finest furniture. His reputation would stand him in good stead should he wish to pursue another career – maybe as a trainer or promoter. The boxing world was changing, becoming more respectable, and there was a great deal of money to be made in accepting challenges from America.

John refused to listen. He needed an outlet for his rage. Needed to be in the ring again with the stink of the crowd in his nostrils, the raucous noise of them in his ears. The money was secondary, the need for a house, a home, not even part of the equation. He was a Romany, a traveller of roads – and if he lost all his money and spent the rest of his life living in the open, it would suit him just fine.

The decision to fight this particular night had been a mistake. The *dukkerin*'s prophecy had taken a further step towards its fulfilment as John's opponent lay at his feet.

He stood there, his breathing ragged as his chest rose and fell and blood trickled down his face. Tierney had fought a dirty fight, Billy had warned John he would – there was no denying he was relieved it was over. Billy was right. He didn't need to live like this any more. This would be his last fight.

Tierney's handlers turned him over. The

boxer's eyes rolled back in his head, his chin dropped and his mouth gaped. 'He's dead!' roared Tierney's manager. 'The gypsy bastard's killed our man.' He leaped to his feet, inciting the crowd. 'Don't let him get away. Murder! Murder!'

John grabbed his precious belt and dived over the ropes with Big Billy at his side. They raced for the cover of darkness, knowing they had only seconds before the baying pack followed. The confusion in the boxing booth was made worse because of the sheer number of people crammed inside, but if they were caught, they'd be torn to pieces.

The horses were tethered nearby and the two men clambered on, spurring the animals across the great expanse of Hyde Park towards the narrow alleyways and hiding places in the rookeries. John's head was pounding, blood and fear copper-tasting on his tongue.

'We should be heading for open country,' shouted Billy. 'Word soon gets around here and we'll have every cut-throat and informer looking for us before dawn.'

John snatched a look over his shoulder. He could already see the flaming torches of their pursuers. 'The rookeries will give us a chance to lose them,' he shouted back. 'They can see us too well out here in the open.'

They rode in desperate silence, slowing only when the lanes were too narrow or choked with rubbish. Curious eyes followed them from the shadows, their gleam sharpened by the knowledge that here were two men on the run. It was a familiar sight – one that might mean a handsome pay-off to an informer.

The hovels and tenements eventually gave way to open fields and woodland, and after making sure they were no longer being followed, they slowed their exhausted horses to a trot. 'I'm going back to my family,' gasped John, his ribs aching, his head still pounding with the pain of his broken nose. He was finding it hard to breathe, hard to keep his balance on the horse. 'I've had it with London.'

17

Kate looked at her sister in disbelief. 'How long did it take you to work this out, Daisy?'

She put all the papers back into the folder and tidied it away, smiling as she turned off the computer. 'Not long,' she replied. 'It was just a matter of putting two and two together, but at least it solves the riddle of Mum's journey to the Hunter.'

'Crafty old bat,' Kate said fondly, breathing out cigarette smoke. 'Might have known she had a trick or three up her sleeve. No wonder she didn't tell the others.'

Daisy poured iced water into a crystal glass. The temperature had been climbing all day and an electric storm was brewing out at sea. 'It'll be interesting to see if she pulls it off. The family rift's been going on ever since her grandmother's day, and even Mum might find it hard to persuade the other side to toe the line.'

Kate snorted and stabbed out her cigarette. 'If anyone can it's her,' she said firmly. 'Once she's got the bit between her teeth, nothing and no one can side-track her. I just hope all this isn't wearing her out. She's already frail, and that long journey, coming so soon after the ructions over Dad's will, is enough to lay anyone low.'

Daisy chewed her lip. 'I managed to get the phone and fax number from Jane, and spoke to someone called Beatty last night. Mum's tired, but seems to be holding up well – in fact she's revelling in the attention.'

'I reckon it's about time she came home,' said Kate. 'If it hasn't worked by now, then it never will, and I don't fancy having to fly to the Hunter to fetch her.' She looked at her watch. 'I've got to shoot through, Daisy. I'm going out to dinner.'

Daisy noticed the rush of colour to her sister's cheeks and the sparkle in her eyes. 'You've got a date,' she exclaimed. 'Come on. Out with it. Who? Where?'

Kate looked down at her manicured toenails. 'He's just someone I met on one of the charity boards,' she said hurriedly. 'No one special.'

Daisy didn't question her further. If things went well with this mystery man, she would hear all in good time. She laughed and chivvied Kate out of the door. With a roar and splatter of gravel, her sister drove out of the driveway and into the gathering gloom.

Daisy looked up at the sky. Lightning was already flickering on the horizon, the ocean gleaming pewter in the dwindling light. Settling into a chair on the verandah, she watched as the storm gathered strength. Great bolts forked above the sea as the deep growl of thunder rolled overhead and a hot wind rustled the trees and made them sway.

The storm was coming and she couldn't help comparing it to the turmoil about to hit the inheritors of Jacaranda Vines. She usually loved watching storms, but wished there was a way to avoid the eye of this particular one. For not only would it damage all of them – for some, it could mean destruction.

The winter encampment was deep in the Ashdown Forest, the *vardoes* in a tight circle around the camp fire, the bender tents sheltered beneath the trees next to the make-shift corral where the horses stood shaggy in their winter coats.

John had been travelling for days, for he had criss-crossed the countryside on his seemingly endless journey south. He knew that to make the journey in a straight line could lead to trouble. The publicity Billy had used to promote his fighting career had played on his Romany background and it would take only one clever mind to realise he would head for his family. Now, as he entered the encampment, it was almost dark, the light of the flames dancing into the trees, casting deeper shadow into the surrounding forest.

He grinned at the smiling faces, winced at the hearty slaps on his back and shoulders, grimaced as he drank the raw wine from the skin pouch he was handed. The children danced around him, clutching at his legs, fingering the shiny, ornate buckle on his champion's belt as the women chattered like sparrows and pressed close. Yet his gaze fell on the one face he'd been seeking since his journey had begun. As he moved silently towards her, the crowd parted to make way for him.

'*Puri daj*,' he breathed as he knelt before her chair and the aged arms embraced him.

'I have waited for you, boy,' she said softly. 'My dreams have been troubled, and I must know the *tachiken*.'

He drew away gently from her frail embrace and looked deep into her eyes. 'The truth is hard, *puri daj*, I have killed a man.'

She nodded as if his confession held little surprise for her. 'It is good you return but there is danger here,' she said softly. 'I have seen the *trito ursitori* – the three spirits – allow me to be the mediator between good and evil, my son, for I see you have *trushal odji*.'

John's shoulders slumped. He did indeed have a hungry soul – how wise his *puri daj* was to recognise that. 'I came only to warn you they will come looking for me, and to ask forgiveness for bringing *prust* to the family. I shall not stay. I have a *lungo drom* to take.'

She shrugged fragile shoulders, eyes sharp with intelligence. 'The fates will not be disobeyed, boy,' she warned as she read his intentions. 'The journey you have chosen will bring you only sadness.'

John wasn't given the chance to reply. A whirlwind of smothering kisses, of long, scented hair and encircling arms, took his breath away. Tina's warmth and obvious delight at seeing him made him blush and he hugged her as he might a sister.

'I leave you to decide, John,' said the old woman as she struggled to her feet. 'Tina knows as well as I what the fates demand.' She hobbled away, the frayed hem of her bright skirts trailing in the damp grass.

'I'm coming with you, John,' the girl breathed in his ear.

He eased away from her, aware of watching eyes and amused smiles from the others around the camp-fire. Leading her by the hand, he took her beyond the orange glow and into deeper shadows. 'I travel alone,' he said quietly. 'The *lungo drom* is dangerous – but I must find my destiny.'

Her dark eyes flashed, the gold coins in her scarf jingled. 'Our destinies are bound together. *Puri daj* has seen it, and so have I. I will follow you to the ends of the earth, for one day you will need me. I'm prepared to wait, no matter how long it takes. I love you, John.'

He put his hands on her shoulders and looked deep into her eyes. 'Don't waste your love on me, Tina,' he said softly. 'You deserve better.'

Her dark eyes glittered from unshed tears but her chin was up, her narrow shoulders shrugging off his hands. 'I'll be the judge of that,' she retorted.

John watched as she walked away. The slender

361

hips swayed, sweeping her long skirts through the grass. The jingle of bracelets and the toss of ebony hair were sounds and images that would stay with him always. And yet he couldn't love her – not the way she wanted or deserved – not as a husband.

When supper was over the musicians brought out their violins and tambourines along with their penny whistles to accompany the clay pots of raw sloe gin that went around the circle. John's lips touched the rough pottery, but he sipped sparingly – he needed a clear head for the next long ride.

He moved away from the heat of the fire and the all-too knowing eyes of his grandmother so he could watch from a distance. This scene must be implanted in his mind so he could carry it with him across the world. He needed to etch the smell of the woodsmoke, the sound of the Romany music and language, and the chill of an English winter on his senses. For this was the last he would ever see of them.

The old woman gathered her skirts and moved from the fire's glow into the surrounding darkness. He noticed how thin and frail she was, how her back bent from the hard life she'd lived, and wished he could bow to her superior knowledge of second sight and ignore the deep need to find Rose. To travel so far to an unknown land where fate could decree untold misery was a risk he must take. For his destiny no longer lay with his people – fate had shown her hand and was pointing the way to a new life. The thought he might never find Rose didn't occur to him, so sure was he of his destiny.

It was the darkest hour before dawn when John crawled out of the bender tent he'd set up beside his grandmother's *vardo*. All was quiet, all was still, and he hitched his bundle of clothes over his shoulder. The low, warning growl of a camp dog was silenced with a soft word. John's footsteps were soundless in the long wet grass as he crossed the clearing and headed for the horses.

With gentle nudges he eased his way through the whickering ponies, his tread light and sure, his hands running over necks and rumps to soothe their fears and avert trouble. He didn't want the whole camp alerted. Cutting out his own horse, he led it through the gate at the far end of the corral. In the deep darkness of the forest, he saddled it up and tied his bundle to the pommel.

He settled on the broad back and turned for one long last look at the sleeping camp.

'Goodbye,' he whispered. 'And may the *Martiya* be with me.' The horse responded to the gentle nudge of his boot heels and began to walk through the trees. John looked up into the canopy of branches and thought he could feel the night spirits watching over him. The *martiya* may only have been part of the Romany legend, but at this moment he wanted to believe in their existence.

As he emerged from the forest and turned his horse's head west, his hands stilled on the reins. The forest sounds had been disturbed by another – a sound that came only from the careful, steady tread of a horse.

John moved into the shadows as the moon appeared from behind the scudding clouds, and with the horse hobbled, he melted into the darkness of a giant tree trunk. He didn't have to wait long.

The delicate legs of the pony picked their way through the debris on the forest floor, the girl on its back crouched low, her soft murmur keeping the animal steady. The moonlight glinted on gold in her ears and on the coins decorating her scarf. The soft jangle of her bracelets was barely discernible amongst the night sounds, but John could hear them clearly as he waited.

The pony drew near and he leaped from his hiding place and grabbed the reins. 'So *keres?*'

After her initial scare, Tina struggled to calm her pony which danced, wild-eyed, shaking its head to free itself from John's grip. 'What does it look like?' she retorted. 'I'm coming with you.'

'No, you're not,' he snapped. 'Go back to the camp where you belong.'

'I belong with you,' she said defiantly. She reached into the hidden pocket of her skirts and pulled out a leather purse and dangled it by the drawstrings. 'I have my *darro,* and permission of the *dukkerin.*'

'I don't want your dowry – and I don't want you,' he said harshly. 'I can travel faster on my own.'

A single tear glinted on her cheek, but her head remained high, her composure regal as she sat on the pony's back and looked down at him. 'I will follow you to the ends of the earth,' she said softly. 'For one day you will realise the truth of the *dukkerin's* warning, and you will need me at your side.'

'I don't need you – I never have. Now go. Go!' John slapped the pony's rump, making it rear up before it galloped back into the woods. He was furious with himself for feeling sorry for the girl, furious he'd had to be so harsh. But Tina was an expert horsewoman, she would survive the mad rush back to the camp, just as she would survive without him.

He leaped back on his horse and kicked it into a gallop. There was a long way to go, and he wanted to travel as many miles possible before day-break.

18

The sun was going down, the dark clouds of an approaching storm hastening the night. Sophie remained on a roughly hewn bench and watched them gather.

All was silence. All was still. And the Hunter Valley held its breath – waiting for the first explosive blast of thunder.

The crash seemed to rock the very core of the ground beneath her feet, and as she raced for cover the forks of lightning rent the clouds with jagged fingers that ran blue and yellow as they sought the earth. Sheets of yellow blanketed the darkness with a light almost as strong as the sun's, flashing like mirrors, turning the world sepia and one-dimensional in their afterglow.

The homestead seemed to crouch on the hillside, the pale light at its windows no match for the light-show outside. Sophie ran up the steps two at a time, tripped over a pair of boots that had been left on the verandah and would have gone sprawling if strong arms hadn't caught her.

'Whoah there, mind how y'going.'

She was breathless from the long run, her heart hammering, and there seemed to be no strength in her to pull away from Jay. The wonderfully familiar scent of him surrounded her as his muscular arms held her close, and she could feel the drum of his pulse beneath her fingers. How safe she felt – how lovely it would be if they could stay like this forever.

'I'll be right,' she finally managed to gasp as she eased away from him. 'Reckon I should get back to the gym – I didn't realise how unfit I was.' Her voice was light, the laugh a little brittle, but she had to do something to break the mood.

'Look fit enough to me,' he said, those dangerous dark eyes gleaming in the half light as he smiled down at her.

Sophie tucked in her shirt – it gave her something to do, something to take her mind off his all-too penetrating gaze. 'Who left those bloody boots there in the first place?' she demanded crossly. 'I could have broken my neck.'

His hand lifted her hair and softly caressed the column of her neck. 'It's such a lovely one, too,' he murmured.

'Stop it, Jay,' she warned. 'Don't play games.'

He was very close, and the electricity between them had nothing to do with the storm raging around them. 'This isn't a game, Sophie,' he murmured. 'Never has been.'

She eyed him for a long moment, her thoughts in turmoil. If he was telling the truth, then why had their relationship foundered? If he was lying – then he was despicable. Yet she wanted it to be the truth, wanted to forget the past and begin again. She was about to speak when the screen door slammed against the wall, making them both jump.

'There you are,' said Beatty briskly. 'Sophie, I think you ought to go and see your grandmother. She doesn't look at all well, but she refuses to let me call a doctor.'

Sophie snapped out of her trance. 'Call one anyway,' she said firmly. 'I'll go and talk to her.' She pushed past Jay and ran into the house.

Cordelia was propped against a mound of pillows, her thick white hair for once in disarray. 'I will not have you making a fuss, Sophie,' she said querulously. 'I'm not crook.'

Sophie noticed the blue tinge around her grandmother's mouth, the dullness of her eyes and the tremor in her hands. She wet her lips, all at once fearful of losing her. 'I know, Gran,' she murmured as she sat on the edge of the bed and took the frail hand. 'But we'd be happier if you'd see the doctor to reassure us it's no more than tiredness.'

The old woman struggled against the pillows. 'You'll do as you're told, my girl,' she snapped. 'When I want a doctor, I'll call one – and not before. I might be old, but I haven't lost my ability to make decisions.' Her thin lips were drawn in a stubborn line as she finger-combed her hair from her face and tried to tidy it. 'And whatever you do, don't let Wal in here,' she added. 'I must look a fright.'

Sophie grinned. Her colour and frailty belied the strong spirit of the old woman, and as long as she had that they stood a chance of keeping her a while longer. She picked up the silver-backed mirror and brush from the dressing-table and handed them to her grandmother. 'Better get you dolled up then,' she said brightly. 'Because he's hovering.'

'Silly old fool,' Cordelia muttered.

Brightness returned to Cordelia's eyes and the twitch of a smile glimmered at the corners of her mouth as she dragged the brush through her hair and eyed her reflection.

She shivered and put down the mirror. 'Nasty inventions,' she muttered. 'They say the camera and the mirror never lie, but every time I look in that thing, I don't see the woman I know – the young woman who's trapped in this tired, wrinkled husk. Enjoy your youth, Sophie. Don't fritter it away by ignoring the things that matter, like I did.'

'I wouldn't say I'm wasting my life, Gran,' she replied, puzzled at this turn of conversation. 'I have a good job and wonderful prospects whichever way the corporation goes. The world's my oyster.'

'Hmmph. Job prospects are all very well, but that's not what I'm talking about.' The penetrating gaze was turned on her. 'Don't waste time dithering, Sophie. We only have one real chance of happiness in this life – and I wouldn't want you to make the same mistakes I did.'

'I don't know what you're talking about,' she replied, her gaze drifting away.

There was a soft chuckle from the bed. 'Yes, you do, my girl. I reckon it's time you and Jay sorted things out between you and made an old woman happy before she dies.' Cordelia smoothed the linen sheet, the diamonds on her fingers sparkling in the electric light. 'Now clear off and tell Wal he can come in for a minute. Though what on earth he wants to see me for, I have no idea.'

Sophie got off the bed and kissed the cool, soft cheek. 'You're a wicked old woman. But then you know that, don't you?' she said fondly.

Arthritic fingers circled her wrist. 'I might be a bloody nuisance most of the time but I haven't done anything really wicked, Sophie.'

She looked down at the wrinkled face she loved so well, suddenly puzzled by the seriousness she saw there. 'I'm sure you haven't, Gran,' she said with a shaky smile.

'Some might say I did what I did out of spite – but they'd be wrong, Sophie. I did it out of love.' She sighed and seemed to come to a decision. 'There's something I have to tell you. I've never been ashamed of it but it's something others might not understand.' She looked deep into her granddaughter's brown eyes and sighed again. 'It happened a long time ago and would have remained a secret if things hadn't worked out the way they have. As it is, I think you have a right to know before we go back to Melbourne.'

Cordelia's words had sent a chill of fear through her. As Sophie perched on the bed again and took her grandmother's hand, she felt an overwhelming sense of foreboding.

'What is it, Gran,' she whispered. 'What did you do that was so wrong?'

Mary was scared. For the first time in her life she was truly alone. There had been no reply to her numerous phone calls – it looked as if her latest boyfriend was away, and she didn't dare call her sisters. She knew she'd alienated her family with her revelations to Sharon Sterling, and had compounded that disloyalty by running away from Daisy – yet she would have given anything to talk to one of them, to have them with her in this tacky motel on the side of the highway leading out of Goulburn.

With restless energy, she began to pace the room. The bright orange walls and swirling pattern on the carpet seemed to close in on her, and the garish oil paintings that passed for art seemed to mock her with their florid colours and amateur themes. What the hell was she doing here? Why this place out of all the others she could have chosen? It was farming country, and although the twin rivers that ran through it were attractive enough, and the town itself was blessed with many fine old buildings, the motel was dumped right across the road from a tacky tourist trap where day-trippers could come and gawp at sheep shearers and learn about farming.

370

She lit a cigarette and stared out of the window at the giant concrete monstrosity that was supposed to represent a merino sheep. A stream of cars was already turning off the highway into the car park. She pulled the blinds and resumed her pacing. The need for a drink was growing but she knew that once started she couldn't stop, so she chain smoked instead.

The irony wasn't lost on her and her smile was grim. 'One way or the other I'm slowly killing myself,' she muttered. 'But who the hell cares anyway? Certainly not Mum or Sophie.'

She eyed the telephone. Perhaps she should call one of her sisters, let them know where she was before Daisy made a fuss and called the cops? The seconds ticked by as she puffed on the cigarette, her mind working with cool detachment. 'To hell with them,' she muttered finally. 'Let them stew. Perhaps they'll forgive me once they think I'm out of their lives or in danger – but I don't care.'

Sinking on to the bed, she stared at the orange walls. 'Oh, God,' she said, her voice cracking with emotion. 'I've made such a mess of things and I don't know what to do to put it right. Everyone hates me and I'm so lonely. So very lonely.'

'You can go in now, Wal,' Sophie murmured as she passed him in the hall. 'But don't be too long. She's very tired.'

The old man eyed her thoughtfully then went to Cordelia. Sophie shivered as the thunder crashed overhead and lightning struck with a crack. Cordelia's revelations had stunned her, making it difficult to think or to speak, even to put one foot in front of the other. Certain pieces of the jigsaw had come together, making a mockery of all she'd known – shifting her sense of time and place, destroying long-held beliefs. It would take only a word, a thoughtless gesture, to shake the very foundations of Jacaranda.

'The tangled web,' she muttered. This family of hers was bound by secrets and lies – by one man's determination to destroy all that was good – by Cordelia's determination to outwit him. She wandered down the gloomy hall and out on to the verandah, her mind going over the story Cordelia had told her, almost unaware of the turmoil in the skies.

'Sophie?'

Jay's voice was raised to compete with the storm and she turned to him blindly. It would have been the most natural thing in the world once for her to creep into his embrace. She still needed his comfort and strength, longed for his warmth. Yet this was neither the time nor the place. They needed to talk, but not with her emotions running high, her thoughts in confusion.

He seemed to catch her mood and made no move towards her. 'It's not Cordelia, is it?'

She shook her head. 'Gran...' She stumbled over the word. 'Gran's just old, Jay. But she'll go when she's ready and not before. She's far too bloody-minded and there's still a lot she wants to do.'

His breath came out in a long sigh. 'We never met before but I can see why you love her. She reminds me of my own great-grandmother.'

Sophie stared out at the strobe lights of the storm that flashed on the hills. The world hadn't changed, hadn't stopped spinning because of what Gran had told her. Yet everything seemed out of focus, unreal in the light of those revelations. 'What was she like?'

He laughed. 'She had red hair that looked as if it was on fire when the sun caught it, and a temper to match. But she had great spirit and a capacity to instil happiness in everyone around her. I was five when she died, Great-gran's favourite. I spent a lot of time with her, listening to her stories, going through that red lacquer box and the scrapbooks. She conjured up a magic world for me of people and places I came to know and understand as I grew up. I still miss her terribly – but with Cordelia here, it's as if she's returned.'

His expression was sober as he looked down at her. 'I can still remember the terrible day she died. It was as if the light had gone out in the house, and a vast emptiness took its place.' He stared off into space, the changing shadows in his face unveiling his thoughts.

'Great-gran was eighty-five, but she did her share of work around the place. She was never still, and sometimes, on a quiet night, I think I can hear those busy little feet tramping up and down the kitchen floor – but of course that's impossible because she never lived in this house. She died long before we moved here.' He smiled down at her, the dark stubble on his chin enhancing his square jaw and sensuous mouth. 'But

I like to think she's here all the same,' he murmured.

Sophie was mesmerised, trapped by his eyes. It seemed to take a great deal of effort for him to look away and collect his thoughts.

'We went out to feed the chooks as usual,' he said finally. 'Me with the feed in a beach bucket, Granny Mu with her heavy pails and the shotgun under her arm.' He grinned. 'She carried that gun every time she left the house and was a bonzer shot too. My word, she could fair beat Dad at shooting cans off fence-posts, I can tell you.'

'So what happened?' Sophie needed him to keep talking. Needed the distraction from her thoughts.

'We got to the hen house and found the wire had been burrowed under. There were chooks flapping all over the place, some of them mangled so bad Granny Mu had to wring their necks. She was furious, and after she'd repaired the wire, she stalked back to the stables and got out her horse and buggy. She was off to get the dingo that had killed her chooks. I raced after her. This would be an adventure. I loved riding in the buggy with Granny Mu. She drove faster than anybody else except Dad.'

Sophie could picture it so well. The little boy and the elderly woman racing off across the grasslands, the child hanging on to the side of the buggy, his face alight with the excitement of the chase.

'We spotted a dingo about five miles out and Granny Mu whipped the horse up. "Put a bullet up the spout, boy," she yelled, tossing me the rifle. "We'll get that no-good son of a gun, and no mistake.

'We were so intent on chasing the dingo that neither of us noticed the deep fissure left behind by the winter rains. The horse swerved violently away from it, bringing the buggy up on to one wheel. We seemed to hang suspended in mid-air for a long time, but it was probably only a matter of seconds. Then we were tilting, hitting the hard earth with such a thud the buggy's side split and the wheel snapped in two. I was young and light on my feet so I managed to jump clear. Granny Mu wasn't so lucky.' He paused as if the memory was hard to talk about.

'The dust finally cleared and I found her lying on the ground in a heap. The remaining wheel was spinning as I crawled under it and tried to wake her. I couldn't understand why she wouldn't answer. Apart from being covered in dust, there wasn't a mark on her.'

Sophie's heart went out to him. 'You must have been very frightened. You were only a little boy.'

He sadly shook his head. 'Death's no stranger out here, Sophie. I might only have been an ankle biter but I'd seen it before, and once I'd stopped snivelling I knew why Granny Mu would never wake up. I must have been quite a sight with my snotty nose and puffed up eyes as I galloped off on the horse to get help.'

'Sounds like your Granny Mu wasn't the sort to die quietly in her bed,' she said gently.

'Too right. She died as she'd lived – in a rush, with no care for the future and no thought for the consequences.'

'An interesting woman,' Sophie murmured. 'I can see why Cordelia reminds you of her.' She looked up at him. 'Granny Mu? That's a strange name – what's it short for?'

He grinned. 'I wondered when you were going to catch on to that one,' he said. 'My great-grandmother was Muriel, the red-headed twin Rose gave birth to here in the Hunter Valley all those years ago.'

Sophie stepped back. There must be something about storms which made people spill their secrets – and yet it was really no surprise, for if she thought about it sensibly, of course they were related. 'We share the same great-great-great-grandmother?'

His grin was wide, even white teeth gleaming against the darkness of his stubbled chin. 'Too right. Rose couldn't possibly have known what she started when she came out here to the Hunter, but here we are, the two sides of the family brought together again. Back where we belong.'

'Wait on a minute,' said Sophie, trying to grasp all the implications of this evening's revelations. 'Did you know this when we were in Brisbane? Is this damn' family feud the reason we split up?'

Jay looked puzzled. 'I had no idea of the connection,' he spluttered. 'Not until I came home and told the family about you.'

Sophie was furious with him then. The worry over Cordelia, and the shock of what she'd learned tonight welled up in a wave of rage. 'You might have had the bloody decency to explain instead of shooting through without a bloody word,' she yelled into his startled face. 'But that's typical of men, isn't it? All balls and no bloody brains.'

She was about to storm back into the house when Wal slammed through the screen and grinned toothlessly at them. ''Bout time yous got sorted,' he grumbled as he sagged into a verandah chair.

'It's not what you think,' she retorted furiously.

'Maybe – maybe not,' he muttered as he stared at the distant hills. Lightning was flashing, throwing trees and rock pinnacles into black relief. 'Reckon the doc won't be coming just yet. Fair crook trying to land a plane in all this, and Cordy ain't too bad – just wore out.'

The three of them stood on the verandah, the tension as electric as the storm. Sophie at last broke the silence. 'Jay was telling me about Granny Mu,' she said during a lull in the thunder. 'He also said she was responsible for the split in the family. Why was that?'

Wal took his time lighting his pipe. 'Reckon Jay's better at tellin' it. Knows as much as me.'

Sophie reluctantly turned to the man beside her. 'Looks like you drew the short straw.'

He leaned back in his chair, his long legs crossed at the ankles, his flat-heeled boots resting on the verandah railings as he stared nonchalantly over the land.

'Great-granny Mu was a woman born before her time. She was independent and almost ruthless when it came to getting what she wanted and wouldn't be bound by the strait-laced rules of the times she lived in. But if you want the whole story, then we have to go back to London and the mid-eighteen hundreds.'

Sophie frowned. 'But I already know about John Tanner leaving England. I've seen the little book and the Champion's Belt. There isn't anyone else left in England who could have anything to do with our family – unless it's Big Billy Clarke.'

Jay grinned as he shook his head. 'Not even warm. Big Billy eventually went to the States to become a very successful fight promoter there. He and John wrote occasionally, but they never saw one another again.'

Sophie nudged him none too playfully in the ribs. 'Stop stringing it out.'

'Fair go, Soph,' he moaned. 'That bloody hurt.'

'Jay,' she warned.

'Righto. The third and final piece of the puzzle which makes up our extraordinary family is Isobel and Gilbert Fairbrother.'

Sophie gasped. 'You're kidding?'

'If you shut up long enough,' he said gently, 'I'll tell you all about it.'

Isobel and Gilbert spent their wedding night in a coaching inn on the road to London. Gilbert had left his bride in their suite of rooms above the bar to prepare for his return and she sat a long while on the lumpy bed, listening to the raucous noises coming from below as she waited for her maid to assist her. The room's low ceiling and dark beams seemed to be closing in. Although the tiny window opened a crack, there was little air to freshen the fetid stench of previous occupants and Isobel felt the first pang of homesickness.

Having slipped on a delicate, hand-embroidered nightshift, she dismissed Sarah her maid and sat up in bed brushing her hair. It glinted pale brown in the lamplight and she arranged it fetchingly so it fell in ripples over the see-through material of her nightgown and hid her breasts. She blushed at the thought of Gilbert's caresses, and smiled as she remembered their stolen kisses as they'd walked in the grounds back at home. Married love couldn't possibly be as bad as Mama had hinted – not when her new husband was so gentle, so attentive.

Time passed and still there was no sign of Gilbert. What could be keeping him? she wondered as her eyelids drooped and she sank back into the nest of pillows. It had been an exhausting day and the journey from Wilmington to East Grinstead had taken its toll. Her eyelids fluttered. She settled further into the pillows, congratulating herself on the triumph of her wedding day. The guests might not have been as grand as Charlotte's would surely be, and their vows hadn't been taken in a cathedral, but nevertheless she was a lucky girl, she thought as she began to drift towards sleep. Gilbert was handsome and popular, their stolen kisses exciting. The nervous tension drifted away. She wished he would hurry up.

The wick had burned low in the lamp when the door was slammed back on its hinges and Gilbert stood silhouetted in the frame.

Isobel was instantly awake, the sheet clutched to her chin as she cowered against the pillows.

She watched him prowl around the room, shedding his clothes, dropping them to the floor. He was unsteady on his feet and a strong smell of ale hung around him like a pall. She slid further beneath the sheet.

Gilbert made the bed springs groan as he flopped on to the bed and struggled with his boots. After much cursing, he finally pulled them off and dropped them with a clatter to the floor. Standing, he shucked off his breeches and stood naked before her.

Isobel stared at the thing between his legs, her eyes wide, the colour rising in her face.

Gilbert fondled himself and the thing grew massive. 'Like the look of it, do you, Isobel?' he growled. 'Well, you wait and see what it can do.'

She shivered. Mama hadn't mentioned anything like this and she wondered if Gilbert was normal.

He ripped back the sheet, tearing it from her clutching fingers. Swaying in the guttering lamplight, his gaze roamed over her body in the diaphanous night-shift. 'We can get rid of that for a start,' he muttered.

The delicate fabric tore in his hands and Isobel cowered away from him, her hands fluttering over her nakedness. This was not the Gilbert who'd been such a gentle, thoughtful suitor. Not the man she'd thought she'd married. For the first time in her life she was afraid. He was demented – out of control.

Gilbert climbed on to the bed, his hairy nakedness looming over her as he straddled her hips. 'Let me show you how it's done – then it can be your turn. You'll enjoy it, I promise. Had no complaints so far.'

His weight pressed down on her, breath foul in her face, knees cruelly jabbing her legs apart as he wriggled between them. She began to struggle.

'Lie still, woman,' he snarled, his hands tearing away the last shreds of her gown, mauling her breasts, touching secret places that made her blush furiously. 'For God's sake, relax. I'm not going to kill you.'

The pain was excruciating, and if she hadn't been so aware of the rowdy bar beneath her, and the people in the next room, Isobel would have cried out. She smothered her screams with her hands as the bedsprings squeaked and the bed-posts banged against the wall.

Gilbert's face was contorted, his breath ragged, his grip on her knees ferocious as he pressed them against her chest and plunged deeper.

Isobel thought she was going to die. She couldn't breathe for the weight of him. Couldn't see for the tears. Couldn't hear for the blood roaring in her ears.

Then at last it was over, and to her deepest mortification there were shouts and whistles from the bar below and a knocking on the wall from next door. They'd heard it all. Heard her shame. Known what they had done. How could she face them in the morning?

As the sky lightened Isobel fell into a troubled sleep, only to be woken by Gilbert fondling her. 'What are you doing?' she demanded, at once tense and alert. Surely he didn't want to repeat what he'd done last night?

'I'm partaking of my conjugal rights,' he murmured lazily as his fingers explored her. 'Nothing like a tumble in the mornings.'

'But we did it last night,' she stammered. 'You can't want to again?'

He fell back on the pillows, his shout of laughter lifting to the beamed ceiling.

Isobel snatched the opportunity to cover herself with the sheet, and sat up, confused and very aware of the sounds of the other guests stirring. 'Hush, Gilbert,' she whispered furiously. 'Everyone will hear.'

His laughter came to an abrupt halt and he leaned on one elbow and surveyed her. 'What does it matter? We're husband and wife, and if I want to have you, I will.' He rolled on to her and pinned her arms to the pillow.

Isobel tensed, waiting for the pain. Waiting for that dreadful moment when it began all over again. And when it did, she realised her husband didn't love her at all – and it broke her heart.

The storm had begun to lessen, the lightning grew pale and less frequent, the rumbles more distant. Sophie stared out into the darkness. 'Poor Isobel. What a bastard.'

'Too right,' muttered Wal. 'But she was stuck with him. Not like today, when any sane woman would have packed her bags and got out. The disgrace of a failed marriage or divorce would have ruined her sister's chance of marriage to Sir James and brought dishonour to her family.' He sucked on his pipe. 'Honour was a big thing in them days. Even when I was a young bloke.'

'Life must have been hell for her, living with a man like that.'

Jay nodded. 'She found things tough if her letters are anything to go by. She wrote to her family regularly, and as the years went on, it was as if they were the only outlet for her isolation and unhappiness.'

'Letters? I didn't see any letters in the box Wal gave me.'

'Beatty's got 'em in her room. I'll get her to give them to you, then you can finish the story for yourself,' muttered Wal.

He struggled to get out of the chair and with a muffled curse finally made it on to his feet. 'Flamin' war wound,' he muttered. 'Gets so crook sometimes.'

They all turned at the distant throb of a light aircraft. 'Doc's here. I'll warn Cordy and take the flak, you go out and bring him in.' Wal slammed through the screens and limped into the house.

Jay and Sophie went down the steps and climbed into the jeep. 'Gran's going to be furious. I feel sorry for Wal,' she yelled above the noise of the engine as they tore through the night.

'He'll be right. He's handled far more dangerous things than a ninety-year-old woman in a bad mood.'

'I wouldn't bet on it,' she retorted grimly. 'You don't know Gran when she's roused.'

Cordelia was dozing when she became aware of someone in the room. Opening her eyes, she realised Wal was standing at the foot of her bed, his disgusting old pipe smoking in his hand. She smiled, too weary to speak.

'We got the doc, Cordy. He's just coming in.'

She shook her head. 'I'll be right, Wal,' she said with a sigh. 'Leave me alone.'

He approached the bed and took her hand, his seamed face close to hers. 'Don't be a stubborn bloody woman all yer life, Cordy. If it means keeping you with us for a while longer, then why not see him?'

She glared back at him, but kept her hand in his. 'Silly old fool,' she muttered. 'Never did listen to good advice.' She closed her eyes, willing the strength back into her body, the band of pain around her heart to ease up. 'I suppose if he's come all this way, he might as well have a chat,' she added grudgingly.

'That's my girl,' he rasped as he patted her head.

Her eyes opened and she smiled up at him. 'Yes. I always was, wasn't I?' she whispered. 'Despite the way things turned out.'

'Reckon so,' he said gruffly before he kissed her cheek. 'Now you rest. Doc'll be here in a minute.'

'I haven't got time to rest, Wal,' she said, energy momentarily returning. 'Sophie has to know the full story, and I can't afford to go dying until I've sorted out the mess Jock and I left behind.'

'John Jay and the boy have done all they can in that direction, Cordy. You rest easy. It's up to them now.' He bent closer. 'By the way, looks like your girl and Jay are starting to sort themselves out though they're aways from knowing it. But give 'em time.'

The colour flowed back into her pale face and her eyes gleamed. 'At last,' she sighed.

They were all waiting on the verandah. 'How is she?' demanded Sophie.

'Mighty fine for a woman her age,' the doctor replied, his eyes dark-ringed from a sleepless night. His medical round encompassed hundreds of miles, and tonight he'd been on call and on the move since he'd checked in to base at three o'clock the previous afternoon. The flying doctor service was manned twenty-four hours a day and until just recently been run on public donations. Now the government had stepped in and there was more money, but that didn't ease the amount of work to be done in his far-flung domain. Women still gave birth in the bush, men still got kicked by horses or trampled by cattle. Fires still burned and rivers ran bankers – and the people who lived in the great wide still got sick.

He dumped his medical bag and accepted a cup of tea from Beatty. 'The long journey out here probably wore her out. Her heart is struggling a bit. I've given her something to help her sleep, and here are some pills if the angina pain gets too much.'

'She won't take them,' said Sophie. 'She hates pills.'

He grinned through his weariness. 'I got the picture there all right. Gave her an injection just in case. Should see her through the next twenty-four hours. The pills are down to you. Crush them up in her food if necessary and keep an eye on her.'

'That's it?'

He nodded and picked up his medical bag. The nurse was already looking at her watch. They still had other calls to make tonight. 'She has a heart murmur, but it's not too serious as long as she doesn't do anything stressful like another long journey.'

'But we have to get back to Melbourne,' said Sophie.

'Not if you want her to stay alive,' he replied firmly. 'I suggest you stay here and make her as comfortable as possible.'

Sophie began to tremble. 'What is it you're saying exactly, doctor?'

'Mrs Witney is very frail. You should prepare yourselves for the worst.' He sighed. 'I'm sorry, but she's lived a long and full life. Although none of us wants to see our loved ones go, there comes a time when we cannot defy the inevitable.' He shook hands and he and the nurse stepped into the darkness where Jay was waiting in the jeep.

Sophie watched the lights disappear down the lane and the cloud of dust rise from beneath the wheels. She couldn't imagine life without Gran. Could hardly bear to think of a future which didn't include her loving kindness.

Beatty put an arm around her shoulder. 'Here, Sophie. Take these and read them. I don't reckon any of us will be getting much sleep tonight, and I sometimes find it helps to ease our own troubles to learn about others whose problems were far deeper.'

The little plane was already taking off. It circled overhead before disappearing into the gloom.

When the buzz of its engine had faded, Sophie looked down at the pile of letters neatly bound with ribbon.

'I doubt I'll be able to concentrate, but thanks,' she mumbled. Turning away, she went into the house and quietly peeked around her grandmother's door.

The old lady was asleep, her thick white hair spread over the pillow, her gnarled hands resting lightly on the covers. Wal was beside her, his soft murmur inaudible as he stroked her fingers.

Sophie gently closed the door and went to her own room.

There was a stillness about the house, an aura of watchfulness after the storm. The humidity lay heavy, making the outback gasp for water, for the precious, life-giving rain – and yet if that rain came, harvest would be ruined.

They lived on a knife edge, she realised. Life and death was with them all. In the elements, in the very earth they used to grow their grapes, even in the surrounding bush and the lush pastures. They were captive in the circle of life that never ceased – perhaps Cordelia was finally ready to step out of that circle and be free – perhaps they should let her go, regardless of the void she would leave behind.

A distant kookaburra chortled, and Sophie smiled. How she loved the sounds and the sights and scents of this vast land of hers. How wise Cordelia was to realise she needed to reacquaint herself with it and learn to look within herself. For it had somehow given her the strength to accept the shock of Cordelia's revelation, prepared her for the changes that would surely come.

She leaned on the windowsill and stared out into the soft grey of another dawn. The distant hills were capped in a veil of mist, their dark pines blue in the deep shadows. The thousands of terraced acres slowly revealed themselves in the thin line of light that was appearing on the horizon, and as the sun touched the tips of the vines it was as if they stretched up to embrace it. The scent of ripened grapes grew with the sun, mingling with the aroma of warming paprika earth and the sound of the rolling warble of the waking magpies. A deep sense of peace filled her as she looked out on this wonderful place. She had indeed come home.

Sophie finally left her window, stripped off her clothes and stepped into the shower, letting the hot needles of water sluice away the dust and sweat of the day. Exhaustion had set in, and yet her mind was alive with all she'd learned and experienced in the past few hours, her senses piqued by the knowledge that life was always surprising.

She knew she wouldn't sleep, and yet she was almost reluctant to read the tightly covered pages with their delicate copperplate swirls. Her fingers plucked at the ribbons, and before she realised what she'd done, she'd placed every letter in chronological order.

She reached for the earliest. The paper was thick and creamy, the folds worn. Charlotte had read her sister's letters often. As the tiny bedside clock ticked away the minutes, the sun burst over the hills and Sophie became lost in another world.

Life in London was a bitter disappointment to Isobel. The women gossiped and spread rumours, made trouble for their enemies and used their influence to promote their friends – but only if it led to a higher position for themselves. The talk was of fashion, of the court and the new young Queen, with much speculation as to her marriage and possible lovers. There were few who wished to discuss literature or politics, few who even read at all, and Isobel found herself once again on the sidelines.

Gilbert had grown distant, his outbreaks of temper frequently leading to sharp punches and hard slaps for Isobel. The once strong-minded, independent girl dreaded his moods, but quickly learned nothing pacified them and the slightest thing could set him off. She knew he drank heavily, and his gambling was eating away at her dowry, but who could she turn to? Who could she tell? And even if there was someone – there could be no solution. Gilbert was her husband. They were bound together until death.

Within three months of their arrival in London, he had moved into his own bedroom so he didn't disturb her when he came in late, and although she realised it gave him the freedom to come and go at all hours it was an arrangement that suited her.

His visits became more rare as the years went on – especially when she was expecting her first child. Gilbert seemed to find her repellent as she swelled up and waddled about the house, and she didn't mind that at all. The baby growing inside her was precious, she didn't want him anywhere near her. But she was bored with London, bored with sitting about the house all day, and couldn't wait to hold her first child in her arms and give it all the love she would have given her husband if only he'd been kind and faithful.

Henry was born in the winter of 1840. The birth was far easier than she'd expected, and when she discovered she was pregnant again the next year, Isobel looked forward to having another little baby to love.

Her second son Clive was born at the height of the summer. His fair hair and blue eyes reminded her of the wheat fields and cornflowers of home, and she loved him with a passion. Gilbert became more distant and his visits to Isobel's room ceased. He had the sons he wanted.

The two little boys were always fighting. Henry was sturdy and square-shouldered, his grey eyes fierce as he bullied the younger, more pliant Clive who liked nothing better than to be with his mama. Gilbert enjoyed the boys once they were walking and talking, and would take them out in his carriage and show them off to his friends. Isobel was never invited and would site dolefully at the window, awaiting for them to return.

It was late in the evening four years later that her world crumbled. She had helped the nursery nurse put the boys to bed, had kissed their cheeks and read them a story before blowing out the candles. Now she was sitting in the drawing room, her tapestry sampler stretched on a frame in front of her, the firelight bringing a warm glow to the chilly, north-facing room.

The front door slammed and the rapid thud of boot heels on the marble floor made her put her tapestry away quickly. Gilbert was in a bad mood. She could always tell.

She sat there, her hands neatly folded in her lap, her gaze never leaving the drawing-room door. Her breath was tight in her chest but she lifted her chin and tried to compose herself. At least the boys would be asleep by now, she thought. They won't hear anything if he gets violent. She began to tremble, her eyes wide with fear.

The door slammed open and he stood there silhouetted by the light from the hall. It was too reminiscent of her wedding night and Isobel's skin crawled.

'We've got to leave,' he shouted. 'London's done for me.'

Startled, she clasped her hands, her knuckles white against the dark bombazine of her dress. 'Leave?' she gasped. 'Why should we leave? This is our home. You chose it especially because it was convenient for the officers' club.' She bit her lip. Gilbert didn't like to be questioned.

He strode into the room and stood before her. 'Notice anything unusual about your husband, wife?' His colour was high, his eyes bright with rage.

She glanced swiftly at him. 'Your jacket...' she began hesitantly.

'That's right. They tore off my epaulettes and broke my sword over their knee.' He ripped off the jacket and threw the empty scabbard on to the chaise-longue. 'I've been cashiered,' he stormed. 'And all because Father refuses to stand by me.'

Isobel sat frozen to her chair despite the heat from the fire. She didn't know what to say, didn't know what he wanted to hear. So she said nothing.

Gilbert loomed over her. 'Did you hear what I said, woman?' he roared. 'The Army have given me a dishonourable discharge. I'm finished. Finished!'

She flinched as his spittle flecked her cheeks. 'But they can't do that,' she whispered. 'You're an officer and a gentleman.'

He sneered, then turned on his heel and reached for the tantalus. Unlocking the polished oak box, he helped himself to a large brandy from the crystal decanter. 'Was,' he snarled before draining the glass and refilling it. 'A so-called fellow officer told our commander I reneged on a gambling debt and tried to recoup my losses by cheating. I've just had to sit through what's laughingly called a court martial.'

Isobel watched as he drained yet another glass of brandy. She wasn't surprised to hear he'd been cheating or that he'd not honoured his debts. Yet she was surprised his father hadn't helped smooth things over as usual. She looked through her lashes at him. 'Perhaps your papa will help once he's had time to consider the consequences,' she murmured.

Gilbert threw the crystal glass to the floor, making Isobel jump as the glass shattered and flew across the polished boards. 'Like hell he will,' he stormed. 'Father has washed his hands of me, he said so this afternoon. And the alternative he's suggested is so appalling I won't even contemplate it.'

Isobel shrank into the depths of her winged chair. Gilbert was now very drunk, swaying on his feet, his large hands balled into fists. 'Alternative?' she whispered.

He stared at her, his expression grim, his blue eyes almost colourless. 'Hell's teeth,' he swore. 'I married a mouse. A little brown mouse without an ounce of sense,' he sneered. 'Sit up, woman,' he roared. 'Talk so I can hear you. I'm sick of your whining and cowering.'

Isobel eased herself out of the chair. It was safer to be standing if he lashed out – the chair would imprison her and she would have nowhere to run. 'What's the alternative, then?' she said as firmly as she could. 'Why is it so terrible?'

'Father has offered to pay passage for us to Australia,' he sneered. 'I'm to be a remittance man – the unwanted black sheep who's been sent to the other side of the world because he's just too embarrassing to keep at home.' He rocked on his heels. 'What do you think of that?'

The words dripped like ice into her consciousness. Australia was a wild, untamed country where convicts wore chains and natives carried spears and ate one another. Surely Gilbert's papa was jesting? Surely he didn't mean for his grandsons to be brought up in such a desolate place? As for her own father, she knew he didn't have the income to help – not now he'd moved in with Cook and Mama took her revenge by shopping.

'What about the children?' she stuttered. 'What about their education?'

'Damn the children,' he shouted. 'What about me? I'll be the laughing stock of London by the time morning comes. We have to leave tonight.'

Isobel was almost overwhelmed with a sense of desperation, and it made her brave. 'You can leave, but the children and I will remain here,' she said firmly. 'We can join you once things are in order.'

'There's no money unless we all go,' he rasped. 'The lease on the house is almost up, and apart from your jewels, there's nothing of value here.'

Isobel frowned? 'No money? What about my dowry, and your income from the military? Or my engagement ring? We could sell it.'

He swept his hand through his hair. 'Gone,' he said brokenly. 'And I sold your ring a long time ago – that's nothing but glass. We have nothing but Papa's charity. You see there isn't really any alternative. We must leave England for New South Wales, or end up in the debtor's prison.'

Her hands covered her mouth as she thought of that terrible place where women and children sold themselves for a crust of bread and men lay in their own filth, beaten by life and the impossibility of ever escaping their debts. 'Then we must go, and quickly,' she breathed. 'I'll wake the servants.'

Isobel slammed the door behind her, the tears already running down her face as she climbed the stairs to the nursery. Gilbert deserved everything he had coming to him, but why should she and the children be punished? Life was bitter and unfair, and although she had no idea of how she could do it, she made a silent vow to make the best of things and see her sons didn't follow their father's nefarious ways. Australia would be a new beginning, far away from everything she knew and understood, but maybe it was a chance to do things differently. To find the independence she'd once had and the strength to make a new life.

HMS Swift arrived in Port Adelaide on 1 July 1845. Isobel stood on deck with the children and watched the approaching coastline. The sea was very blue, sparkling like the sapphires Mama used to wear at her throat. The surrounding hills fell in a dark green tumble to the pale yellow sand of the beaches, and the huddle of low buildings around the dockside were masked by the tall masts of sailing ships and by strange-looking trees.

Gilbert's voice startled her, she hadn't heard him come up on deck. 'There should be a man waiting for us with supplies,' he said pompously. 'These colonials seem to have the measure of things, and Lady Fitzallan has arranged for a bullock driver to take us north.'

She looked up at him. 'Lady Fitzallan? I seem to remember the name but I cannot place the face.'

'A friend of Mama's,' he said as he eased a finger around his tight collar. 'She came out here several years ago. It's a parcel of her land we're renting until we can find somewhere better. The

Barossa Valley is a wine-growing area, evidently. Mama says their wine is rough but beginning to make a reputation for itself. Quite fancy being a vintner – will make a change from the military.'

Isobel bit her lip. Gilbert had no experience with wine other than drinking it – they were heading for failure even before they began. 'Does this land have a house?' she asked hopefully.

He shrugged. 'Doesn't matter if it don't,' he said carelessly. 'Convict labour's cheap. We can soon have one built.'

She looked out across the water. The colours were so bright. The amazing light of this southern hemisphere seemed to enhance the beauty of this new world. Yet her spirits were low for there was no way of knowing what the future might hold for any of them.

19

Cordelia was still breathless after her angina attack, but she insisted upon getting out of bed and was now sitting in a comfortable chair on the back verandah, watching the activity in the stables. She had woken several times during the night to find Wal at her side, his hand loosely clasped in hers, and she had drifted off again, safe in the knowledge she had finally found the peace she'd been looking for all her life.

The air was thick with humidity, and although the storm had threatened rain, the clouds were light and fluffy in the wide blue, with no promise of a downpour. She stared out to the terraces where John Jay and his sons were walking the lines, testing the grapes prior to the harvest. It was a scene that had been with her all her life, and one she would gladly take with her into the next.

Leaning back into the cushions, she closed her eyes and thought about her divided family, and her hopes for the future. Wal had told her Sophie had been given the letters, so perhaps she would understand the rift – yet there was another rift to come – she could feel it in her bones, and there was nothing she could do about it. If her plan failed to re-unite the family and make it strong again, this journey would have been for nothing – and all the journeys of all the previous generations would have been wasted. For those early settlers from their different backgrounds made Jacaranda Vines what it was today – and if it foundered, she would see it as the ultimate betrayal.

She thought about Rose and John and Isobel and Gilbert. Poor Isobel, such a delicate little soul, so lonely and out of place in this vast country, and yet she'd found the inner strength to succeed where Gilbert had failed, and had made a life for herself and her children.

Her thoughts drifted back to a past beyond her memory – to the days when her own great-grandmother was close to dying and felt the need to reveal the final strands of her divided family.

She conjured up the images of those long ago days – the team of dark red bullocks, their horns wrapped in sacking, their wide backs swaying as they pulled the laden carts along the dusty tracks that led north into the wilderness. She could see the bullocky man, with his fearsome whip and his agile, lean figure leathered by the sun and wind as he coaxed the great beasts through deep rivers and encroaching bush.

They were scenes lost forever in the rush for modernisation. And yet, as she sat there in the cool shade of the verandah, she thought she could still hear the ghosts of the men who followed those long, lonely trails, and the slow, steady plod of oxen. Thought she could still make out the rumble of wagon wheels in the bull-dust, and feel the isolation her forebears must have experienced – for the essence of Australia hadn't changed – or the spirit of the men and women who lived in the Never-Never.

Isobel and Gilbert travelled for many days behind a bullock team. The dust rose from the beasts' hoofs trampling the wallaby track, covering their clothes and hair in a fine veil of ochre, choking their throats and stinging their eyes. Sweat stuck their heavy English clothes to their backs, flies swarmed and mosquitoes bit as they jolted along.

The bullock man was taciturn with a face that rarely smiled and hands which could encompass a trunk or barrel with ease. Yet it didn't seem to Isobel that he was a man of ill temper for his quiet voice kept the beasts under control and his horny hands were light on the reins. He chewed tobacco and spat great gobbets into the surrounding bush, but at night could be persuaded from his almost endearing shyness to regale them with stories of his adventures in the outback. These story sessions were of much delight to the two little boys who were in danger of running wild before they reached the homestead.

Isobel was silent for most of the journey, knowing they were travelling further and further from civilisation to a life she couldn't imagine. Gilbert's resentment never left him, and the fear of being marooned with him in the middle of nowhere was something she didn't allow herself to contemplate. For if he could be violent towards her in London, she dreaded to think what he might do in this vast, lawless, empty place.

Yet threaded through that trepidation was the excitement building in her, a thirst for knowledge about the startling birds and strange trees and the funny little bears that sat in those trees and dozed with their babies on their backs. The giant leaping red animals made her smile and the ponderous lurch and roll of the wombat reminded her of the badgers back home in Wilmington.

She refused to dwell on thoughts of home, for unless a miracle happened she would never see it again – yet at night when she could hear the wild dogs howl and the chilling cackle of the kookaburras echo through the bush, she longed for the mist and the rains of England and the mournful lowing of cows underlying the shriek of seagulls.

The journey came to an end at last and in shocked silence they looked at their new home. Isobel saw the great sweep of land stretching as far as every horizon. Could feel the furnace blast of heat rebound from the black soil into the soles of her thin shoes. Could hear only the mournful caw of giant rooks that hovered above her and the chattering cackle of the red and blue parrots that swarmed in great clouds over the deserted land. She turned at last to the dilapidated tin shack that sagged against the lower hill.

'Tell me that isn't the house,' she said under her breath as she took in the rusting corrugated iron, the termite-chewed posts which held up the rotting verandah, and the broken shutters that hung drunkenly from the single window. There was no front door, no glass in the window, and the chimney was a crude metal tube protruding skywards from the tin wall.

Gilbert glowered, a frown etched on his sunburned brow, his hair bleached almost white from their days in the open wagon. 'So much for favours,' he muttered. 'Mama said nothing about living in a hovel.' He turned his back and began to unload the cart. It was as if by not looking at it, things might improve.

Isobel bit down a bitter retort. There was no point in telling him he'd brought it upon himself. But tears were threatening, the hopelessness of it all weighing heavily on her. She looked down at her boys. Their little faces were dirty, their eyes bewildered as they waited for her to reassure them. Smearing away the tears, she took a deep breath, gathered up her skirts and picked her way to the verandah through the rubble and debris that had obviously been left behind by the previous owners. Wary of rotting boards and the dangerous tilt of the whole edifice, she looked into the iron shack.

It was even worse than she'd thought and her spirits, already low, plummeted. The shack consisted of two rooms. One for sleeping, one for cooking. A broken table was the only item of furniture and a monstrous black range squatted in the corner. Thick cobwebs veiled everything. There was a sweet smell of decay mingling with the suffocating heat that bounced between tin roof and dirt floor.

Tears welled again and she angrily brushed them away. She couldn't let her boys see how exhausted and frightened she was. She would have to turn this disaster into an adventure and do the best she could. For they had no servants and no money – Gilbert would be hopeless. It was up to her to make a success of this place.

She stood there in the shade of the broken-down building and looked around her. Despite the awful reality of what they had become, there was a raw beauty here, she realised. An untamed promise of something that could be wonderful if only Gilbert could overcome his hostility. And as she watched the children help the bullock driver, she knew this place would give her far more than the empty life of London. She might not have the luxuries of England, but here, in this vast, empty country, she would be free to use her mind as well as her hands and energy. Free to rediscover the sense of adventure she'd always known was within her. Free of the restrictions her birth had necessarily enforced.

Isobel was thoughtful as she slowly walked away from the shack and sought shelter beneath the stand of trees on the northern side of the homestead. Their delicate purple fronds danced in the warm breeze, their scent almost a memory before it reached her.

'What are these trees called?' she asked the driver.

'Them's jacarandas, missus. Pretty ain't they?'

'Jacaranda,' she murmured. 'Yes, they are.' She smiled for she knew that although life would be tough, the beauty of the jacaranda trees would always feed her soul.

'How y'going, Gran?'

Cordelia opened her eyes and shaded them from the glare with her hand. 'Good,' she replied firmly.

Sophie plumped down on the seat beside her. She had brought the rest of the letters with her, hoping to finish them before tomorrow's vintage. 'You gave us a fright. The doc says you're to stay here until you feel better. He doesn't advise going back to Melbourne.'

'Nonsense,' she retorted. 'I was just thinking about the apartment when you came along and interrupted me. I'd like to see it again before I die.'

'We'll see,' Sophie said, not committing herself to a promise she knew she might not be able to keep.

'And what about you? How are you feeling? It wasn't fair to tell you such things without warning.'

Sophie took the frail hand and smiled. 'I'll always love you, Gran,' she murmured. 'That will never change.' She quickly changed tack. Although the revelations had come as a shock, there was no point in causing the old lady more pain. 'I've been reading Isobel's letters. They're interesting, and so full of detail it's easy to imagine what life was like for her. It's almost as if McCubbin's *Pioneers* has come to life beneath her pen. But she must have been very lonely and frightened, stuck out in the bush with no one but that bastard of a husband for company.'

Cordelia eyed her for a long moment then nodded. 'She was, but she also had plenty to occupy herself with besides Gilbert's beatings. With the help of convict labour, they soon had repairs done to the shack. She planted a vegetable garden, taught the boys their lessons and earned money working for the other vintners during the day while clearing their own plot at night. Their land had reverted to scrub and she needed to know all she could before they began planting their own vines. Isobel had a mind like a sponge. She absorbed information from the other growers, and soon outstripped Gilbert in her knowledge of the grape business.'

'Good for her,' said Sophie grimly.

Cordelia smiled. 'Yes, it's good to see someone regain their confidence and self-esteem, but it had sad consequences. Gilbert didn't like Isobel's new independence and soon grew bored with life in the bush and went off in search of gold. There was a rush down in Ballarat and he thought he could make his fortune and return to England a rich man. Poor Isobel, she was left with a fledgeling vineyard and two small boys to rear. Money was desperately tight with precious few luxuries like a decent stove or even a nearby well. But the people coming into the Barossa at that time were instilled with a pioneering spirit. Most of them were German, escaping the religious tyranny back home, and they helped when they could, soon coming to admire the quietly spoken little English woman who worked so determinedly to succeed in what was really a man's world.

Sophie looked down at the letters in her lap. 'Isobel was a clever woman, I reckon. It's only by reading between the lines that the truth comes out.'

Cordelia nodded. 'Finish reading the letters, Sophie. They tell the story so much better.' She leaned back into the cushions, knowing how the tale would unfold. Knowing how bitter were the tears that nourished the vines in those early years. Yet knowing that if Sophie was to understand the deep commitment she owed those early settlers, she must read it all.

Rose had been travelling for eighteen months. Her inheritance was widespread and, after visiting the outlying vineyards in the Hunter valley, she had gone south-west to Riverina, and then slowly made her way through Sunraysia which lay north of Melbourne, and across to the Murray River where she first saw the Barossa Valley.

Going bush had hardened her and the children. Living from hand to mouth, sleeping in humpies like the natives, they came to respect and understand this country of theirs. There were few changing seasons, just wet or dry – but sometimes the wind blew, howling like a dingo, with a bite reaching to the bone. Rain plummeted causing rivers to run a banker, bending the trees and turning the red earth to cloying mud. Then it was gone as quickly as it had come, leaving the world of the outback steaming in the blazing sun.

They passed few other travellers. Just the occasional native or a swaggy with a bluey on his back and the wear of hundreds of miles on his shoe leather, and one or two drovers and ringers looking for work at the next sheep or cattle station. This was an excuse to climb down from the wagon and brew a billy over a make-shift fire. To share damper bread, hot from the cinders, and strong, sweet tea to wash down salted mutton or dried beef jerky.

The little girls snuggled up to their mother in the glow of the bush fire and listened, their faces alight with wonder, to the stories of the men who walked the wallaby tracks. They learned how to recognise dingo spoor and avoid snakes. Learned which berries to pick from the scrub and which would kill them. Learned where to find water in the middle of the wilderness, and which plants could heal sickness and fever. They slept without fear in the make-shift humpy of grass and twigs, their dreams full of that night's story.

Rose became adept at shooting a gun and snaring a possum for the pot. Most of the stories could be taken with a pinch of salt, but she listened closely when the black fella talked of the different deadly snakes and spiders, and taught her the native trick of stealing honey from a hive high up in the trees. The young black jackaroo had travelled with them a while, fascinating them with his sing-song voice and his mystical tales of the Dreamtime, and they were sorry when he finally left to go walk-about and sing up his country.

The journey was an education, not only in survival but about this wonderful country, of the people and places that were slowly making their mark, and the treasures to be found deep beneath the rich red earth. The talk was of gold – and soon there was many a man tramping the tracks in search for the elusive fortunes to be had in Ballarat, Stawell and Bendigo.

Rose watched her little girls grow tougher by the day. Muriel, with her bright red hair and freckles, had to be guarded against the sun for her fair skin burned, the freckles becoming more prominent as the journey progressed. Emily reminded Rose of herself, dark-haired, with skin the colour of milky tea and eyes that took everything in and stored it in an enquiring, busy mind. Lessons were taken on the road, Rose making the girls recite their tables and their letters, until they could read the books she'd packed in the trunk.

Now the journey was almost at an end. As they followed the Murray River down into the Barossa Valley, Rose knew she had found their new home. The land swept away from them on all sides, disappearing over the horizon in a shimmer of heat-haze. Terraces of dark green vines laced the valley beneath the shade of delicate jacaranda trees, and the glitter of water meandered in a bright ribbon through lush grasslands.

Rose slapped the reins and the weary horses plodded towards the homestead she could see in the distance. Granny Mu had left her two adjacent plots in the Barossa. She was planning to visit the tenants of this one before moving on to the other and settling down for a few years. The previous tenants had given up and gone back to Adelaide and she was looking forward to the challenge of starting again. It would be pleasant to stay here after their long months of travelling. An opportunity to find out what life was like in this wide and pleasant valley that reminded her so much of the Hunter.

Smoke was drifting from the rusting stack and someone had painted the fence posts white around a burgeoning vegetable plot and seared the word 'Jacaranda' into a board above the gate. Rose smiled. The name was appropriate. The new tenants seemed to have settled in nicely, but then they had been there for several years according to the paperwork Granny Mu had left with her solicitor.

Rose had been disconcerted to see the name Fairbrother on the lease, but had decided it could have no bearing on the Captain. For surely he and Isobel would have made their home in London's high society rather than out here in the bush.

She looked around her as they travelled down the dirt road leading to the homestead. The land had been cleared, and there were a few cows and goats grazing in the home paddock. The shack was a typical bush dwelling, but someone had made an effort to repair the roof and paint the shutters. Fields of dark green tobacco waved in the warm breeze and Rose nodded approvingly. It would take between three and six years to produce enough good quality grapes to make a palatable wine; the Fairbrothers were wise to sow another crop to tide them over.

She drew up at the steps, taking in the neat lines of the vegetable garden and the healthy chooks pecking the dirt in their sturdy wire enclosure. Someone had planted roses and their perfume was heady in the heat, the blossoms trailing over the rusting shack in surprising profusion.

Rose was a little put out that someone hadn't come to greet her. These far-flung homesteads were usually an oasis of welcome, for they had few visitors. She climbed down and, with the five-year-old twins scrambling after her, walked up the steps to the verandah.

As she was about to call out, the latch lifted and a woman stood framed in the doorway. A woman whose face she would have recognised anywhere. A woman she'd thought she would never see again, and whose small boys crowded her ragged skirts.

Rose took in the faded and much-patched cotton dress and white apron – the wisps of brown hair escaping the bun and the weary droop of the mouth beneath the dark circles that shadowed grey eyes. 'Miss Isobel?' she breathed.

'Rose?' The eyes widened. The hands hastily screwed her hair back into its bun before returning to her apron and discarding it. 'What

408

on earth are you doing here?' Isobel's tone was almost rude, despite the hunted look in her eyes.

Rose felt the tug of the past tear away her newly found independence and was once again the lady's maid. She dropped a curtsy, aware of her twins' wide-eyed disbelief. This was a side to her they had never witnessed.

'My apologies, Miss Isobel,' she said hurriedly. 'Lady Fitzallan told me this place was leased and I saw the name on the deeds when she left me my inheritance. But I didn't for one minute think...' Rose clamped her lips together. She was running off at the mouth, using mindless prattle against the shock of seeing Isobel Ade in such dire circumstances.

Isobel held the door wide, the bare-foot boys elbowing each other to get a better view of their visitors. 'Seems as if you and I have a great deal to say to one another.' she said quietly. 'Come in and I'll make us a cuppa.'

Rose followed her into the mean little shack. She still couldn't believe this careworn, sun-lined woman was the same delicate young society girl she'd helped to dress all those years ago back in Wilmington. Still couldn't come to terms with seeing the poor sticks of furniture surrounding a woman who'd once lived in luxury.

And yet there was something stronger about Isobel, a certain self-awareness and confidence that hadn't been in evidence before, and as they faced one another across the rough table and she listened to Isobel's story, Rose realised that although their fortunes had turned, the barriers of class no longer existed between them. They were simply two women who shared a strength and purpose that this new life of theirs had demanded of them.

It was to be the start of a life-long friendship – one that saw them through drought and flood, through successful harvest and personal heartache. The two women were drawn together by their will to succeed and they found a support and companionship in each other that would never have been countenanced back in England.

Isobel had never forgiven her mother for the manipulative way she'd arranged her marriage, but still wrote to her sister Charlotte and her father. These letters became less frequent as time went on, for she had grown to love this wild and beautiful country, but when she did write, her letters were filled with hope for the future, despite, or perhaps because of the fact she'd had no word from Gilbert for years.

Rose had dreaded his return – it was the only shadow over her new life here in the Barossa – and although she had never spoken of his rape, she knew how Isobel regarded her erstwhile husband and could feel only relief when the news finally filtered through that he'd died following the riots at the Eureka Stockade.

The gold miners had refused to pay government licence fees and had barricaded themselves into the stockade at Ballarat. The redcoats suppressed the riot on 3 December 1854, leaving twenty-seven dead and many wounded, but the distances involved and the infrequent transmission of news meant they didn't get to hear about it until almost two years later.

Jacaranda flourished and Rose used some of her inheritance to build a new house on the boundaries linking her two plots so they could all live together in comfort. The children learned their lessons in the tiny wooden school house the vintners of the Barossa had built in their fledgeling town. As the time passed the four of them became inseparable.

The years trickled away like dirt through their fingers as the two women battled the elements and the predators to increase their crop and improve their raw wine. They thought their lives were settled and the future mapped out for them all. But fate had another surprise. One that none of them could have foreseen.

Cordelia and Wal decided to take a sedate buggy ride once the sun was lower and the heat just a simmer instead of a scorch. Cordelia held the parasol high, the jolt and rattle of the wheels and the steady plod of the horse reminding her of the youthful days she would never see again.

'See what I see?' mumbled Wal.

Cordelia followed his pointing finger and smiled. John Jay and Beatty were emerging from a stand of trees, their horses led by their reins as they slowly walked into the sunlight. They seemed oblivious to everything but each other. 'Good to see a long-standing marriage still working. Reckon the old place still has its uses,' she murmured. 'Remember how we used to sneak off for a little while alone?'

Wal grinned and nodded. 'Reckon not much has changed, Cordy,' he drawled. 'Cept we never did nothing to frighten the horses – more's the pity.'

She poked him with her parasol. 'Watch what you say, you old larrikin,' she teased. 'I've got a reputation to think of.'

'Ha,' he barked. 'Bit late for that.' He turned and eyed her, his gaze bright with mischief. 'Unless you wanna do something about it, old girl?'

'Wal!' she gasped through the laughter. 'Have you taken leave of your senses? We're both ninety years old – it would finish us off.'

He grinned. 'Yeah, but what a beaut way to go, eh?'

Cordelia chuckled. 'Just you keep your mind on the horse and your hands on the reins,' she scolded softly. 'My word, anyone would think we were their age,' she added nodding towards the two middle-aged silhouettes on the homestead skyline.

'We are, in our hearts and minds, Cordy,' he said as he flicked the reins and urged the horse into a gentle trot. 'Under this decrepit old body beats the heart of a youngster, and I know it's the same for you. Bloody old age – it's a flamin' nuisance.'

'Too right,' she agreed, 'But old age brings a certain peace, Wal. We don't have to prove ourselves any more – our life's achievements have done that.' She looked wistfully into the distance, knowing Wal understood she would have liked to consummate the love they'd shared for seventy years. Too late, she thought – how painful those words were – how many shadows they cast.

412

The echoes of Rose and John seemed to follow those shadows, and as she leaned against Wal, Cordelia's thoughts drifted back to another time and place.

The ship had taken on water as it ploughed through the titanic seas off Cape Horn, but John had not been one of those to take to his bed sick and feverish from the heaving of the timbers. He strode the decks, impatient to see the first glimpse of the land he would make his home, the salt wind lashing his face, ripping through his hair, tearing at his clothes. He laughed with the sheer joy of being alive and free as the sails slapped in the ratlines and the wooden deck shuddered beneath his feet.

A small hand crept into his and, startled, he turned to find himself looking into familiar dark eyes and a wan face. 'What the hell are you doing here?' he demanded.

'Trying not to be sick,' Tina replied. 'How much longer is it going to be like this?'

'Until we round the Horn,' he snapped, shaking off her clinging fingers. 'I told you to go back to the family, Tina. Why are you here?'

'I decided I wanted to see Australia for myself,' she shouted, her words snatched by the wind. 'There's nothing for me back in England.'

John looked down at her, his anger so great he could barely speak. He turned away and, with his hands clenched around the rails, stared out over mountainous seas. 'I left England to find Rose,' he said eventually. 'And, by God, when I do, I'm going to make her my wife. You've come all this way for nothing,' he shouted above the wind. 'You'd do better to get off at the next port and go home.'

'Fine,' she yelled back. 'But until you find your precious Rose, I'm travelling with you. I've just as much right to a new life, and I'm staying put.'

John saw the gleam of determination in her eyes and couldn't help but admire her courage. If the green tinge to her skin was anything to go by, she wasn't finding the trip easy, but her slender figure swayed to the rhythm of the ship as she set her feet squarely on the deck, and her hands clutched the railings with a grip that showed her strength.

'Do as you please,' he said gruffly. 'But I don't want to see you until we make port.'

She yanked the thick shawl more firmly around her shoulders. 'I've got better things to do than hang on to your coat-tails, Mister High and Mighty,' she retorted. 'I'm making a fortune amongst the *gadjikanes*. They love the idea of a *drabarni* telling them their fortune and it only costs me a few pennies to bribe the sailors to look the other way.'

John watched as she stalked unsteadily down the deck. He had to smile. Tina had a lot of spirit for one so slight.

The journey seemed to take forever but as soon as they docked John began to ask questions of the shop-keepers and merchants clustered around the quay. The heat was fierce after the freezing rain-storms they'd come through and he was almost blinded by the glare of the sun on the water. Yet he was too anxious for word of Rose and Lady Fitzallan to notice the bright birds and the bustling energy of this burgeoning town.

They spent a week in Sydney town before John finally had enough information to make a journey into the hinterland. He bought three horses and a wagon and several guineas' worth of supplies to tide them over for the long trek. As he waited for the merchants to load his barrels and sacks, he realised that here was an opportunity to make money. After questioning the merchants more closely, he ordered extra supplies and another flat-bed wagon to carry them, two more horses to pull it with another pair so he could interchange them.

Tina sat in docile silence on the buck-board of the first wagon, her dark eyes following him as her fingers idly jingled the coins in her hidden pocket. 'What do you want that lot for?' she demanded, tilting her head at the sacks of grain and seed and the barrels of lamp oil and rum he was adding to the collection of tools and rope and boxes of nails already lashed beneath the wagon's tarpaulin.

He put a finger to his lips and winked. Tina had to stifle her curiosity until they had left the city far behind them. 'This is a big country,' he confided eventually. 'Some say three, maybe four or five times bigger than home, with people living hundreds of miles from the nearest town. I can sell those stores at a good profit which will buy more the next time.'

'Once a *rom*, always a *rom*,' she teased. '*Puri daj* would be proud to know you're keeping up the traditions.'

They travelled for months along the winding dirt tracks that led into the throbbing heartland of their new country, and although he wished it was Rose who held the reins on the following wagon, John was glad of Tina's company. For this was a lonely, almost desolate place, and a man needed someone to talk to.

Their stock dwindled as they sold it to housewives who greeted them in the doorways of hovels that had been thrown together in the middle of nowhere, to diggers in the rough male world of the mining camps, and to the squatters on the endless grazing pastures that lay beyond the mountains.

With money in his pocket, and the knowledge that his kind were welcome in this hot red country, John began to make plans. He would set up his own store in Sydney town, buying directly from the farms and the incoming ships, then employ other men to take his supplies to the outback stations and isolated mining camps.

But first he had to find Rose and she was proving elusive. The Mission House had burned down, the town was deserted and there were only rumours of Lady Fitzallan having moved to the Hunter Valley.

They returned to Sydney and restocked. He knew what the women wanted, stuck so far from civilisation, and he got Tina to choose bales of material and fancy hats and parasols to stow alongside the picks and shovels, axes and nails. His respect for her tenacious courage deepened as they travelled the lonely tracks together.

The people in the Hunter were little help. Rose

had simply disappeared. John's spirits were low as they returned once more to Sydney before setting out for the interior. The months had turned into a year and there was still no sign of her. His travels had shown him he'd set himself an impossible task. This was indeed a big country, and he knew that beyond the mountains and deserts there lay many thousands of miles he might never see.

Rose was in his heart, but eventually he turned to Tina for comfort one dark night on the wallaby tracks when he'd had too much rum and was convinced he would never find his lost love.

He awoke the next morning, the canvas of the make-shift tent damp with condensation as the sun burned low in the sky and the earth warmed. He looked across at the sleeping Tina, and felt only a few regrets. She might not be Rose but there were similarities between them, he realised. Tina was loyal and strong, with a will that bowed to no man. He was indeed fortunate to have her – even if she didn't fill every corner of his heart.

Tina opened her eyes, the love for him shining so clearly it stirred something in him he'd thought belonged to another. He bent his head and kissed her, breathing in the musky scent of her hair, hearing the tinkle of her bracelets sliding along her arms as she embraced him.

'There can be no *pliashka*, no *tumnimos* or *zheita*,' he warned her softly.

'I don't need an engagement feast or wedding arrangements, and as for bringing the bride home – my house is where you are. My home is here.'

She put her small hand on his chest and rested it just above his heart, and he buried his face in her neck so she couldn't see the shame in his eyes.

20

Rose smiled as Isobel's eldest son Henry kissed her cheek and rushed from the room. He had the good looks of his father, but thankfully none of his character flaws. He would make a good husband for her troublesome daughter Muriel.

She sighed as she stared out of the window of the bluestone house. Muriel's red hair matched her fiery nature. She was popular amongst the young sons of their neighbouring vintners, and her scandalous behaviour in the tightly knit Lutheran community had already caused Rose and Isobel sleepless nights. Unlike Emily, her twin, Muriel seemed to have no regard for the sensibilities of others, with her late-night buggy rides, her flirting and wild dancing at the country fairs – perhaps the rather staid, shy Henry would be a calming influence. He had always loved her, but had bided his time, waiting for the moment Muriel noticed him.

Isobel came bustling into the room. Her brown hair was streaked with grey now and her slender waist had thickened, but there was no mistaking her breeding despite the cheap cotton dress and work-worn hands. 'Well?' she asked.

Rose nodded. 'We're going to have a wedding,' she said.

Isobel frowned. I do hope this isn't another of Muriel's hasty passions,' she said wearily. 'Henry does love her so, I wouldn't want him hurt.'

Rose put her hand on Isobel's arm. She had no illusions about her daughter but firmly believed marriage to Henry would turn her from a larrikin into a poised and happy woman. 'They are mature enough to know their minds.'

Isobel smiled. 'I'm glad our two families are to be formally united,' she said. 'But I must be honest with you, Rose. I thought Henry and Emily would make the match. They're both so quiet, so involved in the wine business – and they spend a great deal of time together. I often wondered if Emily's feelings went deeper than friendship.'

Rose pushed her own doubts aside. Emily might be quiet but behind those dark, smouldering eyes was a determined young woman – if she'd wanted Henry, then she would have had him.

With their arms linked, the two middle-aged women left the house and strolled in the warm breeze through the whispering jacaranda trees. It was an evening ritual begun almost fifteen years ago and they enjoyed the chance to discuss the day and plan tomorrow.

The tobacco crop had been increased to cover them in the bad years and now a vast drying shed for the leaves stood at the southern end of home paddock where they hung throughout the hot summer before they were graded and packed for the long journey by sea to Europe.

The vegetable plot had flourished. Most of the produce was carried to market in Nuriootpa where the diggers from the copper mines of Kapunda came to restock their supplies. From this same market, the women bought material and sewing thread, pots and pans, and all the things that would make the bluestone house a home.

The vines were strung in low, dark green lines. Planted close together, each terrace was about eight and a half feet apart to make hand-picking easier. The quality of the grapes was improving with every year that passed, but none of the vines had yet reached the great age of seventy when, they were reliably informed, the grapes would be at their best.

Their distant neighbour, the German settler, Johann Gramp, could speak twelve languages and had been the first to see the potential of this wonderful wine-growing area once it had been surveyed by Lord Lynadock back in the 'thirties. It was his money that had paid for his fellow countrymen to travel to the valley and settle there. Most of the small towns that had sprung up in the area had German names that twisted the tongue far more than the aboriginal ones.

Gramp's vineyard at Jacob's Creek was one of the best and most successful in the valley yet he had time for everyone involved in the business of grape-growing and his expert knowledge and cheerful advice had helped the two women store and bottle their wine to its best advantage.

Having sent a wagon to Adelaide to import labour from amongst the idle seamen, Rose and

Isobel had giant stone vats built to store their wine. These vats were lined with paraffin wax to seal the walls and make them cool in even the hottest of summers, and when it was time to scour them before the next harvest, the paraffin was burned off and reapplied. For the barrels, they used oak imported from Europe for the red wine, when they could afford it, or jarra hardwood from Australia when they couldn't. Port and sherry could be stored in warm rooms to help it mature, but as the port took at least four years to mature it was an expensive capital investment as well as time-consuming. Each barrel and each bottle had to be hand stacked in dark tunnels beneath the earth, and turned regularly until it was ready to be taken down to Adelaide.

The harvest in that year of 1871 was the best yet, and now the Barossa Valley vintage was over, the wine festival was in full swing. Rose and Isobel stood on the verandah of Nuriootpa's feed store and watched the procession march through town to the accompaniment of a brass band. The long months of uncertainty were over, the grapes pressed and in the storage tanks. With the account books at last showing more black than red, they could begin to plan Henry and Muriel's wedding for the following summer.

Rose put her hands to her ears as the trumpets sounded off key and the big brass drum thundered out the beat. 'You'd think they'd have learned to play the flamin' things by now – they've had enough years' practice,' she shouted above the racket.

Isobel shaded her eyes and pointed towards the

rear of the parade. 'Look, Rose. Don't they make you feel proud?'

Rose smiled as she saw Emily and Muriel riding sidesaddle for once, their smart black riding habits draped most fetchingly over the horses' rumps. The animals' coats gleamed in the sun after hours of grooming early this morning and they seemed to relish being the centre of attention, picking up their hoofs and high-stepping to the music. There were ribbons plaited in their manes and tails, and the girls rode with their heads high, the impertinent little hats tilted at a rakish angle over their brows. At their sides rode the two handsome young men, Henry and Clive, their grins broad, their skittish horses held firmly in line.

'They make a pretty picture, don't they?' murmured Rose. 'Wouldn't it be wonderful if...' Her voice faded into silence as the cavalcade rose past.

'I know what you're thinking, Rose, but Clive and Emily are happy to remain just friends,' said Isobel comfortably. 'I wouldn't want either of them to compromise their future by making the same mistake I did. There were too many years of regret afterwards.'

Rose hardly heard her for something had caught her eye. She peered through the cloud of dust that had been lifted by the marching feet and trampling hoofs, trying to catch sight of it again. Yet she hoped her eyes had deceived her. Hoped the past hadn't caught up with her after all these years – and she would be made to face it.

The small outback town was crowded with

vintners and pickers, field hands and growers, merchants and sightseers, and as the dust settled, they began to climb back on their horses and buggies and head for Jacob's Creek pasture where the pig roast had been laid on with plenty of wine and beer to see them through the rest of the day and into the night.

Rose was barely aware of Isobel chattering at her side as she caught glimpses through the crowd of the figures on the other boardwalk, deaf to everything but the thunderous pounding of the blood in her ears and the pulse in her throat.

'Rose?' A hand tugged at her arm. 'Rose, whatever is it? You've gone quite white.'

She eased away from Isobel and, with her skirts lifted out of the dust, slowly descended the wooden steps to the street. The heat shimmered and danced on the wooden peg tiles of the roofs. The bull dust sifted with the wind along the wide well-trodden track that ran through town. The distant discord of the brass band was displaced by the chattering of a flock of budgies – but she had eyes for only one thing, ears for only one sound, mind tuned to only one person.

He turned as if he'd heard her silent call. His eyes found hers as if he'd been drawn by the same magnet that pulled her towards him.

They met in the middle of the street that was wide enough to turn a bullock cart, the sun beating down from an almost washed-out sky. It was as if the world had spun away from them and no one else existed.

'John?' she breathed. 'Is it really you?'

'Rose. My dearest, sweetest Rose. I can't

423

believe it's you at last.' His hands reached for hers and they stood in awed silence in the middle of that outback town, oblivious to everything around them as they drank in the sight of one another.

Rose noticed how he'd changed. Gone was the carefree boy and in his place stood a man with wings of grey in his long hair and a dashing moustache covering his lip. He was still wiry beneath that prosperous suit, the shoulders firm, the legs tapered and straight. But his eyes hadn't changed. They still looked down at her with love. Were still dark and long-lashed, with a depth that seemed to encompass her and draw her to him.

'I can't believe you're here,' she said finally, drawing her hands away from his clasp. She felt suddenly awkward, aware of Isobel's stare and that of the woman on the far boardwalk who watched them with barely concealed animosity.

'Rose,' he breathed. 'Do you know how long I've been looking for you? Do you have any idea of how long I waited to find you?'

She took a step back. 'I've been in this country for over twenty-five years,' she stammered as all the old feelings returned. 'I never expected to see you again. Never dreamed you would follow me.'

He sighed. 'And now it's too late,' he said, his glance taking in his wedding ring, and the one on her finger. 'Do you love him, Rose? Does he make you happy?'

There was no point in telling him she was a widow. She nodded, the tears making it difficult to focus on his face. Such a strong face, so filled with painful regret. 'But I never loved anyone as much as I loved you – you were always in my heart,' she whispered.

'Aren't you going to introduce us then?'

The sharp voice made them draw away from each other and Rose's glance was caught and held by inquisitive black eyes as the woman tucked a possessive hand into the crook of John's arm.

'This is my wife Tina,' said John. 'Tina, this is Rose.'

Rose took in the rich cloth of her dress and the creamy lace of her parasol and gloves. Tina was as dark as her husband with the same Romany look around her high cheekbones. Rose thought she could remember her as a young girl running through the hay during harvest. She nodded in acknowledgement and received a curious scrutiny in return.

'Max is waiting, John. He wants to drive us to the picnic.' Tina tugged lightly on his arm.

John's reluctance to go with his wife was obvious in the set of his mouth and the lowering of his brows. 'I have four sons,' he said as if stalling for more time in Rose's company. 'But only Max and my daughter Teresa are with us today. The other three are looking after my business interests in Adelaide.'

'And what business is that, John?' Her voice was steady, her tone politely interested, but inside Rose was in turmoil. She was longing to have him to herself so they could catch up on the stolen years – longed to drink in the sight and sound of him once again before they were torn apart again.

'We have one of the largest merchant warehouses in Adelaide, with another in Sydney and one in Melbourne,' interrupted Tina proudly. 'We supply most of these outback towns as well as the cattle and sheep stations further north, and at the end of the year we'll be opening our first emporium in Adelaide. It's the reason we're here: to select wines. But of course the stock must be the finest as our customers will come from the highest in society,' she finished with a sharp look at the home-made dress and hat Rose was wearing.

Rose smiled, not at all put out by the other woman's cattiness. 'I'm glad you've been so successful,' she murmured as Isobel came across the road to join them.

With the introductions made, the women declined the offer of a ride in the buggy to the picnic fields and watched as it bowled past them. Rose noticed how John looked at her as she stood on the side of that dusty road in the searing heat. Saw how his son Max was the image of the young boy John had once been, and her pulse thudded as all the memories of her childhood returned. She knew from that one glance John would somehow find a way for them to be alone – and she wanted it to be so – yet she dreaded the moment for time had moved on and they could never hope to recapture what they'd once felt. No longer had the right to love each other.

Isobel too was strangely silent as they made their way down the street towards the celebrations.

The vintners of the Barossa knew how to celebrate. Jacob's Creek glittered in the sun as blankets and baskets were spread over the lush green grass beneath the drooping trees. A section had been fenced off for the wood-cutting competition, and in the distance a rough race course was set out through the bush and up the lower slopes of Mount Kaiserstuhl. Tables groaned with food and wine, and casks of beer had been set up in a canvas marquee. The celebrations would last well into the dawn of the next morning, the night lit by braziers of hot coals and lanterns hanging from the trees.

Rose and Isobel rolled up their sleeves and were soon hard pressed to serve the food and wine, but when Rose paused to catch her breath, she noticed Emily and Max sitting too close together on the grass, dark heads almost touching like conspirators.

She frowned as her gaze swept over them. This was a complication she had not foreseen. Perhaps she should say something – but what? As she stood there in an agony of indecision, they were joined by Muriel and Henry and Clive, who seemed equally interested in Teresa as Emily obviously was in Max. She eyed them all and bit her lip. What a pretty mess of things, she thought crossly.

She took a deep breath and told herself she was making a mountain out of a mole-hill. They were just youngsters having fun after the long summer's work – not so different from her younger days when a little harmless flirting just added to the excitement. Besides, she thought,

John wouldn't be staying in the Barossa. He had business in Adelaide, and that wife of his wouldn't let him hang around a minute longer than necessary.

The blast of a trumpet made her jump. It was a signal for the wood-cutters to take their places for the competition. She pulled off her apron and rolled down her sleeves. Henry and Clive were competing again this year and both hoped to bring back yet another trophy.

Isobel joined her. They stood behind the rope boundary and watched the men prepare for battle. A cheer went up as the six competitors for the first trial entered the ring. The dark good looks of the long-haired stranger caused a murmur of approval amongst the young girls and Rose watched wide-eyed as he stripped off his shirt and flexed the muscles in his back and shoulders. Max was the image of his father, the sight of him almost too much for her to bear.

She glanced across at Emily. Her daughter was standing on the far side of the enclosure, her gaze fixed on Max as he tied his hair in the same way his father used to, her lips parted, the colour high in her cheeks. Muriel stood by her side, her expression inscrutable to all but her mother. Rose felt a twinge of fear. She'd seen that look before, and she knew it heralded trouble.

Unable to get to them through the press of bystanders, Rose had to be content. She was imagining things, she told herself firmly. Of course both girls were watching Max so keenly, so were most of the others – much to the disgust of the young men around them.

The selected trees had been marked with chalk. As the six men approached them, the sun glinted on the blades of the sharp axes they carried. At the blast of the trumpet, each man swung his axe and it thudded into the trunk, the vibration of that strike trembling through muscled arms. With a pull of strong shoulders and a gleam of sweat, the axes were plunged at speed into the thick wood, splintering bark, making it fly. When the deep triangular cut had been made on one side of the trunk, the men ran to the other side and began again.

The axes rang out. The chips of wood flew past naked shoulders and glistening arms and the crowd roared them on.

Max and Henry were neck and neck, their trees already groaning as they swayed on severed trunks. One last cut each and they stepped back. The crowd held its breath. The trees rocked, the leaves shuffling and falling. Then with a ponderous, almost graceful bow, they leaned towards the earth. Gathering speed, and with a rush of dust and debris, they hit the ground with a thud, and Max and Henry danced nimbly out of the way of snaring branches and the whiplash of leaves. The crowd waited. The judge took the two young men by the hand and raised them both. It was a tie.

Isobel laughed as Max was swamped by his admirers, but Rose saw the way Emily was pushing through them, sharp elbows digging into ribs, feet trampling to get to his side. Noticed how Max laughed down at her and planted a kiss on her cheek as his arm encircled her waist.

'Looks like Emily's got an admirer,' said Isobel quietly.

Rose glowered. 'She's behaving outrageously,' she muttered. 'I'm going to have strong words to say to that young lady when I get her home.'

Isobel raised an eyebrow. 'Taking after her sister,' she murmured, her frown drawing her brows together. Her glance was sharp. 'You're not still in love with John, are you? This isn't bringing it all back, is it?'

'Don't be silly,' she snapped, aware Isobel was probably right. The years had rolled back and she could remember all too well how she'd felt about John – now it seemed her daughter was going down the same road and seeing them together was just too painful.

Rose's voice was tight. 'Muriel's behaviour's bad enough and now Emily's making an exhibition of herself. You know what these German Lutherans are like – we'll never hear the end of it.'

The trumpet blast sounded again and the crowd left the enclosure to the competitors. The great trunks lay on their sides now, the branches hacked off for ease of cutting. Once again Max and Isobel's two sons stepped into the ring to join the others, the long serrated saws dangling from their hands. Wagers flew and money changed hands. Max was favourite after his previous display. Both women could see how Clive and Henry glowered at the newcomer. This was their competition and he was stealing their glory.

The crowd hushed as the men rested their saws

on the rough bark and waited. The trumpet blew and the first rasp filled the clearing. Arms pumped and hair fell over sweaty brows as the lightning flash of steel ripped through wood. Henry's face was dark with determination, his brows coming together in a line of concentration. Clive worked beside him on another log, his mouth grim, his fair hair slicked on his brow. Max wielded the saw with an almost effortless, smooth motion that cut through the wood like a hot knife through butter.

The crowd groaned as Henry's saw became stuck and he fought to release it. Max and Clive speeded up, and the two men stepped back. But it was Max who'd finished first. Max who would collect the trophy.

Rose turned away as the girls once again stormed the arena. She could no longer bear to watch.

It was peaceful away from the arena. Rose ambled down to the creek, her long skirts swishing in the lush grass. When she was far enough from the others, she found a cool, shady spot beneath a pepper tree, discarded her bonnet and sat down. Pulling off her boots and stockings she paddled her feet in the water, watching how the ripples caught the sunlight and startled the tiny fish that swam over the rounded stones.

'I remember you doing that back at Alfriston,' John said softly as he came to sit beside her. 'Seems strange having the past come alive in the present. It's as if there've been no intervening years at all.'

Rose looked at him. His presence hadn't

startled her. She knew he'd been watching her and would find a way to be with her. 'The past is another country, John,' she said sadly. 'A country where we were young and society had different rules. It won't do either of us any good to try and revisit it.'

There was a long silence as they both stared into the shimmering water. 'I should have come for you earlier,' he finally murmured. 'I had the money. But I was greedy. I wanted more. Wanted to have enough to give you all the things you never had.'

She blinked away the tears. 'The sun on the water's blinding, isn't it?' she said hastily, wiping her eyes.

John's warm hand rested on her fingers. 'Why did you run away, Rose? Why, when you knew I'd come back for you?'

She snatched her hand away. 'I didn't know,' she retorted. 'You never told me how you felt. Never said you'd be off to London for months without a word. How was I supposed to know your mind?'

He stroked his moustache thoughtfully. 'I suppose I thought you'd know by the way I was with you,' he said finally. 'I was never much for soft talk, Rose. I didn't think we needed words when we were so close.'

She pulled on her boots and stuffed her stockings into her pocket. She stood up and brushed grass from her skirt. 'You've always been in my thoughts,' she said softly. 'Tucked away in the deepest, most secret part of me. But we're different now, grown up, mature, with families of our own who are ready to spread their wings. Don't destroy that, John.'

He stood and rammed the soft felt hat on his head. His eyes were fathomless in that strong brown face as he looked down at her. 'Destroy? I have no wish to destroy anything,' he said softly. 'I love you, Rose. I have always loved you.'

Rose closed her eyes as she swayed towards him. The heat of the earth, the whisper of the pale green fronds of the pepper tree and the lazy hum of the flies all seemed to come together in an enticing serenade. She felt his arms enfold her. It was as if she'd stepped into an enclosed magic world.

His lips brushed her cheek. She could smell the tang of his soap and the oils in his hair. Familiar scents she'd carried with her on the long, frightening journey to these distant shores. Familiar memories she'd tried so hard to banish.

She tore away from his embrace, stumbling in the long grass, the horror of what she was doing draining the colour from her face. 'We mustn't do this,' she gasped. 'It's wrong.'

He grasped her arms. 'How can it be wrong, Rose, when we both know we were meant for one another?'

She wrenched away from him. 'You have a wife, children, a business,' she gasped. 'Of course it's wrong. It's too late, John. Much too late.'

His eyes were bright with unshed tears as he turned abruptly away. 'Too late,' he repeated, his voice cracked with emotion. 'They have to be the saddest words known to man.'

Rose took a step back, and another. Then, not

433

wanting to prolong the agony, she turned and ran back to the picnic field. She needed to have people around her – needed the distraction of noise and colour to blot out the sadness. Needed time to gather her wits.

The hours and days moved on once the festival was over and the people of the Barossa settled back into the timeless round of clearing, planting, hoeing and watering. Wine from previous vintages was sold in the cities and sent by ship to Europe to make way for the new. The storage tanks were drained, the wax burned off and cleaned in preparation for the next year, and, to Rose's consternation, John Tanner and his family rented rooms in Langmeil's one and only hotel and looked like staying for a while.

Max was a regular visitor to Jacaranda, and although there had been a certain amount of animosity between him and Isobel's sons at first, they soon came to accept him and the interest he took in the vineyard and the wine-making. Day after day he followed them along the terraces, helping to erect wind breaks, learning of the different grapes and the wines they made. He wandered for hours in the cellars, sniffing the sour, rich scent of the fermenting grapes as the process was explained, testing the quality of the wine, checking for too much acidity or too little – looking for the aftertaste that would declare the wine too raw for the cellars of the rich settlers and the European palate.

Rose watched the burgeoning friendship between Isobel's sons and Max and was pleased to see what a quick study the young man was. One day he would make a fine vintner, she realised, for he had an innate talent for knowing the right time to bottle the wine.

Yet she was disturbed by Emily's interest in him. Disturbed to discover the number of times the girl would slip away to the terraces and fields on the pretence of taking the boys their lunch. Max would soon move back to Adelaide with his parents and his sister, and although he and Emily seemed happy in each other's company, she fretted that her daughter was seeing more in the relationship than he did.

Two months passed and Rose received word from John. They would soon be returning to Adelaide. Although she had done her best to avoid further contact, she felt relieved at the thought of not bumping into him unexpectedly again. They had said all they needed to one another. She would have appreciated his friendship but she knew it would have been impossible. Their feelings were still too strong.

The morning of his departure dawned and Rose climbed out of bed and drew back the curtains. The sky was overcast, heavily laden with the promise of rain. Not a good day to travel. She washed and dressed and hurried along the landing to the girls' bedroom. There was a great deal to do in the fields today, and she wanted to make an early start so she wouldn't have too much time to think about John's leaving.

With a sharp rap to announce her entry, she opened the door. Emily stirred, her dark hair spread over the pillows, her eyes bleary from sleep. Rose eyed the other bed. 'Where's Muriel?' she asked sharply. It was most unlike the girl to get up so early – and she'd made her own bed too. A real first.

Emily yawned and eyed her sister's bed as she scraped her hair back from her face. She grimaced. 'Must have gone out early with Henry,' she mumbled. 'They were planning to finish those windbreaks today before the rain set in.'

Rose felt uneasy, but said nothing. 'Hurry up, Emily. Breakfast will be getting cold.' She closed the door behind her, and after a moment's thought, crossed the landing and stood outside the boys' bedroom. With a tentative knock, she opened the door a crack and called through it. 'Henry? Are you there?'

'Yeah?' came the sleepy response. 'Whassa-matter?'

'Henry?' Rose pushed the door open and stepped into the room.

His tousled head appeared over the sheet as Clive carried on snoring in the other bed. 'Have we slept late, Aunt Rose?'

Rose shook her head. 'But breakfast's ready. And there's a lot to do today – looks like rain.' There was no point in worrying him, she was just being silly to think he might have a reason to. She shut the door firmly and hurried downstairs.

The cook was the wife of a free settler who worked his own land in the evening after a day in the fields on Jacaranda. She slammed the metal plate back on the range and hoisted the kettle of water over the heat, her round face already

436

sweating from the heat in the kitchen.

'Have you seen Muriel, this morning, Agnes?'

'No. But I'm missing a side of mutton, some cheese and bread and half of that fruit cake I baked yesterday,' she grumbled as she broke eggs into a vast iron pan. 'And I reckon even Clive and Henry ain't got an appetite big enough for that lot. Looks like we've had a visitor wot don't like making hisself heard or seen.'

Rose touched her shoulder as she passed on the way to the back door. A rapid search of the barns revealed the absence of Muriel's horse, but there was no sign of her on the terraces or out in the pastures.

She returned to the house, suspicions clamouring as she again climbed the stairs to the twins' bedroom. Ignoring Emily's protests and questions, she flung open the drawers. Then in bitter silence she drew back the curtain that hung in front of the girls' dresses. Every stitch of clothing Muriel possessed was gone. Rose slumped down on the bed and buried her face in her hands.

'What is it, Mama?' Emily asked tremulously.

Rose scrubbed her face and looked at her beautiful, dark-haired daughter. 'I don't know, Emily,' she replied honestly. 'But I have my suspicions.'

'Perhaps she and Henry have run off together,' said the girl hopefully. 'Muriel always thought elopement such a romantic thing to do.'

Rose's expression was as grim as her thoughts. 'Henry's still in his bed. Wherever your sister's gone, it isn't with him.'

Emily sank on to the bed, the colour drained from her face. 'You don't think...?'

She didn't finish the sentence – didn't have to – Rose was way ahead of her.

'But she wouldn't,' Emily breathed. 'Not even Muriel would do that. Would she?' The dark eyes were wide, the shadows of fear already noticeable.

Rose stood up. 'I don't know,' she said firmly. 'But I am going to find out.'

She was halfway down the stairs when she heard the thudding approach of hoofs on the dirt track outside. Hurrying to the door, her spirits plunged. For there was John astride a foaming gelding, waving a sheaf of paper in his hand.

'I found this,' he panted as he leaped from the saddle. 'I came as soon as I could.'

Rose scanned the hastily written note, then crumpled it in her hand. 'How dare they?' she breathed. 'How dare they do this to Emily?' Anger surged and she threw the crumpled note in John's face. 'You should have stopped him,' she yelled. 'Should have taught him better than to run off with my daughter. She's engaged to be married. It was Emily who was in love with him.' The tears of rage ran down her cheeks unchecked.

'We didn't know,' he said helplessly. 'How could we? We thought he was just visiting here so he could learn the wine business. Besides, I thought it was Emily he was courting, not her sister.' He fell silent, his hands awkwardly at his sides as he tried to think of a way of appeasing Rose.

Isobel came out on to the verandah. 'He was,' she hissed. 'Making eyes at her, leading her on to think he felt something for her, even though I did everything I could to break it up.'

John frowned as he looked into her furious face. 'Break it up? Why? I was delighted to think our children might find happiness together. It's too late for me and Rose but the next generation would have brought us all closer.' He was uneasy at the sheer venom of her attack. He hadn't realised Isobel disliked his son.

'Isobel?' Rose's voice was hesitant. 'Why are you so against Max? I know he and Muriel have done wrong to run away like this and leave Emily and Henry heartbroken, but...'

'Don't spout all that romantic nonsense to me,' she shouted. 'It was always too late for you and Rose – it was never possible.'

She came to an abrupt halt as they stared at her in confusion. Frightened, Rose grabbed her arms and shook her. 'What are you saying, Isobel? What's the matter? Why are you talking like this?'

Isobel's face had lost all colour but she maintained an electric silence that sent shivers down their backs.

Rose shook her again, her voice icy with calm. 'What did you mean, Isobel when you said it was never possible?'

She tore away from Rose and sought shelter at the far end of the verandah. They let her go, helpless in the face of her strength of feeling, confused and fearful of the things she was finding so hard to say. They watched as she folded her arms around her waist, and knew she was trying to bury some deep anguish that was threatening to break her.

'There's no easy way to tell you,' she whispered finally. 'No kind way to break your hearts.' She looked back at them then, her eyes awash with tears, dark with pain.

John reached for Rose's hand and grasped it tightly. He shivered as if the ghosts of his ancestors touched him. 'What is it, Isobel? For God's sake, tell us,' he whispered fearfully.

'There's a curse on any union made between the Tanners and the Fullers.'

The words knifed through him as Rose gave a sharp little cry of anguish and stumbled against him. 'No,' he whispered in agony. 'Please tell me this isn't true? It can't be. I'd have known. *Puri daj* would have told me.'

'It was your precious *puri daj* who encouraged your mother to put the curse in place,' Isobel spat. 'And although I've always believed the whole thing to be nonsense, your turning up here, and this betrayal by your son and Muriel, has made me think again. The curse is all too real.'

'My mother?' he gasped. 'What did she have to do with all this?' John watched as Isobel turned away and knew she couldn't face them. Couldn't bear to see the anguish in their eyes. He had loved Rose so much, had searched for her across the world. Now everything he had ever known was being destroyed – and the pain was unbearable.

'You're lying,' shouted Rose. 'How would you know such a thing?' The grip of John's fingers was the only anchor to reality.

Isobel's muffled voice seemed to be torn from her grieving depths. 'John's father had an affair with your mother, Rose. It was shortly after Davey's accident, and John's mother was dying of the lung infection she never shook off after giving birth to him. Max and your mother were planning to run away – she was expecting his child.'

Rose tore away from John and strode across the verandah. She slapped Isobel hard on the face. 'Liar,' she screamed. 'It's not true. It can't be.'

Isobel stood there unflinching, the marks of Rose's fingers livid on her cheek. 'They were overheard planning their escape by John's mother,' she continued softly. 'It was she who put the curse on any union between the two families. She who could never forgive Max's betrayal and the dishonour he brought to her noble family. The *dukkerin* gave her blessing to that curse, but she didn't have the power to lift it when she saw what was afoot between you and John.'

Rose had lost all colour. 'You're lying,' she whispered. But the dread of belief was already in her eyes.

'Max and your mother tried to forestall the curse by finishing their love affair. Your mother went back to Brendon who forgave her. He was willing to give the child his name, and protect Kathleen from scandal – but it wasn't to be. The baby was born with terrible afflictions and died two days later. The curse was in place, the evidence clear for all to see.'

Silence fell as each thought of the dying woman and the terrible punishment she'd meted out to

441

those who'd betrayed her and brought disgrace and shame to her tribe.

'Your mother confided in my father before she left Wilmington. She'd always planned to go back to Ireland and leave you with us in the hope the curse would go with her and leave you unscathed. Papa wrote me a long letter just before he died, telling me everything. He left it to me to decide whether to tell you or not, and until now there was no need.' She sighed. 'I didn't believe in curses and gypsy warnings – thought the whole thing ridiculous nonsense. But after what's happened here this morning, I fear it is all too real.'

Rose watched stony-faced as the tears ran down the reddened cheek. She was numb.

'I didn't tell you because I love you and think of you as a sister more than a friend,' Isobel sobbed. 'Why hurt you more after your mother left and never wrote again? Why reveal this terrible secret when John was on the other side of the world and you would probably never see one another?' She reached out to Rose, fingers plucking at her sleeve. 'I did what I thought was best. How was I to know what the future held?'

Rose crumpled. There was too much pain in all of them, and she loved Isobel too well not to forgive her her silence.

John looked up at the sky and saw the remnants of the stars still glittering as dawn broke. He felt a chill as he remembered his grandmother's words from so long ago: '"When Orion rules the skies and Gemini is split asunder – then you will know what the fates have in store for you should

442

you ignore my warning"' he murmured through the choking sobs. 'Grandmother tried to warn me, but I refused to listen. But why didn't she just tell me straight?'

Rose hugged her waist as if chilled to the bone. 'Maybe she was frightened by the strength of your mother's powers, ashamed she couldn't take the curse back,' she murmured.

'I can't believe she wouldn't tell me. She knew how much I loved you. Knew I would stop at nothing to find you.'

Rose turned to him, her tears dry, pity for him in her eyes. 'What we have to do now is find them before it's too late,' she said softly. 'They cannot marry, John. The curse could destroy them and any children they might have.'

'And if we don't?' He knew his face was grey, his eyes dull beneath the dark brows.

'That is in the hands of fate,' she said sadly. 'But curse or not, Muriel will not be welcome here after what she's done to her sister and her fiancé.'

There were sightings of the two runaways, but nothing that led to their being found, and it was with a mixture of sorrow and relief that Rose heard John and Tina had eventually returned to Adelaide.

Emily was inconsolable for months, drifting around the house and terraces like a wraith. Henry worked harder than ever, spending night after night poring over the accounts, refusing all advice, locking himself away in his misery. Then, after the first year had passed, he and Emily found consolation in each other and were married in the little Lutheran church that had been built by Jacob's Creek.

Another year passed and still no word from Muriel and Max. Clive made his annual visit to Adelaide with the vintage for the Europe-bound ships and returned with the news that he and John's daughter, Teresa, were to be married the following summer.

Rose and Isobel's friendship was stronger than ever and they greeted this news with relief and happiness. At last John and Rose would be united, if distantly – and she hoped it had made him happy. Yet there were other things on her mind – things that would affect them all.

The weather that year was perfect. The grapes were abundant as they clustered green on the vine waiting for the long warm days to swell and colour them, and Rose and Isobel were looking forward to a record harvest. It would mean hiring extra hands, but so far the rumours the English government would no longer be sending convicts to Australia had come to nothing and cheap labour was still plentiful. But if the convict runs ceased, then the farmers and vintners would see their stock prices rise to cover this unexpected outlay, and it would make it even harder to compete in the world markets.

Then the price of wool dropped without warning. The traditional bidding took place in Cornhill in London by the measure of a lit candle – when it had burned an inch, the bidding closed – and suddenly few voices bid for the wool, the wealth of the colony, and it went for so low a price, it was hardly worth the effort of sending it. The impact was a disaster. It reverberated across the vast sheep runs and the laden bullock drays with their unwanted cargoes. Thousands of hopeful settlers were ruined. Banks failed, sheep were sold for sixpence and farmers despaired, giving away their runs and moving into the towns. Few could afford the price of a mug of beer, let alone a bottle of wine.

The vintners of the Barossa and the Hunter held their breath as they were besieged by gaunt-faced men begging for work. They realised that if the slump continued, the colony would soon be bankrupt. Yet, in one respect, the vintners were luckier than most, for they had wisely grown other crops like tobacco and hops and could store their wine and market it at a more propitious time. For unlike livestock, wine cost nothing to keep and in fact improved with age, but if the slump went on for too long, there were be no money to replant – no money to pay wages.

With every barrel and cask full and the cellars stocked from ceiling to floor, Isobel and Rose looked to their tobacco plantation and waited it out. The Governor of the colony was blamed for everything, as politicians always are, and there was much discussion of his methods of allotting land and reputed convict sympathies. Things got so bad even the drought and the following winter rainstorms appeared to be his fault. Rose and Isobel laughed at the ridiculous need for people to pin the blame on anyone but themselves or the Almighty.

The following winter saw the return of Max

and Muriel. They arrived unannounced late one afternoon in a dust-smeared carriage that was pulled by a matching pair of chestnut mares. Isobel was away for a few days visiting friends. Rose heard the horses and peeked through the net curtains. Her fingers covered her mouth and her eyes widened. As Max helped a heavily expectant Muriel down from the carriage and guided her up the steps to the verandah, Rose could feel nothing but disgust for what they had done to Emily and Henry. She had no wish to speak to them. No wish to see them – but could hardly leave them for all the world to watch on her doorstep.

She snatched the door open, leaving the screen firmly between them. 'What do you want?' she asked coldly.

'I wanted to see you, Mum,' said Muriel softly. 'We're going to have a baby.'

'I can see that,' she snapped. 'You aren't welcome here after the trouble you caused.'

Muriel had the decency to blush, and Rose noticed how Max's protective hand held her waist. 'I know, and we're both sorry, Mum. But it was the only way.'

'It was not,' she declared stoutly. 'You caused your sister to have a breakdown and your fiancé shame. The gossip and rumours kept Isobel and me locked in this house for almost a year.'

'Father told us about the curse, but it was too late by then,' said Max gruffly. 'Despite it I have no regrets about marrying Muriel. As far as I'm concerned, all this nonsense about a curse is just so much Romany tosh.'

'So you defy the laws of your Romany heritage?' she demanded, anger rising at his arrogance. 'Let's pray that the child doesn't carry the mark.'

'Mum, please,' begged Muriel. 'If we could just come in and sit a while. We've travelled a long way and I'm very tired.'

'There's a hotel back in Tanunda,' she said coldly. 'You're not welcome here.'

'But we have nowhere else to go, Mum,' she begged. 'Max has been working as a manager on a vineyard in the west, but the new owners don't need him. I wanted to be with my family when the baby comes... Please don't turn us away.'

Rose saw the tears and the trembling lips and remembered how she'd felt when her own mother rejected her. She relented. 'All right. Come in and rest,' she said wearily. 'But you can stay only a few days. I will not have Emily and Henry upset. They're expecting their second child in a few weeks, and I don't want either of them to see you.'

'I wish she could forgive me,' murmured Muriel as she took off her hat and gloves and sank into the soft upholstery of the parlour chair.

Rose looked down at her, and for the first time realised how difficult it must have been for her proud, rash daughter to have made this journey. 'She will never forgive you, Muriel,' she said softly. 'You hurt her too badly. But if you're willing, you can move out to the Hunter Valley and take over from Hans. He's ready to retire and I need someone I can trust to run Coolabah Creek.'

Their faces lit up with excitement and hope. 'Does this mean you'll forgive me, Mum?' breathed Muriel.

Rose's heart ached for her. 'You are my daughter and I will always love you. But I find it hard to forget what you did to the others. If you wish to take up the offer of Coolabah Creek, then consider it done. But don't expect to heal the rift with your sister. It's too deep.'

21

Sophie returned the long letter to the envelope, the tears drying on her face as the sky lightened and the magpies began to chortle. Poor Isobel, she thought. To have carried the burden of that secret for so long, only to have to expose it so cruelly. No wonder the rift was never healed.

She returned to the red lacquer box and sifted through the neatly bound papers, some of which were yellow with age. It was then that she finally understood the power Cordelia possessed to turn things around for Jacaranda Vines. This journey had been a homecoming for her grandmother, a chance to heal the damage done so long ago and rise phoenix-like from the ashes. Yet it had also been a rite of passage for Sophie – for now she had an inkling of the plan in Cordelia's head. Understood why it had been necessary for her to come here.

She threw back the sheet and clambered out of

bed. There was a vitality in her this morning that couldn't be dulled by lack of sleep, and she was really looking forward to the board meeting.

But first it was the beginning of harvest. The reaping of what they had sown – and like this divided family, it was a chance to clear away the old and plant the new. A chance to begin again.

The kitchen was already humming with activity. Beatty was crashing pots and frying bacon as the men stood around drinking strong coffee. The talk was loud, high with expectancy and excitement as they watched the cavalcade of trucks and cars and motorbikes pass the house on the way to the terraces. The last of the pickers were arriving.

Gran was already ensconced at the head of the table, a healthy plate of scrambled eggs and sausage in front of her, and as Sophie planted a kiss on the soft cheek, she received a sly wink. 'Don't look like you slept much. Something on your mind?'

Sophie grinned as she poured coffee and took her place at the table. 'I was up all night reading the letters and going through the documents in that box. It's good to understand the rift, and the background to our divided family, but I'm pleased things are changing. Those documents have given the whole argument over Jacaranda a new perspective. I'll be spending tonight slaving over my computer to put a package together.'

A liver-spotted hand covered her fingers. 'No need, darling. Wal and John Jay and I already have a "package" as you call it, in hand.'

'What is it?'

Cordelia tapped her nose before tucking into her breakfast. 'You'll find out soon enough,' she said enigmatically. 'But there's something far more important for you to put your mind to in the next few days – and I'm not just talking harvest, either.' She nodded towards Jay who had just strolled sleepily into the room. 'That young man's in love with you, and if you can't see that, then you're blind. It's about time you two sorted yourselves out. I can't hang around forever, you know.'

Sophie blushed furiously with anger and embarrassment as silence fell in the kitchen and all eyes turned to her and Jay. If only Gran would learn to keep her opinions to herself, she thought despairingly. *I will not be blackmailed.* She dropped her chin and concentrated on her breakfast. But it might as well have been sawdust for all the taste it had. She was too aware of Jay's presence. Too aware of him watching her from the other side of the table.

With breakfast over, the dirty plates stacked in the sink for later, the family moved out on to the verandah. Cordelia would ride with Wal in the covered buggy and keep a watchful eye on everything. Sophie hopped in the ute next to John Jay and Beatty, leaving the brothers and their wives to travel behind them in their own utilities and cars.

The cavalcade moved slowly along the dirt track, the dust rising from the wheels, masking their surroundings. Expectation was high. There was no sign of rain, the frosts had not come this winter, and although the heat shimmered and

450

danced on the horizon, there were no signs of electric storms or sudden winds.

Far out on the northern side of the terraces stood a low building that squatted along a fold in the hills. The wooden walls and sloping corrugated roof encompassed the sleeping accommodation for those pickers who didn't have their own campers or tents. The accommodation was mostly dormitories, with several rooms put aside for families. There was a kitchen, a row of shower cubicles and dunnies, and a large comfortably furnished room where they could watch television, read or play board games after their long day in the fields.

John Jay drove into the courtyard. Sophie noticed the vast barbecue pit off to one side and the benches and tables that had been set in the lee of the giant pepper tree. The pickers clustered in groups, drinking tea from thick white mugs and munching on the bread and sausages Beatty had brought up earlier.

They all seemed to know one another, Sophie realised as she heard the excited chatter of the women as they renewed old friendships and caught up with the gossip. The men's voices were a low rumble as they stood in their stained and much-worn moleskins, their boots showing the scars of many years' labour. Checked shirts and sweat-stained Akubras seemed to be the uniform, even amongst the teenagers who were joining the group for the first time.

John Jay and his sons strode from one group to the next, laughing and chatting, greeting many of them as old friends – which they were, for Beatty had explained that Coolabah had a tradition of employing the same families year after year, and some of those here today were the third or even fourth generation of pickers.

Cordelia bullied Wal into helping her down from the buggy and settled herself on one of the benches. She was soon in conversation with another elderly woman who looked far too frail to be standing in the hot sun all day.

Sophie began to feel isolated. She knew no one and it had been many years since her last vintage back at Jacaranda so she wasn't sure what was expected of her. Standing slightly off to one side, she watched the crowd shift and re-form before her, the chatter high, the electricity in the air almost tangible.

One of the younger men brought out a mouth organ and began to play a hornpipe. He was soon joined by someone with a penny whistle and the onlookers shifted again into a natural circle and clapped in time as two of the girls did an impromptu dance. Sophie laughed, sharing the fun. What a wonderful way to begin vintage.

The music died and people rammed on hats against the sun's glare and began to move towards the terraces, each carrying a long basket and special secateurs. There was no mechanical picking on Coolabah, for it damaged between ten and thirty percent of the vines over a ten-year period and fewer grapes could be grown.

'Follow me,' said Beatty. 'I'll show you what to do. There's no mystery to it.'

Sophie watched as she cut a cluster of ripe black grapes from the vine and laid it in the basket. 'You won't get much done as it's your first time, but I'd rather you took care not to get sunstroke so rest if you get tired. Forecast's for up to 46 degrees today.' Beatty handed her the secateurs and strode off.

Sophie tugged down the sleeves of her cotton shirt to protect her arms from the sun and rammed the soft felt hat more firmly on her head. She was already sweating and prickly with heat and yet it was only just past seven in the morning. Cupping a cluster of black grapes that were silvery with bloom, she snipped and moved on to the next.

The chatter and snatches of song went on around her as she concentrated on her task. The sun beat down with hammer blows to her head and neck, sweat evaporating as the mercury rose. Jay worked in the terrace above her. Now and again they glanced across and grinned at one another. Sophie eased her back and wiped the sweat from her face as she took a breather and looked around. It was a glorious sight, this land of black soil and dark green vines, the hills mauve and grey, the sky so blue and wide it seemed to encompass their lilliput lives and put things into proper perspective.

The raucous belch of a klaxon heralded tucker break, and Sophie was amazed to see the vast hampers Beatty was unloading from the back of the ute. There was cold chicken and ham, cold mutton, fresh bread and home-made pickles. Tomatoes and cucumbers nestled in boxes of lettuce and there were crates and crates of water and light beer to quench the thirst.

Jay brought a basket to Sophie's terrace and they sat on the warm earth between the two rows of vines. She tipped back a bottle and drank thirstily. It didn't seem as if she'd ever quench the dryness.

'Go easy, Sophie. You'll make yourself sick. Here, take these and keep them by you for when you need them. You'll get through several pints of water before the day's through, but it's better to do it gradually.'

She smiled up at him. 'I'm glad we can be friends,' she said through a mouthful of delicious cold mutton and pickle. 'And I'm glad I've had the chance to work at the sharp end of a vineyard again.'

'This place isn't typical by any means,' he warned thoughtfully. 'Dad's got a good reputation amongst the pickers because he's a fair employer and pays good wages as well as providing food and comfortable accommodation. You should see the state of some of the places these people have to move on to when they leave here. No better than hovels, with no running water or anything.'

Sophie finished the mutton sandwich and took another drink from the bottle. 'I'm surprised he makes a profit after feeding everyone so well,' she remarked as she took an orange and began to peel it.

'Other vintners think he's eccentric but it pays off in the end. We're never short of pickers and these are the best in the business,' he said, looking out towards the others who were finishing their lunches. 'Some of these men and women first came as children, now they bring their own. It's a family thing, I reckon.' His dark eyes looked across at her, holding her gaze.

Sophie wrapped the last of her orange in a paper napkin and tucked it into the breast pocket of her shirt for later. 'Better get on,' she said with a brittle laugh. 'I'm already miles behind everyone else.'

The afternoon sped by as the heat simmered, the flies buzzed and the smell of warm, ripe grapes filled the still air. The chattering never ceased, neither did the singing nor the dirty jokes that flew between the terraces. But Sophie was worn out, with a headache lurking behind her eyes she couldn't shift.

As the sky began to lose its colour and the sun slowly sank behind the hills on that first day of vintage, she wearily climbed back into the utility with Beatty and John Jay and headed for the homestead. She ached in places she didn't know she had and the sun had burned a triangle of skin where her shirt peeked open. There was no way she had enough energy to join the pickers for their barbecue that night.

She almost fell asleep under the shower and had to force herself to remain upright long enough to climb into bed. She was asleep and dreaming of vines and grapes before the others left to join the pickers for their night's celebration.

The week sped past. As Sophie became more used to standing in the sun all day, she began to enjoy it more and take a greater part in the story-telling and singing. Jay made a point of bringing the tucker basket to her and as they shared the cold provisions they began to mend the rift between them.

Yet neither of them mentioned the reason for their breakup and Sophie wondered if perhaps it was better to put it behind them and look forward. She had learned a salutary lesson from those letters – rifts were the death knell to families and relationships if they weren't quickly mended, and now she and Jay were being given a second chance.

It was their final day. The vines had been stripped, the last basket emptied into the back of the lorries that would carry the grapes to the winery. Sophie took off her hat and wiped away the sweat. Her hair was plastered to her head. She unpinned it and shook it loose.

'I'm glad you never had it cut,' said Jay softly. 'It's so beautiful, even when it's tangled and sweaty.'

She turned to face him. Their growing intimacy had made her less scratchy with him. 'Flattery will get you nowhere,' she teased. 'I'm off for a shower and shut-eye before the party tonight. I'm knackered.'

He took her hand, stopping her from walking away. 'There's something you should do first,' he said mysteriously. 'Follow me.'

She held back. 'What are you up to, Jay?' she said warily.

He smiled that slow sensuous smile that still made her insides go weak. 'Nothing crook, I promise.'

She eyed him thoughtfully, decided she was

being over-cautious and smiled. 'As long as it involves something cool,' she said lightly. 'I'm frazzled with heat.'

'Good on ya,' he said, pushing his hat back from his forehead. 'Come on.'

They walked over to one of the utes and climbed in. Minutes later they were eating the dust of the last of the grape lorries. Jay drove into the cobbled courtyard that formed a square between the processing plant, the bottle plant and the visitors' reception area. 'Come on. I'll guarantee it's cool in here.'

Sophie got down from the ute, gave up on trying to brush the dirt from her clothes and sweating face and followed him into the cool shade of the winery's reception area. Their boot heels echoed on the stone floor and up into the cathedral arch of the roof. As she breathed in the perfume of wine and oak barrels, she felt the tension of the past week fall away.

'You've been on Coolabah for nearly three weeks. I reckon it's time you saw the nuts and bolts of the place.'

She heard the soft accusation in his voice and silently admitted he was right. 'I always seemed to be doing something else,' she stammered. 'It wasn't deliberate.'

His eyes were shadowed by the brim of his Akubra as he looked down at her. Then without comment he strode across the reception area and headed for a heavy oak door. 'We're closed to visitors so we won't be disturbed,' he said as he unlocked the door and stepped inside. 'Mind how you go,' he warned. 'It gets slippery.'

Sophie followed him into the long dark tunnel that seemed to wind its way down into the earth. The walls were cold to the touch, the ceiling low with only an intermittent light to show the way on the broad stone steps. She turned the corner and stood in awe at the sight before her.

'Beauty, ain't it?' he said proudly as he lit the candles on top of a battered table.

'Too right,' she breathed as she looked around the vast cavern that had been hacked into the core of the earth. The ceiling was high, the floor and walls of stone, and the enormous wooden vats were the height and breadth of an English terrace house. But it was the smell of fermenting wine that took her back to her childhood, and the gurgling witches' brew that simmered in those titanic vats which reignited a thrill she'd thought long forgotten. 'It takes me back,' she whispered. 'Reminds me why we do it.'

He took her hand. 'Follow me.'

Sophie felt the electric shock of his touch. As she followed him down another long tunnel and into the gloom of the racking cellars, she kept her gaze fixed to the floor. She was afraid of what he would read in her eyes. Afraid he would break the spell by doing something rash.

He let go of her hand and didn't touch her again as he pointed out the different vintages and explained how they were made and stored and matured. His enthusiasm for his work made his eyes shine. As he marched her through one long tunnel into another, it was almost as if she'd been forgotten.

Sophie bit her lip. She'd wanted him to kiss her,

wanted to feel his arms around her, and yet at the same time she knew things had to be taken slowly if something was to develop between them again. Theirs was a fragile relationship which had been damaged once already – a relationship forged when they were still very young. Now they were mature, with different lives and differing priorities, it would be silly to risk everything for a moment's madness they might both regret.

John carefully extracted a bottle of vintage Champagne from the rack and, after twisting off the wire, eased the cork out. Pouring it into two glasses, he held one out to Sophie. 'Here's to the future,' he said softly. 'To Jacaranda and Coolabah and all who slave in them.'

Sophie sipped the cool dry Champagne and let the bubbles burst on her tongue. It was an excellent vintage.

His fingers gently lifted her chin, forcing her to look up into his eyes. 'Penny for 'em,' he murmured.

'Old currency, mate,' she joked, the Aussie twang reasserting itself. 'Reckon I'm just tired and overwhelmed by everything.'

He was standing close – too close – and she moved away. She'd seen her own reflection in those brown eyes and knew he wanted more than friendship. But could she trust him again? Could she let by-gones be by-gones and risk getting hurt? The questions went round in her head. Although she knew she would have to find an answer, time was running out. They were leaving in two days.

The sun had sunk behind the hills, the soft night cast velvet shadows across the land as the extended family followed John Jay and Beatty to the winery. Each of them carried a lantern, and the soft chatter and laughter and the quick footsteps made Sophie wonder if these people ever got tired. The lack of sleep combined with her week of back-breaking toil under the sun had been shattering for her, the weariness not helped by Jay's obvious need for answers.

The winery chilled her now the heat was gone from the sun. As she entered the long tunnel for the second time that day she shivered and drew her sweater across her shoulders. There were too many ghosts here. Too many reminders of what was between them both and had remained unsaid. Perhaps it was better to leave things as they were, she thought as she followed the others into the vaulted cellar where the sour, tingling smell of fermentation filled the air. Jay would never leave this place and she was a city girl with a high-flying career. It wasn't meant to be.

John Jay stood beside the giant vats, several bottles of a previous vintage already open on the table behind him. He waited for his wife to pour each of them a glass then lifted his in a toast. 'I drink to Coolabah Creek,' he said, voice echoing in the arches of the great cavern. 'To Rose and John and Isobel, and to all the generations that followed. May we find peace and prosperity from now on.'

Sophie joined in the hearty response and sipped the dry, full-bodied Cabernet Sauvignon. It was as good as, if not better than, the wine from Jacaranda – but perhaps it was merely the atmosphere and her heightened awareness that made it appear so.

Cordelia licked her lips and held out her glass. 'It's good for the blood,' she declared as Beatty raised an eyebrow. With her glass full once more, she raised it and called for silence. 'Here's to a bloody good party.'

They laughed and finished their wine, then headed for the pickers' accommodation where there was a whole pig roasting on a spit, and as much wine and beer and rum as they could drink. Like the pioneers of Jacob's Creek, Coolabah Crossing knew how to celebrate vintage, and Sophie thought they did it in style.

The harmonica and penny whistle were joined by a guitar, a violin and someone who could play the spoons. An Irish woman brought out her tambour, and the ancient piano was hauled out of the recreation room and enthusiastically pounded by Wal. No one seemed to mind that half the keys didn't play and it hadn't been tuned for years.

John Jay and Beatty led the dancing and Sophie was whirled around with more nerve than verve by men young and old who stomped on her feet, held her too tightly, or had no sense of direction. She was soon breathless and sweating, but the pickers seemed tireless and she caught their enthusiasm and danced until her feet hurt and her ribs ached.

Seizing her chance, she slipped away from the boisterous circle of dancers and found a quiet cool spot in a corner where she could sip an ice-cold stubbie and take a breather. She watched the colourful swirl of checked shirts, heard the shuffle and stomp of flat-heeled boots and the enthusiastic yells as they danced reels and tried out the steps to the latest line dances.

Yet she was all too aware of Jay, clasping the waist of a young and very attractive redhead. He swung her up in the air and planted a kiss on her cheek then passed her on to the next in line. His glance told Sophie that he knew she was watching and she looked away quickly. There was no point in letting him know how much that quiet moment of Champagne and cool darkness had affected her. No point in trying to repair what was broken. Their lives were so different, their expectations and ambitions poles apart. She would be gone after tomorrow, back to Melbourne. It was for the best.

Daisy had done everything she could to prepare for the board meeting. The weeks had seemed to fly past but they had given her a chance to recoup the energy and enthusiasm she'd once had for Jacaranda and made her realise how much she could offer the family corporation.

There were now less that forty-eight hours to the meeting and she and Kate were accompanying Charles home from hospital. The by-pass surgery had gone well. Although he would need care over the next few months, Charles had insisted upon coming home.

'Hate the damn' places,' he grumbled as they approached the house. 'Reminds me of boarding school with all those rules and regulations. D'you know, they even stopped me smoking my cigars?'

Daisy laughed. 'Of course they did,' she said. 'You have to give them up if you want to come good.'

He grimaced as the car turned into the driveway. 'Gonna be a fair drag if you ask me,' he grumbled. 'What's a man supposed to do without a drop of whisky or a glass of wine with his dinner and a cigar to follow?'

'Eat less, give up smoking and only take a little wine now and then,' said Kate drily. 'Best of luck, Charles, you're going to need it.'

'I'm retiring after the meeting,' he said wearily. 'Whichever way things turn out, I've had it with the whole bloody shooting match. If it weren't for Jock, I'd have given up a long time ago.' He turned to Daisy. 'What about you?'

'I've got plans for Jacaranda's future,' she said enigmatically. 'But you'll have to wait until the meeting before I tell you anything more.'

'Thought you hated the place? What's changed your mind?'

'A sense of my own worth,' she said with quiet pride.

Jane paced the floor of the silent apartment. Newspaper cuttings and scrapbooks lay strewn across the carpet, photographs and letters scattered over the coffee table. Her past was catching up with her – the need for the truth to be revealed growing more urgent as the meeting drew nearer.

She stopped pacing and looked out of the vast picture window to the city that sprawled beneath her. So many lives, she thought. Little lives that went on regardless of the pain and suffering around them. Little beings who played out their dramas within the walls and streets of this rambling, rowdy city without a care for others. It was how she'd led her life in her youth, when she'd had her looks and her fame. Now her sins were coming home to roost and she didn't know how she would face up to them.

With a sigh she sat down again, her fingers running over the black and white publicity shots of her taken so many years ago. She could see why Jock had fallen in love with her, understood his need to have a beautiful woman on his arm and in his bed. It was all a part of his gigantic ego – and if she was being truly honest a part of hers too. It had done her career no end of good for her to have a rich and powerful man as a lover, and because she'd loved him deeply, she'd hardly given a thought to Cordelia and her children.

Until she'd needed them. Until Jock knocked over that glass of whisky and threw the money at her. She'd stared at that spilled drink as he told her to get out of his life. Watched the notes become wet and dark as he forbade her to return if she didn't do what he wanted.

She looked down at the discoloured snapshots she'd kept hidden for almost a third of her life. This was what it came down to. This was the reason for the lies and the deceit which spun the web so tightly around her it was almost suffocating.

Snapping out of her thoughts, she began to clear away, a new vigour returning as the decision was finally made. She had spent too many years in the shadows. It was time to walk in the sun again.

Sophie stood in the bedroom, bags packed and ready at her feet. The soft, rolling croon of the magpies and the piercing sweetness of the bell-birds' ring echoed over the land as the shadows were chased away by the sun. And in the extra-ordinary light unique to the outback, the pale delicate leaves of the eucalyptus trees became a soft haze above the rough brown of their bark and the glare of silver grass.

She sighed. She would miss the sound of the birds in the early morning, miss the smell of the warm earth and ripening grapes, and the cool blue shadows of the encompassing hills and dark green vines. But most of all she would miss this happy, boisterous family. Jay was a lucky man to be surrounded by such love.

She turned from the window. There was no point in feeling sorry for herself. She had been the one to reject his advances – the one to mistrust his intentions – the one too cowardly to make the first move towards a proper recon-ciliation. Snatching up the bags, she slammed out of the door. Silly bloody cow, she thought crossly. Why do you have to take everything so damn' seriously?

The kitchen was quiet for once, with Beatty mucking out the stables and the men busy preparing the terraces for the new season of planting and growing. Wal was smoking his morning pipe on the verandah, if the squeak of the rocking chair was anything to go by, and there was no sign of Cordelia. Sophie realised suddenly she hadn't had a smoke for most of the time she'd been here. Crispin was right – she didn't need it any more. With that enlightening thought, she helped herself to a mug of tea from the ever-present pot and, after tasting it, added sugar. It was stewed and very bitter but it woke her up.

Cordelia shuffled into the room and stood by the table, leaning heavily on her sticks. 'Good party, wasn't it?' she said with a sigh. 'Reckon it'll be me last, though. Getting too old for all those late nights.'

'You've got plenty of time to rest, Gran,' Sophie said quietly, 'and I promise I'll come down and visit as often as I can.'

Cordelia grimaced and sat down. 'I'll be a long time dead,' she snapped. 'So don't put me in a box until I've breathed me last. I'm coming back to Melbourne with you. I've warned the others.'

Sophie gave an exasperated sigh. She'd known this would happen. Gran had been far too compliant when it was first suggested she should remain at Coolabah Crossing. 'The doctor advises against it,' she said firmly. 'You can keep in touch by phone during the meeting or give me your proxy vote.'

Cordelia waved her hand dismissively. 'Not bloody likely. I want to see their faces when I tell them what's planned for Jacaranda. Can't do that over a bloody phone,' she said contemptuously.

'Gran, you have to listen to advice for once,' Sophie insisted. 'You've got low blood pressure and angina. It could be dangerous to fly in your condition.'

The pale eyes regarded her solemnly. 'I would agree with you if I was going to flap my arms and take off from the top of that hill, but as it's metal and engineering doing all the work, I think I'm capable of sitting about for a few hours doing nothing.'

Sophie struggled to keep her exasperation under check. 'You don't need to be there. Give me the package you and the others have put together and I'll read it up on the plane. I'm perfectly capable of arguing your corner.'

'You don't think I'm going to trust anyone else to run things properly, do you? she barked. 'I've been a member of that board since I was twenty-seven and never missed a meeting. I'm not about to change the habit of a lifetime.'

Sophie was fighting a losing battle. 'What happens if you die in the attempt, Gran? Who's going to keep an eye on us then?'

Cordelia folded her arms and glared back. 'I've made contingency plans,' she said firmly. 'Now, get me my breakfast and stop whingeing. I need to keep my strength up for the journey and we're wasting time.'

Sophie did as she was told. When a plate of scrambled egg and toast was put in front of her grandmother, she sat and sipped coffee and waited for her to plough through it. The angina attack hadn't even dented the old girl's appetite, she noticed with a wry grin.

'I was reading about the curse on the Fullers and the Tanners,' she began.

'Curses only work when you believe in them,' muttered Cordelia through a bite of toast.

'It must have seemed very real to John and Rose for them to react the way they did.'

'Things were different back in those days. Superstition was high, and you've got to remember, Rose was Irish and John Romany. Both cultures believe very strongly in spells and curses.'

'So Muriel's baby was born safe and sound?'

Cordelia wiped her mouth on a napkin and leaned back in her chair. 'She had a strawberry birth mark on her thigh – but that had little to do with curses and spells, and every baby since has been hale and healthy.' She gave a smile, her eyes almost dancing with mischief. 'So if you and Jay should decide to do something about the way you feel for each other, there's nothing to stop you.'

'Only time and distance,' Sophie murmured. 'We've left it too late.'

Cordelia helped herself to another piece of toast and dipped it into the milky coffee. The thick, creamy drink helped liven her a little, and as she munched the soggy toast, she thought over her plans for the board meeting.

With a sly smile, she wondered how the others would react when she sprang her surprise. It was fun to be in charge again –scheming kept her alive.

Having made the best of her breakfast, she hobbled to the back verandah. 'I'm going soon, Wal. Thought it best to say goodbye in private,' she said gruffly.

He stood up, the rocking chair tilting as he knocked against it. His arms went round her shoulders as he pulled her close and kissed her brow. 'Goodbye, old girl,' he murmured softly. 'Reckon we won't see each other again – not in this lifetime anyways. But I'm glad we had these last few weeks together.'

She held him close, remembering the wasted years, the times when she'd wept for what she'd lost. 'Goodbye, Wal,' she whispered. 'Thanks for giving a silly old woman a chance to turn things around. I wish...'

His grip tightened. 'No, Cordy. Never wish for more than we've had, 'cos it was the best we could do in the circumstances.'

She finally drew away from him. Looked into the dark eyes that were faded by the years and too much sun. Saw the creased brow, the blurred features of old age and knew she would love him to the end. 'I'm going to miss you, you bloody old reprobate,' she said through the tears.

He kissed her cheek, his grizzled chin like a rasp. 'Nah, Cordy. We have each other in our hearts, luv. That'll see us through till we meet again.'

'You reckon there's something after all this?' she asked in surprise. Wal had never been a religious man.

'Too bloody right,' he answered firmly. 'Otherwise we've all been wasting our bloody time.'

Cordelia gave him a hug and returned to the house. She had nothing else to say to him he didn't already know – there was no point in prolonging the agony. Yet, as she slumped on the bed, she felt the anguish rise in her and had to muffle bitter tears in the pillow.

Sophie wandered out to the stables in the hope Jay was helping his mother. She hadn't seen him since the vintage party and had a nasty suspicion he was avoiding her.

Beatty was mucking out Jupiter's box and welcomed Sophie's offer of help. As they cleared the night's bedding and replaced it with fresh straw, she kept up a stream of inconsequential chatter about people and places that meant nothing to Sophie but were a means of filling an awkward silence.

'Where's Jay?' Sophie asked finally when there was a break in Beatty's prattle.

She looked back as she filled the buckets from the tap. 'Gone up country,' she replied. 'John Jay needed something done and Jay volunteered.'

Sophie turned away, hoping Beatty wouldn't notice the disappointment in her eyes. But she hadn't been quick enough.

'He didn't want to be where he wasn't wanted,' Beatty said without rancour. 'So he thought it best to stay out the way until you left.'

'But I *did* want to see him,' Sophie protested. 'There are things I need to sort out, things I should explain. I was real crook to him last time we spoke and I wanted to apologise.'

Beatty's gaze was very direct. 'Strikes me you've had time enough already. Jay told me he's approached you more than once but you brushed him off.' She sighed as she placed the buckets in the stalls. 'There's only so much a man's pride can take, Sophie. Jay loved you very much once. I reckon you didn't give him a fair go then and you aren't now.'

Sophie was unable to speak for the tears in her throat.

Beatty grasped her shoulder. 'If things are meant, then they'll work out,' she said calmly. 'Be patient – don't give up on him yet.'

The small plane took off and Cordelia looked down on Coolabah for the last time. 'Goodbye,' she whispered, her fingers resting on the window.

The waving figures below grew smaller and smaller as they faded into the distance. Cordelia finally rested back in her seat and closed her eyes. She would carry the scent and the sight of that beautiful corner of Australia with her to the end. Would remember the people, the way the magpies woke her in the morning, and the squeak of Wal's chair on the wooden verandah. But most of all she would remember the scratch of a stubbled chin on her cheek and the slow drawl of the man she had secretly loved for most of her life.

A twinge of pain shot through her chest, making her gasp, leaving her breathless. Surreptitiously she popped one of the doctor's pills under her tongue and waited for it to ease. The young bludger was right, she thought grimly. I feel terrible. But I'm determined to make that meeting tomorrow. Determined to leave my mark on Jacaranda Vines before it's too late.

Jane had waited nervously all afternoon. She had

only a vague idea of their time of arrival and hoped she'd thought of everything. The apartment had been cleaned and there were bunches of sweet-smelling lilies in the vases. Tea was laid out on the dining table. Cordelia's bed had been made up with fresh sheets and a hot water bottle because Jane knew she felt cold even in the height of summer.

The key rasped in the lock and she turned towards the open door.

'Hello, dear. Here I am, back home,' said Cordelia brightly.

Jane tried to disguise her shock as they hugged. Cordelia looked ghastly, her pallor grey, her lips blue and trembling. She would have to revise her plans – put them on hold for a while. Cordelia needed her. 'Come and sit down,' she said quickly. 'I've made a pot of tea.'

Cordelia hobbled slowly to her chair and collapsed with a grateful sigh. 'The apartment looks lovely, Jane. As always, you've made me feel special.'

Jane blushed, knowing what she'd planned – and feeling disloyal.

Cordelia took the cup and saucer. She looked up at Jane, her eyes bright with curiosity. 'What's on your mind? Come on, spit it out.'

Jane was flustered. She might have known Cordelia would miss nothing, but she hadn't expected this so soon. 'It's nothing,' she said hastily, 'Now isn't the time.'

'I always know when something's bothering you, Jane. You get that shifty look.'

Cordelia was not to be side-tracked and Jane

knew she would worry at it until she was forced to tell her. 'I'm moving out,' she began. 'You've had me crowding you for too long. It's time I stood on my own and did something with my life.'

'What's brought this on?' demanded Cordelia.

Jane made a helpless gesture with her hands before clasping them together. 'I've never been a part of this family – not really. I've had no voice, no part to play, and although it might sound silly coming from a woman of my age, I need to feel wanted. Need to know I can achieve a semblance of self-sufficiency before it's too late.'

She took a deep breath and rushed on before Cordelia could interrupt. 'There's an apartment going over by the gallery and I've been accepted for Chair of the Arts Council. It's a chance to do something with what's become an empty life, Cordelia, and although I shall miss you terribly, it's time I moved on.'

Cordelia sighed. 'Don't be too hasty, Jane. I shan't be here much longer myself, and I was hoping to leave this apartment to you in the knowledge you would care for it and regard it as home. It's the least I owe you for all you've done for me in the past.'

Jane sat down, surprise making her legs weak. 'You don't owe me anything,' she protested. 'It's what you've done for me I can never repay. When I think...'

Cordelia cut her off in mid-sentence. 'Not now dear. We'll talk about it tomorrow when I've had a good night's sleep.' She dug in her handbag and brought out a large brown envelope. 'This is something that will give you a voice, Jane. You deserve it, and I hope you use it wisely.'

Jane frowned as she took the envelope. After turning it over in her hand, she broke the seal and pulled out the pieces of paper inside. 'You can't do this,' she gasped when she saw what Cordelia had given her. 'I have no right – no right at all.'

'You have every right,' Cordelia said firmly. 'It's your voice, your turn to make your mark. Don't disappoint me Jane. I'm counting on you.'

22

The boardroom doors were open. As the two women approached they could hear the buzz of conversation and the clink of cups and saucers.

'Sounds like a full house,' muttered Cordelia. 'Are you ready for this?'

Jane nodded. With one guiding hand hovering at Cordelia's elbow, she stepped into the room and was greeted by nine pairs of startled eyes.

'What's she doing here?' Mary demanded.

'I might ask the same of you,' retorted Cordelia. 'What do you think you were doing, running off like that without telling anyone where you were? You should be ashamed of yourself.'

Mary lit a cigarette. She'd obviously been drinking, and her hand shook. 'None of your bloody business,' she snapped. She glared at Jane through the smoke. 'That woman has no right here. She can't vote and isn't a family member.'

'Jane has as much right as any of us,' Cordelia said mildly. 'I gave her some of my shares.'

There was a stunned silence.

'That's our inheritance,' spat Mary. 'You can't just give it away to that – that – tart!'

Cordelia noticed how Sophie put a hand on her mother's arm to placate her. It had little effect, for Mary shrugged it off, her colour high, her mouth a thin angry line.

'They're my shares and I'll do what I want with them,' she retorted. 'Mind your own business, Mary, and if you can't keep your temper, I suggest you shut up.' Cordelia ignored the howl of protest, gave Jane a look of support and made her way to the end of the table. The meeting had started badly. How on earth would they react as things moved on? Yet, strangely, she was almost looking forward to it.

Edward finished his coffee and waited for the others to take their places. Cordelia took the chance to greet her daughters and watch as they all settled around the table. It was interesting to note none of them commented on the extra chairs.

Charles was in a wheelchair, propped up with cushions to ease his breathing, but his colour was good, and apart from a slight tremor in his right hand, Cordelia thought he appeared to be recovering well. Her gaze turned to the twins, Michael and James. She had read the reports from Jacaranda late last night when she couldn't sleep. The vintage had been good in the Barossa too, and the twins seemed happy as they quietly talked together to the exclusion of the others. Philip looked like a cat who'd swallowed the saucer as well as the cream. And Mary...? She'd have been better if she hadn't had a drink so early in the day and wasn't glowering.

She smiled at Daisy, seeing the bright young girl once again in those intelligent eyes and the self-confident way she carried herself. Gone were the matronly glasses, there was a new hair-cut and smart clothes as well as manicured nails and a hint of make-up. Perhaps Daisy had finally found herself, not before time – but Cordelia hoped nothing would happen at this meeting to destroy what she suspected was a fragile confidence.

Kate, she thought fondly as her gaze settled on her eldest daughter. Still acerbic, still calling a spade a shovel, still smoking. There was a light in her eyes too, and colour in her face, and Cordelia joyfully realised her daughter was in love. Good luck to her, she thought. About time my Kate had someone again. She might think she's independent, but there's a soft centre to that girl and she needs a man in her life.

Edward cut through the conversation. 'We all know why we're here so I won't bore you with it again. Would someone please close the door?'

'Leave it where it is,' Cordelia demanded. 'Not everyone's here.'

Edward frowned. 'What are you talking about, Cordy? There's no one else to come.'

She smiled with deliberate sweetness. 'There is,' she said triumphantly. 'Here they are now.'

All eyes turned to the door as John Jay entered, closely followed by Beatty and their eldest son. 'G'day,' he said cheerfully. 'Sorry we're late, but the bloody plane wouldn't start and we had to wait for spares to come up from Sydney.'

'Who the hell are they?' demanded Mary. 'This is a circus. First the freak then the clowns. What are you up to, Mother?'

Cordelia's withering stare quelled the outburst. 'This is John Jay Tanner, his wife Beatty, and their eldest son Jay. They are your cousins.'

Edward stared, then recovered his manners quickly and shook hands. 'Well, well,' he muttered. 'This is a surprise, I must say.' He looked across at Cordelia. 'I'm glad you've invited the other side of the family, but I don't quite see why they've come to this meeting. Jacaranda Vines has nothing to do with them – and as such, I'm afraid I'm going to have to ask them to leave until our business is concluded.'

'Jacaranda has a great deal to do with them,' Cordelia said clearly into the silence. 'They are shareholders.'

'Since when!' stormed Mary, her voice rising above the babel of surprise.

'Since I arranged it,' said Cordelia calmly.

'You...?' Mary seemed to be lost for words as she stared at her mother. Then she turned on Sophie. 'Why didn't you stop her, you silly bitch?' she screamed. 'You must have known what she was up to.'

Sophie recoiled but before she could answer Mary had turned her invective elsewhere.

'Family rift healed profitably enough, you

bastard?' she snarled in John Jay's direction. 'Hope you're happy because your thirty pieces of silver have merely made the rift worse.'

She turned on Jane. 'And as for you, you conniving cow – I bet you helped Mum cook this up, didn't you?'

Jane's gaze never wavered under Mary's glare. 'I had nothing to do with it,' she said calmly. 'I suggest you sit down and stop making a fool of yourself.'

'Don't tell me what to do, bitch,' she spat. 'You're nothing – d'you hear? Nothing. You've leached off mum for years, wheedling your way into her life like the worm you are. No wonder Dad finally saw sense and dumped you – once a cheap tart, always a cheap tart!'

Cordelia held her breath. She could see the silent battle Jane was fighting and knew she would soon be unable to hold back. She broke in quickly before things went too far. 'That's enough,' she snapped, her hand coming down hard on the table.

Mary slumped in her chair, her breathing shallow, her eyes gimlet sharp as she glared at Jane and the Tanners.

Cordelia waited for them all to quieten down. 'I did what I did because I want this family – such as it is – to be reunited. For all of us to have a voice in the future of Jacaranda Vines. Divided we fall, but united we'll be stronger than ever.'

'Sounds to me as if you're buying votes,' rasped Charles. 'That's a deliberate breach of the constitution, Cordelia. I can't allow it.'

'The proportion of shares hasn't changed, just

moved about a bit. The shares are theirs, regardless of how they vote,' she declared stoutly.

Edward shuffled the papers in front of him. 'Then let's get on, shall we? There's been enough unpleasantness.' He looked around the silent room before carrying on. 'The last vote was split down the middle, so I need to have one spokesperson from each side to put their case before we vote again. I remind you that should the vote be a draw, I shall have the final decision.'

Cordelia exchanged glances with Sophie and nodded encouragement. She noticed her look at Jay before pushing back her chair and wondered how long it would be before the two silly young fools kissed and made up.

Sophie shuffled papers and cleared her throat. She had everyone's attention. The time had come to put her plan of action on the table, even though she knew how things would probably turn out. She and Cordelia had had a long talk on the flight home.

'Gran has taught me a great deal over the past few weeks,' she began. 'I learned the story behind the foundation of Jacaranda Vines and the ultimate split between the two sides of the family. It's good to welcome John Jay and his family here today. Good to know they now have a voice in Jacaranda's future.'

'Get on with it,' growled Mary. 'We all know how we're going to vote, I don't see why we should listen to this nonsense.' She folded her arms and looked around the table, but was met with chilly disapproval.

Sophie carried on as if she hadn't been interrupted. 'At the last meeting I was in favour of Jacaranda going public. I still am.' She looked down at her grandmother and just managed to avoid winking.

Cordelia looked suitably disappointed and remained silent.

'If we are to survive in today's market as we are, going public is the only option. We must sell the satellite companies and use the proceeds to clear our debts and bring stability to the company in readiness for the stock market flotation. The family will lose their ownership of the company, but as shareholders, we can all expect a handsome windfall in return. With Jacaranda strong again, the opening share price should be high, and we can look forward to a prosperous future.'

She looked around the table. 'The winery isn't the weak link in the corporation. Not even Jock could destroy that. It's the retail outlets and the rest of the smaller companies Jock set up just before he died. He deliberately threw good money after bad, and although a great deal of it could be claimed as a tax loss, the rot has got to stop. Getting rid of those companies is the first step towards financial stability and it must be done immediately.'

She saw the nods of approval and carried on. 'The French have offered us a fortune for Jacaranda, and it's a tempting offer for those who wish to see the back of the corporation. But consider this. They will merely sell off the loss-making sections of the corporation and make their own stock market launch. They can see the potential in Jacaranda and will exploit it to the full.'

She looked around the table again. 'Is that what we want? Do we really need to throw away the chance of recouping our losses and seeing Jacaranda flourish again? I don't think so. The French offer is a clear signal the corporation is worth a great deal, and we'd be fools to let it slip through our fingers out of revenge. Revenge was Jock's way – it shouldn't be ours. He did his best to destroy us all in his lifetime. Why give in and finish what he started? Why not fight for our inheritance? Our ancestors did. They fought the elements, the government, drought, fire and flood to keep their vineyards going. They lived and died on the land we so carelessly wish to hand over to strangers, survived personal heartache and two wars to carry on the tradition and leave an inheritance to the following generations. Don't let's waste this opportunity to respect what they've done for us. We might not have full ownership of the corporation any more if we go public, but we'll still be at the core of the decision-making.'

Sophie sat down. Her legs would no longer hold her and her mouth was dry. She caught Jay's look of admiration and, to her shame, blushed. What was it about him that made her behave like a kid in high-school she thought crossly. For heaven's sake, pull yourself together, girl.

Mary scraped back her chair and swayed to her feet. 'Sophie is to be congratulated on her emotional speech,' she said drily. 'But we shouldn't be persuaded by a lot of emotive talk about the past – sentimentality has no place in the boardroom. We no longer exist in the world of the pioneer, but in one that fights dirty. The stock market may seem a good compromise between bankruptcy and the sale to the French but let's get real about this and look at what it would mean to each of us.'

She glanced around the table, seeing the hostility in their eyes, knowing she would have to recoup the damage she'd done. Her loss of temper had done her little good. Although she didn't really care much how they felt, she would have to work hard to regain even a small measure of their respect.

'Dad knew what he was doing when he began to destroy the corporation. He could see the world was changing and the competition growing fiercer. His bully-boy tactics wore us down, and I think he realised that once he was no longer at the helm, the ship would sink – he knew we'd want our revenge. All he did was puncture the good ship Jacaranda below the waterline and help it on its way.'

She saw they were listening and took a deep breath. The need for a drink was getting worse and she hoped she could last out. 'I have no love for the corporation but I can see Sophie's point about not letting it slip through our fingers before we get our due rewards from it. But if we go on the stock market that's exactly what will happen. United or not.'

She glanced at John Jay and his family who so far had wisely remained silent. 'We'll remain tied to it as shareholders but the real decisions will be made on the trading floors. It will be a repetition of all the years we had to put up with Dad. Nothing will have changed. The promised windfall's not guaranteed. Markets are unstable. We might show a united front but the hawks will recognise it for the sham it really is and fly in for the kill.'

Mary looked around the room and waited for the murmurs to die down. She was coming to the end of her speech and hoped she'd done enough. 'Let's sell to the French, take the money and run as far as we can from Dad's influence.' She sat down and took a long swig of water, wishing it was gin.

'My, my,' murmured Phillip. 'Who would have thought there was a brain behind those inches of make-up? Almost had me applauding.'

'Oh, shut up,' she snapped before lighting another cigarette.

Edward banged the gavel on the table to silence the arguments that flew round the room. 'We've heard both sides. It's time to vote,' he rumbled.

Daisy felt very calm as she stood up. 'There aren't just two sides to the argument,' she said firmly. 'I have a third proposition.'

'What's that?' said Mary nastily. 'Sit back and let the corporation fall around our ears while we do our knitting? Sit down, Daisy, before you make a complete idiot of yourself.'

She eyed her sister coldly. 'You've had your say. Now it's my turn.' She looked away and addressed the rest of the meeting, her pulse racing, sweat gathering at the nape of her neck.

'It's time I made my position clear. I might not have had anything to do with the management of the corporation when Daddy was alive, and I know you think of me as a bit of a joke, but I have a degree in business studies, accountancy and statistics, and the thesis for my doctorate was the marketing and managing of a family corporation approaching the new millennium.'

A gasp of amazement went round the room, and Daisy felt a thrill of achievement as she looked down into her mother's proud face. 'It was your encouragement that made me enrol on that first course and I've been waiting for this moment for years.'

'Come on then, Daisy. Let's hear your proposal.' Kate grinned at the astonished faces around her. 'It's the quiet ones you should watch,' she said proudly. 'You'll be surprised to hear what she has to say.'

'So get on with it then,' said Mary sharply.

'I propose we neither sell any part of Jacaranda nor go public,' said Daisy. She waited for the objections to fade into silence before she carried on. 'My advice is to turn the entire corporation into a trust.'

'Can't be done,' rumbled Charles. 'There's nothing in the constitution to permit it.'

Daisy took a sheaf of papers from the folder in front of her. 'There are ways of amending the constitution, as you well know. It's been done before during expansion, and as long as the Board approves, it can be done again. What it already states clearly is that certain measures may be taken to protect and conserve the corporation in part or as a whole. That is what I propose we do.'

'What would this trust entail?' asked Philip.

'The trust would be set up in a series of hierarchical levels. Think of a pyramid, with the chairman and ruling board directors at the top. Then there would be a central council made up of the district managers, accountants, sales directors and shop stewards. At the bottom of the pyramid is the wide base of the local councils. This will be made up of the workforce.'

'You're asking for trouble, letting the workers have their say,' declared Charles. 'We'll end up with rebellion, strikes and union interference. The Australian cobber can be a bloody-minded bastard, and many a company's gone to the wall over union troubles.'

Daisy knew she had to convince him, even though she knew he was right to be concerned about the unions. 'It may seem as if I'm spreading the responsibility for the company too thin, but hear me out, Charles. Please.'

He grimaced. 'All right, but I don't agree with anything you've said so far.'

She swallowed. It would be hard enough to convince them she was right without Charles sticking his oar in. His knowledge was respected, his opinion regarded as law amongst the others – she had a tough task on her hands.

'There are several large corporations who have never had to go on the stock market, and have been run as successful trusts for many years. The John Lewis and Waitrose group in the UK is a prime example, having set up their trust back in

1926. Their organisation is not as old as ours but the similarities are uncanny, with retail outlets and supermarkets under their corporate umbrella. I've prepared a run-down of my proposal that I hope will make things clear, and perhaps answer some of your questions and concerns.'

She handed out the neatly prepared portfolios and nervously watched as the pages were flicked through.

'The staff on all levels of the pyramid will be known as partners. They will have annual bonuses and perks directly relating to each year's performance of their section of the corporation and their position within that section. In that way, the trust would be a sort of red herring. It will fulfil the aim that all partners will obtain the advantages and privileges of ownership, but without actually owning anything but a percentage of voting rights. The chairman, who must be voted in by a majority, will wield sixty percent of the shares in the trust, effectively giving him the power to throttle rebellion should it arise. He will be handsomely paid, as will all the directors in the ruling council.'

There was silence in the room as they tried to take in what was being proposed.

'We will be a hierarchical organisation, which some will say is much like it was when Daddy was alive. But this time everyone will have their say and be allowed to vote through their different representatives at their councils' levels. You cannot be a flat organisation if you are in retailing because you have people out on the floor or in the market place selling for you, and they know what's going on at the sharp end of the business, and need to be listened to.'

'And what if we set up this trust and the workforce decide they want a piece of the action by going for a flotation on the stock market? The windfall they'd stand to gain then isn't to be sneezed at.'

Charles' question stilled the rustle of pages and every pair of eyes turned towards her.

'That's why I propose the pyramid of councils. I agree the windfall idea is something that would be hard to resist. But if we maintain a constant open line of communication between the three pyramid levels and encourage serious debate about issues that concern everyone, then I think it can be avoided. The perks and bonuses would disappear if we went public, so would the management. Workers would find themselves once more on the shop floor with no say in how the company is run – their grievances wouldn't be taken into account – there would be no one higher up to forward their complaints to the board. The principle of this trust is to run the company like a co-operative, where every man and woman involved is paid fairly for their experience and justly rewarded for their commitment and input.'

'How are we going to afford all this?' asked Cordelia.

'By splitting the share issue sixty-forty and selling the lesser amount off to the workforce.'

'And if they aren't willing to buy?'

'Then they will have no say in the future of Jacaranda – no vote,' said Daisy firmly.

'I think we need time to digest all this and discuss where we go from here,' said Edward. 'I suggest we break for a few hours and return later on this afternoon.'

Sophie wasn't hungry so she skipped lunch and remained in the boardroom working through the afternoon on Daisy's proposal. There were flaws, but it had the potential to be an excellent solution if Gran hadn't already put certain factors in place. She nibbled the end of her pen, still stunned by the self-composure of her aunt and the hidden resourcefulness behind that meek exterior. Yet she recognised the skill that had gone into preparing the package and realised Daisy would be an important part of the company's future – whichever way the vote went.

'So which way do you think things will go?' Cordelia plumped down beside her, breathless from the effort of making the journey back from her penthouse apartment.

Sophie leafed through Daisy's proposal. 'This has tremendous possibilities, but there are certain things I would change if we had to go through with it.'

Cordelia's eyes were bright, her face animated as she settled back in her chair. 'Tell me what changes you would make.'

Sophie eyed her suspiciously. 'What are you plotting, Gran? I thought...'

Cordelia winked. 'Just tell me your thoughts on this proposal of Daisy's and I'll tell you mine. I have the feeling our solution was very nearly rumbled.'

It was four o'clock in the afternoon by the time Edward had commanded silence and they were once again grouped around the table. There was an almost tangible sense of expectancy and excitement amongst them, a tension that manifested itself in startled jumps as Cordelia banged on the table with the handle of her stick.

'As the eldest one here, I'm entitled to have my say.'

Mary groaned. 'Not now, Mother.'

Cordelia ignored her. 'What Daisy has proposed is an excellent idea and I congratulate her on a superb show of skill. But what I propose is even better.' She looked around at their puzzled faces and smiled. 'Sophie and I got our heads together and discovered we are of the same mind. For, you see, Daisy's proposal came as no surprise to me.'

She saw the disappointment in her daughter's face and smiled. 'You're a clever woman, Daisy. Don't hide your talents any more. Be proud of them.'

Turning back to the room she carried on. 'I realised shortly after the last board meeting that a kind of trust was the only natural progression for our corporation if we were to keep it in our possession – and I began to make contingency plans. Of course I can go no further until I have the board's approval, so I would appreciate your full attention.'

Silence fell as everyone watched her. The tension was almost unbearable.

Cordelia eased forward in her chair, her hands

lightly clasped on the Huon pine table. 'I have listened to all the arguments and found things to agree with in all of them – but each has its flaws, each relinquishes our hold on our inheritance. We are Australian and should remain so. This is a family corporation and should look to itself for rescue, not to the stock market or the French.'

She paused to take a breath and put her thoughts in order. She had rehearsed what she was about to say, but now, in the moment of truth, she was almost afraid of the consequences. for if the vote went against her, it would be the end of all she had ever known, all she had ever believed in.

'I propose we sell off the supermarket chain and the bottle shops. They will bring in enough capital for us to reinvest in the shipping and road transport side of the business as well as pay off our most pressing debts.' She held up her hand for silence as a storm of voices rose around her. 'Let me finish,' she demanded. 'Then you can argue all you want.'

Silence fell again and she carried on. 'Jacaranda Vines made more profit this year than ever before and much of that is owed to the twins, James and Michael. Coolabah Crossing has also made a healthy profit this year with overseas sales steadily rising. But let us look at the wider picture. Let us examine the rest of my portfolio.'

She opened up the folder in front of her, fully aware she had everyone's attention. 'Jock might have thought he knew everything but no man is infallible,' she said firmly. 'His interest lay in Jacaranda, nothing else – so I was free to nurture my own little empire.'

She shoved a stack of papers towards Sophie. 'Pass them around, dear. There's enough for everyone.'

Cordelia waited and smiled as she saw the look of astonishment on their faces. 'As you can see, Great-grandmother Rose left me the vineyards that Muriel Fitzallan willed to her. I have added some over the years, but the core remains, and each of them has flourished. During my stay at Coolabah, John Jay was kind enough to contact each of the tenant managers for me, and after lengthy discussions over the telephone, I had these agreements drawn up in Sydney.'

Another sheaf of papers went the rounds and Cordelia waited until their contents were read before resuming. 'Daisy's idea of a trust is close to my own. But I would prefer a co-operative where the shareholders hold a real stake in their investment, not just a proportional voting right. Jacaranda and Coolabah are the largest of the fifteen vineyards and I propose the chairman be chosen from one or the other. But the rest of the vineyards will have their spokesmen, and like Daisy's pyramid idea, those spokesmen and women must be listened to, their advice and opinions taken seriously. A referendum and vote will be taken to elect the board of directors who will be monitored closely by all of us.'

She looked around at the stunned faces. 'By uniting in this way, and by keeping our rail and shipping companies working for us, we will become a force to be reckoned with. Some of our competitors might have sold out to the French –

but we won't need to. Let's give them a run for their money, let's show 'em the Aussies haven't lost their spirit for a bloody good fight.'

Bankrupt of energy, the spirit almost knocked out of her by the effort of speaking for so long, Cordelia slumped in her chair and waited. She had done all she could.

The applause was led by Sophie and swiftly rose to a thunder of approval and respect for the grand and determined old lady. Mary resolutely kept her hands in her lap and wondered if anyone would notice if she took a nip from her hip flask.

'Are we ready to vote now?' Edward called above the hubbub.

'Don't let all this sentimental tosh go to your heads,' Mary warned loudly. 'Just remember what it's been like all these past years. Things aren't going to change – we'll still be tied to Jacaranda – still have to live in its shadow. Vote for reason and common sense. Vote to take the money and run. Get a life.'

'Have you quite finished?' Edward raised a bushy eyebrow. 'Then let's take the vote. All those in favour of flotation?'

There was silence in the room as they looked at one another. No hands were raised.

'All those in favour of accepting the French offer.'

Three hands went up.

Mary scanned the faces of those who had not yet voted. She was outnumbered. 'Put your hand up, Jane,' she ordered. 'We all know you were only in this for the money. Why spoil the habit of a lifetime?'

Jane's face paled but her hands remained resolutely in her lap.

'Come on, you bitch!' screamed Mary. 'At least have the balls to show us your true colours. This is your chance to line your pockets – you won't get another one.'

'I'll vote as I see fit,' she said calmly. 'And I vote for the co-operative.'

'All those in favour,' said Edward hastily.

A resounding 'Aye' echoed round the room as all other hands were raised.

Sophie gathered up her papers and returned them to her briefcase. With a smile of triumph at her grandmother, she rounded the table and gave her a hug. 'You did it, Gran,' she murmured. 'Well done.'

'I didn't do it on my own, Sophie. Rose was behind me, as well as John Jay and the others. Without them, we could never have saved Jacaranda.'

Sophie glanced across the room. Jay's dark gaze was fixed on her, the smile on his lips for her alone. She smiled back and was unaware of the noise around her as he pushed back his chair and made his way towards her. Perhaps now they could talk. Perhaps now they could start to pick up the pieces and begin again.

As Jay stood before her she looked into those dark eyes and knew that this was the moment she had been waiting for. He held out his hand and she took it. 'Let's get out of here,' he murmured.

'We need to talk.'

She nodded and let him lead her to the door.

The crash of a fist against the table startled everyone. Sophie and Jay turned in the doorway. The silence was absolute, the electricity of Mary's rage filling the room.

'You two-faced bitch,' she hissed at Jane. 'Not satisfied with stealing my inheritance, you've ruined my chance to make some money and get out of this bloody business.' Her nails were like claws as she reached across the table. 'I hope you drop dead before you get a penny more out of us.'

Mary heard Cordelia's mewling efforts to pacify her and ignored them. She was suddenly fascinated by the strange, almost fearful expression on Jane's face.

'And I wish you'd never been born,' Jane said quietly. 'You were trouble from the moment you were conceived. I should have done what your father ordered and had you aborted.'

Mary gasped as she felt the colour drain from her face and the hatred was replaced with shock. She must have misheard. 'What did you say?' Her voice was strangled, the effect of the alcohol making her mind sluggish.

'You heard,' said Jane clearly. 'Jock refused to have anything to do with me once he discovered I was expecting his child. He ordered me to have an abortion – said he didn't want a bastard in the family. I wish now I'd taken his money and his advice, but how was I to know what a vicious bitch you'd turn out to be?'

494

'You're lying!' Mary shouted. 'You've just thought this up to get back at me.' She gasped for breath, making an enormous effort to regain some kind of control. 'It's not clever and it's certainly not funny. I demand an apology.'

'What's the matter, Mary? Afraid to face the truth?' Jane retorted. 'You so nearly got it right in that magazine article – and if you'd stopped to think instead of just venting your spite, you might have realised the truth in the old adage of no smoke without fire.'

Mary's confidence faltered in the face of Jane's cold calm. 'Mum?' she said, looking to Cordelia for support. 'She's lying, isn't she? She's got to be.'

Cordelia's face was a mask, her eyes pleading for understanding as Sophie put a protective hand on her shoulder.

'She's not your mother – I am,' said Jane sharply. 'Cordelia never formally adopted you, but she gave you her name, brought you up as if you were her child. And look at the thanks she got. Look at the way you've treated her over the past years with your drinking and your men, your temper tantrums and constant scandals in the gossip columns.'

Mary sat down with a thump, the fear dark inside her as she looked from face to face in an urgent quest for support. 'But how?' she stammered. 'You were Dad's mistress, she was his wife – you should have hated one another.'

Jane sighed. 'I'm sorry, Mary. I should never have told you. I promised Cordelia long ago that I'd keep it a secret.' She hung her head. 'But now you know, you should be told everything. You deserve the truth after all these years.'

'How could you, Mum?' Mary turned to Cordelia in a last desperate attempt to make sense of it all.

'I did what I thought was best,' she replied quietly, 'but it's Jane's story – not mine.'

Jane was talking, her voice low and devoid of all emotion. Mary reluctantly turned back to her.

'Your father and I had a long and happy relationship. I knew he was married, knew he had children. But he swore it was a marriage in name only and that one day we would marry – only his wife was religious and it could take some time.'

She raised her head and Mary was chilled by the agony she saw in her eyes. Her dislike for this woman was intense but she recognised and understood the suffering she was going through. It echoed what she'd experienced when her father banished her.

'We lived in a different world from the one you know, Mary. Divorces weren't easy, there was a lot of disgrace and dishonour attached to everyone involved. I was happy to go on being his mistress all the while I thought I knew the truth about his marriage.' She fell silent, almost unaware of the others in the room.

'Then I got pregnant. He flew into a rage, lashing out at me, quoting the Bible, calling me names. I was terrified, never having seen him that way before, and when he threw a wad of money at me and ordered me to "get myself seen to before I came back to him", I left the money and ran.

'But where could I go? I was twenty-five years old, pregnant and unmarried, with no money and no home. My parents disapproved of my career, and would certainly have shut the door on me if I'd appealed to them. All I could do was try to convince Cordelia that a divorce from Jock would set her free. In my youthful naivety, I thought he would change his mind and make me and his child respectable with marriage.'

She gave a bitter smile. 'How wrong I was. I saw Cordelia, and she was gracious and kind and so very understanding. But she had valid reasons for not divorcing Jock. Once she'd explained the situation, I understood more clearly how he'd been leading me on. Yet that meeting led to another and another. We forged a friendship that has lasted to this day. I will always treasure it.'

'That doesn't explain how Mum got away with pretending I was hers,' said Mary bitterly.

Jane rubbed her forehead with trembling fingers. The memories were painful, but she knew she had to bring them out in the open if she was ever to exorcise them.

'I went and stayed in a rented trailer down on the southern coast of Tasmania. Everyone there and at the hospital where you were born, knew me as Mrs Witney. Which is why you couldn't find any misleading birth certificates or adoption papers. Witney is a fairly common name, after all.'

She took a sip of water before carrying on. It was a painful exorcism, remembering those lonely days and nights in that caravan at Snug. Remembering how the gulls sounded so mournful as the sea crashed on the rocks and bent the trees as winter tore up from the Antarctic. There had been no one to confide in – no one to share her fears – for she'd had no idea of what to expect when the time came, and was terrified of not getting to the hospital on time. It wasn't an age of childbirth trusts and helpful clinics that explained the process of giving birth. Not an age when a single woman could hold her head high and feel little shame. It was a time of suspicion, of gossip and scandal, with mouths chattering behind hands, watchful eyes and constant speculation. Her disguise as a young widow had probably fooled no one.

'It was easy for Cordelia to do what was necessary to fool Jock into believing she could be pregnant. You see, after her twins were killed in the Spanish Civil War, she and Jock had grown closer – a reconciliation in the face of tragedy. First Kate then Daisy were born from that reunion and if it hadn't been for me ... who knows? Cordy and Jock might have stayed together. But she was truly hurt to discover he was still up to his old tricks, and this was her chance to get her own back. They still slept together occasionally when he was in town, even though he'd sworn to me they hadn't – and to this day neither of us can forgive him his lies and deceit.'

She fell silent. The atmosphere in the room was electric as they all waited for her to resume.

'He went away to Europe on business and Cordelia waited for me to contact her. She came over to Tasmania when I did and once I was

498

released from hospital, she brought you home as her own.'

'So Dad never knew?' Mary was unaware of the mascara streaking her face, just the chill of shock, the almost numbing sensation that the world was slipping away.

'You were his daughter,' said Cordelia. 'He thought I was your mother. It was the best revenge I had on him for all the years he was such a bastard to me, and I was determined you would want for nothing. I love you, Mary, even though you try my patience to the limit and do your best to destroy us as well as yourself. There're a lot of your father's less lovable characteristics in you, but I chose to ignore them, to guide you on a less destructive course. I held you in my arms when you were just a few hours old, and I felt the same love for you as I did for the others. That hasn't changed. I might not have given birth to you but I still feel I have the right to call myself your mother.'

Mary looked from Jane to Cordelia and burst into tears. 'I don't believe this,' she sobbed. 'I just wanted to be loved, to be your and Daddy's favourite. Then he banished me, Sophie's father left and ... and...' She stared from one face to another, her thoughts in a swirling dark cloud.

Cordelia struggled out of her chair and hobbled around the table. She put her arthritic hand on Mary's shoulder and slowly drew her into an embrace. 'It doesn't matter, darling. I know. I understand the demons troubling you. But you have me and Jane, and your own daughter who loves you very much if only you'd give her the chance. Let that be enough for now.'

Mary breathed in the familiar perfume and closed her eyes. Everything would be all right. The clouds were thickening, becoming darker, swirling in her mind as the sounds of the board room faded and she withdrew into her own world.

23

The private nursing home was on the Mornington Peninsula, elegant bay windows overlooking the sea, lush gardens meandering down to a sandy cove. Sophie parked the car and, armed with flowers, hurried to the suite of rooms her mother had been allocated for her stay. It had been four weeks since her breakdown but there were finally signs of improvement, both in her health and in her attitude to the rest of the family.

She opened the door and smiled. Philip was here again, reading to Mary from the gossip columns, making her laugh with his outrageous mimicry of the celebrities being lambasted by Sharon Sterling. Who would have thought it? Sophie mused as she kissed her mother's cool cheek and arranged the flowers in a vase. Philip and Mary. Yet perhaps they had more in common than she'd once thought for, after all, they had always been the outcasts of the family, the ones who stood apart from it.

'Phil and I have been talking about you,' said Mary as she eased herself up the pillows.

'Nothing bad, I hope,' Sophie replied lightly.

Mary eyed her thoughtfully. 'I might not be the perfect mother, Sophie, but I can see you have a lot of good points. Working to the exclusion of everything else is not one of them.'

Sophie looked from one to the other and frowned. 'There isn't time for anything else but business,' she said regretfully. 'What with setting up the co-operative and getting everything back on line, I don't have a minute to myself.'

Mary lit a forbidden cigarette and shared a secret exchange of looks with Philip. 'Then it's time you did,' she said firmly. She began to cough and hastily stubbed out the cigarette. 'Run downstairs and see if Mum's on her way. She's going to need a hand getting up here.'

Sophie frowned. Cordelia had visited every day and had managed the elevator quite easily. But she saw the impatient tightening of Mary's lips and decided she had her reasons.

The gardens were lovely, the scent of roses filling the still air with their perfume. She breathed deeply, content with the way things were working out between her and her mother. They would never be close, she realised, but the tentative threads of friendship were enough for now.

Yet the contentment was marred by the fact that she and Jay had had little time together since the board meeting. Mary had been rushed to hospital, and he'd been needed back in the Hunter. A few telephone calls had kept them in touch but it wasn't the same as seeing him. Sophie sighed. She supposed she couldn't have it all – not now she was so busy with the family business – but Mary was right. She had to take time out to see to her own needs, and those of Jay.

The Rolls-Royce purred up the gravelled drive, black coachwork gleaming in the sun. Sophie smiled and waited until it drew up beside her. Cordelia was making her entrance in style.

It wasn't until Sophie reached to open the door that she realised her grandmother wasn't travelling alone. 'Jay,' she breathed.

He unfurled his length from the car, and as the chauffeur helped Cordelia to her feet, came to stand beside Sophie. 'I couldn't stay away any longer,' he said softly.

She smiled up at him, for once lost for words.

'Let's hope this time there won't be a family quarrel to interrupt us.' His eyes twinkled and laughter tugged the corners of the sensuous mouth.

'We're a fiery lot, the Witneys,' she breathed.

'Don't I know it,' he drawled. 'Been on the end of one or two snipes myself.'

She looked down at his boots. They were scuffed and the leather had been stained red by the earth. 'Sorry about that,' she murmured. 'But you shouldn't play games with me – not when the stakes are so high.'

He was suddenly very close, and the electricity between them was tangible. 'This isn't a game, Sophie. Never has been.'

She looked up at him. Hope and disbelief made

a strange brew of emotions. She so wanted it to be the truth – wanted to put the past behind her and begin again. 'Then why, Jay? Why go off to France without a word? Why get your brother to take my calls? Why not write or contact me in all those years?'

His eyes held hers, his hand reaching out, drawing her closer until their breath mingled. She wanted him to kiss her. Wanted his lips on hers, his arms tight around her. Yet she needed answers before she could commit herself further. 'Jay,' she began, her hands pushing against his broad chest.

Her protest was abruptly cut off as he pulled her roughly to him and kissed her. Despite all her misgivings, and all the pain he'd caused, she melted into him, her legs almost refusing to hold her, the blood coursing like fire through her veins. She put her arms around his neck, her fingers buried in the thick black hair that curled just past the collar of his shirt. The surroundings faded, the world spun and nothing else existed but that joyous feeling of having come home.

He released her finally and held her at arm's length. 'I've been wanting to do that since the first moment you stepped down from the camper,' he said with a sigh. 'But you were so prickly, so distant, with a scowl fit to sour milk – I was scared to approach you.'

Sophie was still reeling. She hadn't been kissed that thoroughly in years. 'I didn't know how things would be between us,' she said, the tremor in her voice betraying her inner turmoil. 'I was furious with Gran for taking me to Coolabah, and determined not to let you see how much I was still hurting. When you deliberately seemed to be ignoring me, I decided two could play that game,' she finished.

He cupped her chin, tilting it so she would have to look into his eyes. 'Hurt you? How did I do that, Sophie? It was you who finished it between us, and until that morning we met in the bush and you got all tangled up in your hat, I thought you no longer felt anything for me.'

She pulled away. She couldn't think straight when he was that close. 'What do you mean? You stopped writing – not me.'

Jay frowned, his gaze thoughtful as he looked down into her face. 'I admit you were the last to write,' he said finally. 'But after reading that letter, there seemed no point in replying. I'd lost you. I had to get on with my life and leave you to yours.'

Her pulse was hammering. 'What letter?' she demanded.

'The typed letter from Jacaranda Towers,' he said warily. 'Even for a "dear John" it was harsh.'

Sophie clutched his hands, her nails digging into the flesh as suspicions took form. 'What was in that letter, Jay? Can you remember?'

'It doesn't matter, Sophie. It was a long time ago. We've found each other again, that's all that matters.'

'Fair bloody go, Jay! There's been a great deal of harm done. Now tell me. I have to know what was in that letter.'

He chewed his lip. 'I remember every bloody

word,' he said grimly. 'It wasn't long, but the message was clear enough.

This is to tell you I've met someone else and by the time you get this letter I shall be married. Don't contact me again. Thanks for the memories.
Sophia

Sophie swayed and had to clutch his arm for support. The suspicions were crowding in, clamouring to be heard – but they made no sense, no sense at all.

'It arrived as I was packing. I was on my way to Melbourne to ask you to marry me and come to France with me. The engagement ring was new and shiny in my pocket. When I read that awful letter I went out into the paddock and threw the ring as hard as I could into the bush. I never bothered to try to find it afterwards.'

'I didn't write that letter,' she whispered tearfully. 'I would never have written that letter – least of all signed it Sophia. You should have known something was wrong.' The tears were streaming down her face as she looked up at him. 'There was no other man – no wedding – not for another four years. That long silence was terrible, Jay. I didn't understand what I'd done wrong. Couldn't understand why you'd gone off to France without a word of explanation.'

He enfolded her in his embrace, held her to his chest and rocked her. 'If only I'd known,' he murmured. 'If only I'd caught the next plane out and come to see you. Asked you face to face why you were marrying someone else. I should have fought for you – should have made sure.'

Sophie snuggled against his chest. 'Why didn't you?' She rather liked the thought of him racing across Australia, just as John had crossed the world looking for Rose.

'Dad told me it was best to leave things as they were. He said a man should never plough the same field twice and there had been enough trouble between the two sides of the family. Me storming into the middle of a wedding ceremony wouldn't have helped. Grandad Wal was more philosophical. He said that sometimes things work out in a most unexpected way and I should wait. If it was meant to be, then it would happen.'

She sniffed. She was making his shirt wet with her tears but he didn't seem to mind. 'How right he was,' she said softly. 'And how crafty Gran's been. I wonder if she knew and was trying to make amends? She said some pretty strange things when we were back in Coolabah – hinting not everything was as black and white as we thought.'

He stroked her hair, calming her as he would a half-wild pony. 'I think she does know, but I'm certain that letter was none of her doing.'

'It was Jock,' said a weary voice.

Sophie turned within Jay's embrace. They had forgotten Cordelia's presence, so wrapped up in each other.

'He sent that letter but I didn't find out until years later and as Sophie was married by then it was too late to do anything about it. I thought it best to leave things to sort themselves out. It looks as if I was right.'

Sophie looked at the elderly woman she loved so much. 'But what about the letters I sent to Jay trying to get an answer?'

'Jock had the maid take all your mail to him before she posted it. I suspect he destroyed your letters.'

'But why? What did he have to gain?'

'He could see how intelligent and ambitious you were. Could see a fine career in corporate law for you. He didn't want to lose a potential asset to his business. Didn't want you going off to get married to a man he considered beneath you. That's why he changed the habits of a lifetime and allowed one of his "girls" go to university. He chose London because it was out of reach.'

'Spiteful old bastard,' growled Jay.

'Forget him,' Sophie whispered as she turned back to him. And as his kiss swept all thoughts of treachery away, she thought she heard the rustle of skirts and the joyous crescendo of a Romany fiddle. The Jacaranda rift was finally healed, the curse banished.

Epilogue

It was winter in Sussex as the dawn of the new millennium lightened the horizon and turned the mist pink and orange. Jay and Sophie stood on Windover Hill, their hands clasped as the church bells began to peal in the valley.

The past three years had brought them success as well as sorrow, with the co-operative up and running, and her own flourishing chambers finally organised in Sydney. Life might have been hectic, but she and Jay were blissfully happy. Her relationship with Jane had evolved into a close and loving one – yet Cordelia would always remain in her heart as her true grandmother, and the revelations made during that journey across Australia had never changed that.

Mary was almost over her breakdown and at last trying to come to terms with life, having forged a surprising bond with Philip. She and Sophie had also called a truce, but there was too much water under the bridge for them to find the mother-daughter closeness that Sophie yearned for. Perhaps the news that Mary would soon be a grandmother might go some way towards healing the old rifts?

Cordelia had passed away, as Rose had done, in her sleep. It had been the eve of her ninety-second birthday, and she had been surrounded by the sounds and scents of Jacaranda – at peace with her re-united family. Her passing had left a great void for Sophie, but she firmly believed her spirit would always remain by her side.

'I'm glad we came,' Sophie murmured as the light began to chase the shadows from the Long Man of Wilmington. 'It somehow brings the story of Rose and John full circle.'

Jay kissed her cold cheek and put his arms around her. 'Our roots are here, and it's almost as if I can feel their presence.'

And as they stood there in the chill of an English winter and watched the dawn of the new millennium bring light and colour to the world, Sophie felt the baby move in her womb. She smiled as she remembered the words of the Aborigine Wyju. The song lines had been laid across the world, linking the past to the present with each sacred site, each new generation – they had simply gone walk-about, and were following in the footsteps of their ancestors.

The publishers hope that this book has given you enjoyable reading. Large Print Books are especially designed to be as easy to see and hold as possible. If you wish a complete list of our books please ask at your local library or write directly to:

Magna Large Print Books
Magna House, Long Preston,
Skipton, North Yorkshire.
BD23 4ND

This Large Print Book for the partially sighted, who cannot read normal print, is published under the auspices of

THE ULVERSCROFT FOUNDATION